AT ANY MOMENT

A GAMING THE SYSTEM NOVEL

Brenna Aubrey

Silver Griffon Associates
Orange, CA

Publisher's Note: This is a work of fiction. Names, characters, places, and incidents are a product of the author's imagination. Locales and public names are sometimes used for atmospheric purposes. Any resemblance to actual people, living or dead, or to businesses, companies, events, institutions, or locales is completely coincidental.

Trademarked names appear throughout this book. Rather than use a trademark symbol with every occurrence of a trademarked name, names are used in an editorial fashion, with no intention of infringement of the respective owner's trademark.

Book Layout ©2014 BookDesignTemplates.com

Cover Art ©2014 Sarah Hansen, Okay Creations

Professionally edited by Eliza Dee, Clio Editing.

Ordering Information:
Quantity sales. Special discounts are available on quantity purchases by corporations, associations, and others. For details, contact the "Special Sales Department" at the address above.

At Any Moment/ Brenna Aubrey. – 1st ed.
First Printing 2014
Printed in the USA
ISBN 978-1-940951-08-9

For all survivors and for the beloved memory of those who didn't.

ACKNOWLEDGEMENTS

I owe many thanks to those who helped this book come into being: Sabrina Darby, Courtney Milan, Kate Mckinley, Minx Malone, Tessa Dare, Natasha Boyd, Leigh Lavalle, and Carey Baldwin. A big thank you to my production team: Eliza Dee, S. G. Thomas, and Sarah Hansen.

Thank you to my amazing fellow authors for your support: Bella Andre, Roxie Rivera, Mimi Strong, Maya Rodale, Marquita Valentine, Elena Dillon, Debra Holland, Michelle Pickett, S.M. Butler, Viv Daniels, . Shout-outs to the NAAU peeps, the Awesome Authors, the LOL ladies, the SPRT guys and gals and the Romance Divas.

Many thanks to all the readers and bloggers who have loved, read, reviewed and talked about the Gaming the System books. Adam and Mia are every bit as much yours are they are mine. <3

All my gratitude to my family. Thank you to my husband, sometimes affectionately referred to as "the publisher." Hugs and kisses to my sweet little guys, heroes to some lucky future heroines. Love always xoxox.

The Do Over

"Respawns, Do-overs and What Video Games Can Teach Us About Life"— Posted on the blog of *Girl Geek* on December 16, 2013

*T*HE HANGOVERS FROM THE FIRST ANNUAL DRACOCON HAVE FADED, *and the sleep is wiped from our eyes. Our anticipation for the next Dragon Epoch expansion is only increased and that ever-elusive secret hidden quest still beyond our grasp. I take this moment to consider that some gaming truths can teach gamers the cold, hard realities of life.*

Seems like a weird idea, no? You are thinking that Girl Geek has finally lost her mind. You play to blow off steam and hang out with your friends online and have fun. Life lessons, Girl Geek? You're a looney!

But think about when you are faced with a difficult quest, a seemingly impossible foe to defeat or a trap-riddled dungeon that you just can't make it through. Once your character's life is reduced to zero, what happens? Respawn!

You show up at your home point as a ghost and after a minimal wait period, your character's belongings and health are all restored. You take what you learned from the previous encounter with that monster whose attack took

1

you by surprise or that trap that caused you to get run through with a spear and pinned to the wall. You go back to that encounter with increased knowledge and maybe, after a few—or a few hundred—more tries, you accomplish what you set out for.

Wouldn't it be awesome if life had a respawn button?

Oops, did you accidentally tell your girlfriend the truth about how her ass looked in her new jeans? Or did you take that dreaded moment to actually look at her ass when she asked you? Big mistake! And by now I'm sure you are suffering the consequences. But if there was the ability to hit the respawn button, you could go back to that split second with the knowledge that one hesitation, one extra second to actually catch a glimpse, will get your head bitten off. Respawn button. "No, baby, you look absolutely beautiful in those new jeans!" Lesson learned!

The lure of a do-over is attractive with more serious mistakes in life, too. Why can't we respawn after screwing up, so we can do it over—even if it means showing up as a chainmail-bikini-wearing ghost?

We are fortunate that our beloved Dragon Epoch doesn't feature the Hardcore Mode, which leads to the dreaded permanent death. Permadeath would be one damn depressing way to end your game. Your fiftieth-level Barbarian mercenary has just died? Time to start over in the meadow as a first-level Fire Mage picking daffodils for General SylvenWood. But even then, worst case you can start over with a new character, dump all your baggage and have a totally clean slate.

Don't you wish you could hit a button and start parts of your life over again?

In so many ways, as we learn, we are also screwing things up. And in the process of bumbling our way through life without that wonderful respawn button, we make it nearly impossible to untangle the very mess we are creating while we are learning those important lessons.

I'd like a respawn button for life. Time for a do-over.

1
MIA

THIS WAS THE ONGOING STORY OF HOW I COMPLETELY AND utterly fucked up my life. I guess cancer had some part in the whole mess, too, but it was definitely off the rails before all the medical stuff happened. I wished I could blame the cancer, but it wasn't cancer of the brain. No, apparently something else had gone wrong with my brain before the cancer showed up.

I'd always tried to be an optimistic person. When life gave me shit, I made lemonade. Absent father? Sick mother? Monstrous tuition? I set up an auction to sell my virginity in order to make the money I'd needed.

I could always think my way around a crappy situation in the past. But this...this...I wasn't prepared for it and it had bowled me over. I couldn't think straight about any of it. Now we were in the middle of a nightmare and I had no do-over button. Given the vacant, zombie-like look in Adam's dark eyes, I could tell he was wishing for one, too.

So here it was finally Monday morning after a completely gut-wrenching weekend. We had both just found out about my pregnancy and Adam had just found out about the cancer. I glanced over at him without turning my head. His eyes were on the road, both hands gripping the white vinyl steering wheel of his vintage Porsche. He couldn't see me studying him but there was no mistaking his stiff bearing, the undeterred focus that he usually put into his driving. In spite of those appearances, he was clearly distracted. His mind was always running, like one of his computers. It never shut down and right now, he was in problem-solving mode.

Trouble was, not all problems could be solved, not even by a boy genius.

"So, um, I'm going to need for you to wait in the waiting room..." I said.

His cheek bulged as he clenched his jaw. "I have a lot of questions for the doctor."

"But—but he's going to do an examination and..."

Ridiculous. I sounded half out of my mind. Well, I was beyond exhausted, but the thought of letting him see me with my shirt off...no. Just no.

He glanced at me out of the corner of his eye—probably to determine if I was serious or not. I took a deep breath, hoping he wasn't in the mood for an argument, because I sure as hell wasn't.

He pulled into the parking lot and parked. Then, before getting out, he turned to me. "Please let me be there. I'll wait until you get undressed to come in the room, but...I really would like to be there."

I looked out the window for a long time. It was only fair, really. This affected his future, too. "Okay. I..."

He took my hand in his. "You don't have to explain yourself. I understand. But this is important. We need to have all the facts, okay?"

I looked down and nodded, swallowing. I knew what "getting all the facts" meant. Adam was on a mission to convince me that my decision to carry the baby to term was the wrong one. Sure, he'd assured me that it was my decision, that he'd agree with whatever I ultimately decided, but I still wasn't a hundred percent sure he wasn't going to step in and dominate this situation like he always did. I took a deep breath.

He touched my cheek with a brush of featherlight fingers and then turned and opened the door. Before he could come around to get mine, I'd opened it and sprung out. He didn't say anything when he came around to my side, raised his brows, and shut the door behind me.

"Adam..."

"Yes?"

"Thank you for being here...but I need for you to not do your thing where you try to take over."

His lips thinned, but he nodded. "I'll behave myself. I promise."

I kissed him on the cheek and he gave me a faint smile. He took my hand and we walked in together.

Things were still weird with us, but better than they had been in months. We were at least trying to hold it together during this wretched turn of events in our lives. We'd spent the last few days constantly in each other's presence and things were strained but okay.

But the tension in that doctor's examining room could be cut with a knife.

Once Dr. Metcalfe entered and asked me to open my paper gown for my exam, I cast a self-conscious glance in Adam's direction. He lowered his head, focusing on his tablet. The doctor looked over the scar and indentation on my left breast, where the tissue had been removed, and commented that it was "nicely healed." Then he performed the usual breast exam.

"Any tenderness?" he asked.

I pressed my lips together, then swallowed the nervous lump in my throat. "Yes, actually."

The doctor straightened and I adjusted the paper to cover myself again. "Which breast?" he asked.

"Both."

"Any specific location?"

I cleared my throat, avoiding Adam's gaze from across the room. "All over."

The doctor frowned at me. "Could you—"

"I'm pregnant," I blurted before he could finish his sentence.

Dr. Metcalfe sucked in his bottom lip and looked at my chart again. "It doesn't say—"

"I just found out. Home pregnancy test."

"And your last period was...?"

And then I had to go into detail about how I hadn't had a period in months because of the hormonal treatment I'd been on. How I'd thought that meant I wasn't at risk of getting pregnant. He shook his head. "You can still ovulate even with the hormone therapy."

Yeah, obviously. I swallowed a sob of frustration and rubbed my forehead. Dr. Metcalfe seemed to get over his momentary astonishment.

"Well, this certainly means we can't start the chemotherapy as planned."

I saw Adam stiffen in his seat out of the corner of my eye. He cleared his throat, stood and approached my examination table. I pulled the stupid paper frock tighter around me.

"What are her options?" Adam asked.

The doctor cast a furtive glance at me before answering. "It depends on whether or not she decides to terminate the pregnancy."

"If I don't?"

"Then we wait until fourteen weeks—how far along did you say you were?"

"Six weeks," Adam answered. I jerked a look at him. He'd figured all that out, apparently. Thank goodness, because I had no idea.

The doctor's brows shot up. "That's at least an eight-week delay."

"What are the risks of waiting?" asked Adam. He was stiff, facing the doctor like he was conducting a business negotiation. It was almost like I wasn't even there.

"With her type and stage of breast cancer—had she been able to start now, without this complication and with the full round of chemo, she would have had an eighty-five percent survival rate."

The doctor had Adam's full attention now. He seemed focused in on everything Dr. Metcalfe was saying, his jaw tightening, obviously not happy at the eighty-five percent number that I already knew about.

"And now? If she continues with the pregnancy and delays the chemotherapy? How does that change the prognosis?"

The doctor glanced at me and took a deep breath. "That's difficult to say. You want an exact number? I can't give that to you. You want a rough estimate? She has hormone-sensitive carcinoma and is not only delaying treatment but also exposing her breast tissue to pregnancy hormones. Also, if she proceeds with the chemo at the second trimester, a less aggressive drug will need to be used, one that is not as successful with her type of cancer. At best, I'd say a fifty-five percent chance of survival."

My jaw dropped, along with my heart—and my stomach, too. Things were happening in slow motion. I was in a dream, underwater. Adam was firing questions at the doctor as quickly as the doctor could answer and I was sinking deeper into myself. Their conversation echoed in the distance. I blinked, trying to fight back the shock, the anger, the helplessness. *Now wouldn't be a good time to puke up my guts.*

While they talked, I slid off the examination table and made a beeline for the sink, huddling over it, pathetically clutching the white crepe paper "gown" while my stomach upended itself.

When I finally straightened after rinsing my mouth out, I almost fell over from the head rush. Hands reached out to steady my shoulders. I leaned up against a solid body supporting me from behind. His arms slid around me and it felt painful and sweet. I leaned against him, relaxing, calming. But inside, things were tender and prickly. His touch simultaneously hurt and comforted me.

"You okay?" he whispered.

I couldn't speak. I didn't trust myself to. I shrugged.

"The doctor's gone. You can get dressed if you want. Did you have any more questions for him? He said we can sit in his office if you did."

I shook my head. He slowly released his hold on me. I almost wanted to cry from the loss of his arms around me. I'd missed him so badly. And now he was back—but under these circumstances, it was hardly a thing to celebrate. There was that ache that wouldn't go away—that ache I felt every single day since we'd broken up.

I swallowed the emotion rising in my throat. He was tense. I could feel it in every muscle as he hovered near me. He was preparing to do battle. And he was anticipating that it would be epic. He wasn't wrong.

I turned from the sink, wiping my mouth with the back of my hand, and went to grab my funny padded bra and shirt.

"Can you turn your back, please?" I said. My voice was raspy, hoarse. He watched me with his unreadable eyes. It was a ridiculous request, really. He'd seen my naked body hundreds of times before—touched it almost as often. God, how he'd touched it. My cheeks heated at the memory and I looked away.

He turned around, snatching up his tablet and typing furiously into it. Likely he was looking up some of the terms the doctor had used.

I pulled off the paper covering my torso and glanced down at my breasts. The right one was perfect, untouched. The left one had an angry red scar slicing into it and a scoop-shaped divot taken out of it. I shot a look at his back. Maybe he'd find the disfigurement disgusting. He'd never been shy about expressing his appreciation of my breasts before. I slipped on my bra and hooked it. It wasn't a sexy bra—those little lacy things I used to love wearing when I had the money to splurge on one. This was more of an old lady's bra. Sturdy, supportive. Functional.

Thanks to cancer treatment, I was slowly but surely being robbed of my youth, between scars on my body, hormone therapy and the dreaded chemo-beast, which loomed near, like one of those giant dragons scrawled across the edges of antique maps. Soon I'd be as shriveled as and even balder than my grandma.

As the child of a surviving cancer patient, I knew what I was in for with chemo. I'd seen my mom go through it all. The thought made my gut twist in dread. Maybe the pregnancy was my unconscious way of engaging in the ultimate procrastination where that was concerned. Knowing what I knew, I probably would have jumped off a balcony and broken both my legs to delay the inevitable.

After I slipped on my shirt, Adam turned around, closing one app on his tablet and opening another. It looked like a calendar.

"Your next appointment is at one."

My head shot up as I grabbed my bag. "Next appointment?"

"The second opinion we discussed. You're going to need to sign some papers on the way out to get your records and test results."

I signed the papers and copies of my tests and records were transferred onto a flash drive that Adam had handed to the office staff. When they gave it back, I snatched it and stuck it in my pocket. Damned if I was going to give him access to pictures of my maimed boob. Hell no.

Since Jordan, Adam's playboy best friend, had been setting Adam up on "hot dates" lately, Adam had probably been rubbing elbows— and God only hoped no other parts—with models and actresses. To say nothing of the swarm of interns at work that I had mentally nicknamed the "Adam groupies." They liked to catalogue what he wore to work and rate how hot he looked from one day to the next. It had been hell having to sit around and listen to that shit day in and day out while attempting to ignore it.

Not that I thought he'd ever date any of those interns. They were like eighteen and nineteen. But they had perfect bodies and I was sure not a one of them had a big divot taken out of their left breast. Nor would any of them soon be balder than Captain Jean-Luc Picard of the Starship *Enterprise*.

I caught Adam watching me a couple times. Well, it was more like I could *feel* him watching me. Adam's dark eyes had a way of drawing your eyes to him like a magnet.

"What?" I said finally.

He shook his head, unlocked his car and opened the door for me, patiently waiting for me to get in.

I paused and folded my arms against my chest, turning to him. "You're up to something."

He frowned. "Why do you think that?"

"Aside from the fact that you are *always* up to something, you haven't mentioned Dr. Metcalfe's prognosis numbers yet."

He rested an arm across the edge of the open door and looked at me—*really* looked in that way that usually felt intimidating. "What's there to say, Mia?" Then he took a deep breath and looked away. "Those numbers speak for themselves. You're an intelligent woman. And hopefully you're going to be an oncologist. If you were in that doctor's place, what would *you* recommend your patient do?"

It suddenly felt a little harder to breathe, like a band had been wrapped around my chest. Instead of replying, I dropped my arms to my sides and sank into the passenger seat. Adam gently closed the door for me and came around to the left side of the car to slide in behind the wheel. I bent my head, rubbing my temples against the beginning of a headache. His use of the word "hopefully" was not lost on me. Odds were good that if I went ahead with the pregnancy, I would not be starting medical school any time in the near future.

He didn't start the car, just sat and watched me. I pressed back harder into my seat and sighed, looking at him. I shook my head. "I can't do this. He is one opinion, one estimate. His number might not even be right."

We stared at each other for a while—long after it had become awkward. I wanted him to reach out and hug me. And it was strange...if I wanted him to hold me so much, why didn't I ask, or—

better yet—lean forward and take him in my arms? I swallowed and blinked, my eyes stinging.

"I need to stop off at the office for a few minutes to grab some of my stuff," he said.

"You aren't going into work today?"

He gave me a look like I must be crazy for asking him that and turned to start the car.

Twenty minutes later, at the campus of Draco Multimedia, Adam's company, I rolled down the windows of his car, telling him I'd wait while he got his stuff done inside. He promised me he'd be no more than ten or fifteen minutes but I knew better, because his secretary would catch him to sign some papers or someone would call or he'd get stopped a half dozen times on the way back to his office. I could have gone in with him, but I wanted to avoid that awkward return to work. The Friday before, I'd hurriedly packed up my desk with no explanation whatsoever while Mac, my superior, and the interns I worked with watched me with slackened jaws. I hadn't cared, though. All I could think about at that point was the pregnancy test I'd just taken and the subsequent angry confrontation with Adam in his office.

I played a game on my phone to avoid having to sit and think about everything that was happening. I'd done too much thinking throughout the weekend and was starting to get exhausted and nauseated by it.

But the game was interrupted when Heath, my roommate and best friend, texted me.

Hey, did you make it to your dr. appointment okay?

I typed out my reply:

Yes. On way to 2nd appt.

Alone?

No. A is with me.

Ok. I'll be home when you get here.

Just as he'd promised and in spite of my fears to the contrary, Adam returned about a quarter of an hour later with his laptop case slung over his sturdy shoulder. He got in and we went to the next appointment.

The second doctor was in some fancy medical building in Newport Beach, right next to Hoag Hospital (half country club, half medical response to the rich and sometimes famous). Adam's search for "the best" in OC must have led him there.

After taking twenty minutes to page through my tests and charts from the flash drive, she looked up at me, grim-faced. Her numbers were not as good as Dr. Metcalfe's.

Less than fifty percent if I went through with the pregnancy. She was dead serious and adamant that I not pursue this course.

"I strongly recommend termination and immediate rounds of chemotherapy."

And that's when, slumped on her fancy exam table, I felt the tears filling my eyes. I met Adam's gaze through my hazy vision. His face was cold, impassive. I imagined him telling me, "I told you so." I looked away and blinked, unable to breathe.

The whole world around me felt like it was sinking.

2
ADAM

I WATCHED EMILIA CLOSELY AS THE DOCTOR DELIVERED HER prognosis numbers. She bravely tried to hide the emotional reaction that I knew was near the surface. The doctor excused herself and I stood, approaching her as she sat on the exam table. She didn't look up or move at all, her eyes fixed on some point in the middle distance, her mind far away from this point in time.

I swallowed, feeling the same old guilt almost suffocate me, but by necessity, I shoved it aside. I couldn't let emotions get in the way—not now. This was a critical time and we had to act fast. My sole concern was Emilia's health and survival. Everything else could be taken care of later, when she was healthy again. Hopefully by then there would be enough pieces of us to pick up and put back together.

I prayed to a God I didn't really believe in that she listened to what the doctors had told her today. Since I'd had the time to recover from the shock of discovering that not only was she pregnant but she also had cancer, I'd taken the time to analyze the way I'd handled it, determining that I should have done everything in the opposite way of what I'd done.

So I'd spent the whole weekend strategizing and coming up with a plan. These doctor visits were part of that plan. I hoped, rather than knew, that she would follow the medical advice. Emilia was a very smart woman, but at this point she was being driven by pure emotion. Since we'd argued on Saturday morning about her need to terminate the pregnancy, and faced with her adamant refusal to do it, I'd decided to back off and be there for her. We hadn't mentioned the subject again because I feared that the more she fought me over it, the deeper she would dig in her heels.

I hoped that she'd listen to the medical advice, but if she wouldn't, I wasn't going to give up—I'd find something or someone she *would* listen to. For this reason, I had set up a back-up plan.

Emilia was quiet the entire walk down to the parking structure. I opened the car door for her and she slid inside, her shoulders rounded. When I sank into the driver's seat, she was staring straight ahead. I reached over and took one of her hands in mine. It was cold and lifeless, and she didn't return the pressure when I folded her hand inside mine.

"Mia," I said quietly. "Are you okay?"

She blinked. "What do you think?"

"I'm sorry."

"It's not your fault." She buried her face in her hands and laughed bitterly. "I bet you wish you'd hooked up with that model of Jordan's instead of hopping into the sack with me."

I pulled her into my arms. She laid her head on my shoulder. "Now you are just being silly."

She grabbed my shoulders, holding me against her. "Adam, I'm sorry."

"I don't want you to apologize. All I want is for you to have the best chance possible."

After holding each other in long silence, she quietly said, "Can you take me home now?"

I hesitated. Home. For me, her home was my house, where we'd lived together until our breakup two months before. And it hurt when I realized that her reference to "home" meant Heath's condo. I turned and gave her a quick peck on the cheek, then pulled away.

I started the car, on the way to set my back-up plan in motion, but it didn't involve taking her to Heath's place.

By the time I got on the freeway, she was dozing in the seat next to me—thankfully. I knew she was exhausted. I'd kept the top up to minimize the wind inside the car so it wouldn't keep her awake. She hadn't slept enough lately. Her head lolled forward and all I could see was that ridiculous white fluff of hair that she had recently bleached white and dyed in rainbow colors to match her fairy costume for the company costume party at our convention in Las Vegas. The hair coloring had been permanent—presumably because she'd anticipated it would soon be falling out from the chemotherapy she was supposed to start this week. She looked like a faded punk rock star from the '90s.

I took the long route, so she didn't start to stir until I exited the freeway. Rather than head straight up Chapman Avenue to Heath's house, I turned right, toward North Tustin and my uncle's house instead.

She blinked, coming awake, groggily asking, "Why are we going to Peter's house?"

When I didn't answer, she glared at me, realization dawning. She straightened in her seat. "Adam, stop the car."

Instead I shifted, pressed the gas and headed up the hill toward the high school.

"Adam," she said between clenched teeth.

"You need to tell her sooner or later."

She hissed through her teeth like I'd just punched her in the stomach. "Stop. The. Fucking. Car."

We were about two blocks away from Peter's house. I pulled over to the nearest curb and turned off the ignition. I hesitated, staring out the window in front of me, gripping the wheel. Emilia sat stiffly beside me, fuming. I'd been willing to risk her anger because if Kim was the only one who could talk sense into her, then she was my secret weapon. At this point, I was willing to do whatever needed to be done. I was that desperate.

I waited for her to catch her breath, her cheeks even paler than normal, her hands white-knuckling the edges of her bucket seat.

I took my hands off the steering wheel and watched her carefully.

"Mia...She's your mom. You have to tell her."

She pressed the heel of her shaking hand to her forehead. "I don't *have* to do anything."

I took a deep, calming breath, staring out the windshield, trying to collect myself.

She fidgeted in her seat next to me. "Take me back to Heath's, please."

After a long pause, she turned to stare at me expectantly.

"I'll take you back to Heath's under one condition. You hear me out first."

Her jaw tightened and then relaxed and finally she nodded, her eyes avoiding mine.

"When we were just online friends, I recall sitting up with you online until six a.m. the night you found out about your mom's cancer. Do you remember that?"

She bit her lip. "Of course."

"I know how painful that was for you. I also know you are trying to protect her now—"

"Don't make this about me. *You* are angry with me because I didn't tell any of you, but what you need to understand—"

I held up a hand to cut her off. "We're not talking about me right now, Mia. We're talking about your mom. She has a right to know. She has a right to be the strong one for you, to help you. You're going to need people. That's probably harder than hell for you to admit."

She rubbed her forehead with a shaky hand. "I know I need—but—I—God, I remember how I felt when she told me. I remember how it felt to be the helpless one standing by, not able to do a single goddamn thing. It was the worst thing I've ever gone through in my life and I wanted to spare her"—she looked at me—"and you."

I bit my tongue to keep the irritated reply where it belonged—unspoken in my mouth. *Because finding out the way I did was so much better than your not telling me.*

Her eyes widened in reaction. Apparently she saw what I was thinking and I cursed myself for not hiding my thoughts better. I used to be so good at that.

She took a deep breath. "I know it was my own cowardice, too. I can't explain what was going through my head because it sounds so ridiculous. It started out just a small thing. First a suspicion, a biopsy. But then the diagnosis came and I...It was like getting cancer was somehow letting you all down. There were all these problems between us before and then this...I thought it would finish us. I was like damaged goods."

I exhaled in surprise but didn't say anything. She swallowed, casting a nervous glance at me before continuing.

"I know these sound like silly excuses."

"Yes, they're excuses," I replied quietly. "There's never a good time to have something shitty happen to you. But to lock everyone out? *That's* how you make it worse for everyone else—and for yourself. Because by doing that, you made us more than helpless. And whether you'd want to admit it or not—You. Need. Our. Help."

She sighed. "I thought it would be a quick surgery and some radiation. So I didn't think it really necessary to bother anyone with it—"

I scowled. I couldn't help it. Fucking *cancer* and she didn't want to "bother" us with it.

"Let's not worry about the past, okay? It's done. Let's talk about today. Now. Your mom needs to know. She deserves to know. And she deserves to hear it from you." *The same way I deserved to hear it...*

She shook her head. "Don't force this on me."

"I won't. But...think of it like this. What if she had never told you about her cancer? You were away at school. She could have kept it from you for months without a problem. How would you have felt after finding out that she'd gone through all that alone? She *will* find out, eventually. You can't hide this from her forever. Please, Mia."

She pressed the palms of her hands to her eyes and began to sob, her entire body shaking. "I'm scared, Adam! Okay? I don't know which I'm more scared to tell her about, the cancer or the pregnancy."

I reached out and pulled one of her palms away from her face, took her hand in my own. My fingers closed around hers. "I'll be there. I'll help you."

She was still and silent for a long moment. Took a deep breath and, with her head bowed, finally nodded. "Okay," she whispered, and her hand tightened around mine.

After a long pause, I slowly removed my hand from hers and turned to start the car again. A few minutes later, I was pulling into Peter's driveway. Kim had stayed over another day when I'd contacted her yesterday, asking her to. Heath would be here shortly, too. This was Emilia's intervention.

3
MIA

I SLOWLY GOT OUT OF THE CAR, MY MUSCLES STIFF WITH annoyance. Adam had been prepared to handle this in the same high-handed fashion he handled most things—until he'd heeded my pleas to pull over. But I hadn't been prepared for his calm, cool reasoning. His gentle pleas. That was different...

I took a deep breath, my heartbeat racing. Adam hesitated, hovering nearby. I stared at the red-trimmed front door to Peter's house, knowing my mom was in there, knowing I was about to drop a bomb when she had just found a new love and things were starting to look up for her. "Give me a minute," I muttered.

He didn't move, looking away and putting his hands in his pockets. "Take the time you need."

Adam did have a point—it was time to tell Mom. I'd been wondering when I could tell her and I'd kept putting it off. Might as well get it over with in one quick and painful blow.

A weight sank in my stomach and everything tightened in my chest as I nodded and he turned for the front door. I numbly followed him up the porch steps. He opened the door without knocking—like he always did—and called inside, "Hey, we're here."

Mom was the first person I saw and Adam stepped aside so that she could greet me, throwing a hug around my neck. I could tell by her face that she didn't know. Her features were clouded with uncertain worry. I'd like to think I'd know what her face would look like if she knew about the diagnosis. I'd seen that face a thousand times when I'd imagined telling her. In my own thoughts, I never got past the first word or two before utterly breaking down at the thought of having to destroy her like this.

I knew how that had felt two years before when she'd gotten her diagnosis. It had gutted me, and Mom was only very recently cancer-free herself. What if the stress of my diagnosis made her sick again?

I pulled away from Mom, unable to meet her eyes. She put her hands on either side of my cheeks. "Mia," she said quietly. "Whatever it is, we'll get through it, okay? I'm here for you."

I looked into her brown eyes, so much like my own, and I couldn't keep it inside anymore. I started sobbing. Again.

Her arms wrapped around me. We were now alone in the kitchen. Adam had already stepped away. I tilted my face into my mom's shoulder and muffled my crying as best I could, but I was shaking so hard I couldn't even gather a thought, much less collect myself.

"Shhh," she said, smoothing my hair like she used to do when I was a little girl.

She led me into the living room where Adam and Peter sat in chairs across from us. Mom guided me to sit down next to her on the couch. Somehow the presence of others forced me to try to pull myself together and stop bawling like a baby. Adam got up, fetched a box of tissues and set them on the coffee table in front of me. I grabbed a handful of them and mopped my face.

"Adam, maybe we should step out," Peter said quietly.

"No," I said finally in a shaky voice. "It's okay. You should be here for her."

I turned to my mom, who'd raised her brows at my words. I put a hand on each shoulder, sniffed and squared my own shoulders, trying to find the strength to say those horrid words. "I—uh—" I began in a shaky voice. I cleared my throat. "I have cancer, Mom."

Mom didn't react at first. Then, after about a three-second delay, she looked like someone had stomped on her feet with steel-soled boots and she was trying not to show a reaction.

So I took a deep breath and kept talking. "It's, um, it's a carcinoma, stage two, in my left breast. I had a lumpectomy in October and hormone therapy and, uh, I need to start chemo."

My mom's lips disappeared into her mouth and I could tell she was trying her hardest not to cry. She was trying to do that thing I'd done when she'd told me about her diagnosis.

Finally, after a minute of trying to contain it, she broke down. "Oh God, baby," she said, taking me in her arms, pulling me close. No one understood the road ahead of a cancer patient like a cancer survivor. My mom knew intimately every torture in store for me.

Almost every torture.

"Why didn't you tell me?" she said tightly.

"I didn't tell anyone."

"Not even Adam?" she said, pulling away and looking at him.

And that was when I finally felt like dirt for the first time. I'd thought I was being strong for them. I'd thought I was choosing to brave my battle—a battle that only I could fight—without burdening them.

This was the first moment I realized how selfish I'd been.

I sat back and looked at Adam. His face was blank but his eyes were heavy with accusations and hurt. I looked back at my mom. "I only told Heath."

My mom shook her head, clearly not understanding. A million excuses jumped into my head. I was scared. I didn't know what to do. I was confused. I wanted to be strong. I wanted to fight the cancer on my terms.

But every excuse was dust and ashes. Meaningless to the people who loved me.

"So you made Heath keep this from us? Oh, Mia, that was so unfair to him. But—" She put her hand on my arm, shaking my shoulder so that I'd look at her again. "Now is not the time to discuss how you've handled it. Now, we talk about what comes next. When do you start chemo? And where?"

I straightened, pulling away from her. I kept my eyes fixed on her. I couldn't meet the gaze pinning me down from across the room. This was what he'd counted on. He knew that it would rip my heart out to tell my mother that I was going to refuse chemo. I clenched my teeth, trying to swallow that bitter pill.

"Kim, there's a complication," Adam spoke up in a quiet voice. "Mia can't start chemo this week because she's pregnant." I closed my eyes—mostly to block out my mom's reaction. But I was such a coward because of the relief I felt that Adam had told her for me. I felt like falling at his feet in gratitude.

My mom's head jerked back toward me. She opened her mouth to say something, but, apparently unable to find the words, she shut her mouth again. Her face went white as the wall behind her.

The doorbell rang and Adam stood up to get it, walking quickly down the hall. Peter leaned forward. "Kim, can I get you some water or something?"

At her vigorous head shake, he leaned back, watching her carefully. Mom turned back to me, her jaw slack again, gaping like a fish.

Adam re-entered the room with Heath, who immediately walked over to my mom. She stood up and practically leapt into his arms, clasping him close to her and weeping into his shoulder. Adam must have notified Heath to come. I realized now that I had been right earlier when I'd told Adam that I knew he was up to something. He'd scheduled a meeting so they could all sit around and tell me what I needed to do. I shot him a look but was distracted by Mom's sobs.

I watched them, feeling like a knife had impaled me through the sternum. A wave of nausea smacked me and my stomach roiled. I swallowed bitter bile at the back of my throat.

Mom finally stepped back from Heath and scooted over on the couch to make room for him at the end. Then she turned to me, wiping her face with the back of her hands. Heath leaned forward, grabbed some tissues and handed them to her. She wiped her eyes. Without looking at him, she said, "Heath, I'm sorry I was so angry with you at Christmas when you wouldn't tell me what was going on with Mia. This must have been impossible for you."

Heath put a hand on Mom's back and didn't say anything. He looked like he might start crying, too. I pressed the heels of my hands to my eyes as if to dam my own tears.

"Do you want to talk about what you are going to do?" Mom asked.

I was too chicken to uncover my eyes. After minutes of silence, I muttered, "I know what I want to do." I took a deep breath and then dropped my hands, sitting up. I looked at Adam. He was as still as a statue, as impassive and unreadable as he'd been in the doctor's office today. "But it means not getting the chemo."

Mom grabbed my hand and pulled it into her lap, squeezing it tight. "Mia, you need the chemo."

I let out a shaky breath and shook my head. I couldn't say it. I couldn't tell her that her daughter was choosing to forgo therapy. From the corner of my eye, I could see Adam stand up and put his back to the room while he stood stiffly, staring out the window. I studied his tense shoulders.

"Mom, what if you'd chosen not to have me? I can't do this."

Mom's jaw dropped. "My circumstances were completely different. I wasn't fighting for my life, Mia. You can't compare yourself to me!"

"I might never be able to have a baby, after the chemo—"

"Is that worth giving up your life for? A full life? You're twenty-two years old—a baby yourself!"

I opened my mouth to reply but she interrupted me, gripping my shoulder firmly as if hanging on for dear life. "You have everything ahead of you—you're going to go to medical school. You're going to be a doctor. You're going to save lives. But right now you have one life that is the most important to save—*yours.*"

I fought to catch a breath. My chest felt like it was compressed under tons of steel. This was a nightmare. They all wanted the same thing. No one—not one—could see my side of the issue. That there was life—a future *child*—growing inside me. A child who deserved a chance to live.

Then another voice spoke up—another whisper inside my brain—didn't *I* deserve the best chance to live, too?

Before the diagnosis, before that call from the doctor's office, I'd been on top of the world. I was waiting for responses from medical schools—had been accepted to my dream school—and I had an amazing man who loved me—whom I loved. That ache of loss diffused into my chest again. It had been as much a part of my daily life for the past few months as the endless blood tests and harsh medications I'd been forced to put in my body. And what loomed ahead was worse still.

"Is it really so bad that I believe in my child's right to live?" I said in a tiny voice.

Mom looked at me, frozen. Then she touched my cheek. "No, honey, it's not bad at all. But—I need to beg you to remember *my* child's right to live—to finish her life. Don't sacrifice *my* baby, I beg of you."

I suddenly felt as if I would collapse from the weight of everyone's eyes on me. Everyone except Adam watched me as if waiting for some pronouncement…some decision.

I put my hands to my temples, rubbing them. "I need to think. I can't make a decision like this right now. Please. Can you understand?"

My mom looked at me, her eyes so sad that it broke my heart. She actually bit her lip to keep it from quivering. But she nodded.

"Okay," she said. "You've still got a little time? Please—please don't shut us out again, okay? That's all I ask. All I beg. Let us love you."

Let us love you. Was that what I had been doing? Pushing them away, refusing to allow them to feel these feelings? I turned and looked at Adam, who was watching me again with veiled dark eyes. We held each other's gaze across the room and my insides felt heavy, tight. I could hardly breathe. I didn't want to think about this. Didn't want to do this. I wanted to lie back and wait for things to happen to me. I had no desire to ponder these difficult choices. My life was starting to feel like an epic failure. And there would be more failure along the way before I could pick things up, start again, if I even had the will left to do it.

I declared myself exhausted and in need of sleep. I hadn't slept very well in almost a week. Since finding out about the pregnancy and the big explosive confrontation with Adam. The day he'd found out about the cancer. All of it.

New Year's Eve was tomorrow and I didn't want to welcome in a new year that would be full of sadness, broken hearts, and tension between Adam and me.

I went to stand beside the passenger door of his car before determining it would probably be more practical to go home with Heath, since I lived with him now. Things between Heath and me had been strained since before this big blowup. He'd been pressuring me for weeks to tell them all. And I'd refused. I'd taken advantage of his loyalty to keep him silent. He'd had to face Adam and my mom demanding answers as to what was really going on with me. I owed him big time for it all.

I turned to walk toward Heath's car when I felt a hand on my upper arm, stopping me. Peter stood on the front steps with his arm around my mom's shoulders, and Heath was speaking to her in a low voice while she sniffled into a wad of tissues.

I turned to face Adam. His hand tightened on my shoulder and then slid down my arm. "You okay?"

I sighed and looked away. "I was pissed at you for bringing me here...planning all this." I swallowed a big lump in my throat. "But now I feel like a weight has been lifted off my chest."

He nodded. "I'm sorry that it upset you."

At least he didn't say that I deserved it. I glanced up into his face again before my eyes darted away. I knew perfectly well he was still angry with me. He hid his feelings so well that sometimes it took a stray glimpse, a brief tightening in the muscles of his face or an even briefer flicker in his eyes to figure out what was going through his mind.

I knew that I'd hurt him. We'd hurt each other. A lot. And I could only see more hurt down this road before we could start to heal, if we ever could. Fresh guilt clutched at my throat again. If he could set aside his anger at a time like this, then I could, too.

He cleared his throat. "I know you're too tired right now, but can we talk in the morning?"

I wondered if he'd have anything new to say. Would it be more of the same? Would he yell at me again and insist I get the abortion? Fatigue pulled at every inch of my body, weighted it down. All I wanted right now was to stop struggling, stop fighting. I found that, in spite of everything, I wanted him with me, holding me. I almost asked him if I could go home with him tonight instead.

"Umm. Yeah, of course."

"Pick you up for breakfast?"

I hadn't eaten breakfast in over a week. That was the time of day when I was sickest. But I really didn't feel like starting something with him. And as much as I'd tried to avoid him in the past few weeks, it seemed that now I needed his presence as much as I needed to breathe.

I could pick at a piece of toast and sip some juice if it meant we could spend some time together.

"Yeah, come get me whenever."

He bent to kiss my cheek. When he leaned in, I caught a whiff of his amazing scent and my heart skipped a beat. I wrapped my arms around his waist and pulled him close. He hesitated—it was only for a split second but I knew it. His bearing was stiff before he relaxed, his arms sliding up my back to rest on my shoulder blades and then the imperceptible movement of his head as he turned to smell my hair. I pressed my face into his shoulder and he held me. I closed my eyes and relished that salty ocean smell and that smell of man. I breathed it in.

It felt good. So good. But it was over almost as quickly as it had begun. He pulled away from me, first with a small jerk, then slowly, as if reminding himself not to be too abrupt—as if handling a fragile puppy or kitten. It physically hurt. That separation cut like a knife, deep into my heart.

"Adam...I'm sorry," I whispered.

He reached up and smoothed my cheek. "So am I."

That look we shared in the low light made my chest tighten, and new tears threatened, burning the backs of my eyes.

A respawn and a do-over at this point would be fantastic. If only.

If only I could have restarted things back to that day I'd gotten the letter of acceptance to Hopkins. I *really* could have handled that better. But I'd been so wrapped up in that accomplishment—that monumental achievement that had been my single hope and dream for the past few years. One that I thought I'd failed miserably at when I'd failed the MCAT exam.

That had been the point when we had both started making the big, stupid mistakes.

Adam pushed a strand of hair behind my ear. "We have to stop saying it over and over, okay? We're moving past it. No recriminations, self or otherwise, right? That was *your* rule, after all."

I smiled wryly. "You're all about the rules, aren't you?"

"Life is all about rules. Even games have rules."

I nodded. This was no game—far from it. I opened my mouth and almost, *almost* asked him if I could go home with him tonight. I wanted him to hold me. I wanted to feel him lying beside me, to listen to the peaceful sound of his breathing in sleep. It had been too long. Way too long.

But I was too afraid he'd say no, so I silently hoped he'd offer it to me instead.

"Sleep well," he said in a soft voice.

I closed my eyes, feeling something drop inside me. Things were not the same and wouldn't be the same for a long time, if ever. There was something missing or guarded in his voice and the way he looked at me. And in that instant, I knew exactly what it was—trust.

He no longer trusted me. And no, I didn't fully trust him either.

"You, too," I said.

He walked me to Heath's Jeep and opened the door for me. Previously, he would have insisted on being the one to drive me home, even if he knew that Heath was going that way anyway. But not tonight.

4
ADAM

FTER YET ANOTHER LONG AND SLEEPLESS NIGHT, I found myself driving almost on autopilot back to Orange. I could probably make the trip with my eyes closed by now. I'd hardly ever driven this route before I started seeing Emilia.

It was early in the morning on New Year's Eve and the traffic was lighter than normal. People probably only had half days at work—like those still working at Draco—and were planning to cap their holiday celebrations with bright and hopeful expectations of the new year.

I wondered what that must feel like. Because any way I looked at it, this new year ahead of us did not look very cheerful. Emilia and I were speaking again, at least. But our shaky relationship was about to get hit—very, *very* hard—by some dark shit. For us, there wasn't much to celebrate.

I stopped by a nearby specialty bakery to pick up a few things for breakfast and then went to get her at Heath's.

She opened the door. Her strange rainbow-colored hair was pulled back into a ponytail and through the back of a dark blue baseball cap with the Draco company logo on it. She wore baggy jeans and a denim jacket. Her mouth curved into a wan smile when she opened the door.

"Hey," she said.

"Hey. I thought we could go eat breakfast at the park. And maybe talk?"

She visibly paled at the mention of breakfast—even her perfect pink lips were almost white. She looked like she was about to puke on my shoes. But her smile didn't falter and she nodded gently.

Walking back to the car, she slipped her cold hand into mine. I closed my fingers around hers, almost without thinking about it. I should have been pissed at her. Part of me was still demanding I remain pissed at her. But most of me could see her for what she was: lost, alone, as terrified as I was, and the woman I loved more than anything in the world.

We drove to a nearby park that had hills and big trees and hiking trails—a line of pines almost a mile long and a semi-private place for us to sit at an empty picnic table. She sat across from me, keeping her face down as I set down the tray of coffee and pastries.

She glanced at the box. "I hope you aren't offended if I don't eat anything."

"I won't be offended, but I do think you should eat something. You need to keep your strength up."

Her brow arched. "I can do that this afternoon, when my strength doesn't come up with my breakfast."

I grimaced, grabbing one of the cups. "Well, at least have some coffee."

She looked at the coffee cup and then away. "I shouldn't."

I froze, my cup halfway to my mouth. I knew what she was implying with those two words and they infuriated and scared the shit out of me at the same time. I plunked down my cup, but I didn't say anything.

She watched me, unsurprised by my reaction. I was probably as pale as she was now.

"So you've made a decision," I said flatly, my voice as dead as the rest of me felt at that moment.

She looked away, rocking in her seat. Two joggers bounced past us, a little too close. I glared at them. She cleared her throat into her fist and took a deep breath.

"I know I said it's my body and my decision. And it is, but...I'm not going to shut you out."

I laced my fingers together on the table in front of me, studying them instead of looking at her. "So what does that mean?"

She turned to look at me, but even with the weight of her eyes on me, I didn't look up. "It means we talk about it. In clear, quiet voices. We do what we haven't been able to do in months—*communicate.*"

I looked up then and our eyes met. It was powerful, like a physical blow. My chest felt tight and it was difficult to breathe. I reached out and clamped my hand around her delicate wrist. "Thank you."

She didn't smile. "Don't thank me yet."

I held my breath.

"I want to keep the pregnancy."

I swallowed a golf-ball-sized lump in my throat. "So that's the end of the discussion?"

She shook her head. "No. It's the beginning. You tell me what you want."

I blinked. "I want *you*. I want you healthy. I want you to have the best chance of surviving you possibly can. Eighty-five percent isn't the greatest number, but at least it's better than—"

She pulled her hand away from my hold. "No, don't do that. Don't talk numbers and percentages. Tell me what you are *feeling*. Tell me what you want."

I clenched my teeth in frustration. "I can't *not* talk about the numbers, Mia, okay? Everything in my life is about numbers and percentages. Everything. It's my job. It's the way my brain works."

She took a breath and looked away as a light breeze caught some strands of her long, white and multi-colored hair, sending it dancing around her shoulders. "We're talking about an embryo. A new life—a little you and me. In eight months it will be a baby—*our* baby. How does that make you feel?"

The only feeling I had inside was icy numbness, certain dread. "I don't feel anything but cold fear, to be honest. I can't lose you."

Her dark brows bunched together. "If we end this, I may never be able to bear another child. You may never be a father."

I shook my head and looked away. "For one thing, that is not the most important thing to me right now—"

"It will be, someday."

"Maybe. But I know what I want *now*. I *need* you to be healthy again. I need for you to do everything you can to fight this."

Emilia blinked. "Okay, and what was the other thing?"

"The other thing is that there is more than one way to become a parent. If and when that becomes important to me, there will be other ways."

"For *you*, maybe, but not for me. Chemo has a big chance of putting my body into permanent, early menopause."

I shifted my seat on the hard bench. "I spent the entire day yesterday researching this. You can't do an egg retrieval because of the hormones involved and the timing, but you can have part of your ovarian tissue frozen—"

She wasn't looking at me. Her face was blank, like she had zoned out.

"Mia—" I said, shaking her hand. She looked up at me—looked *through* me.

"You aren't telling me anything I can't find out myself from Google or my doctor. You aren't telling me what only *you* can tell me."

"I can't tell you what you want to hear. That I'm happy you are pregnant. I'm not."

She exhaled slowly, clearly frustrated. "I don't want you to tell me what I want to hear. I want to hear about what you *feel*. What do you feel?"

I paused, looked away, studied the long morning shadows we were casting on the trail behind us. I cleared my throat past the sudden tightness. "I'm afraid."

She gave a curt nod. "And?"

"That's all there is. Fear. I love you and I need for you to survive this. I need you to have the best chance of doing that."

"And…what about the baby?"

"It's not a baby."

"In eight months—"

"In eight months, if I have anything to say about this, you will be finished with your chemotherapy and be declared cancer-free and I will finally be able to breathe again."

She frowned. "I've never had much family. It's always just been me and my mom. I wanted brothers and sisters growing up, or even cousins and aunts and uncles. I had my grandma and we saw her once in a while, but—I always wanted a family. Thought that after I became a doctor, maybe I'd have a child..."

"You and I can be a family. We have each other."

Her hand came up to rub her forehead. "Someday you'll need more."

"This isn't someday, this is now."

She looked up at me with exasperation in her eyes. "Someday *I'll* need more. And this is my only chance."

"We're young. We shouldn't have to face this shit now, but we are. Life isn't fair."

"Adam," she said in a low voice, trembling on the second syllable of my name. I waited while she collected herself, cleared her throat. "There is still a chance I won't make it. If I don't, you'd still have the baby—*our* child."

My hand tightened into a fist on the table in front of me. "I'm not going to respond to that because that is *not* a possibility. I'm going to have to borrow your mom's words here. Please don't sacrifice yourself. You have so much to live for. Med school in the fall—"

She shook her head. "I'm not going to med school."

I tensed, utterly frustrated now. "Stop this. You are giving up your dream, now? You are already letting cancer win."

"I want to live. I'm not giving up."

I took a breath and let it out slowly. There was no manipulating her here. If I even tried, this fragile door that we'd opened between us would be slammed shut and barred. I'd already learned that manipulating her to do what I wanted only made things worse. I'd fucked up badly in the past, but I wasn't an imbecile—at least I learned from my mistakes.

I took her hand again. "I can't pretend to understand what this is like for you. I only know what it's like from the outside. But for God's sake, there are so many of us who want the best for you. Who *need* you. Me, your mom, Heath, all your friends..."

Her head tilted down, the brim of her cap hiding her face.

"Mia," I whispered. "I'm sorry that we can't have everything. I wish to God we could. But we have to choose what's most important here. For me, that's you. For you, I hope that's you, too."

She put her free hand to her face and only nodded.

I got up from my side of the table and slid onto the bench next to her.

She melted into my side before I even put an arm around her. She felt limp, her posture relaxing immediately. I practically had to catch her against me to hold her up. She turned and pressed her face into my chest. My arms tightened around her.

I held her like this for long, long minutes. She had grabbed handfuls of my shirt and was hanging on for dear life. She didn't move and I could hardly tell if she was breathing. And I would have given every last dime I had to know what was going on in her head. I was holding my breath, too, hoping she'd make the choice I needed her to make.

She turned her head to the side, laying her cheek against my collarbone. She wasn't crying, but when she spoke, her voice trembled. "If I do this, I will regret it forever."

"If you do this and live to regret it, put that burden on me. I'll take that on my shoulders. They're sturdy. They'll take the weight."

She sighed and I held her.

"I need time," she whispered after an endless stretch of minutes.

"You don't have much," I reminded her.

"Please, Adam," she said, her voice muffled against my shoulder.

I opened my mouth, wanted to push her to make the decision now so that we could take action today, but I couldn't. This had to come from her. And I was helpless, utterly helpless to take this into my hands.

"Whatever happens, whatever you decide..." My voice faded and I cleared my throat. "I love you."

"I know."

"Do you want to spend the day together or do you want to be alone?"

"Can we be together?"

I held her, bending to kiss her face. "Of course."

I had no idea what tomorrow would bring. I had no idea if this pain would eventually split us up for good, but for now—today—she wanted us to be together and I wanted it, too.

And maybe, just maybe, we could make some enjoyable memories where I could forget this cloud of doom hanging over us and be in the moment, be with her, be in love.

5
MIA

W E SPENT NEW YEAR'S EVE IN ADAM'S AUDIOVISUAL room—his private little movie theater. We watched the *Doctor Who* Christmas special almost a week late. Then we binged on reruns of *Battlestar Galactica*, pretending that that horrid last episode didn't exist. So we spent an hour making up our own stories about what happened to the characters instead of them landing on a primeval earth forty thousand years in the past and deciding to die out as dirt farmers and cavemen.

When I dozed off in my recliner, Adam carried me up the two flights of stairs to his room and laid me gently on the bed. By the time we got there, I was partially awake again.

"Is it after midnight?" I asked in a groggy voice.

"It's twelve fifteen."

"Hmm. It's a new year."

The bed dipped as Adam sank beside me. "Yes," he said, smoothing my hair back from my face.

He cleared his throat. "You want to sleep in your clothes?"

"Can I have a T-shirt?"

He got up and pulled one out of a drawer, at the same time grabbing one for himself and some pajama bottoms. I watched as he undressed, his beautiful body outlined in the dim, silvery moonlight that poured in through the windows. His chest and hard abs were a sight to behold—one that I'd missed. My throat tightened and suddenly I was very awake and aching to have him close to me. I might have been sick and pregnant, but I wasn't dead. Not yet, anyway.

Once dressed, he came around to my side of the bed and I rolled onto my back. He reached down and unbuttoned my jeans for me. Was he going to undress me? Oh, that was too much, but I didn't move. I relished the feel of his hands on me. The last time...well, better not to think about the last time, right? We'd both been drunk off our asses and it had led to disaster.

But again, I wasn't dead and I still wanted him so much it hurt. He had the waistband of my jeans in his hands, ready to tug them down my legs. "Lift up," he murmured.

So I did, like a helpless child, and shivered as the denim slipped over my legs, exposing them to him. Adam liked my legs a lot. I knew he did. But in the dim light, I couldn't tell where his eyes were or whether he was looking at them. Maybe he was too focused on the task at hand?

I sat up to pull off my shirt. "Can you look away, please?" I whispered.

He didn't say anything, just froze. I cleared my throat to explain myself. "It's—I'm sorry. I feel ugly there."

I hated the thought of him seeing my disfigurement, of his possible disgust at my scars, at the tiny black dots that had been tattooed on me to mark the spots that needed radiation therapy. Of the long, angry and still pink-red scar down the left side of my breast, where it puckered around missing breast tissue.

He raised a hand to my face, smoothed my cheek. "There's no way in this world you could ever be ugly. You've never been anything but beautiful to me."

His words made me ache even more but before I could reply, he shifted on the bed and turned away. I didn't say anything but hurriedly pulled off my shirt and bra and slipped on his big T-shirt to sleep in. Before he could turn back, I clamped my arms around his neck and kissed his rough cheek.

I really loved the sandpapery feel of his cheeks when he kissed me at night or early in the morning before shaving. After making love, I felt tender everywhere that he'd kissed me, and I savored the slightly sore reminder that he and his scruff had been there.

I wanted to be able to turn everything off, the constant ache inside, the thoughts that threatened to drive me insane. I wanted to feel...him, his hands, his kisses all over me. But when he turned and kissed my lips, his mouth stayed closed, despite my best efforts. I sank back against the bed, pulling him with me. "I need you," I said. There may have been more than a little pleading in my voice.

Instead of lying on top of me, he slipped beside me, still kissing me, pulling his mouth away from mine to pepper my jaw and neck with kisses. I felt his desire stir against my leg, but there wasn't any passion in the way he kissed me. It was more...affectionate.

"Please?" I asked.

He didn't reply immediately, but he stopped kissing me, pulling me tight against him. He was hard, so I knew his body wanted it, but apparently his mind didn't agree.

"I'm tired..." he began. But I knew that wasn't the reason. I knew Adam and he rarely, scratch that, *never* passed up the chance for sex— at least in the few short months that we'd been together as a healthy couple.

"You're still angry with me," I said. It wasn't a question.

He hesitated. "No."

"Then...?"

"It's too soon. It's—I'm sorry, but I can't stop worrying about you, in this condition."

I nodded, unable to explain or even understand this hurt that rose up like prickles in the back of my throat.

He seemed to sense it. "Mia, I want you. I do. But we shouldn't do anything tonight."

It was hard to explain the bitterness that drowned out the hurt. Maybe the timing was wrong. Maybe it was because everything was completely uncertain...

But he wasn't being honest with me. He was angry, resentful. I needed him but that didn't matter to him. I took a deep breath and his hands were gentle on me as they guided me to rest against him.

I reminded myself that he needed time, too. That mind of his, it was always going, and likely he wouldn't rest easy until something was settled between us...one way or the other.

We had no idea what our future would be even two days from now. But in his arms, I'd always felt beautiful, like the most important, desired and gorgeous woman in the world. The center of his universe.

I laid my head against his shoulder and his arms came around me. I wanted things to go back to the way they'd been, before we were broken.

I wanted it more than anything else.

But that would never happen, would it? Our normal, those few short months of happiness, were now wrecked forever.

I pressed my cheek to the center of his chest and fell asleep, lulled by the rhythm of his heartbeat.

***

When I woke up, bright light was pouring through the windows and the bed was empty beside me. I could hear the shower going so I lay flat on my back and looked up at the canted wooden ceiling. I'd been agonizing over a life-changing decision. One that I knew I wasn't grown-up enough to make.

My birth certificate might have stated that I was twenty-two years old, but inside I still felt like a girl, immature, scared. Afraid to come out of her shell, open herself up, take a risk. Deep down I was that girl inside the body of a woman. Everyone around me seemed so much more together, so much more in touch with who they were as adults. Especially Adam.

He might not always have been right, but he was always certain of what he wanted and what he did. I closed my eyes, feeling a stab of pain as I thought about him.

Without realizing it, my hands went down to my belly, resting atop my womb. I had his child inside me. Until five days ago, I hadn't even known it existed. But now that I did, I wanted it more than anything—maybe even my own life. But how could I tell him that? Or my mom or anyone else?

And how could I want this more than my own life? I was a scientist. This life form was not viable and soon my body would not be a hospitable place for its own systems, let alone a completely dependent one. This option made absolutely no sense to my biologist's brain. My scientific mind knew that it wasn't a baby yet. It knew that one in four early pregnancies spontaneously aborted on its own—oftentimes before the woman even knew that it existed.

The same could happen to me. I couldn't make this decision lightly, but was it my decision alone to make?

As a feminist, I strongly believed in a woman's right to choose. Every woman deserved to determine what happened to her body. I'd fight for the right for a woman to choose, and I'd never, ever dictate what that choice must be for anyone else. It was a thing so personal, so dependent on circumstance. But what I faced—was it really a choice at all?

That was what rankled me most of all, what left me nearly breathless with helplessness. I was being robbed of my choice.

Because my life wasn't *just* about me. It was about all those who loved me—Adam, my mom, my friends. It was about my future, all the years I still had before me to live for myself…for them.

Anger and bitterness stung the backs of my eyes. I'd make this choice for them, because I loved them and I wanted to live for them. But it wasn't fair. It was *so* not fair. In order to save my own life, I had to destroy that tiny life inside of me before it ever had a chance.

When Adam came out of the bathroom, one towel around his waist and another around his shoulders to towel his hair dry, he found me like that. Lying flat on my back, both hands on my stomach. His expression blank, his dark eyes zeroed in on my hands, narrowing slightly before he turned away. He'd easily deduced what was going through my mind. It wouldn't have been hard.

It had been going through both of our minds constantly for the past few days.

I sat up, staring out the window as he dressed. When he was done, he came and sat beside me on the bed.

"Hi," he said.

"Good morning."

"Want some breakfast?"

I shook my head.

"Not even a little tea or dry toast?"

I shook my head harder.

"You're green."

I nodded.

"You're also not talking."

We held each other's gaze. My heart leapt into my throat. He felt distant from me, guarded. I wanted him so damn much. I wanted to stay here and be with him. I wanted his love. It felt less accessible now than ever before. Like a distant dream I never had any hope of attaining.

And what I wanted more than anything was to live. For him. For my mom. For my friends. I'd find a way to live with myself later.

"I'll do it," I finally croaked.

His brows drew together. "What?"

"The termination. I'll do it."

Adam looked like he was about to fall over in relief. For long minutes, he didn't move, didn't smile, didn't breathe. He just watched me.

"Tomorrow?" he asked.

I nodded.

He sighed. "Okay."

I felt cold inside. Numb. Why should I feel guilty for trying to save my own life? I couldn't answer that question. Part of me wanted to shrivel up and die right there. Part of me, a larger part, was gearing up for the epic battle ahead.

"I need you," I said. "I need your help."

He put his hand to my face, cupped my cheek. "I'm here. I'll always be here." I fell against his body and he pulled me to him. I closed my eyes and tried not to think about the part of me that was curled up and rocking in the corner, already wanting to weep with the loss we were about to face.

6
ADAM

EMILIA SPENT THE REST OF NEW YEAR'S DAY IN HER ROOM AT Heath's after I dropped her off. Connor, Heath's new boyfriend, was there and they were on the couch watching *Sherlock*. I stayed for a few minutes to trade pleasantries with them. Things between Heath and me were still tense. I was pissed at him for helping Emilia keep her secrets. He was pissed at me for getting her pregnant.

It would blow over—maybe, eventually. I hoped it would, because I liked Heath. Nevertheless, I did plan on depriving him of his roommate. I'd have to discuss living arrangements with Emilia soon. Once things settled down, I was going to make a good case for her to come back and live with me. I needed her near, needed to know she would be okay. I needed to take care of her.

But for now, I needed to give her some time alone. She'd made an agonizing decision, and though I was so relieved I couldn't even think straight, I knew she must have also been dealing with a lot of doubt and self-loathing. I hoped it wouldn't last long. She needed all of her strength, all of her fight to face what lay ahead.

I followed her into her room. "So...should I come get you tomorrow morning?"

Emilia was picking up discarded clothes from the floor and throwing them into a laundry bag, apologizing for the mess.

She cleared her throat. "Yes...I'll have to make an appointment."

"I...uh...I already did, after we talked this morning."

She straightened and looked at me for a long, tense moment.

I shifted weight on my legs where I stood. "Are you—are you okay with that?"

Her mouth thinned and she took a deep breath before releasing it. "You can't just do that..."

I froze. Damn it...I'd fucked up again. I ran a hand through my hair. "I'm sorry. I didn't even think about it. I was trying to be—I wanted to save you the trouble of having to do that. I know how hard this is for you...or at least I'm trying to understand how hard it is."

She frowned and then bent to sit on the bed and didn't say anything. Then she patted the spot next to her. Slowly, I sat down beside her.

She looked up at me, grim-faced. "We can't keep doing this—making the same mistakes over and over again. I know you meant well. I know you were trying to help...but look at this from my point of view. It looks like you were jumping on the situation and making that appointment so quickly because you were afraid I would change my mind."

I swallowed. Maybe that thought had been in the back of my mind, too, but it wasn't the reason I'd done it. "I'm sorry. I fucked up." Then

I took a deep breath and let it out. My throat tightened. "You can, you know..."

She tilted her head to the side, a question in her eyes.

Fear made my heart feel like it was spearing my chest with every painful beat. "You can change your mind."

She blinked and looked away. "Either way I choose, there's somebody's gaze I won't be able to meet—either all of yours or my own, in the mirror."

I needed for her to do this—we *all* did—and so, giving her that out was all I could do. And yes, I'd said those words because I'd had to—because I had no idea what it must feel like to be in her position.

"You're strong, Mia. You'll get through this and I'll be with you every step of the way, if you want me."

Her eyes remained drenched in misery, but a faint smile tugged at the corners of her mouth. Her head sank to my shoulder. "Yes, I want you."

I closed my eyes, turned my head, smelled her hair, that peaches-and-vanilla scent which overwhelmed my senses. This rush of protectiveness washed over me, infusing every muscle. But no matter how much I vowed to watch over her, I was helpless to protect her from the greatest threat of all.

We made plans for me to pick her up in the morning and I left. There was an awkward moment where I think she wanted me to kiss her goodbye. And I would have, but Heath tucked his head in at that moment to make sure Emilia was okay—or probably to make sure I wasn't up to something with her, given the glare he gave me.

The second oncologist we had seen had provided me the information for a doctor who would see her immediately for the procedure, given the circumstances. His office was the one I'd called that afternoon. I'd also called the oncologist to set up the follow-up appointment for afterward.

I was at Heath's place again early the next morning. It was a cold, crisp day that promised moisture later on. A dark, dreary sort of day. Suitable, really, for what we were about to do.

I hadn't let myself become emotionally involved. I was in problem-solving mode. I had to be the strong one for her. It was my job—one that I took seriously. I only hoped she could do what I'd asked her to do—to put her burdens on my shoulders. I was ready to carry that weight. Emilia had once called it a baby—a child, *our* child. But I'd refused to think about it that way. Instead, it was an obstacle to her becoming healthy, a possible threat to her life. I wouldn't think about it otherwise.

We said little on the way to the doctor's office. She kept her pale face pointed downward, staring at the clenched hands in her lap. I didn't bother with small talk. She never looked up once, and that was the first time that I began to wonder what kind of long-term effects this whole thing would have on her, beyond the cancer. Would it affect her will to fight it? I clenched my jaw. One step at a time. We'd tackle that problem later.

I filled out the paperwork when we got there, leaving blanks for her to complete with information I didn't know, like her medical history. She underwent a quick examination to confirm the date of conception. Then the doctor handed her a small plastic cup with two pills inside and a glass of water.

"You'll come back for an exam and more medication in two days and a blood test in seven. Remember to follow the guidelines in the paperwork if there are any unusual symptoms."

Emilia gave a vague nod and took the water in one hand and the pills in the other. The doctor left the room and we were alone. She hadn't looked at me or directly addressed me since we'd arrived at the office. Now she stared at the pills like they were coiled rattlesnakes.

"I can't do this."

That same cold fear clutched at my throat. She was changing her mind. "Mia—"

She wrinkled her brow, focusing on the pills, her hand beginning to shake. "I thought I could."

I gently put my hands on her shoulders and stooped to get at eye level with her. "Look at me."

But she didn't. "August eighteenth. That's the due date. I looked it up." Her lip trembled.

I moved my hands so that they were on her cheeks, holding her. Finally, her gaze met mine.

The tears pooling in her beautiful eyes shredded my heart. Valiantly, she blinked them away and swallowed. I soothed her cheek with my thumb.

"Adam..." she whispered. "I can't."

My attention narrowed on her so that she was my entire focus, my entire world for those few critical moments. "You *can*. Mia, I need you—so much. *Please*." My voice died out and I was incapable of saying a word with my throat closed up, clogged with fear and agony.

She froze, her gaze dropping. Any color she'd had in her cheeks was long gone. She was so pale, in fact, that she looked like she might pass out.

I swallowed. "Do you need a minute? I'll step out. I'll—I'll do whatever you need. And—" I gulped air, suddenly feeling sick. "If you can't...if you change your mind, I'll be here for you for that, too."

Her eyes flew to mine—as if to ascertain whether or not I was serious. I was, but God—I prayed to any and all of them that she wouldn't choose to carry to term. We stared into each other's eyes. "You'd do that?" she choked out.

"I want you in my life for as long as possible—one way or another. This is your choice. You know where I stand. But I can't pressure you beyond telling you how much you mean to me. And I can't even find the words to tell you that in any adequate way. But I'll go and be right outside the door and give you a moment to figure this out."

"No," she said, her voice half a shaky sob. "I need you to hold me. Please. Just hold me and don't say anything."

I nodded, taking her in my arms. She turned so that her back was to me and I tucked her head under my chin, wrapping my arms around her waist. She felt thin, frail, breakable.

"Tighter," she whispered. *The cure for all that ails me,* she'd once said about my hugs. Now my words had no power. She knew what I wanted...but what I wanted meant nothing right now. I was lost, at her mercy.

For long, silent moments, she was still, making no sound. She wasn't weeping. She wasn't shaking.

Then, after an agonizing string of minutes, she put the cup with the pills to her lips. She began to tremble and with a sob murmured quietly, "I'm sorry—I'm so sorry."

She jerked her head backward, following up with the water and swallowed. Then she went limp in my arms. It really felt like she was coming undone. Every muscle shook. I buried my face in her hair and she stilled. I wished, somehow, that there were a way I could transfer my own strength and health to her. For the battle she was about to face, she would need them. She'd need everything she could get.

But first and foremost, she needed to heal from this. She needed not to blame herself. Even if it meant blaming me.

She finally pushed away from me to go to the sink and splash some water on her face. I noted that she still wasn't crying—hadn't shed a tear since telling me yesterday that she was going to go through with this. I didn't know whether that was a good sign or bad.

Bending over the sink like she might fall over, she looked sick. Then, she started to laugh—an ironic, wounded sound—like she was laughing and crying at the same time. "I'm sick as hell with morning sickness. But if I puke this up, it's not going to work. How weird is that?"

She put her face in her hands. I came up behind her. "You going to be okay?" It was a stupid question. Of course she wasn't okay. On so many levels.

Stiffening, she stepped away from the sink, away from me. "I'm fine," she said in a flat, raspy voice. "Take me home, please."

My stomach dropped. "Sure. Can I—do you want me to stay with you?"

She looked down. "I'm not going to be pleasant company."

"I'm here for *you*, not the other way around."

"But Heath—"

"—will understand, I'm sure." I scratched my jaw for a moment, studying her, wondering why she was being evasive now. Was she already starting to blame me?

I drove her back to the apartment. The cramps were already starting and she was as pale as a stone. I walked her to her room and she lay down on the bed without my even having to ask.

"I'm going to run out and fill your pain med prescription and get some other things. Text me if you need anything. I'll be back soon."

I got back an hour later and gave her the medicine, which she refused to take, telling me it wasn't that bad. She was curled up on herself in bed, her forehead clammy, and even I could tell the pain was considerable.

"Mia, please take your meds."

"I will, just not now. Please don't pester me about it?"

I pulled out my laptop and used my special login to give her access to Dragon Epoch. It was the beta version of the completely new and unreleased expansion that wasn't due out for months yet. She sat up, somewhat interested as I showed her some of the new features. She leaned on my arm, breathing heavily. I fought the urge to try to get some pills down her again, wondering why she seemed averse to pain medicine now when she'd had no qualms about injectable medication during her earlier cancer treatment. Eventually, she slid down on the bed, eyes half-closed.

"Adam," she whispered. I tucked away the computer and turned to her. "Can you hold me for a little while?"

"Of course," I said, lying down beside her. She turned toward the wall and settled back against my chest. "Are you okay?" I asked quietly.

She took a long time to respond. When finally she answered, her voice was groggy, on the edge of exhaustion. "I need to sleep. For a long, long time. When I wake up, it will all be over. Maybe I'll wake up and this will all have been a nightmare."

I didn't answer, as I felt her go slack in my arms. I wondered which parts of this last year she wished away. Did she regret us and the pain our messed-up relationship had brought into her life? She'd fought so hard not to be pulled into this. Maybe on some level, she'd known something that I didn't. Maybe, once she was well again, she'd decide this wasn't healthy for her.

I pushed that nagging fear aside, reminded myself that I was here for her. I was the healthy one. I'd protect her until my last breath, if it came to that.

7
MIA

MY BODY FELT LIKE IT WAS BREAKING IN HALF AND MY heart along with it. For a week I only left my room to go to the bathroom. Heath brought me food and so did Adam. And I ate a little, because neither of them would leave me alone until I did. But I didn't take the pain meds and Adam actually started an argument about it before I shut him down.

After that, I would take a few of the pills out of the bottle and throw them away when he wasn't there to see. But he wasn't stupid. It was impossible for me to hide the pain, and he knew I wouldn't be like this if I had taken them.

After our argument, I only got the deeply concerned looks when he thought I wouldn't notice them. I wasn't against medication at all. But for this...well...I couldn't explain it fully. Something inside of me strongly compelled me to feel everything, the emotions of what was happening, the physical pain. I was afraid to be numb about it. So I felt it all.

Because one thing I couldn't afford was to fall into depression. That would defeat the purpose of why I was going through all this in the first place—depression would only inhibit me from surviving the cancer. And I had to survive, especially after this. I'd done this for everyone who loved me so, because of that, I wouldn't give up.

But Adam didn't understand and I lacked the words to explain it to him. All I could feel, in his every stiff muscle when he visited, holding me in his arms when I asked him to, was worry, concern, and yeah, deep guilt. It made it hard for us to talk and, to be honest, I don't think either of us could have even if we'd wanted to.

On one of the days when Adam had to put in a few hours at work in the afternoon, and when I was feeling well enough to migrate to the couch and watch TV, Adam's cousin William paid me a visit with a plastic box tucked under his arm.

"Hello, Mia," he said with a nod as he sat down on the chair, facing me where I reclined on the couch. His mannerisms were formal and stilted in social situations. I was used to his autistic quirks by now, but sometimes I could tell that they made Heath uneasy. I sat up, racking my brain, trying to remember if I'd brushed my hair this morning. I ran a self-conscious hand over it, gathering it behind me into a makeshift ponytail. William hardly noticed.

"How are you feeling?" he said, his eyes on the floor in front of him.

William didn't know about the pregnancy or specifically why I was feeling under the weather at this time. But Peter and my mom had told him about the cancer. They'd broken it gently but Mom had told me that he'd been very upset, suffering an anxiety attack. Peter had been able to calm him down, but they'd all discussed it and decided it would be best if he didn't visit me until he felt he could handle it.

Apparently, this was that day. So I was going to make extra sure to put him at ease. While the thought of doing that should have exhausted me, it actually was comforting to know that I could step outside of my own misery and worry about someone else for a little while.

"I'm doing just fine, William."

He nodded, bringing his eyes up to my chin before they drifted down again. He rubbed his hands across the front of his jeans and appeared out of things to talk about already.

"How's work?"

He grunted and shrugged. "It's okay. There is a lot to do. We have deadlines to meet for the new expansion."

"Yeah, I can't wait until that comes out."

He frowned. "Well, unfortunately, you have to."

I smiled at his literal interpretation. I usually tried not to use figures of speech around William because they weren't his forte.

He rubbed his palms over his lap again a few times before bending to snatch up the box he'd set next to him when he'd come in. "I have something for you." And he presented me with the box.

I took it from him. "Oh, thank you."

It looked like a portable box for fishing tackle. I knew, because Heath had one like it, which was actually full of stuff he took on his camping trips. I gave William a fearful look and he said, "Do you want me to open it for you?"

"Uh...no, that's okay. You know I don't fish, right?"

William stared at me like I'd spoken to him in Martian. So instead of saying anything further, I opened the box. Inside, each tiny compartment that had been designed to hold fishing tackle items was instead filled with pieces of foam cut to fit each square. Resting in the middle of each piece of foam was a tiny pewter figurine—the figurines he loved to paint in his old room when he was visiting his dad's house.

I touched one, gently taking it out of its resting place. "Oh, William...they are so gorgeous." One dozen carefully painted figurines, all in different poses and portraying different types of characters. There was a jester and a knight in full plate armor, a scholar and a man holding a map and a sextant.

"Those are the ones you've admired when you have visited."

I blinked, looking back at the box, and noting that he was exactly right. These were the figurines that, in the past, I'd pulled off the shelf behind his worktable to take closer looks at them. Among hundreds of figurines that he'd had sitting there, he had remembered every single one I'd specifically admired.

I took the figurines out of the box and arranged them on the coffee table in front of me. "I'm going to find a special place for these. So I can always see them. They must take forever to paint."

"Not forever. Or I'd never finish more than one. Depending on the figure, they take about six to nine hours to complete. First, I need to prime them with base paint, then I do the biggest amount of base color..."

And he went on like this for the next ten minutes, tirelessly explaining every step while I nodded and smiled and examined each figurine in turn.

Heath brought him a beer at some point—maybe hoping that would break his monologue—but William didn't quiet down until Adam arrived. William grew visibly uncomfortable at the sight of his cousin.

"Hey, Liam," Adam said as he sank down on the couch beside me and leaned over to kiss me on the cheek.

William gave Adam a cold nod. I raised my eyebrows, and Adam frowned and pretended not to notice the brush-off.

William looked at his watch and then, with dismay, at his nearly finished bottle of beer. "I need to wait another forty-five minutes or so to metabolize the beer before I can drive home."

"I think you're probably good, William," Heath said. "You're tall and it's just one—"

But Adam cut him off with a hand gesture. "Yeah, best to drop it, Heath, and just let him stay. There's no point in arguing it."

Heath got up to answer a text message, and I reached out and took Adam's hand. William watched with interest, so I held our hands up and smiled. "See, William? All's good with us. You don't need to be mad at Adam anymore, okay?"

"I was angry with both of you," he said simply. "You were both behaving immaturely."

Adam and I exchanged a startled look. I hadn't meant to open that can of worms. There was an awkward silence but then William continued. "If you would have talked to each other, you wouldn't have had the problems that developed."

"You're absolutely right," Adam said, his hand tightening around mine. "But we really don't want to talk about all that right now. It's not productive."

William peered at his cousin through slightly narrowed eyes and then nodded. "How did you two...how did you start dating?"

Adam and I shared another long, uncomfortable look. Of our friends, only Heath knew the sordid circumstances of our beginnings—the virginity auction, Adam winning the bid and pretending he hadn't been my online friend already for over a year. It was all a complicated mess that was either a) too hard to explain, b) too embarrassing to explain, c) none of their business, or d) all of the above.

"We met in the game, Liam. I told you that," Adam said.

"Yes, but you were only friends then. When did you ask her to go out on a date with you and how did it happen?"

I shifted in my seat and fought the urge to giggle at Adam's discomfort. It was funny, actually, watching him sweat it out, but I decided to let him off the hook and answer. "Adam and I decided to meet, and then after we hung out for a while—as friends—things developed into more."

Adam's dark eyebrows rose briefly at my careful arrangement of the truth, which William seemed to accept. Adam's cousin frowned and then rubbed his thumb along his forehead. "So how do you go from knowing someone—maybe even being a friend—to having a romantic relationship?"

Adam opened his mouth to answer and then shut it, looking utterly lost as to how to answer that. By now I was suppressing laughter behind my free hand. William really was asking the wrong person that question! Adam had had no romantic relationships before me. Just a series of standing hookups with various partners over the years—not so affectionately referred to by me as "fuck buddies." In fact, our mutual inexperience in the relationship department was a big part of why our relationship had run into trouble in so short a time.

I turned back to Adam's cousin. "William? I'm curious, is there someone you've been thinking about asking out?"

William looked down, a small smile on his mouth before he blushed and then straightened in his seat. "Yes."

Then he stood up and grabbed his keys. "It has only been forty minutes, but I can spend the last five minutes walking to the car."

I went to stand up but Adam stopped me.

"William, can you spend fifteen seconds of that giving me a hug?" I said. And he stiffly bent and allowed me to give him a hug. "Thank you for the figurines. I love them."

And he was gone. Adam locked the door behind him and sat down beside me again with a smile on his lips, shaking his head. "Poor guy has no clue that I'm the last person he should be asking for advice about women."

"Hmm," I said, leaning over to rest my head on his shoulder, relishing the feel of his arm around me. "I think you do quite well with the ladies...*too* well, as a matter of fact."

He laughed and tucked me into bed not long after that. But I noticed, when he thought my eyes were closed, that he picked up the pill container and checked the level on it.

***

One week later and with the help of a blood test, I was declared officially no longer pregnant and ready to start rounds of chemo. It was honestly as matter-of-fact as that, like being told my red blood cell count was low, or something.

I tried my best to show a brave face to everyone around me. To make sure those feelings of hollow worthlessness at what I'd done didn't show on the surface. Heath checked on me regularly. My mom came over every day to spend hours with me. We'd talk about other things, never about what was happening to my body...how I had allowed my fight against cancer to kill the little life inside me, one rapidly dividing cell at a time.

And Adam. He spent lots of time over at my place. Things were tense between him and Heath for the first few days, but after that, they seemed to begin to go back to normal.

Adam and I got along great on the surface. But beneath that, it was weird—as if there were some kind of unseen barrier between us. Ironic, since we had both shed all our secrets. It seemed like we were finally open to each other, yet neither of us could really turn and look at the other and see them for who they were.

Would it get better? Or was the demise of our relationship only a matter of time? We had way more baggage than any two people our age should have. And we were currently wading through the worst of it now. I worried about what our future would be—even more so, I think, than my own future. I took for granted that I'd still be around to worry about all of this stuff.

Sometimes I caught him looking at me, his dark eyes nearly unreadable, but I could detect a sharp sort of worry. That look made my heart hurt. I didn't doubt he still loved me. But there was some essential ingredient to that love that seemed to be missing now. We'd hurt each other and he hadn't quite been able to see past it yet, despite all his earnest attempts to focus on the bigger problems in our life at the moment.

"So," Adam began when we were sitting side by side on my bed, each with a laptop resting on our legs. I was still a little weak from the pain but aware enough to pick up the subtleties in his behavior. "With all this going on, I didn't get a chance to tell you that the hidden quest has been unlocked."

I hesitated and studied his face. He was looking at his screen and typing at his crazy-fast pace.

"I, uh, I know," I said.

He stopped typing and looked at me with a faint smile. "I know you know."

I blinked. "How did you know it was me?"

"You left your rig on the login screen the other day. I knew the name of the character that unlocked it."

I raised a brow. "So what does this mean? Are you going to disable my account?"

He frowned. "Why would I do that?"

"So I won't blog about it."

He shrugged. "You can blog about it if you want. And you can blog about it how you want."

I looked askance at him. "You mean...you're okay if I spill all the secrets?"

He looked at me again. "I have no control over how you dish your scoop."

I frowned...there must be things he wasn't telling me. Or maybe it was my own discomfort at the thought of reporting on his beloved project that he'd spent so long developing. "But it's your big secret quest. You love that quest."

"It was meant to be enjoyed by players. It's time. I'll think up something new and even more frustrating for them to look for next."

I snorted. "More frustrating? I'm not sure that's possible."

"You know me, don't you? It's entirely possible."

I nodded. "Oh yes, you've cornered the market on frustrating."

"Besides, you've unlocked it but you haven't solved it. And you don't even know what the quest is supposed to accomplish."

"Yes, I do...Save the poor, helpless elf princess Ally—uh—Alloreah'ala—or however the hell you pronounce it. How *do* you pronounce it, anyway?"

He shrugged. "I have no idea. I jumbled a bunch of vowels and apostrophes together to make it look Elvish. Do you know how to pronounce half the Elvish names in Tolkien's books?"

I smiled. "Nope. But I do know this quest is a standard save-the-princess type of quest."

His sensual mouth turned up at the corner. "You don't know that for sure."

"What else could it be besides that? She's been captured and dragged away, imprisoned under the mountains by big, nasty trolls. Of course the quest is to go and save her."

He leaned back against the wall, watching me. "Okay. If you want to think that."

I narrowed my eyes at him and his smile grew. "You suck," I said.

That gorgeous dimple I loved so much appeared just below and to the left of his mouth. "Sometimes, yeah. And I like it."

I smacked him on his hard bicep with the back of my hand and went back to my blog post—a commentary on another game that I'd been beta testing. That article had been started and left unfinished due to recent chaotic events. I was almost done when Adam, who appeared to have finished whatever he'd been working on, turned to me.

"There's something I want to talk about," he began. I held up a finger to finish typing my thoughts before hitting the save button and closing my computer.

I turned to him. "You want me to move back to your house," I said matter-of-factly.

His dark eyebrows rose. "Umm, yeah. That's a neat trick. Do you read minds now?"

I smiled. I wished. I'd have loved to know what went through his mind most of the time. He hid his feelings and thoughts so well.

"Nope. But I know you well enough to predict that you'd be angling for this soon enough."

"I'm not 'angling' for it. I wanted to know if... Well, I'd like to take care of you."

I hesitated. Things had not gone well between us the last time we'd lived together, and I didn't want to upset the shaky ground we seemed to be standing on now. "I don't need anyone to take care of me."

His jaw tensed. "Bullshit."

"Maybe I'm tough enough to get myself through it okay."

His mouth thinned and irritation flashed in his dark eyes before he looked away. "Maybe you are. But maybe there are people here who want to help you anyway."

I sighed. "Let me think about it. The last time we lived together—"

"This won't be like last time. I'll do everything I can to make sure of that."

He was tense and I rested my head on his shoulder. "I'm sorry. I know you want to take care of me. But I'd like to think I have my independence for a little while longer."

Despite what I'd just said to him, I knew that soon I'd be very sick and at the mercy of anyone willing to help me.

***

On the night before my procedure to insert a port for the chemo—and to have a portion of my ovarian tissue taken out to be frozen for possible later use (since this procedure was still experimental), Adam had to work. I assumed he was clearing the deck and setting things in motion so he could take more time off later to spend with me.

I sat on the couch and read the latest *Game of Thrones* novel while Heath banged about the condo. He appeared to be organizing, moving things around. After he removed his fourth box of crap to take out to the garage, I looked up. "Hey, what's going on?"

He shrugged and didn't look at me. "Just making some room in here. It's getting pretty cluttered and my storage unit is almost full."

I raised my eyebrows. Heath was not the tidiest person I knew and he usually spent his free time playing games instead of cleaning. He paid someone to come in and clean his place every week.

I cleared my throat. "You okay?"

"Shouldn't *I* be asking *you* that?"

"Just wondering. I haven't seen Connor in the last few days. Everything okay?"

He sighed and sat down. "Connor was getting a little...needy."

I leaned forward, alarmed. "What do you mean 'was'? You didn't break up with him, did you?"

Heath looked at me and then away. "No. I'm not *you*, after all."

I sat back, deflated. That had stung. "I guess I deserved that."

He ran a hand through his hair. "I'm sorry."

I didn't say anything. Instead, I fiddled with the edges of the pages of my book and swallowed a sudden lump that had formed in my throat. Heath's words smarted, but it was true—I'd deserved the comment. I'd broken up with Adam after one fight—albeit a huge fight. He'd done something to utterly betray my trust, but instead of giving him the opportunity to explain, or even a second chance, I'd shoved him away. I'd thought it would be easier. It was almost as if that fight had given me the excuse to spare him this whole cancer thing. I'd been like a one-woman crusade, vowing I was strong enough to overcome it all by myself. But I'd leaned on Heath—far more than I should have.

I looked up at him. Was he finally feeling bitter because of it? My throat tightened. He got up and sat next to me on the couch. We stared at each other and then he stretched out an arm. "I'm sorry. Come here, dollface."

I leaned forward and his arms came around me. "I hope things are okay with you and Connor," I said, looking over his huge shoulder at nothing while he hugged me.

He let me go and I sat back. "They'll be okay. He's wanting to spend more time with me and there aren't enough hours in the day."

I pressed my lips together, watching him. What he wasn't saying was that he felt obligated to be around the house to look after me and drive me to my appointments. Even though I'd told him repeatedly that he didn't need to.

I reached out and grabbed his hand. "Thank you for putting up with my idiocy."

"Hmm. Yeah, I wasn't doing you any favors."

I blinked, my eyes stinging. "Thanks for being there for me even though I'm not perfect."

He didn't say anything.

"Heath?"

He glanced up at me. "Yeah?"

"I'm sorry. I never told you that before, during all of this. I'm so sorry. I put you in a crappy position."

"You were afraid. I get it."

"I still am."

His eyes narrowed as he stared at me. "Yeah, we all are. But, the difference is that most of the time we don't let fear lead us to do stupid things. Who was it that said…something about courage not being the absence of fear but the triumph over it?"

I sighed, rubbing my forehead. "That was Nelson Mandela or Eleanor Roosevelt or someone like that."

"Hard to get those two mixed up." He laughed. "I'm trying to say that you can't let fear rule you all the time. You've got to stand up to it and overcome it. Let it help you grow as a person."

I smiled, throwing a playful pretend-punch at him. "When did you get all wise and stuff?"

"Wise and wiseass—there ain't a big difference."

"Good point." I smiled. "Why don't you ask Connor to come live here?"

He threw me a glance out of the corner of his eye. "I've been…thinking about it."

I laughed. "Is that what this unprecedented cleanup job is all about? Decluttering to make room for the boyfriend's stuff?"

"So you wouldn't mind?"

"Why would I mind? This is *your* place. You have the right to ask your boyfriend to live with you."

"You and I were roommates before Brian and I got together. Then I moved out, forced you to move to that dive studio."

"It wasn't a dive!"

"You know what I mean. I don't want you to think that if Connor moves in, you have to leave."

I leaned forward and patted him on the shoulder. "Well, thank you. I appreciate it. Now ask him."

When he pulled me into a hug, thanking me, I couldn't stop thinking about his words—about fear. That it was exactly what kept me from accepting Adam's offer to move in with him again. Would fear of all that lay ahead lead me to make more poor choices?

8
ADAM

EMILIA HAD HER MINOR SURGICAL PROCEDURES DONE AND THEN a few days later we showed up at the hospital for her first round of chemotherapy. She would endure a total of twelve treatments, one every week for the next three months.

And this morning, at the bright and early hour of eight a.m., we sat in a private room in the UCI Medical Center while a nurse went down a checklist and pricked Emilia's finger to get some quick blood work done. Emilia didn't say much. She sat in a comfortable recliner with a big IV stand next to it and she had that same dead stare she'd had for days. Her golden eyes hadn't glowed for—what was it, weeks? Months? She hardly seemed like the same Mia I'd fallen in love with. It was like she was becoming a shadow of herself.

She reached down and gripped my hand. "You didn't have to come, you know…but thanks."

I didn't have to come? What the fuck was that? I frowned. "So you wanted to do this alone, too?"

She gave a light shrug. "I'm sorry. I didn't mean it that way."

"But you did specifically ask me and your mom not to tell any of your friends that you were coming in today. Was there a reason for that?"

She took a deep breath and let it go. "This isn't easy..."

"Asking for help? Yeah. I'm noticing that it's damn near impossible."

She grimaced, avoiding my eyes.

"Have you considered that it's more than just wanting to help you—it's *needing* to help you? To feel that in some way we are doing something and not standing by feeling utterly helpless and shut out?"

Emilia blinked and frowned, as if the idea hadn't even crossed her mind. "I don't want to shut you out...not anymore."

I sighed. "This is one of those things that can't continue on between us like it has in the past. Like when I made the appointment for you without asking you. I can misinterpret your intentions just as easily as you did mine. You don't want to show weakness by asking for help—so you're saying that you don't need me. Or you don't *want* to need me—and your other friends."

She looked up and met my gaze, her brows pinched together, that tiny valley appearing in her forehead between them. "I'm sorry. You're right." She let out a long sigh as if it hurt her to admit it.

Putting my hand behind my ear, I said, "What was that?"

I smiled and she made a face and stuck her tongue out at me. "I'm only going to say it once."

"Seriously, though, Mia...let us be here for you. Please?"

We stared at each other for a long, silent moment and then she let go of the breath she was holding. "I will. I'll try my hardest."

"Do, or do not. There is no try." I broke into a cheesy grin.

Finally, a wide smile from her. "Whatever you say, Master Yoda."

I checked my watch.

"Your mom will be here any minute."

She suddenly looked very afraid, shifting in the huge recliner. I reached up and smoothed her cheek. "You're going to be fine."

"I'm going to be Pukey McBarferini."

I grimaced. "That's a lovely image."

"So is the one with me bent over a toilet for the next twenty-four hours. You don't need to be around for that."

I raised my eyebrows and cleared my throat.

Her lips formed an o-shape when she realized why I was correcting her. Then she shook her head. "Wow, it comes so automatically."

At that moment, Emilia's mom walked into the room with a brave smile already fixed on her face. "Hey, you!" she said in a cheerful voice. She bent down and kissed her daughter on the cheek. "I brought you some stuff from home." Kim pulled out a bag with a battered stuffed animal, some fuzzy socks and an empty insulated plastic cup and straw to fill with ice water, presumably so Emilia could keep hydrated during treatment.

Emilia's face flushed deep red. "Mom!" she groaned, grabbing the stuffed dog and tucking it quickly behind her in the recliner. She threw me a look and I fought a smile.

"Is that your stuffed dog?" I asked. "How cute."

Her eyes narrowed and she held up a closed fist. "Don't say nothing to me, mister, or you'll regret it!"

"Mia!" Kim chided.

Emilia stuck her tongue out at her mother. "No interruptions from the humiliation committee, please."

I grinned. "I might be afraid of the violent threats if they put something like super soldier serum in that IV."

She looked over at the bag of glowing orange medication sitting on a tray, ready to be injected into her body in short order. With a grimace she said, "It looks radioactive. Maybe it will turn me into Spider-Woman."

I grinned. "A helluva lot more sexy than Pukey McBarferini."

"No doubt."

After a few more jokes, she seemed at ease, but my heart twisted in my chest when, after the nurse re-entered and explained the process, she inserted the IV into the port in Emilia's chest. I pretended not to notice when Emilia quietly pulled the stuffed dog from behind her back and cuddled it next to her.

Instead, I got up and went to the window, stuffed my hands in my pockets and tried to disguise the worry, fear and heartbreak in my own features before I turned back to her again.

9
MIA

"Not All Secrets Stay That Way Forever"— Posted on the blog of *Girl Geek* on January 19, 2014

*E*VER HAVE A SECRET YOU WERE DYING TO TELL BUT KNEW YOU'D BE IN *big, big trouble if you did? What is it about the weight of a secret that makes unburdening oneself of it so satisfying?*

Well...I've got a secret. It may just have something to do with that *secret. You know the one.*

And it's not Victoria's Secret, although the chainmail bikini armor sure looks like she could have designed it. Sometimes I expect my character to come strutting down a catwalk with angel wings pasted to her back, all covered in mandrool.

It's not the Secret to Everybody from the Legend of Zelda.

And it's not the secret cow level in Diablo.

And no, I wasn't teasing you. I've got a secret. A secret from Dragon Epoch. That *secret.*

But unlike the hack sites who prefer to use crowdsourcing to solve an intricate and long-hidden quest in hours, I will act as your guide instead of your guru.

Have you scoured every inch of the Golden Mountains, killed every computer-generated monster a zillion times, examined every single last bit of loot, questioned every non-player character that lives in that zone and every zone adjacent?

Well, no wonder you are frustrated. You are looking in the wrong place.

Girl Geek's first clue is to begin at the beginning.

Lest you don't believe me, I'll be posting a screenshot (with telling details blurred, of course) that proves I have unlocked the secret quest.

Now if you'll pardon me, I have a princess to save.

***

I think it was day two AC (after chemo) that I finally came to in the dark of my bedroom at Heath's condo. I had no real way of ascertaining the date. It might have been day three or five or ten, for all I knew. But I did know that I was dog thirsty. I could have lapped up a lake, but the water bottle by my bedside was empty.

So I ventured outside of my tiny shelter of a room. My joints ached and the skin on my hands and feet felt like it was too tight. Classic signs of water retention. I was likely about to start sloshing around like a whale before I peed it all out.

And that didn't even touch on the blazing heat in my chest or the pounding headache. At this moment I didn't know which was worse, the cancer or the medication to fight it. Chemo was making me wish for a quick death. I almost wanted to sob at the thought of eleven more rounds.

I fumbled toward the kitchen, my water bottle in hand. I was halfway there before I had to pause from exhaustion. The apartment was dead quiet and dim but for the light coming from the living room. Heath must have gone out. Good for him...and here was my chance to prove that I didn't need to be babysat like a toddler.

I straightened after a few minutes, took a few more steps before I bumped up against the cabinet door in the hallway. Suddenly, someone was standing beside me.

I opened my mouth to begin a rant about how I hated life, this world and everything in it, including the air I was currently breathing. "Heath—"

My vision swam as I turned my head, registering the figure next to me—not quite as tall as Heath and with dark hair instead of blond.

"You need more water? I didn't hear you come out of your room," Adam said, reaching for my metal water bottle. "I should have checked, but you were sleeping and I didn't want to wake you."

I pulled the bottle away from him when he reached for it. "What are you doing here?"

He straightened. "Giving Heath the night off. I told him I'd camp out here in case you needed anything overnight. Heath's out with Connor at a movie."

"I was going to fill this up myself."

"But that's what I'm here for."

I suspected he'd been here all weekend and wasn't just staying over tonight to give Heath a break.

He pulled the water bottle out of my hands, which I released with only a little resistance. "You want ice?"

I nodded and he guided me to sit on the couch in the living room where he'd been sitting. I could feel the warmth that his body had left and instead of being annoyed because I was already burning up, I sank into that warmth. There was an ache at the back of my throat, a prickling behind my eyes. I sucked in a shivery sigh. Emotions clashed inside me, chaotic, striking sparks off one another like atoms locked in a chemical reaction.

He returned with the ice-cold bottle and handed it to me. I pulled my knees up under me on the couch and he sat beside me, watching me closely. "You feeling okay?"

"Oh, peachy," I rasped between desperate gulps. "I can see why the chemo defeats cancer. It's so miserable and shitty that even *I* don't want to be inside my own body anymore. I'm sure that's why cancer decides to take a hike."

He smiled halfheartedly, as if laughing at my joke would be too much—maybe even disrespectful. I rubbed at my hands. They felt swollen and yet they weren't.

"Your hand hurts?" he asked.

"Everything hurts. I think I even have a migraine headache."

His eyebrows twitched together. "I'm sorry. I at least know how much those suck."

I shook my head. "Seriously, I can't believe you deal with this shit all the time," I said, pressing my hand to the throbbing ache in my forehead.

"You learn to live with it," he said, watching me closely. "You've been sleeping a lot. Like, for days straight."

I continued to rub my brow, the only part of my face I could still stand to touch. "Yeah, what day is it, anyway?"

"Sunday night."

Two days. I'd lost two days. I blew out a breath. "Fuck."

"You need to eat something."

I shuddered and shook my head.

"Please. I can get you anything. Even if it's a dry piece of bread."

I cocked a brow at him.

"Or...not, I guess."

My eyelids felt heavy over my eyes and my head was still pounding, but I didn't want to go back into the dark and be all alone again. I'm sure that after two days in bed, I reeked. It was a good thing I couldn't smell myself.

"What were you doing out here?"

He shrugged. "Just playing around on my tablet."

"You're not bored out of your skull sitting here all weekend?"

He fixed me with his dark gaze. "Nope. Why? Trying to get rid of me?"

"I think it would probably take several sticks of dynamite and a couple anvils to get rid of you."

He smiled. "So I'm like that coyote in the cartoons?"

"Yeah, only Road Runner can't run very fast these days." My head sank to his shoulder.

"She looks pretty exhausted, I have to admit. Guess I won't need my Acme motorized skateboard to chase after her." He shifted, pulling me against him. I closed my eyes.

It felt good, even through the plethora of suckitude going on inside my body. I swallowed. "Maybe she stopped running because she doesn't want to be chased anymore."

"So when is she going to move in with the coyote so he can take care of her?"

I frowned through my brain haze. In truth, I was a little surprised that he hadn't brought the subject up again before this. "Meep. Meep,"

I breathed with a light laugh, hoping he'd let me evade the subject with a little grace.

He didn't reply, running a light hand over my back. "What do you need? Do you want to sit and watch a movie or...?"

My eyelids grew heavier by the second. "This feels good...right here..." My words were stumbling over each other, my tongue suddenly feeling thick.

His head shifted and he kissed my hair. "Okay. We can just sit like this, then."

I fell asleep to the sound of his voice coming from inside his thick chest, relishing the feel of it vibrating against my cheek.

10
ADAM

I LEANED BACK AGAINST THE COUCH AND LISTENED TO HER SLEEP. I knew I should have carried her to her room then. She'd hardly get the rest she needed leaning up against me. But I kept telling myself, "Just five more minutes." I turned my head and smelled her hair. It smelled like *her*—straight and undiluted, not masked by hair products. I closed my eyes, that tight feeling pulling at my chest again. The sense of smell was a gatekeeper to vivid memories. I savored the ones that arose from this small sniff—the first time I'd kissed her in the hallway of her tiny studio apartment, the first time I'd really touched her in Amsterdam in that gorgeous, glittering black dress. The feel of her healthy, glowing skin under my hands.

I pulled my head away, turning to stare at the wall, unwilling to torture myself any further. The happy times—those brief flashes in our near past—only made the stark present hurt more.

I glanced down at her pale face, wishing I could be the one to take care of her. That I could do more than the measly amount of babysitting I was doing tonight. I held her in my arms for almost another hour before Heath and Connor came in through the front door and crept into the room quietly.

"Did she eat anything?" Heath whispered.

I shook my head but pointed to the water bottle. Connor took it and went into the kitchen to refill it.

I slowly extricated myself from Emilia, lifting her from my chest and then bending, I picked her up to carry her to her bedroom. I tried not to think about how much lighter she was in my arms than she used to be, how much frailer she felt. I gently laid her on the bed and when I straightened to go, she reached up and clamped her hand tightly around my wrist.

"Adam," she said. I paused and then sat beside her on the bed, smoothing her cheek. "I need you."

Something about that simple admission struck me like a blow in the center of my chest. I took a deep breath. "I'm not going anywhere."

With that, she seemed satisfied and soon her breathing was steady and rhythmic again. I bent to kiss her.

I felt powerless, helpless. And these were two feelings that I wasn't accustomed to. Feelings that angered me. Feelings that I usually avoided at all costs. I knew how to keep my distance emotionally. And with hardening resolve, I decided to do so.

I left her when Heath came in to take my place at her bedside with the refilled bottle of water. Then I drove home, my work for the evening only beginning.

11
MIA

"**Y**OU NEED TO DO IT, MIA."

I sighed, watching my mom as she finished folding my laundry. I was crammed in the corner of my small room at Heath's condo, sitting in a chair with my novel on my lap while Mom finished pairing all my socks.

"I don't *need* to. I could just—"

"It's not fair to Heath. And it's not fair to Adam, either."

My mom was trying to convince me to move back into Adam's house. She needed to go back and see to the ranch. Her favorite mare was due to give birth any time now and her caretaker wasn't equipped to handle that. And in any case, she'd been away for weeks longer than she'd originally planned due to my surprise cancer-bomb.

I fiddled with my book, flipping the pages between my thumb and forefinger. "Maybe."

"What are you afraid of?"

Of history repeating itself? Of going back to the fighting? "We rushed into it last time. I think it will jinx us. I know that sounds silly and superstitious, but..."

Mom's mouth quirked to the side as she pondered that. She looked at me with hooded eyes. "How hard did you try, Mia?"

I frowned. "What is *that* supposed to mean?"

She picked up a stack of folded T-shirts and pulled open a drawer in my dresser. "Well, as far as I understand it, you moved out after one fight. It's not like he kicked you out."

I clenched my jaw. Mom didn't know the half of what had gone on between Adam and me. The heat of indignation rose in the back of my throat. I felt judged. "He gave me an ultimatum. I don't do those."

She shook her head. "I'm not saying he didn't make mistakes, too. You both did."

My lips pursed with irritation. "But somehow my mistake was bigger than his?"

Mom returned to sit on the bed, her hands on her knees. "No. But the last time I checked, Adam didn't try to hide a serious illness from everyone close to him."

The air left my chest. So here it was. I was wondering when Mom would confront me about this. Apparently, she'd judged that I was now feeling well enough. "I know you are still mad at me and I know I deserve it, but—"

"I'm not so much mad as...disappointed—hurt. I know you and your legendary stubbornness, kid. I've known it since you were a baby. But you have to stop it. You have to grow up sometime and realize that not everything can go your way all the time."

A wave of bitterness washed over me. "Things haven't been going my way much lately."

My mom's face sobered so suddenly I thought she was about to burst into tears. My chest tightened to see it. "I wish to God I could do something about that, Mia. I honestly do."

I blinked, suddenly feeling prickles in my eyes as well. "I'm sorry, Mom. I'm sorry I hurt you. I'm sorry I hurt all of you."

She bit her lip, watching me. "I know you are. I know you are trying to do the best you can."

Apparently my best wasn't good enough. Not really. I looked down, avoided her eyes, hoped she'd drop the subject of my moving in with Adam.

She didn't say anything for a long time. Then, as if for lack of anything better to do, she turned and scooped up my socks and started stuffing them into my top drawer—where there was not much room for them. I rubbed my forehead.

"So, you won't even consider it, then?" she finally asked.

"Why do you think it's such a good idea?" I folded my arms over my chest. Best way to avoid a difficult question was to ask another question. But I also knew that she was no stranger to this tactic.

She looked at me through narrowed eyes. "Because you *can't* do this alone. I know you. I know you want to do everything by yourself. God knows what a frustrating experience it has been to be your mother and to have to deal with that stubbornness. You used to insist on tying your own shoes even when you didn't know how. Then you'd trip until you skinned your knees bloody before you'd let anyone help you tie them. But it's one thing when you are six. It's quite another thing to face the medical treatments you have ahead of you with no help at all."

"But I have Heath..." And even as I said it, I knew that she was right—it wasn't fair. Mom caught it pretty quickly.

"You've already put a hefty burden on his shoulders, Mia. Sometimes I think he's about to crack from it. You need to give him a break. And you need to give him a chance to be able to spend some time with his new boyfriend and not play nursemaid for you."

I sighed. "You've made good points. I'll, um, I'll think about it, okay?"

Her eyes narrowed. "I can't leave until I know you are going to be taken care of properly, since I won't be able to do it myself. You can call me at Peter's when you've made your decision."

"But Mom, what if Rusty goes into labor—"

Mom gave a tight shrug and that's when I knew that she meant business. "Horses have been giving birth in the wild for thousands of years."

My jaw dropped. "Mom..."

Her brows rose. "You got that stubbornness from somewhere, kid. Don't even try it."

I put my head down and rubbed my forehead. Inexplicably, tears stung my eyes—tears that would never slip down my cheeks. I blinked fiercely, unwilling to allow it.

"What are you afraid of, Mia?"

I sucked down a breath of air and shook my head, shrugging. "Blowing it again? Because even if we didn't ruin everything, it's all hanging by a thread."

"You've been through a lot in a short amount of time."

"It's all like a blur," I murmured, blinking my eyes. My vision seemed a metaphor for my life. "It's like one moment everything was going great. Wonderful. All these pieces were falling into place and then..."

"And then?"

"Is he just with me because I'm sick—because of everything that's happened?"

My mom patted the bed beside her and I looked up. She nodded reassuringly, and I stood up and went to sit next to her. She slipped an arm around my shoulders. "I'm going to tell you the truth. I don't know. You don't know. Heath doesn't know. The only one who knows? You need to ask *him* those questions."

I didn't say anything for a while, watching the spotted carpet beneath our feet.

"How about you? Are you just with him because you're sick? Because of everything?"

There were those feelings again, the jumbled ball of heaviness at the center of my chest. It was hard to breathe. I didn't want to talk about this with her. I shook my head. I supposed if I sat down for a few hours and thought about nothing else, unraveled this ball like it was a tangled spool of yarn ends and examined each piece, I might be able to tell her what every nuance and twinge meant—love, hurt, longing, distance, loneliness, distrust, regret, guilt. They were all there bunched up in knots. And my heart was tender and vulnerable for it.

"I'm afraid if I go there, if we live together, that it will ultimately be what makes us fail."

"Or, it could be what makes you stronger. Maybe you should believe in yourself more."

I put my head in my hands. "Why do I have to deal with this now?"

"You don't have to do anything but let the people who love you take care of you. Your job right now is to get better. Okay?"

"Mom, you have to go back to the ranch."

She looked at me. "And what about you?"

I avoided her eyes. "I'll talk to Adam."

She seemed to relax beside me. "Good."

***

Later that day, Adam came by after putting in some time at the office. He brought me a box of fresh cinnamon rolls, cinnamon bread and a pack of cinnamon gum. Since getting any sort of appetite back after the first round of chemo, I'd been craving cinnamon to get rid of the rusty, metallic taste in my mouth. I'd mentioned it this morning when he'd called to check up on me and now, here he was, like some sort of Cinnamon Sugar Plum Fairy bearing gifts.

He'd grabbed a sandwich for himself and we sat at the table in Heath's kitchen. Heath had gone to pick up some of Connor's boxes to move in. I nibbled on my cinnamon roll, licking the icing from my fingers. Adam watched me carefully while trying to make it appear that he wasn't. I got down about one third of the roll before I set the rest aside.

"Milk?" he said.

"Can't. It's on the 'no' list," I said, referring to my dietary restrictions.

He nodded and bit into his sandwich thoughtfully. My hands fidgeted on the table in front of me. "Umm," I finally said.

He chewed and swallowed, looking at me expectantly.

"If—if that offer to stay with you is still open... I'd like to accept it."

Adam wiped his mouth with a napkin, his eyes brightening. "Sure—yeah. Yeah, of course it is."

"I just want to tell you something, though." I cleared my throat. "Um. I'm a little scared about this. Because of what happened last time."

Adam reached a hand across the table and took mine. His warm palm enveloped it. "Last time was different. We both made a lot of shitty mistakes."

I nodded. "Okay..."

"No recriminations, remember? I think we can move past this. Do you?"

I frowned but nodded slowly. "I hope for it, anyway," I said.

He was moving his hand on mine, idly tracing my palm with his index finger. His touch tingled, burned. My fingers closed around his, but I didn't know whether I was grasping at him to pull him closer or to stop him. It was so confusing.

"Grab your bag and toothbrush. Let's go."

I looked up, stunned. "Now?"

His brows drew together. "Sure. Why not?"

"Um."

He stood, boxing up the leftover pastries and stuffing everything back into the bag he'd brought them in. "Come on. I'll get my assistant over here tomorrow to get the rest of your stuff."

"But—"

He stopped and turned toward me, waiting for me to finish.

I remembered that night when I'd first told Mom about being sick. When the thing I'd wanted most was to go home with him, for him to hold me. I had a vague memory of two nights ago, when I'd emerged from my chemo coma and he'd been here—camped out on the couch all weekend. He'd carried me back into my room and I hadn't wanted to let go of him, hadn't let go of him until I'd fallen asleep.

I took a deep breath. Time to stop being so scared. "Yeah—I'll, uh—I'll get my T-shirt and some clothes for tomorrow."

His mouth turned up in a small smile and he nodded. "I'll go shove this in the car and come back for your bag. Be right back."

With shaking hands, I quickly gathered up my stuff and texted Heath to let him know where I'd be. And then I hopped in the car and we left.

A half hour later, we stood at the bridge that crossed the small bit of harbor water to take us to Bay Island. Adam insisted we take one of the little army of golf carts waiting at the end of the bridge instead of walking the hundred yards to his house. When I hesitated, he insisted, saying I looked tired.

I probably just looked like shit since shit was my new look, compliments of the chemotherapy. And I wasn't even bald yet, though I knew that was coming soon. I could have walked but I didn't push the issue. Adam wanted to take care of me. He worried. So I'd humor him. After all we'd been through, I realized that arguing over something as simple and as trivial as this was just pointless. There were more important things in life to fixate on.

We got out and he took my backpack, gripping it as if it and I might both vanish if he didn't grab on tight. He'd been waiting for me to say yes, to come stay with him. Though he didn't show it, I could tell he was quite pleased that I'd finally agreed. Why else had he rushed out of Heath's apartment as if he were afraid I might change my mind if I stayed there one more night?

It was late afternoon when we walked up to his front door with our long shadows preceding us. A fresh breeze blew off the harbor and the familiar scent of the Back Bay assailed me. Only in Southern California, during an unusually warm winter, could we boast eighty degrees in January while the rest of the country was locked under a massive sheet of ice.

Adam unlocked the front door and opened it for me, guiding me in with a light hand pressed to the small of my back. My muscles tightened under his touch, suddenly aware of how long I'd been craving something more than just a hug or a squeeze of the hand. Now that the crappiness from the first dose of chemo had mostly faded, I was only mildly feeling like ass rather than weakly wishing for my own quick and painless death.

I was bouncing back. I'd read about this. With every treatment it would take me slightly longer to bounce back, with fewer and fewer days of feeling good in between. I tried not to think about what lay ahead and instead chose to adopt my new philosophy of living in the now. I vowed not to fret about what might come tomorrow, choosing to accept and appreciate what I had today.

And today I had a very attentive, very hot young man at my beck and call. Tonight, we'd be lying in the same bed together and I hadn't felt his touch in that way in far too long. My heart raced with anticipation. It didn't matter that I still had a dull headache or that my joints still were a little stiff. I was still alive, goddamn it, and for today, why not enjoy it?

Adam checked his watch when we hesitated in the entry hall. Before spending the night on New Year's Eve, I hadn't been here in almost two months, since just after our trip to Vegas and the god-awful fight we'd had when he'd found the painkiller syringes in my bag. I swallowed a ball of nerves stuck in my throat and glanced around. Everything was still exactly the same. The house looked as unlived in and spotless as ever.

"Miss Emilia!" Adam's housekeeper, Cora, cooed as she came out from the kitchen and greeted me with her usual bright smile, a hug and a kiss on the cheek.

Then she put her hands to my cheeks. "You look tired. I made some dinner. Mr. Drake told me you were coming."

I raised a brow at Adam. He shrugged. "I texted her when I went out to the car."

"Dinner's in the fridge. You can reheat it whenever you want."

She spoke with Adam, telling him the chef would be here in the morning to make breakfast. He said he needed to prepare a shopping list for her with my diet restrictions.

"Hey, I'm going to run upstairs and freshen up," I said, interrupting them.

I turned to move past them when Adam caught my wrist while he finished giving Cora instructions to pass along to Chef.

I paused, fidgeting beside him. He glanced at me. "Just a minute, okay?"

Cora brightened. "Mr. Drake has a surprise for you."

I turned to look at him. He grimaced at Cora, as if she'd said something she shouldn't have.

She threw her hands up at him and shook her head. "I'm going to go. You are okay for everything tomorrow?"

"Yes, we're fine. Thank you for everything," he said while escorting me toward the stairs.

I threw him a look. "I used to live here, in case you forgot. I know the way to the bedroom."

There was a small smile on his sexy mouth, which he hid almost instantly. "That's not where we're going."

I puzzled at that, following him up the stairs. I knew better than to ask him what the hell he was talking about. With Adam, all was revealed in due time—*his* due time. So when we turned left in the upstairs hallway instead of right, which led to the master suite, I mentally scratched my head.

Holding my hand, Adam led me into the guest suite. "Step into my TARDIS, young lady."

"It's bigger on the inside!" I said almost automatically, staring around me in wide-eyed wonder at the transformation in the room.

Adam smirked. "That's what *she* said."

I made a face. "Perv."

The entire time that I'd lived here before, for a month before Adam had left on his hike, the month during the hike, and a month after that when we'd been together before I'd decided to move out, I'd only been in this room a handful of times. The suite was nearly as spacious as the master suite that I'd shared with Adam.

But today it looked completely different. It had been redecorated and, in some cases, renovated. There were different windows—huge ones that went all the way up to the ceiling from a brand new upholstered window seat that lined the entire thing. The room was decorated in two shades of green, my favorite color, and crème. The designs were muted and soft with forest and mint green accents. There was a modern, ergonomic lounge in the corner with a retractable desk, complete with a brand new laptop computer. The bathroom, which had been gorgeous before, had been redecorated to match. It had a beautiful shower tiled in jewel tones, but I noticed steam jets had been added and the sunken tub beside it was new. It sat flush against the tile floor and was backed by a new recessed gas-lit fireplace. It was an overflow bathtub with a lip all the way around it that allowed water to go right to the edge and then drained away any excess.

"This is amazing!" I said. "You've been busy the past few months."

Adam smiled. "The past three weeks, actually. My decorator organized a rush job."

I raised my brows. "Expecting some important guests?"

"Yep," he said, watching me closely. "You."

My heart stuttered a little bit, but I wasn't quite sure whether it was from pleasure or disappointment. He'd done all this—a huge undertaking in a short amount of time, a major modification to part of his home—for *me*. But it was for me to live in...to stay in. To sleep in. Alone. While he slept down the hall.

I turned away from him so he wouldn't see the mixed emotions on my face, walked out of the bathroom and back into the beautiful bedroom. I stared out the huge windows at the view that looked out on part of the Back Bay of Newport Harbor. Sailboats were motoring in after a long day of leisure on the ocean. Small electric boats full of tourists and locals alike were tootling along the calm water while maneuvering around the bigger motorboats.

"The best part about this room is the windows," Adam said, coming up behind me.

"They are nice windows," I said quietly.

He picked up what looked like a remote control from the marble-topped nightstand. "But they aren't always windows. Sometimes they're a wall." He pressed a button and suddenly the windows went opaque and turned a flat eggshell color, as if part of the wall. We stood in semi-darkness, the only light coming from the bathroom skylight behind us.

"What the hell just happened?" I said, confused.

"No blackout curtains necessary. Just hit this button at night and the room stays dark until you hit another button in the morning. Or you can even put it on a timer so they go transparent again at a certain time of day. Or if you only want to let a little light in..." He pressed another button and the window was back, only with a frosted, muted effect.

"Can I project movies and video calls on it like Tony Stark's windows?"

He grinned. "Not quite yet. When they invent an Iron Man window, that's going into *my* room first."

There it was again, that twinge in my chest when he said *my* room. There was my room and there was his room. There was no "our" room. Did that mean there wasn't an "us"? I turned away from him again.

"They're more than windows and wall, though—they are also lighting." He hit another button and the windows went opaque again but glowed with a golden light that mimicked indirect lighting. He pressed another button and a bunch of tiny white lights appeared along the seam of the walls where they met the ceiling.

I wandered over to the low bookcase that stretched the length of the wall perpendicular to the window and its seat. On top, there were a series of framed pictures. One of my horse, Snowball, who was still up at the ranch in Anza. One of me and Heath on a visit to Palm Springs when we were in tenth grade. One of my Mom riding her favorite mare, Rusty. One of Heath's gorgeous desert sunset shots taken at Anza-Borrego State Park. And one of Adam and me standing next to Diamond Falls—that spectacular cataract in St. Lucia—the morning after the night we'd first made love. My chest tightened to look at us then, so happy, so in love even though neither of us would admit it to the other—or even ourselves—at that point. I picked up the picture, instantly fascinated that these two people were the same ones standing in this room, getting along swimmingly even though we felt miles apart from one another.

"So what do you think?"

I swallowed and set the picture down. I wouldn't dare let him know about my disappointment. He'd done a magnificent, wonderful thing. Made a very kind gesture. I plastered on a smile and turned back to him.

"I can't believe you did all this. You didn't even know if I was going to come back."

He set down the remote and shrugged. "Well, I hoped for it. And I wanted to make sure you'd be comfortable. So I had it done. Just in case."

Just in case. He'd spent thousands and thousands of dollars on a rush remodel "just in case."

He approached me, peered into my eyes. I was still faking that rapturous smile. He put a hand on my cheek and my eyes fluttered closed. Every touch from him was like magic, like a thousand words, feelings and gestures wrapped up into one split second. His fingertips grazed my cheek. "Like I said, I want to take care of you."

He did. He did want to take care of me—from fifty feet away, down the length of a long hallway and separated by two doors.

He frowned. "You okay? You seem distracted."

"I think I need to puke. And you don't need to see it." I forced down a wave of nausea that had washed over me like a tsunami of sick.

I turned, slipping into the bathroom and falling to my knees, into the familiar position of praying to the porcelain gods. Even though the initial wretched days of my first round of chemotherapy were behind me, I still felt sick—at least once a day, sometimes more. Maybe that was the real reason Adam had decided to put me up in my own room— so he wouldn't have to hear me hurl daily. Hopefully that meant he'd stay in the other room while I took care of this.

12
ADAM

I STOOD FROZEN FOR A MOMENT WHILE EMILIA HEAVED INTO THE toilet. Uncertainty stilled me because the first thing I wanted to do was go in there and comfort her, but she'd specifically told me to stay away.

I went to the closet and grabbed a spare throw and some pillows and took them to her. It was puzzling because she'd hardly eaten a thing at Heath's. What could she have possibly had in her stomach to throw up?

She was on her hands and knees, her head down over the toilet bowl and her long hair strewn all around her. I reached down and pulled it back for her.

"What part of 'you don't need to see this' didn't you understand?" she choked, but from the tone of her voice, she was more dismayed than annoyed or angry. I didn't move, just kept her hair back for her while I set down the pillows and blanket beside her.

"What's that for?" she asked.

"For your knees, and the blanket is in case it's cold down on the floor."

She choked again and then sat up, wiping her mouth with the back of her hand. I filled a glass of water from the tap so she could rinse her mouth out. "You are incredibly sweet."

I sat beside her on the ground. "Shh. Don't let that get around. My dev team would never believe it, anyway."

After rinsing her mouth, she sat back and watched me again with that long, enigmatic look. She seemed...sad. My chest tightened. She always looked sad these days.

Resting on her heels, she gave me a small smile. I took the empty cup from her. "You need help up?"

She was fiddling with her hair, running the part I'd held back from her head through her fingers. "I, uh, I like to stay down here for a little bit, just in case."

Darting me a look, she grabbed one of the pillows I'd brought and stuffed it under her butt, sighing in satisfaction. The other one she crammed against the wall and rested against it.

"Hmm, maybe I should get you a little lounge to sit on for these episodes."

"A toilet lounge?" she grinned. "Your decorator would have a fit."

I shrugged, leaning back on my own piece of marble-lined wall, the chill seeping through my shirt. I was glad she had the blanket to keep her warm. I wasn't kidding. I'd email my decorator tonight and get her to find something to fit the bill. Call it a toilet lounge or a commode couch or whatever.

"So there was one more thing I wanted to give you," I said. I pulled the box from the front pocket of my shirt.

She took one look at it and swallowed, and I realized her hesitation was because it was a jewelry box. Good things had not happened the last time I'd handed her a jewelry box. I flipped it open to allay her fears that it was another engagement ring. Besides, who the hell would propose over a toilet?

Her brows went up when her eyes landed on what was inside and then she frowned, clearly intrigued. She reached a hand out and stroked the inside of the box.

"Take it. It's not going to bite you."

She stuck her tongue out at me. "You do *not* want me to breathe my barf breath on you, dude."

"No, I have a feeling that could be a lethal weapon."

"There isn't a dragon even you could dream up even in *your* twisted imagination that would have breath more lethal."

I leaned forward and she pulled the piece from the box, the gold chain dangling down. She peered at the object at the end of it and looked up at me with a questioning expression. "A compass?"

I nodded.

Another rush job, this time from a jeweler, who had designed the face of an antique gold compass with a flat backing of dark blue lapis lazuli and a pattern of small diamonds in the form of a constellation on the surface.

"That looks like your company's logo."

I was glad she recognized it. "Kind of. They are both patterned after the constellation Draco the Dragon."

She nodded, fingering the surface. "Is there a special meaning to it, then? Beyond your company name?"

"I wanted to get it for you...as a reminder."

She slipped the chain around her neck and it rested low on her chest. The chain was long and it dangled just above her breasts over the loose gray T-shirt she wore. "What is it supposed to remind me of?"

"Draco is a constellation in the sky, near the North Star. It's always in the sky, no matter what time of day and no matter what season."

She nodded, watching me, her face unreadable. Her fingers smoothed over the glass surface. "Uh huh..." she said, sounding like a child listening to a story, prompting the storyteller for more.

"It's the lost zodiac constellation." I pointed to the diamond that represented a star in the head of the dragon. "This is Thuban. Four thousand years ago, this star was the North Star. Now it's forgotten because the earth's axis has shifted. I chose it as the symbol for my company because it reminded me never to take my eyes from my goal, my true north. So I thought I'd get this as a reminder for you."

She concentrated on the tiny recreation of the constellation. "My true north. And what is that?"

I wanted so badly to supply that answer for her. Us. *We* are, I wanted to say. I watched her for a long moment, hoping she could figure that out for herself. It wasn't something I could ever provide for her. "It's what you have to figure out. It's your reminder to be strong. To have hope. To keep being the warrior I know you are."

Her lower lip disappeared into her mouth, her eyes teary. The rest of her froze. Then suddenly, she leapt toward me so fast I thought she would crash right into me. But she hooked her arms around my neck so tightly that she was in danger of cutting off my airway.

"Easy now," I chuckled. Wow...this got me a much better reaction than the engagement ring. I'd really screwed that one up, hadn't I?

She held me tight, her knees practically in my lap. My arms came around her to hold her lightly to me. She rocked in my arms before turning her head. "If I didn't have barf breath, I would kiss you so hard right now."

I turned, kissed her cheek and released her. "Are you safe from puking again?"

"Probably. I'm going to brush my teeth."

I got up and went out into the bedroom while she dug through her bag and brushed her teeth. I was messing with the kick-ass windows when she came in. "I had them install these in my room, too. The whole house gets them next. But I had to wait and put them on order while they make them. They also control how much heat comes into the room, and they can make the window one-sided so people can't see in even while you can look out."

"You're such a gadget addict," she said, watching the windows go from opaque, to frosted, to transparent, and back again, one time abruptly and another time gradually.

I pressed a few more buttons. "You say that like it's a bad thing. This remote is also an intercom."

"An intercom? You mean so we don't have to shout down the hall to each other?" she said, and her voice shook a little when she said it. I glanced at her but pretended not to notice. I was still getting that weird, nervous vibe from her. She'd said as much—that she feared us walking down the same crappy road we'd traveled down before. Not if I could help it. Hopefully I had enough safeguards in place to prevent it.

"Yeah, in case you—well, in case you need me." I showed her the button to press. "There's one in your bathroom, and I've got one in my room and my office and downstairs, too."

"Can't I just ring a bell instead? And have you bring me a tray in bed while dressed only in a Speedo and bow tie?"

I suppressed a laugh. "I don't wear Speedos."

She eyed me playfully. "Too damn bad."

Suddenly, a rush of heat rose under my collar. The way she was looking at me...I had to take a deep breath and remind myself that she was sick. There would be none of *that*, no matter how much my body protested. She'd just been on the floor, puking.

Before I could stuff in another thought of protest, however, she stepped gingerly toward me, slipping her hands around my neck, lacing them at the back and pulling me down to kiss her.

I tasted the peppermint of her toothpaste and another taste, strong and medicinal, like she'd rinsed with mouthwash. Her hands tightened around my neck and her kiss deepened, her mouth opening. She pressed her chest against mine and—wait, what was I supposed to remember again?

My hands slipped to her lower back, pressing her against me. She was saying something, but I barely heard over the rush of desire roaring in my ears. She was thanking me for the room, telling me she'd missed me. I opened my mouth and slid my tongue into hers. I angled my head to press her for more and—

This was getting out of hand. I pulled my head away gently and lifted on her tiptoes to follow me. So I took a deep breath and stepped back, still holding her at her waist. She stared up at me with those lovely brown eyes, a tremulous smile on her lips.

"This was so sweet of you," she whispered. "I can't—can't believe that you did all this. But..." Her eyes flicked away.

"But what?" I prompted. If she wanted us to communicate better, there was no time like the present to begin improving.

She backed off, suddenly looking embarrassed. Her teeth clamped down on her luscious bottom lip and her brows lowered over her eyes in a pensive frown. "I just thought we'd...that I'd..." She took a deep breath and I waited, a little nervous as to where this conversation would go. "I thought when you wanted me to come back that you wanted us to be a couple again."

I put my hands on her cheeks to hold her still. "We do need to work on our relationship. I agree. But right now is about you getting healthy again. I don't want you to feel any pressure about us. I don't want to let the difficulties we've had get in the way of you getting better."

"What makes you think they will?"

My hands dropped back to my sides. "This isn't a good time for drama. And there's been a lot of drama between us. It's like what you said before¬—that we can't keep making the same mistakes. So we just need to be careful."

She was watching me, hardly masking her disappointment, fingering her compass while looking at me with wide eyes. "So it's not because I pushed you away before?"

I shook my head. "No. This isn't about shutting you out, Mia. It's...it's supposed to be your place, a little sanctuary. So you can get better."

"And you won't stay here with me." Her voice was quiet, calm, but it shook just a little. It wasn't hard to detect her hurt.

"Of course I will...when you want me to. But I think it's really important that we stay positive and go slow."

She raised her brows in surprise, but understanding was dawning in her eyes. "Go...slow?"

"So...one step at a time, okay? We have a long road ahead of us and a lot of time to cover that ground. But not today. We will figure this out, but the most important thing right now is you—your health, your happiness and well-being...okay?"

She nodded slowly, not looking entirely on board with this plan. "I'm willing to give it a try," she began quietly.

"Good." I smiled.

"But it might get lonely sometimes," she started, a smile tugging at her lips.

"Hmmm..." I said, feigning deep thought. "You didn't bring your little stuffed dog to keep you company?"

She smacked me on the arm with the back of her hand and we laughed. Not long after, we went down to the kitchen, hand in hand.

***

Emilia went in for her second round of chemotherapy a few days later. This time, Heath and her two closest girlfriends, Alex and Jenna, were there, along with her mother and me. But instead of going home to Heath's afterward, and me having to dream up excuses for camping out on his couch all weekend, she came home with me, where she belonged.

13
MIA

"Meta-Gaming, or The Lives Our Characters Lead, Without Us"—Posted on the blog of *Girl Geek* on February 15, 2014

I REMEMBER THE FIRST TIME I LOADED A SIMULATION GAME—YOU KNOW, *the ones where your characters actually simulate real life. They have a house, a job, relationships. All of these require work to maintain. Clean the house by getting your character to scrub the toilet. Get up at six a.m. to get dressed for work. It was hugely entertaining at first. I spent long hours those first few days pinned in front of the computer, clicking away while my own real-life dietary and cleaning needs were ignored. After that, I never touched the game again. I realized that my characters' lives were more boring than even my own.*

Not so with the other games we know and love. The exciting adventures, zooming through the streets of LA in a stolen car or careening through space exploring the universe in your own spaceship. Or...questing your way across Yondareth with a magical weapon in hand.

But what happens when we hit that log-off button? In the world of massively multiplayer roleplaying games, where thousands of people interact on a server, the world goes on, but our character vanishes from it until the next moment we log in. It's like our character takes a little vacation from life, stepping into a stasis.

What if, instead of those fantastical adventures our characters lead—or even the more mundane ones of the world-famous simulation games—we logged in to a game where our character logs in to a game to play a computer game?

Wouldn't that be the ultimate form of meta-escapism?

***

This second round of chemo didn't floor me for long. Thank God. I hoped that boded well for the future. I had a chart sitting on the nightstand beside my bed. It had twelve boxes and two of them were now checked off. Two down, ten to go. *Just kill me now.*

Or maybe I was waiting for my superpowers to kick in. My chemo oncologist, a wonderful man who had male pattern baldness, admired my still full head of hair and warned me that it would most likely fall out soon. Running his hand over his own bald pate, he said, "But at least yours will grow back in!"

Of course, getting cancer wasn't worth the jokes, but I'd take them over self-pity.

I flipped the chart over on the nightstand with no desire to even think about the ten rounds remaining. Instead, I studied the group of figurines that William had given me. They were so intricately painted, detailed and shaded—even the tiny pewter bases upon which they stood were painted to simulate grass or earth or stone. There was the Guide with a map and sextant. The Bodyguard dressed in a full suit of armor. The Jester with the funny hat and wildly colored clothes. Sometimes I'd pass an hour staring at them, rearranging them. Pretending they represented people in my life.

I also spent a lot of my downtime on the laptop playing Dragon Epoch. Since these were times when none of my friends—except Adam—could log on, I worked on the secret quest that he was completely hands-off about. I knew better than to ask him about it or to try and wheedle more clues out of him. He'd once thought himself the height of generous by giving me the uber-elusive "yellow" as a clue. In the end, it had been a very valid clue but so generic as to be useless.

After our talk about asking for help, and the very simple fact that I needed help constantly, working on the quest by myself was a way that I could assert my independence and do things on my own. I spent long hours lying in bed, my laptop propped on my knees, looking for answers on how to proceed with the quest.

But I was getting nowhere and once I was feeling better frustration drove me out of bed. I decided to take a shower.

Though I'd prepared myself for the inevitable loss, it still hit me as a shock when the first clump of hair came off in my hands. It was dry and dead like autumn leaves, and it left my head with little to no resistance.

With a quick intake of breath and a sharp stab of alarm, my heart battered against my chest in fear. I pulled out four or five handfuls and let them fall to the floor. Though this loss was nothing to what I'd already suffered, it was still something to remind me of all that cancer was robbing me of. This loss may have been temporary, but it served as an all-too-poignant reminder of all that I had lost. My breath came in shivery gulps and tears prickled my eyes.

The drain was starting to plug up with the excess water running out of the showerhead before I finally stopped yanking and pulling at my own hair. I reached up to touch my patchy scalp. The skin there was tender, sensitive.

I think I tried for about sixty seconds to be brave, but it was soon overwhelming and I was shaking with rage and anguish as tears trickled down my face to match the rain of the showerhead. Fuck you, cancer, for succeeding in stealing yet another thing from me...my hair and all it represented—youth, beauty, femininity.

By the time the shower started overflowing onto the bathroom floor, I was on the ground, sobbing and trying to pull the hair out of the drain to unclog it.

The world around me turned and my stomach flipped. I felt like throwing up, but fortunately I held it in. I was not as successful with my tears. Because of that, I could hardly see what the hell I was doing and the water began to get cold as I became more frantic.

Suddenly, there was a rush of cold air and the showerhead turned off. I huddled on the shower floor, a mess, bent over myself.

Adam knelt in the water beside me. "Mia. Get up."

But I didn't move. I buried my face in my hands. "I don't want you to see me."

"I've seen you naked before. Come on. You're shivering."

"Get me a towel," I sniveled.

He'd seen everything, yes. But not like this. Not this scarred, maimed, skin-and-bones version. I would disgust him. I knew I would. I disgusted myself every time I stared in the mirror.

This cowering wimp was a far cry from the empowered, confident female who had once shucked my bathing suit to expose myself to him before luring him to take a shower with me. I'd been confident in my body then. I'd wanted him and I'd wanted him to want me. And he had. He *so* had.

This body belonged to a sick woman. A husk. A sniveling, pathetic weakling. Because along with the physical losses—the weight, the pregnancy and now the hair—there were those that couldn't be seen—confidence, independence, empowerment. Cancer was slowly yet surely breaking me. I didn't know this girl. She wasn't me. She was the furthest thing from me I could have ever imagined. And I had no doubt in my mind that he felt the very same way. I swallowed that ever-present shame. It stabbed in my throat like a jagged piece of glass.

In seconds, Adam was holding out a towel in front of me, his head turned to the side so that he couldn't see. "Stand up. I'm not looking."

Slowly I stood and walked into the towel he held out, wrapping it around myself. He kept his eyes away from me as he went to grab the fluffy bathrobe off the hook in the corner and held it up while coaxing me into it. Then he turned and looked at the shower, which was still backed up. He grabbed the trashcan and sloshed into the shower, the legs of his jeans now entirely soaked. He proceeded to unclog the drain, pulling out clumps of my hair. The water ran down the drain with a hearty gulp.

Shaking, I watched his impassive face in the mirror. "*I'll* clean up the mess. Please...let me."

He didn't look at me, grabbing extra towels to soak up the excess water on the floor. "No, you won't."

"But—"

"You aren't cleaning *anything*. Don't even try."

"Adam—"

He stopped, straightened and looked at me in the mirror, bathroom trashcan still in hand. He met my gaze, his face dead serious. "Don't argue with me, Mia. You aren't cleaning. You're a guest. My guests don't clean."

A *guest*. That word sounded so weird. I'd lived here. For three months this had been my home. Adam had once called it *our* house. But now I was a guest. Moving out in a huff must have demoted me to guest status.

He turned and finished up with the wet towels, grabbing them and throwing them in the second sink. "I'll have Cora call the cleaning people in the morning."

I hadn't had a chance to turn my attention to my reflection in the mirror until that moment. What I saw almost made me gasp in shock. My head looked like a sheep that had some kind of weird molting sickness. Patches of hair hung by barely a thread. Huge clumps had been pulled out and some of it was still firmly rooted in its place.

I'd been mentally preparing for this moment since I'd been prescribed chemotherapy. But it still struck me, almost taking my breath away. I sniffed and blinked, ferociously fighting new tears. Adam finished tidying the bathroom and then straightened, watching me watch myself in the mirror.

"Mia, take a deep breath."

So I did. It was shaky and weak, like the rest of me. "I look like a leper."

He came up behind me, reaching around to belt my robe, which I had left hanging open (but, mercifully, I was still covered by the towel). The feel of his arms around me was both thrilling and alien at the same time. I wanted him to pull me to him, whisper in my ear that I was still beautiful to him. I avoided his gaze in the mirror.

I wasn't beautiful to anyone.

"Come with me," he said, taking my hand and leading me out of the bathroom. He pulled me through my bedroom and into the hall toward his bedroom.

"Where are we going?"

"My room," he said matter-of-factly.

"I can see that. Why?"

"Trust me."

I let him tow me along, his grip around my hand tightening. We went through his room and straight into the ensuite bathroom. He stopped and bent to pull something out of the bottom cabinet. He had an ironic smile when he straightened.

In spite of myself, I laughed when I saw what it was. Electric clippers.

"May I do the honors?" he said, waggling them in front of him. "I may have fantasized about shaving a beautiful woman's head."

"Sicko." My eyes narrowed at him. "Shut the fuck up and turn those on."

He grinned. "Oh God, please talk dirty to me. Hurt me, baby."

I playfully slapped his chest with the back of my hand. I grabbed a towel and laid it across the sink. "Don't want to be responsible for plugging any more drains."

Then I bent over the towel while he plugged in the clippers. He gently placed them against the back of my neck and moved the clippers forward. They were cold and tickled my scalp, buzzing across my sensitive skin. I closed my eyes, waiting for it to be done.

"Good riddance to this white hair with the pink and purple. It's god-awful My Little Pony hair. I've never been so glad to see hair go!"

I swallowed my laugh. "It's platinum blond, you dolt."

"Dolt! Ah, you can do better than that. Come on, hit me hard."

The clippers slipped against the back of my ear, tickling me. I started laughing. "Bastard. Fucktard. Asshole."

"I'm shaving all your hair off. You're going to be the chick version of Humpty Dumpty."

"Fuck you, prick," I ground out between gritted teeth.

"Damn, the reflection of this light off your head is blinding me. Can't see a thing."

He purposely set the clippers against the sensitive back of my neck and I shrieked, laughing. "Pencil dick."

"Are you married to Mr. Clean?"

"You better run when you're done with this shit, 'cause if I catch you, I'm so kicking your ass."

"Sounds exciting," he said, clicking off the clippers. "Done."

I didn't move for a stretch of minutes, taking a long breath.

"You ready? You need me to psych you up?"

"Shut your hole, asshat," I said, then cleared my throat and straightened, looking at myself in the mirror.

Yeah, I was speechless. I looked like Dr. Evil from *Austin Powers*. My eyes flew to Adam, who was watching me very closely, probably expecting another meltdown.

So I took my pinky finger, raised it to my lip and said, "I shall call him 'mini-me,'" in the best imitation of Mike Myers that I could manage.

Adam's handsome face broke into a smile. His stance relaxed, as if he was relieved.

I raised my hand to my naked scalp. "Shit, this feels so weird."

He held up the clippers. "Wanna do me now?"

"Don't even think about it. How would the horny little interns fantasize about running their fingers through your hair if you were as bald as me?" *And what would I fantasize about?* I mentally added.

He rolled his eyes in response. I ran my hand over my head again. "Feel this shit. It's weird as hell."

He set down the clippers and obediently ran a hand over my head. He shot me a seductive look in the mirror. One that, in other circumstances, might have made my panties hit the floor fairly quickly. "Shit. I'm getting so turned on right now."

I elbowed him lightly in his hard stomach and he gasped as if I'd slammed him with a two-by-four.

"You are the hottest bald woman I've ever laid eyes on."

"Fuck you."

He threw his hands up. "What? I'm serious. Ilia from the very first *Star Trek* movie? Did you see that? The one from the seventies?"

I narrowed my eyes at him. "A long, long time ago."

"Yeah, she was this Deltan chick. So hot that sex with her killed any human dude who tried to screw her. Still not as hot as you."

I turned around and faced him, folding my arms across my chest. "You're so full of shit."

"Am not. You see *V for Vendetta*? The bald chick in that one— Natalie Portman. She was hot. Very hot. But again...not as hot as you."

I bent my head now, trying to hide the fact that I was laughing. "You know of any other bald women?"

"Demi Moore in *G.I. Jane*. Not even close to your level of hotness."

"Did you do an Internet search to look this up or something?"

He gave me a funny look. "I watch a lot of movies."

I turned back to the mirror and ran a hand over my scalp. He came up behind me and put a hand on my head again. He bent toward me as if he might kiss me. My heartbeat raced and I tilted my head back slightly in anticipation. Would he kiss me? Did he want me?

But before he connected, I watched him stiffen and draw back almost as quickly. We locked gazes in the mirror and I swallowed.

"Ripley," he said.

"What?"

"Ripley from *Alien*. You know... Sigourney Weaver."

I frowned at him. "She had hair."

"Not in the third one. She was bald—bald as you."

"You actually saw the third movie? I heard it sucked so much ass it could be a black hole."

"You are still hotter than bald Ripley from the ass-sucking *Alien* movie." He shrugged. "I've seen a lot of bad movies, too."

I looked at myself again. "At least I still have my eyebrows and eyelashes...for now."

Adam shrugged. "You could possibly still keep those."

I glanced at him and shrugged. "Maybe, maybe not. It's not like I'm out to impress anyone." Except him.

"Are you going to get a wig?"

The thought of putting a heavy wig on my head was not appealing to me in the least. It would make my head sweaty and hot, and I just didn't see the point. "I think I'll just wear a hoodie every day."

He tilted his head, studying me. "Not a bad idea. I think I have a knit cap or two. Something to wear when it's not eighty degrees out."

"Can't stand the thought of a wig."

"You could wear bandanas. But be careful what color you wear in whatever part of OC you're in."

I flashed him a phony gang hand sign. "Yeah, because there are so many gangs in Newport Beach."

He grinned at me and it made my heart flutter more than a little bit. He looked so much like the guy I'd fallen in love with. That brilliant, sexy man with the little boy's impish grin.

"I think this night calls for some ice cream and *Farscape*."

I frowned at him. "*Farscape?*"

He raised his brows at me. "Seriously? You've never seen *Farscape*? It's only the best science fiction that has ever been televised. I will have to force you to watch a marathon someday so that you, too, can appreciate the genius that is *Farscape*. And there's a hot bald woman in that, too. Zahn. She's not as sexy as you, either. And she's blue."

I laughed. "Glad to know I'm sexier than the blue bald chick."

Except I couldn't eat ice cream. The chemo diet did not allow dairy, nor did it allow soy. I was doubly screwed in that department. No frozen yogurt, either. He muttered something about ordering a snow cone machine instead.

We sat in recliners in his home theatre to watch the episodes of this show from the early 2000s. I made it all the way through the first two episodes—the bizarre but amazingly done fantastical journey of John Crichton, hunky, brilliant astronaut from Earth who'd inadvertently discovered how to create a wormhole and ended up on the other side of the universe, where plants had evolved into humanoids, giant spaceships were creatures that were alive, and a strange, controlling race that looked exactly like humans, called the Peacekeepers, ruled with an iron fist of tyranny.

It was late when the second episode ended. He clicked off the widescreen TV and came to stand in front of me. "Off to bed with you, baldy."

"I could so kick you in the nuts right now," I muttered, yawning.

"Yeah, you aren't very frightening when you can't even keep your eyes open."

"Where's my paintball gun? I could so *shoot* you in the nuts right now."

He gasped as if in remembered pain. "You are going to trigger my PTSD from the paintball war with talk like that."

I halfheartedly kicked my foot in the general direction of his crotch and he caught my leg around the ankle, laughing.

"Bed. Now."

And I didn't have the energy to argue. It had been a long, harrowing day.

***

The next morning, a tiny pixie-like woman with blond hair and the highest heels I'd ever seen showed up at the house with several garment bags slung over her shoulder. I'd met her once before, when I'd lived here with Adam before the breakup. Sonia was Adam's shopper, and she stopped by every month or so with new clothes for him.

That was the day I'd discovered that what I had once thought was Adam's knack for dressing well wasn't really a knack at all. He relied on Sonia to dress him. And she did a good job. Not only did she have great fashion sense, but she knew enough about him to determine his own particular style. Not that Adam would ever wear something he didn't want to, and he did send some clothes away every time a delivery came.

Sonia usually just had clothes delivered to the house from the department store where she worked at Newport's exclusive high-end mall, Fashion Island. But today she paid a visit in person, and I'd learn later that it was at Adam's request that she stop by.

Because now Sonia wasn't just Adam's shopper, she was mine. And though the idea of someone else buying clothes for me didn't thrill me at first—especially when she started talking about head-covering options and wigs—her suggestions soon intrigued me.

She took my measurements and we looked through some magazines. She asked me a long list of questions about my own sense of style and she had color swatches. She showed me the different things I could put on my head, from creatively tied scarves to berets to "buffs"—thin, tubelike knit caps that hugged my scalp.

When she left, I gave Adam a tight hug and a kiss, thanking him. I actually didn't need an excuse for wanting to be close to him, but I took advantage of one whenever it popped up.

14
ADAM

OVER THE NEXT FEW DAYS, ALL SHE SEEMED TO DO WAS SLEEP, eat and watch *Farscape* with me. I wasn't sure if it was the natural fatigue from the chemotherapy or depression. I crammed my work into the times when she was asleep, opting not to go into the office. Jordan, my CFO, brought me the important stuff I had to see to every few days and—to his credit—asked about her health and seemed concerned.

Though I was expecting "the talk" and eventually I got it.

"So, uh…can I ask—what's going on with you two, anyway?"

I looked at him over the paperwork he'd lined up for me to sign but didn't answer.

"Are you two, uh…you know…?"

I started signing. "Friends? Yeah, we're friends."

"But you're not…together…"

"In what way does that concern you?" I asked, whisking the top paper off the stack and proceeding with the next one.

He held out a hand and looked away nervously. "Okay...I'm just trying to watch out for you, man. After last time—"

I clenched my teeth. "This isn't last time."

"Are you sure about that? Adam, you have a big heart and I know you feel sorry for her, but she had you tied up in knots for months."

My pen froze and I straightened. "I don't feel sorry for her. I love her. We've moved past that...or at least we're trying to, until well-meaning people bring it up again."

Jordan took a deep breath and let it out. "Fine. Okay. Just...just be careful, okay? You have no idea how this is all going to...shake out..." His voice died out and he grimaced as if, in hearing what he was saying, he realized how ridiculous he was being.

As if he had to remind me that I didn't know how this was going to end up. Her eighty-five percent chance had done that for me. That number hovered at the edge of my thoughts every damn day. It had stunned me speechless the first time I'd heard it at the doctor's office, and I'd buried it under a brave face ever since. Of course, I had no idea how this was all going to turn out, but I didn't need Jordan's reminder of that all-too-real fear.

I didn't say anything for a long while, burning my way through the stack, skimming each page to make sure of what I was signing. Then I straightened and put the cap back on the pen, looking at him. "Listen. I get what you are saying, but I'm okay. And she will be, too. She'll pull through this."

He nodded, bent to take up the stack and then stopped, looking at me. "Yeah, she will. But after she does? What about then?"

"I realize that she's not your favorite person—" Likely because he preferred his women dumb as toast and Emilia far exceeded his maximum IQ limit for a woman. Some men were genuinely intimidated by a smart woman. But I had no patience for this today, no matter that it was well-meaning. I clenched my teeth. "She needs friends now. Support. Why don't you be that instead of the constant critic?"

Jordan frowned and didn't say anything, shifting his weight from one leg to the other.

"I know that my advice in the past has only made things worse for you, but...well, if you ever want to talk about it, I'm here for you, man."

"Your advice is shit." I laughed and he tilted his head and smiled self-deprecatingly.

"Hey! I was wondering if you wanted—" Emilia rounded the corner from the hallway and into my office, obviously unaware that Jordan was here. She halted in the doorway and locked eyes with Jordan, who she sometimes referred to as her nemesis.

They stood and stared at each other in silence. She didn't have anything on her head and Jordan was the first person besides me, her mom and my housekeeper to see her with no hair.

"Hey, Jordan," she managed weakly, her face flushing red and the color spreading across her naked scalp.

"Mia!" he said in a bright voice as if our previous conversation had never taken place. "Wow, you're looking—"

"Bald?" she interrupted, putting a self-conscious hand to her head. "Shiny?"

Jordan hesitated awkwardly. "I was going to say 'a lot better than I thought you would be looking after two weeks of chemo.'"

Mia's brows rose. "Oh—oh...thanks."

"I hope you are feeling okay?"

Her mouth thinned a little, but she didn't look at me. "I'm feeling great, actually. Never better."

Jordan didn't react to the obvious lie. Good for him. He fidgeted for a moment and then gestured to the stack of papers in his hand. "I better be getting along, but I'm glad I got to say 'hi.' I'm glad to see you are doing so well."

A brief frown crossed Emilia's face, but she thanked him and then Jordan grabbed his stuff and left.

"Wow," she said when the front door downstairs had shut. She turned back to me with a sardonic smile curving her lips. "He must think I'm on the verge of death or something."

I grimaced. "No, he doesn't. Why would you say that?"

"Dude has *never* been that nice to me."

I laughed. She laughed.

"I guess if he's going to keep being that nice, I'll bother to powder my head next time." She rubbed her scalp again.

"You brazen hussy," I said. "Flashing all that skin!"

She stuck her tongue out at me.

"Now you're just torturing me," I said.

She slunk around the desk in an overtly seductive manner, swiveling her thin hips in her yoga pants, and came up next to me. "Is it working?" she whispered into my ear as she put her arms around my neck.

"Mmmaybe." I closed my laptop and turned my office chair to face her, hooking my arms around her waist and landing a light kiss on her cheek as she sank onto my lap. She pulled her knees up, leaning in against my chest.

"Whoa," I said, suddenly very uncomfortable at the closeness. I may have been joking around but it had been a while, and she was now sitting on me in her very sexy yoga pants and thin T-shirt. I had to fight a mental battle with myself not to cop a feel of her ass. Because, damn, I really wanted to.

"What's up?" I asked a little shakily.

She shifted against me, sending a not-unpleasant jolt to parts south. "Nothing. Just wanted to say 'hi.'"

"Okay," I said, my mind racing to find a way to get her off my lap without hurting her feelings.

"You aren't going to work today?"

"Naw."

"Why not?"

"You have another round tomorrow. I thought maybe we could do something before...before you aren't feeling so great again."

She sighed. Her hand came up to press flat against my chest and rub it lightly. I bit down on the inside of my cheek and tried to think about something other than the fact that it had been months since I'd had sex.

"You okay?" I asked.

"Sure. Never better."

"Jordan and your mom aren't here now. You don't need to lie to me."

"Well, I'm good, really. Just got a weird email, though."

"Who from?"

"From another gaming blogger. The owner of GameGlomerate. He wants to buy out *Girl Geek*."

"Are you kidding me?" I stiffened, leaning back to look into her face.

She smiled. "I do bullshit you a lot, but not this time."

"Those guys are tools. Why do they want *your* blog?"

She pulled a face at me and then rested her head back against my shoulder. She fiddled with a button near the collar of my shirt. "Don't act so surprised. It's a good blog."

"It's an excellent blog. But what are they planning to do with it?"

She shrugged, avoiding looking into my eyes. "I think they are buying up several smaller popular blogs to expand their platform and readership."

I laughed. "They could just do that the old-fashioned way by writing their own content. But they'll never be as clever as you are."

She didn't say anything for a while, just continued to fiddle with my shirt. I studied her. "You aren't thinking about it, are you?"

She shrugged.

"You aren't selling your blog, Mia."

She looked up at me. "It's *my* blog."

"You'd really tolerate someone else swooping in and picking up your platform that you took years to build? All the content you've written, all the connections with your readers, other bloggers and commentators. What would you do without it? Why would you sell it? You don't need the money."

She was silent for a moment, then she quietly unbuttoned one button, opening my shirt at the neck. "I didn't say I was selling it. But sometimes...blogging about DE can get awkward...especially with all the new traffic I'm getting about the secret quest."

I swallowed and looked away. Her hand slipped to the next button at the base of my neck.

"What's so awkward about it?"

She shrugged. "It feels wrong, somehow...because you and I are—because we live together." Her verbal gymnastics were not lost on me. She was as in the dark about what this was between us as I was.

Her fingers unbuttoned the second button. I decided it would be safer to change the subject and get her the hell off my lap. "Hey, I was thinking we should take the Duffy boat out and go down to the end of the jetty. Or we can go to the Fun Zone..."

"Or...we can stay here," she said, her hand slipping inside my shirt.

I took a deep breath and willed my hormones under control. Her hand on my bare skin was doing strange things to my ability to even think straight. I reached up and gently pulled it out of my shirt.

"Aren't we getting together online with Heath and Kat today?" Heath couldn't come over because he had a cold and Emilia couldn't be around anyone who had any type of illness. The chemo made her highly susceptible to bacteria and viruses due to her suppressed immune system.

She frowned, watching me. "I think they wanted to, yeah."

"Good. Do you want to go outside and go for a walk or something before we do that? You'll be stuck inside for a little while after tomorrow."

She blinked and slid from my lap, standing up. I almost sighed in relief.

"Uh. Yeah, sure. Let's do that."

I stood up and moved past her to grab our sweatshirts and put my shoes on. I tried to ignore the puzzled look she gave me as I passed by her. It was a mixture of surprise and hurt. I was aware I'd just rejected her advances—and that it had probably hurt her feelings. I made a mental note to discuss it with her later. But not now.

Because right now, if I didn't get out of here, I was likely to do something I'd regret—something I *really* wanted to do—like pull her back onto my lap again and kiss her senseless. I'd assured her we should go slowly, and if I didn't stick to my guns, disaster was likely waiting in the wings. So I ordered my body to calm down and we headed outside into the fresh air, where there was no danger of temptation.

15
MIA

"TAKE THAT, YOU GREEN-FACED FUCKTARD!" I YELLED into the mic of my headset. Shooting off another fireblast spell, I pasted a stray orc against the wall of the fortress we were fighting our way through. Obediently, the orc burst into flames and was no more.

"Such violence, Mia," Heath's laughing voice came through the earpiece on the headset.

"Mmm. I'm in that kind of mood," I replied, using another high-level spell on a very low-level monster and thus vaporizing it. Hell had no fury like a sexually frustrated woman who'd just been rejected by the object of her lust.

"What up, girlfriend?" Kat asked. "Everything okay?"

I gritted my teeth and fired off another over-the-top spell. "Just fucking peachy."

"Okay. So...does anyone know if FallenOne is going to log in?"

I bit my tongue. After our walk along the beach, he'd left me to go get started with our group while he finished up some things in his office, promising to join us as soon as he could. I'd hardly heard most of what he'd said because I was still mentally licking my wounds from earlier. He'd been perfectly sweet to me during the entire walk. But I knew he was still mad at me. Why else would he keep pushing me away? And just how slow did he mean we should go? I'd only been here a couple weeks, but I already hated this plan of his.

Unless there was another reason...and that was the other thing that smarted. Because I wasn't an idiot. I saw myself in the mirror every morning. I was perfectly aware that I was beginning to look like the Queen of the Borg from *Star Trek*. Between the pale, sallow skin, the darkening veins in my arms, and the bald head, I was sure I made up the perfect sexy picture. I frankly couldn't blame him for being revolted, though I'd hoped he wouldn't be.

I blinked away the sting of that feeling by reminding myself that this was all temporary. These losses wouldn't be forever, unlike others...

I focused on the computer screen in front of me. A horde of goblins came running around the corner of our corridor where we'd slaughtered their orc cousins. I wasted them all with my highest-level spell.

"Mia!" Heath hissed. "Stop wasting all your high-level magic. We're going to need that later when we get to the boss." Heath referred to the big bad monster that was the one carrying all the best loot, the one we'd most likely find at the end of this foray.

*Your friend, FallenOne, is now online.

I blew out a breath. Well, apparently he was done with work now.

"Damn, maybe Fallen can talk some sense into you, woman," Kat said.

Heath barked a laugh. "I seriously doubt that."

I rattled off a private message to Heath.

You tell Fragged, "Knock it off or I'm pasting you next!"
Fragged tells you, "WTF did I do?"
FallenOne has joined your group.

"Hey, Fallen," Kat said. "Can you get to us? We are halfway down the south corridor and Mia is going apeshit with her magic. We're going to need some help when we get to the boss."

Adam's voice came across my headset. "I think I can fight my way down to you."

I took a deep breath and looked out the window. I was sitting in the window seat, propped up on pillows, but it was a little hard to see because of the sunlight reflecting off my laptop screen. Also, my butt was starting to get numb from sitting in one place, so I got up and moved to the bed. As I did, Adam came in through the doorway, his headset on and laptop balanced on one muscular forearm.

He put a hand over his mic so the others couldn't hear him. "You okay?"

"Sure. Never better," I said, giving him my canned response.

He grimaced, a flash of irritation passing through his dark eyes. "Do you not want to play today?"

I shrugged. "No, I'm fine. Just jittery about tomorrow."

"What's tomorrow? Who are you talking to, Mia?" Kat said.

Silence. Heath sneezed. Shit. I froze. Kat still didn't know that Adam and I were—or had once been—a couple. She had no idea who

FallenOne really was. She was as clueless as Heath and I had been this time last year.

All she knew was that I'd held an auction to sell my virginity—had given me her blessing, as my only friend who *had* approved. And later, when she'd asked, I'd told her that it hadn't gone through—we'd had that talk during the time after Adam and I had split up in St. Lucia and then never really discussed it again. One thing about online friends was that you could always hold them at more of a distance than face-to-face friends. And since these past few months had been about keeping my face-to-face friends—and my boyfriend—at bay, I'd shoved everyone away and was still paying the price for it.

Adam still had his hand over the mic. "She still doesn't know?"

I gave him a guilty look and then leaned back, resting the computer on my knees.

"Fallen, are you coming or what? Let's get this party started," Heath said, clearly trying to distract Kat from her questions.

Adam sat on the edge of the bed without another glance at me and turned his attention to the game. He started making his way through the same fortress in which we were fighting orcs and goblins. Our group had to backtrack over territory we had already crossed in order to meet up with him.

"*I* know what Mia's problem is," Kat said, that familiar mischievous tone in her voice.

"What's that?" Heath asked.

"Sexual frustration."

I choked, looking up from my screen toward the end of the bed. Adam hadn't looked up from his laptop, engrossed in some battle against a group of goblins that had just jumped on his character.

"That's you projecting, Kat. You probably really need to get laid," I retorted.

"Oh, I'm *certain* it's your problem. But you just don't know it because you're too pure and virginal."

Adam threw me a sidelong glance and Heath started hacking on the other end of his mic. I couldn't tell whether he was coughing or laughing—or both.

"Um," I said. "No, that's not my problem anymore."

"Shut up!" she said. "Did our little virgin finally lose it after her scandalous auction fell through? Who was it? Was it that hot guy you were dancing with at the employee party in Vegas?"

Oh, for the love of God... I looked at Adam. He had his head down as if concentrating on the screen, but his shoulders were shaking like he was trying to keep the laughter inside.

"He wasn't *that* hot," I said, and when Adam looked up at me again, I stuck my tongue out at him. He squinted at me.

"Incoming!" Adam cried out as his character came running down the hall toward the rest of us with at least five big orcs behind him.

I pressed the button for one of my big nuker spells. Again, total overkill, but it was too enjoyable to watch them all drop like rocks.

"What the...?" Kat muttered.

"Again...we could have used that spell against the big boss, Mia. What the hell are you going to fight him with now? Sticks and rocks? It's going to take you an hour to get that spell back." Heath was clearly irritated with me.

I shrugged, though I knew they couldn't see the gesture. I knew I was being immature and probably should just log off due to my pissy mood. I'd do less harm leaving than I would shooting off my good spells left and right.

"Mia isn't feeling well," Adam said, looking at me.

And he was right. He'd said that at almost the exact moment I'd felt a headache clamp down over my head. It felt like someone was driving a spike through my skull. And I got hot and sweaty.

Suddenly, I could hardly hold the keyboard in my lap as I started shivering. Without another word, Adam stood up and set his laptop aside. "Hold on, you guys, I'm AFK and so is Mia," Adam said, giving the universal gamer's code for unavailable—AFK meant "away from keyboard."

He tore off his headset and had my laptop off my legs in seconds. Grabbing the fleece wrap on the end of my bed, he enfolded me in it.

"Lie back," he whispered.

"Ugh," I said, putting my hand to my head. "Usually I get so excited in my lady parts when you say something like that to me."

Adam's expression looked grim as he pulled the fleece blanket over me, tucking it around my body. I continued to shiver.

"Why did you keep playing if you were feeling sick?"

I shrugged. "Helps me keep my mind off of everything." He pressed the back of his hand to my forehead. "I'm fine—go help them take care of their dungeon crawl."

But he didn't move. "I'd rather take care of *you*."

My teeth chattered. "God, this sucks. Kat has no idea, either. I just...haven't told her."

Adam's thoughts were unusually transparent on his handsome face when he gave me the "I am so not surprised" look.

"Yeah, yeah, I know," I muttered between shivers.

"Can I get you anything? Some water or something?"

I stared at him for a moment. "Get me my headset."

He frowned before turning to grab my laptop and headset and set them near me. I pulled the headset onto my head and glanced at the screen. Kat and Heath were in the middle of fighting goblins while arguing.

"How come no one's told me this whole time that Mia and FallenOne are a couple and have been living together?"

I sighed. Oh, I had a lot of splainin' to do to poor Kat. I swallowed. "It's not his fault. It's mine. And it's a super long story that I should tell you on the phone or over Skype without the guys around..." I glanced up. Adam had grabbed his laptop and was sitting next to me on the bed, putting his headset back on.

"Oh yeah, well, I'm fine with doing that now. They can go off and play while we talk." There was an edge to Kat's voice, one of hurt and confusion. Because it wasn't enough that I'd stomped all over Heath's, my Mom's and especially Adam's feelings. Now I was being made to suffer from the stupidity of my actions on every level and with everyone I cared about.

"Not now, Kat. But soon, I promise. I'm feeling kinda shitty right now and I need to log off."

"What's wrong with you? Did Heath cough on you or something?"

"No, Kat. I have cancer." Those three wretched words weighted everything down like an anchor—or an anvil falling out of the sky.

Adam's hand curled around mine but he was looking at his screen, managing to help the other two fight off monsters one-handed. Only he could do something like that. I squeezed his hand tight.

"Ha ha, yeah. Okay. No, really, what the hell is wrong with you? Fallen didn't give you the clap or something, did he?"

"I wish I was kidding," I answered.

Silence.

I heard Heath cough on the other end. Adam and I shared a look. I tapped my mic. "Kat, are you still there?"

There was a long sigh and then Kat cleared her throat. "Uh. Um, yeah. I'm here," she said, her voice trembling. She sounded like she was seconds from tears.

"I'm—I'm sorry. There's a lot I haven't told you."

The only thing I heard on the other end of the line was a long sniff.

"You okay, Kat?" I finally said.

"No. No, I'm not okay," she said in a trembling voice. "I've got to log off. See you guys later."

My stomach dropped as I watched the screen. Persephone, her character, teleported away from the dungeon at a critical moment where there were a bunch of goblins—too many for us to handle, really—attacking our characters. She was our healer and we had no way, except for my crappy healing spells, to survive.

In seconds, our characters were dead, hovering as ghosts in the graveyard. Heath heaved a long sigh. "Well, that was excellent timing," he muttered between coughs.

"I'm sorry," I whispered. "I had no idea she'd take it that hard."

"Mia, I love you but sometimes you are just fucking clueless," Heath said.

I glanced up at Adam, whose jaw had set at Heath's words. But he didn't say anything. I couldn't tell whether he was agreeing with Heath or preparing to go to battle for me. Instead, he was silent.

"I know," I agreed. "Maybe I just need to grow up."

"Doll, there isn't a person alive who loves you more than I do. And I don't want you to be down on yourself. I will talk to her. She'll be okay. Just keep your strength up. I wish I could be with you tomorrow. But it's round three. Only nine more to go after that."

I fell back against my pillow, tears prickling my eyes. Only nine more rounds of sheer and utter hell. Yay.

We logged off and Adam sat beside me for a long time.

Finally, I got the courage to ask him the burning question that had been on my mind all day. "So this afternoon, when I was sitting on your lap...did you not like that?"

He didn't answer for a few long, heavy minutes. Then, he cleared his throat. "I liked that. A little too much, probably."

I blinked. That made me feel a little bit better. "You say it like it's a bad thing."

He shifted next to me so he could look into my face. "We're supposed to be going slow, remember?"

"That was your idea, not mine."

Another beat of silence. "True."

"So...how slow is 'slow'?"

He took a deep breath and let it out. "Maybe we could play it by ear."

"So does this mean like...no kissing, no groping, no making out?"

He appeared very uncomfortable. "Let's...play it by ear?" he repeated.

I sighed heavily and he smoothed his hand across my bare head, my cheek. I drifted off to sleep but felt his kiss against my smooth scalp before he got up to leave me.

Heath was right. I was fucking clueless. And now that I was becoming self-aware, it seemed I had no idea how to get myself out of these pits I'd dug myself into. I found myself needing the people around me more than ever, but because of my own actions, they were more distant. Mia Strong was an island, all right. But she was fucking lonely and dying to have someone save her from her solitude.

I dreamt of William's figurines. They were life-sized and animated, yet still made of metal. They could only speak to me in the quietest of whispers, but it seemed they all spoke at once and I couldn't hear them over the roaring wind and storm all around me. But I knew—I just knew that they had important things to tell me. Vital things. Things I needed to know for my own survival. But I couldn't hear.

I woke up at two a.m., sticky with sweat and burning up. My mouth was dry, my pajamas were soaked and I had a headache as big as the mansion I now lived in. Stumbling out of bed, I went to splash cold water on my face and all over my head, soaking my T-shirt and yoga pants even more.

It was damn unfair that my last night of freedom before more chemo was being ruined by this taste of menopause. Like I really needed that reminder that I was now as barren and lifeless inside as the moon. And probably as inviting, as my rejected advances toward Adam had indicated.

I stumbled from the bathroom, now completely wet, and peeled off my clothes, grabbing a thin tank top and pajama pants. But I felt stifled, suffocating in the still air of my room. And I still had no idea how to open my new, fancy windows.

Plus, I had no desire to go back and toss in my bed for hours, thinking about the certain doom that would be injected into my veins in a matter of hours. The night before each round of chemo was a lot like how I imagined it must feel for an ex-inmate anticipating his next incarceration. He knew exactly what hell was in store for him, and he also knew that he was powerless to avoid it once the jury declared, "Guilty on all counts."

The IV injection would feel like the cold weight of manacles around my wrists and ankles. The almost instant metallic taste in my mouth and dull headache would be the sounds of the jail door clanking shut, locking me in for days.

I hated chemotherapy almost as much as I hated the cancer. And now it was slowly bleeding me of my will to live, to survive, to fight.

With a shaky sigh, I rubbed my hands over my smooth scalp, my new substitute for twirling my long hair with my fingers. I slipped through the threshold of my little sanctuary—soon to be my prison— and I glanced down the hallway toward Adam's room.

I opened and closed my fists several times, fighting the urge to pad down the hallway and slip into bed beside him. I wanted it so badly— wanted *him* so badly. I wanted to listen to his peaceful breathing, cuddle up to his hard body, feel his arm curl around me. Feel his lips caress my neck. But I couldn't forget our short conversation before I'd fallen asleep—his insistence that we take things slow.

Could I blame him? He seemed as scared about this as I had been to move back in here. And we were getting along rather well, so maybe there was some wisdom to it. But it still annoyed me.

I thought about that as I felt my way downstairs in the dark and flipped on a dim light over the wet bar. I could see my way to the glass doors that led down to the private beach on this side of Bay Island, where Adam's gorgeous home overlooked the Back Bay of Newport Beach. As I exited, the cool night air caressed my burning skin and I took a deep breath, already feeling calm, peace washing over me though my heart raced.

I fingered the pendant around my neck. I never took the compass off. I still wasn't fully clear on what Adam had been trying to tell me the day he'd given it to me, but having it next to my heart was my constant reminder of him—of his kindness and his love, and of my love for him. Not that I needed much of a reminder of that last one. Every time I thought of him, that pinch in my heart did it all on its own.

I lay across the cool sand, looking up into the murky sky, shrouded in thick clouds. I thought about us for long moments, the compass pressing against my sternum. I hoped, rather than knew, that we would survive this. But we hadn't been strong enough once, and in the wake of all that had happened since, I honestly had no idea how we could be.

16
ADAM

I'D DRIFTED OFF TO SLEEP AGAIN, MY HEAD AGAINST MY ARM AS I hunched over my desk. I rubbed my aching neck and checked the clock, remembering that I'd have to take Emilia to the hospital in the morning. I'd better get at least a few hours of sleep in a bed so I could be there for her. Forcing myself to work—and therefore keep myself distracted—did not seem to be as effective as it had once been.

I moved down the hallway toward her room, determined to look in on her before going to bed alone. She'd been weak and shaky tonight, upset at Kat's abrupt reaction to her news. She'd managed to fall asleep in spite of all that and I was grateful. She'd need all her strength for tomorrow. But when I got to her room, I found the door wide open and her bed empty. The clothes she'd been wearing were wadded in a pile on the floor.

Maybe she'd gone downstairs to grab a bite to eat? Hopeful that this was the case—because she probably wouldn't be eating again for days, if her previous rounds were any indication—I jogged down the stairs, but the kitchen and bar area were empty. However, a dim light had been left on over the alcove near the glass doors that led out to the beach, one of which was ajar.

Had she gone for a walk at this time of night? It was perfectly safe, of course, but what if she'd gotten weak and passed out somewhere? I was out the door in a second, and after a moment of letting my eyes adjust to the darkness, I scanned the stretch of sand in front of me. The chairs and lounges were all empty, but after striding toward the shore, I became aware of a human-shaped form spread out on the cool sand, just feet from the shoreline. I cleared my throat loudly to let her know I was there without startling her.

Hopefully, she hadn't fallen asleep out here.

Her head turned and she came up on her elbows, looking behind her. It was a dark night out. What little moon there had been was obscured by the ever-present coastal inversion layer. I came up behind her and sat on the sand nearby, the cool seeping through my jeans immediately.

She was only wearing thin pajama bottoms and an even thinner tank top, but she did not appear cold.

"Are you okay?" I asked without preamble.

She nodded, speaking almost as an afterthought. "Yeah."

I paused and she seemed to be avoiding my eyes, turning her gaze back up to the sky. "What are you doing out here?"

"I couldn't sleep. I was feeling really hot." She shrugged. "It was nice and cool out here. I could breathe."

"What's wrong?"

She waited to answer me, keeping her gaze glued to the sky. "I can't find Draco."

I looked up again. There were no stars to be seen. The black of night was completely covered by the dull gray of low coastal clouds.

She took in a shaky breath and then shot me a look before her eyes darted away like skittish birds. "You told me that Draco is always in the sky—no matter what time of night, no matter where you are in the northern hemisphere. You can always find it. But I can't see it tonight. What does that mean?"

I reached out and touched her smooth, cool cheek with the back of my knuckles. She was trembling so slightly that it was almost impossible to notice. "You can't see Draco because you can't see any stars tonight. It's the marine layer."

Her breath shivered out between her lips and she closed her eyes. I continued to stroke her cheek. "I want to see it. I *need* to see it."

"You just have to trust me. You can't see it, but it's there, I promise. Do you trust me?"

Her head sank as she lay back flat on the sand. I bent over her, looking upside down into her eyes. Our gazes locked. Suddenly, it was hard to breathe. I stroked her cheek again. Her eyelids fluttered like butterfly wings. She was as delicate as one of them. As fragile. And I'd never thought of her in those terms before.

She was vulnerable. And in many ways she was, at the mercy of everyone around her. Including me. My throat tightened.

She watched me for long moments, reaching up and hooking her hand around my neck as if afraid I would pull away. "You know what I love most about your eyes?" she asked.

I frowned, confused at the abrupt change of subject.

Her thumb moved across the back of my neck and I tried to ignore the tingling her light touch evoked. I wanted to pull her hand away but she was so breakable. And I'd pushed her away earlier.

"They are so beautiful—your eyes. And so different."

I sighed, trying to laugh it off. Emilia's intensity was unusual but not surprising. It didn't take a genius to understand why she'd be feeling somber tonight. "Men don't like being called beautiful."

She grimaced at me and I saw a glimpse of my Mia return. "Whatever. Deal with it. Your eyes are *beautiful*. In a totally manly way, of course."

I smiled but didn't reply.

She tightened the clamp of her hand around my neck, pulling me closer to her. Our eyes were inches from each other, but I didn't look away though the intensity of her gaze made me feel like I was staring into a 1000-watt spotlight.

"They are so dark, so mysterious. I used to think of them as curtains, or shutters. To close off what was going on inside. But tonight I think of them as...mirrors. Reflecting everything. I can see myself in there."

My breath stuttered a little. "Oh," I answered in the smallest whisper that seemed to get swallowed up in the ambient sounds around us, the regular lap of the water on the shore, the distant hiss of the freeway even in the early morning. "Oh, you're in there, Mia. You are most definitely in there."

And then without thinking, just feeling, my mouth sank to hers. I was bent over her, our heads facing different ways, my top lip sealed over her bottom lip, and she opened to me and I tasted her. I was kissing her upside down. This kiss held more than passion, more than a declaration of desire. It held love. My love. Her love. They collided like waves crashing against a barrier that prevented them from meeting. Like that rugged, unmovable jetty that protected the harbor from the worst of the weather on the south-facing coast.

"Spider-man kisses," she murmured against my mouth. I kissed her chin, her cheeks and the tip of her nose. She'd referred to the famous kiss Spider-man shared with Mary Jane in the first Marvel movie. Completely unaware that Spider-man was her next-door neighbor, Peter Parker, Mary Jane had peeled back his mask from the bottom half of his face and passionately kissed him in the rain as he dangled upside down from his web. Spider-man kisses.

But was I as disguised to her as Peter Parker had been to Mary Jane? In many ways, I was. I wore a mask because this wasn't the time for us to deal with all the bullshit that had gone on between us. My lies. Her lies. Our respective secrets. They'd created that barrier between our hearts and there was no telling if they were surmountable. But now was *not* the time to test them. These days I cared about one thing and one thing only. Her survival.

A thin, silvery tear leaked from the corner of her eye. I pretended not to notice, pulling back, stroking her cheek.

"I'm sorry...for everything," she whispered.

"I know. I'm sorry for everything, too."

She took in a shaky breath. "How will we ever get over this? Is it even possible?"

"Shhhh," I quieted her, placing a finger over her lips. "Now isn't the time."

She watched me again. Her tears stopping, her eyes widening slightly at the realization that I was brushing this aside. Would she dissent from that opinion? Force the conversation that we'd been avoiding since the moment I'd found out about the cancer, her pregnancy, the huge gap that had widened between us when we hadn't been looking?

"When will it be the time, Adam?"

I took a breath and let it go, touching her cheek again. "When you are strong and healthy again. Come on. You need to sleep. It's going to be a long day for you tomorrow."

And just when I was readying myself for her protest, trying to outthink her argument, she only nodded and moved to stand up without my help. I rose beside her and she slipped her small hand in mine. I clasped it firmly, pulling her toward the doorway. She sighed and leaned against me.

"I don't want to sleep alone tonight. Please...can I sleep with you?"

I wanted to tell her no, encourage her back into her room. I wanted to push her away again. Because she was getting too close. The safeguards around my feelings and that tiny bit of reluctance to let go of past resentments stood to take a battering. But she needed me. And I needed her to need me.

She came to my room and I changed, lay on the bed and pressed her close against me, wrapping her in my arms and burying my face against her neck, immersing myself in her smell. That ever-present sting, like a scab that had been ripped off my soul, intensified.

She was asleep in minutes, so still and frail in my arms. And my mind was wandering through all the possibilities that the future held for us—even to those unthinkable yet too likely ones that I never allowed myself to consider.

If I lost her, I'd lose everything.

But there was more way than one to lose her. She would survive. She had to. But that didn't mean that *we* as a couple would. I had to admit it...I had my doubts. We were human, after all, and there was a lot of water under that bridge—a lot of hurtful things had happened between us. It would be a long, hard road to mutual and self-forgiveness. The love was there...oh God, it was there. But obstacles like this required more than love to overcome.

My eyes finally closed hours later, and in what seemed like seconds, my alarm was blaring in my ear and the space beside me where she had been was empty and cold.

17
MIA

"Online Friendship: Is It the Real Deal?"—Posted on the blog of
***Girl Geek* on March 3, 2014**

WHAT'S A "REAL" FRIEND VERSUS AN ONLINE
friend? Are those relationships the same or even similar?
Should they be stuck with the same label? Recent studies on the
online social media phenomenon have shown that a person usually has far
more virtual friends than real-life ones. These same studies, however, claim
that the virtual friends can be no substitute for "face-to-face" friends because
real-time experiences cannot be shared in the same way through text chat
and comments on your favorite social site.

With online gaming, such is not the case.

It can be argued that with our online friends, we have complete control
over how we present ourselves. We have time to formulate responses to them.
We can be selective in the information that we share. We don't have body
language or weird tics or insecurities to hide. These facts can lead to the belief
that your gamer friends cannot possibly know you like your face-to-face

friends do. The medium of online gaming allows us to form a buffer for ourselves, erect a façade of the written word. We can even provide an avatar as a visual in order to prevent exposing our real identity.

But those same online friends we hold at such a distance are, in many ways, our close comrades in arms. We go off to battle together, spend long hours working on quests together. We adventure together, virtually. We sit for long hours waiting for the right spawn to show up with the items we need. We joke. We play around. We make memories. And they may be memories shared over bits and bytes rather than stories swapped over the campfire, but is there really a difference? These are our companions. We fight virtual wars together. We comfort each other through disappointments.

And sometimes...sometimes we meet in person. And we find that that same chemistry that brought us together as friends over the game exists even more in real life. Because aside from forming that bond based on geography, as you would with random classmates or roommates from school, you have shared epic experiences. Events that, at some later time, you'll still chuckle at and start your sentences with things like, "Remember that time we were fighting the Cinder Dragon in Ashenstorm Castle and it took us eight hours to clear the place because we all kept dying over and over again?"

We've spent hours and hours in each other's presence, helping each other, problem-solving. And at times, when things got more personal, we helped each other with real-life problems, sometimes talking with one another through the night, to fight the loneliness and isolation we sometimes feel.

Sometimes those virtual friendships have blossomed into something more. Face-to-face forever friends. Or lovers. Or lifelong companions.

And when you really think about it, even though the interaction is different, are the feelings any less worthy of the label "friendship"?

No, indeed.

***

My third round of death by IV was dealt by smiling nurses and a very kind oncologist, Dr. Rivera, who I would have loved to have had for a grandpa. He was head of the oncology division at the UCI Medical School and had brought some students with him on chemo rounds. After talking to me for a few minutes, he sent the students on ahead and sat down opposite me.

"I hear that you are going to be a medical student yourself, Mia. Is that so?"

I sent a glance toward Adam, who sat beside me, reading. My mom was still up in Anza with the overdue mare and Heath was still sick, so it was just him and me. And I was suddenly wishing that he wasn't here to listen in on this conversation. "Um. Well, I would have been. But that's on hold for now."

The doctor looked thoughtful. "You'll be well and done with your rounds of chemo by the fall. Dr. Tahan from Johns Hopkins says he's looking forward to having you in his program."

I shifted in my chair. Adam appeared to be reading email on his tablet, but I knew he was following every word. "I'm probably not going to be in his program. I notified him—"

"Mia, dear," Dr. Rivera said, placing a hand over mine. "It's okay to plan for the future. You've been through a lot, but don't lose sight of your dreams and goals."

"I haven't," I said.

He smiled. "Of course, you could always stay in lovely SoCal and attend our school. We'd be ecstatic to have you—and I see you requested the deferment from us as well. But I'll be the first to admit we probably can't compete with JHU in the field you want to study."

I smiled. "We'll see. At this point, I'm just trying to figure out how I'm going to keep my lunch down today. I'm not really at the stage where I can give it much thought."

Dr. Rivera sobered, his shaggy brows puckering over deep-set eyes. "Have you attended any of the group therapy sessions, Mia? I think they might be good for you."

"I'll look into them," I said. My way of brushing him off, of course. I had no intention of going to group therapy. I couldn't spill my soul to the people I loved most in the world. How could I rattle off the string of tragedies to a bunch of strangers? And I'm sure that there'd be plenty of judgment meted out for the decision I'd made to get chemo right away, too. It wasn't too far-fetched to anticipate, after all. I judged myself for that decision every damn day.

Adam never spoke up, but I caught him watching me for the rest of the chemo session. I started popping anti-nausea gum, playing dumb by avoiding his gaze. I knew we'd keep on playing this weird unspoken game between us where we went through the motions of being perfectly healthy without discussing the biggest issues between us. It was almost as if we were both hoping that if we pretended these problems went away, they would. But he didn't want to deal with those things now because he thought I couldn't handle it.

"That doctor had a point," Adam said on the drive back home to his house. I wasn't yet feeling the rumblings of the usual nausea, but the headache was starting to beat down on me. I slumped down in my seat and looked at him. His features were completely unreadable behind his designer aviator sunglasses.

"I draw the line at group therapy."

"Okay, but what about private therapy? It might be good for you."

I glanced at him sidelong. "Yeah, it might be. And it might not. I think I'll be fine without it." I punctuated this statement by folding my arms over my chest.

"And what about what he said about medical school?"

I didn't say anything, just massaged my forehead, hoping the body language was enough to get him to drop the subject.

He glanced at me again. "I think it's a good idea for you to make plans for the fall."

He meant it was a good idea to make plans that didn't involve the possibility that I wouldn't survive this. I squeezed my upper arms where I held them. I wished I could push away those nagging fears that told me I was somehow in that fifteen percent that would not make it. I wished I could assure him—like he obviously needed to be assured—that I hadn't given up hope.

The hope was there, but it had been bruised and battered along the way and it was hard to see. I looked at Adam again. I wasn't going to fight him on this. If he needed to see me not giving up, then I'd somehow find a way to give it to him.

"I'll do that at some point...when I'm feeling better."

***

This round came and went with the usual brand of grossness. But after about four days, I started to bounce back. I was even eating a little, so Adam thought we should go out.

I didn't like to go out, though. I was still self-conscious about my looks and anywhere nice wouldn't let me keep my hoodie up. And— just my luck—the winter was an unusually warm one and knit caps grew sweaty and uncomfortable.

But Heath was feeling better now, and Adam suggested grabbing takeout and going to his house for a visit. That I could get behind. We grabbed some Greek food—my favorite—and headed over.

I had a key to Heath's place, but now that he was living with Connor, I never used it. Instead, I knocked at the door while Adam lagged behind me to get the food out of the car.

But what happened when the door opened totally floored me. A beautiful red-haired woman of medium height and curvy figure opened the door and stared at me, her jaw dropping. We'd met in person for the first time just a couple months before at DracoCon.

I gasped. "Kat?"

"Nice to see you, too, bitch," she grumbled and then pulled me into a tight hug. "You're bald, by the way."

"As a Ferengi, yes, I know. Attractive, isn't it?"

"Fuck no. But you're still hotter than me."

I gasped, laughing. "What the hell are you doing here?"

"You keep cancer a secret from me and you are asking me to explain myself? Maybe I wanted to come see you."

"Heath helped you pull this off?"

"Yeah, I'm staying with him and his BF for a while. He said I could crash here as long as I want."

I heard a rustle and figured Adam had caught up with me. Kat looked up, eyes widening. "Fallen?"

Adam grinned. "Kat. Glad to meet you in person at last."

"Yeah…glad to finally be in the loop."

I turned to him. "You knew she was here?"

"Yep."

I made a face at him. "Nice work."

Kat was staring at Adam through narrowed eyes. "You look so familiar, Fallen. Don't tell me you were at the Con and I didn't know!"

Adam laughed and looked away shyly. "I'm going to go put this in the kitchen," he said as he squeezed past both of us.

"I'll get my hug later, then," Kat said as he moved past her, his arms laden with kabobs, gyros and different varieties of hummus dip. She watched him pass and when he turned his back, she waved her hand as if she was trying to cool her face. "He is fucking hot, Mia. No wonder you wanted to keep him a secret. Figured I'd take him away from you, huh?"

I laughed. "Something like that. Men lose their shit for redheads. And well, since I've got no hair on my head, there's no way I could compete."

"Seriously. Fuck me. Does he have a friend as hot as he is?"

I raised my brow. "No one's as hot as he is. But there are a few who are close."

"We'll talk about that later. I'm going to go get my hug from him and see if his body is as hard as it looks."

"Slut. If he looks at your ass, I'm beating the shit out of you."

"You're a bit too skinny for those kind of threats, my friend," she said, turning around and leading us toward the kitchen. Heath stopped me on the way in. "Hey, doll," he said, pulling me into a hug. "Feeling better?"

"I should ask *you* that, Typhoid Joe. You aren't going to give me your disease, are you?"

"If by disease, you mean awesomeness, then no. I can't pass on my awesomeness that way. You've been wishing that for years." He landed a peck on my cheek.

I wiggled out of his hold. "I'd better get in there. Kat has the hots for Adam."

"Well, no fucking duh. Who doesn't?"

I heaved a sigh.

"Go on, then. Defend your territory," he chided. "Not that you really need to, you know."

I shrugged.

Heath stopped me, putting a heavy hand on my shoulder before I moved through the door. "I mean it. I know you are feeling and looking like shit these days—"

"Wow, thanks—"

"But you don't need to worry about him. He's by your side until the end."

I swallowed a sudden dry lump in my throat and looked up—way up—at Heath. He was a lot taller than me so I had to tilt my head back to do it. "The end of what?"

He frowned. "Goddamn, I'm sorry. That was a shitty choice of words."

I turned to go through to the kitchen. "I agree. But we are all permitted our lapses."

"Lapses? What lapses?" Kat asked, backing away from apparently having hugged Adam.

"Lapses in judgment. Like letting a saucy redhead leave her new job to travel here from Vancouver—over a thousand miles—"

"—to see a sick friend," Kat interrupted. "And I'd lose my job again in a heartbeat. Just like I know you'd do the same for me. You aren't getting rid of me, Geek Girl."

I grinned. "Good!"

"What's good?" Heath laughed. "You aren't the one who's stuck with her and her Lucky Crispy Sugar Flakes addiction. She seriously eats the shittiest sugar cereal in existence."

Kat waggled her brows. "I have a cute dentist. I like to have an excuse to visit him."

"So is that true?" I asked. "You really lost your job to come down to see me?"

"Pfft." She waved her hand. "It was a crap job anyway. I'll look for another when I get back...if I get back. I have to say the weather here is ah-mazing. How could I go back to Vancouver after spending a winter here?"

"There might be something for you at Draco, Kat. Maybe something cool like playtesting. Because I know you'd be honest as hell," Adam said

"A job at Draco? That would fucking rock. You know someone with an in?"

I glanced at Adam, raising my brows. "Does the CEO count?"

"We are talking about the gaming company, right? The owner of the game we are all hopelessly addicted to? Because this would be hella disappointing if you all were talking about Draco garbage delivery or Draco burger joint."

I started giggling and both Adam and Heath watched me, open-mouthed. I closed my mouth, self-conscious. "What?"

Heath glanced at Adam and then turned back to me. "I think we are both just happy to see you laughing again. It's been a while."

Kat snuck up beside me and slipped an arm around my shoulders. "Then my visit has been good for something."

Adam watched both of us, his gaze intensifying thoughtfully. "I'll be the first to agree with that." He turned to her. "Kat, if you want to stay, then I can make sure you have a job."

Kat raised her brows at Adam. "Oh, and how will you do that? Do I need to blow the CEO at Draco or something?"

I opened my mouth to answer but Heath's snicker interrupted me. "No, that's Mia's job." My face flushed with heat and I didn't look at Adam, though I would have liked to. I was starting to feel better again after that last round and when that happened, my sex drive usually kicked in, too. And it had been a while. A long while.

But Adam seemed more interested in taking it slow.

We sat down to eat the Greek food and explained the entire thing to Kat. She was still gap-jawed and pale from shock when we left a few hours later.

**

The next day Kat was sitting with me in my room at Adam's house. We'd all agreed that she could stay as long as she liked at Heath's place. I'd lend her my car, since I really wasn't using it. And not having a car in Southern California really wasn't an option. It was just too difficult to get around without one. Heath was more than willing to let her stay in the guest room and she'd look for work, hopefully at Draco.

We were sharing playlists over the sound system in my little sanctuary. Adam had gone in to work, which was what he usually did for the first few days after I was feeling more myself after a round. Kat threw surreptitious glances at me and I could tell she wanted the details of what was going on between us.

"You might as well just ask me," I sighed after more than a half hour of her out-of-place coyness.

"Is he as hot in bed as he is to look at?"

My mouth dropped open. "I'm not going to talk about *that*." Especially because it had been so long, I almost couldn't remember. Almost. Adam was hot to look at, sure. And he was even hotter in bed. But he wasn't sharing any of that with me anymore.

"To be honest, the memory is starting to fade..."

Her eyes widened. "You haven't gotten any since you've been sick?"

"Who can blame him? I'm starting to look like Skeletor, after all."

She snorted. "Oh, come on, you are still *so* pretty."

"I'm a far cry from my ideal weight..."

"Girl, your ideal weight is Adam Drake on top of you."

In spite of myself, I laughed. Kat didn't know about the added complications—the pregnancy, the agonizing decision to terminate, the abortion itself. I didn't even like to dwell on those things, let alone discuss them. Aside from the two of us, only Heath, my mom and Peter knew. And, in my opinion, that was far too many.

I swallowed those usual dark feelings and tucked them aside. I'd become quite practiced at it. "Yeah, maybe he thinks my body parts will fall off like my hair," I said, trying to laugh it off.

"But like, there're other ways, you know. You don't have to be, like, going at it like animals in order to have a little fun."

I watched her as I considered the fact that the highlight of my sex life these days was getting myself off when I couldn't stand waiting any more. Or that the only time I got felt up was at the doctor's office during a routine examination. The subject of my sex life was more than depressing.

"Well, like, how about oral? I mean...you have *no* hair on your body at all, right? Not even...down south?"

"I'm bald everywhere, except my eyebrows and eyelashes."

"Consider the advantages to this. I mean, aside from the puking, of course, you don't have to shave! No waxing your legs. No Brazilians. You're as clean as a whistle down there. This should be like the heyday of getting some good oral in. You don't have to worry about him hacking on hairballs like a cat or getting razor burn."

I gasped and then choked out a laugh at the mental image her words evoked. I tried to ignore the flush of heat that rose from the center of my being as I pictured Adam's dark head between my legs, licking and sucking, bringing me to climax. God, I could use some of that. I really could.

"And, you know, when you are better, you'll get some reconstruction work done, eh? You could, like, ask for any size you want."

I raised my brows and then threw a self-conscious glance at my less-than-impressive chest. "I'm a perfectly respectable B cup. And besides, the surgery was only on one breast and I have to keep them the same size, of course."

"Bor—ing," Kat replied, her deep blue eyes brimming with humor. "No, you see, this is how you play this. You want a nice C or even a D. He will go bonkers for that. More than enough to make a handful! You can get them both fluffed up, and since everyone knows what you are going through, you wouldn't get judged for going a little bigger. Or even a *lot* bigger."

I shook my head. "I don't get reconstructive surgery for a while yet. I'm not even letting him see these babies until then."

Kat's ginger brows shot up on her forehead. "You aren't going to let him see or touch the ladies and yet you are wondering why you aren't getting any? Girlfriend, I bet if you walked into his room tonight and pulled your shirt up, he'd be all over you."

I thought about that for a moment. About the angry scar slicing from my armpit to my nipple and the puckered flesh underneath. I was repulsive and the thought of it repulsed him, too. He hadn't actually seen, though he'd come close. But he'd gone out on dates with Jordan's model friends while we'd been broken up. There was no telling how far he'd gone with them or if he'd gotten breast gropage in the meantime. There was no way he could even remotely be interested in mine and that thought stung more than a little.

"Maybe."

Kat watched me, her gaze softening, her jokey manner fading. "Try it. I bet he will..."

I nodded. "Okay."

She stayed a few more hours. We'd actually broken out our laptops so I could show her my work on the secret quest, but I was well and truly at an impasse.

When Adam got home, she opted to leave of her own accord. When she hugged me goodbye, she mimed pulling her shirt up and then pointed at Adam's back, nodding knowingly. I grinned and told her she was an ass and kissed her cheek.

And that night, I almost did it. When he walked me to my room after we'd spent the evening watching more episodes of *Farscape*, I hesitated at my doorway, turning to him like a shy teenager wondering if her first date was going to kiss her on the porch. I wanted more than a kiss. I wanted him to push me up against the wall, press his hard body to mine, pull my clothes off, push into me. He'd done it before and the memories of his touch burned me. I missed it. I missed him.

I went to kiss him and his mouth landed on my cheek. I clamped my arms around his neck, kissing him at the base of his throat. "Adam," I whispered. "I want you. Tonight."

He tensed. It was for a split second before it was gone. He said nothing, stroking along my spine with one hand. "I'm really tired tonight—"

He didn't want me. I swallowed and almost pulled back, almost pulled up my shirt like Kat had suggested. But it was very difficult to change Adam's mind once he set it on something. And he seemed dead set against touching me. I just wished I knew why. Was he really that scared about us making the same mistakes? Or was it his anger, still, at the circumstances around our breakup? Was it fear that he would hurt me? My stomach dropped...was it resentment over the pregnancy and the abortion? Or was he just not interested?

"I know you said you wanted to go slow, but I didn't think that meant at a glacial pace."

A smile tugged at his mouth and he ran the back of his finger across my cheek. I swallowed and closed my eyes. "I'm sorry, Mia. I promise we'll hang out all day tomorrow. I'm not going in to work again until next week."

I blew out a breath and he bent and kissed me again, this time on the mouth, as if that would appease me. I almost—almost—grabbed his head and forced the issue. Even tired, he had to be at least a little horny.

I had no clue how to even go about finding out what his issue was. I could ask him, of course. But would I get the truth or some bullshit answer about how he was too tired to answer me? I let out a small sigh and pulled away, planting a brave smile on my face. "I'm sorry about the long work days. I know you were just trying to get over those, and it seems like with the time you take with me while I'm sick, you have to work twice as hard when I'm feeling okay."

"I don't mind. I want to be here for you."

"Kat can be with me now on those days. It can't be pleasant listening to me puke my guts up all day." And probably the biggest turn-off ever. How could I possibly expect him to desire me after that?

He frowned. "She can be here for you, too. But that doesn't mean I'm not going to be. You are my top priority."

"I love you," I said, my voice growing more and more quiet as the conversation continued.

He leaned in and kissed my forehead, the tip of my nose, my chin. "I love you, too. Goodnight, sweet Mia."

I slumped into my room but didn't close the door. I didn't close the door these days, full of hope that he'd be tempted to slip inside. There were enough barriers between us. I didn't need the physical ones. I knew that if I lay down on the bed now, I'd be tied up in my own sexual frustration for hours. So instead, I went into the bathroom—leaving that door open, too—and filled up the large overflow bathtub with hot water.

After a few minutes of soaking, I fantasized about him coming into the bathroom, pulling his clothes (for some reason they were wet and clinging to his muscular frame) from his body and sinking into the bathtub with me. He'd rub me down with his soapy hands until every inch of me was tingling and screaming for his touch. And then he'd pull me on top of him, entering me while putting his mouth on my breasts.

I moaned and put my hand between my legs, picturing his beautiful body. The last time I'd seen him naked was when we'd been together in Vegas. But that time, it hadn't been about making love. There'd been very little love that night. That had been us coming together because we couldn't stay away. It had been explosive and erotic and utterly intoxicating. But it had resulted in disaster. A moment that had forever changed our lives and that had possibly broken us. And that, at least, had been all my fault.

Getting myself off these days was always tinged with that guilt—as if some part of me didn't believe I deserved to feel sexual pleasure ever again. I still did it, but I couldn't enjoy it the way I had before. The way we had enjoyed each other. And it occurred to me then that this might be the real reason that Adam couldn't touch me. Because of that last time.

And now it was occurring to me that that last time might possibly have been our last time ever.

18
ADAM

AFTER BRUSHING MY TEETH AND CHANGING INTO MY pajamas, my thoughts roiling with our conversation over and over again, I decided to go back into Emilia's room...just for a little while. I hadn't touched her in any sort of erotic way for over three months. Sure, I was starved for it, and apparently she was, too. I'd been keeping her at arm's length, but I could tell she was growing exasperated.

We'd have to have a talk about it sometime soon. But for now, I trusted myself to give her what she needed without allowing it to go too far. We weren't ready for that yet. *I* wasn't ready. And fuck what my body wanted, because I knew the rest of me wasn't there yet.

I padded down the hallway and slipped into her dimly lit room, glancing at her empty bed. The light was on in the bathroom and I could hear the sound of splashes from the bathtub. I took a step toward the bathroom before I remembered how shy she was about me seeing her altered body now. I froze next to the doorway, pausing with indecision until I heard her sigh. I took a step back but didn't move again when she let out a very quiet moan. I closed my eyes, well acquainted with those sounds.

Emilia was getting herself off, likely out of desperation because I wouldn't touch her. And though it felt like an invasion of privacy to listen at the doorway, I didn't move, transfixed, my own body reacting to her sighs and moans, remembering how it felt to be the one to evoke that pleasure in her. I loved being in control of her body, being the one responsible for those sounds, that gratification. Was she fantasizing about me while she touched herself?

I got hard, remembering that it had been just as long for me as it had been for her. And every bit of me wanted to march into that bathroom, pull her wet, naked body against me and do deliciously dirty things to her. But I didn't move. Instead, I leaned against the wall and listened like a perv voyeur. It didn't take her long before she was gasping quietly with her release. There was nothing explosive or overwhelming about it. Just a natural expression, probably no more exciting than a sneeze or a cough. I went to leave, to give her back her privacy, but couldn't move a muscle when I heard the first sob.

Her crying was louder than her orgasm had been. I squeezed my eyes shut, feeling an inexplicable tightening in my chest. She sniffed and sniveled and sobbed, and I felt sick inside. Because I was powerless to change what she was feeling

Was it rejection? Was it loneliness? Was my behavior leading her to believe that I found her ugly? She was likely running every scenario inside her head but the real one—the deep, bone-wracking guilt that permeated every breath, every heartbeat. The real reason I couldn't look her in the eyes. Because the last time we'd been together had not been an act of love on my part, but an act of possession. Like a caveman, I'd staked my claim, declared her mine over and over again and taken her. Even the memory of it made my body flush with arousal but my gut writhe in disgust. The result of that night's events had threatened to take her life.

I stepped quietly out of her room and retreated back to my own like a whipped dog. If I'd had a tail, it would likely have been wedged firmly between my legs.

Needless to say I didn't sleep very well, but I was determined that we would make it through this. We could talk about it. So the next day I asked Chef to pack us a picnic lunch that Emilia could manage to keep down. Simple, organic foods and the requisite ginger chips, which, together with the anti-nausea medicine, worked well in keeping her from being too miserable in between her rounds of chemotherapy.

We'd go out on the Duffy boat, putter around the Back Bay, eat a bit of lunch, maybe get a famed frozen banana at the Balboa Fun Zone before heading back home. With a cheerful smile, Emilia donned a knit cap, wearing her hooded sweatshirt over some jeans, though it was not that cool. She had to be warm, but there was no way she was exposing her bald head to the world. Even out here where no one would really notice.

We passed numerous boats docked in their slips, sea lions lazing in the sun on top of the buoy at the entrance to the ocean. Emilia watched the stretch of mansions go by, remarking on the different lavish homes belonging to the rich or famous of Southern California.

And we talked about everything. It was like old times. She smiled and laughed like nothing wrong or awkward had passed between us the night before.

"So Heath was telling me about this new thing about the *Star Wars* movies."

I cocked an eyebrow at her. "What, about the new one coming out next year?"

"Not really. But, the good news is that after the prequels, it probably can't suck any worse, so there's that. And even though all the original actors are pretty old, at least they'll be in it. So we get to see what Han Solo will be like as a grandpa."

I rolled my eyes. "Sounds exciting."

"Heath says that there's a new canon among the first six films. That people should be watching them in what he called 'machete order.'"

"Machete order? What the hell is that?"

"It means you behave as if Episode One had never been made."

I raised my brows. "Well, that sounds promising. And does this 'machete order' involve hacking out Jar Jar Binks from the other episodes with a machete?"

She laughed. "Sometimes the way your mind works really disturbs me."

I nodded. "Thank you."

"No, machete order states that the *Star Wars* saga, instead of being about Anakin Skywalker's rise and fall, as George Lucas would have us believe, is actually about Luke Skywalker."

I frowned. "Okay. I'd buy that with Episodes Four, Five and Six, but what about the other two? He's not even born until the last five minutes of Episode Three."

"Yeah, so machete order states that you should start watching the saga with Episode Four, *A New Hope*, then Episode Five, *The Empire Strikes Back*."

"Okay. I'm with you so far. Those two are my favorites of all of them. Then you stop there, I take it?"

She frowned at me. "How can you stop there? *Empire* ends with Han frozen inside carbonite and a prisoner of Boba Fett."

I shrugged. "I could live with that mystery if it means I don't have to sit through three hours of Ewoks in *Return of the Jedi* to discover how it resolves."

"Well, machete order doesn't involve editing out Jar Jar or the Ewoks. It just states that since the saga is about Luke, you watch *A New Hope* and *Empire Strikes Back* first, and then treat Episode Two, *Attack of the Clones*, and Episode Three, *Revenge of the Sith*, as flashbacks. Then conclude with *Jedi*."

"So the only thing machete order does is eliminate the existence of *The Phantom Menace*."

"Yep. But it's worth it, isn't it?"

"Hmm. Would be more worth it if someone pulled out a machete and hacked Jar Jar's head off in the first scene. *That's* what *I'd* call 'machete order.'"

She giggled, nibbling on one of her ginger chips. I watched her, a gray knit cap pulled tightly over her head, her beautiful brown eyes peeking out just under the edge. "So how are you feeling?"

Her mouth twisted and she gave me a look.

"Yeah, I know I ask you that a lot, but I still want to know."

"I'm fine. Just great. For a few more days, until the next dose of death."

I frowned. "Just means we need to enjoy these days even more, then, don't we?" She darted an unreadable look at me and turned. Grabbing her glass of ginger ale, she sipped, looking out over the harbor as we puttered along at a measly three knots in the little electric boat. The sea air was bringing a healthy pink flush to her cheeks.

I took the opportunity of her distraction to admire her. She was lovely, even when obviously ill. And she kept her head up. She was braver than anyone else I knew. My heart swelled with pride to recognize that in her. I just wished I knew what monologue was going on inside that head of hers when I saw those flashes of pure sadness pass like a ghost through her eyes.

I wished we could do things over, apply a brand of machete order to our own lives. There was a lot about how I'd handled things between us that I wish I could just cut out. But there was no way out of this hell but straight through it, with the dogged hope that our love would still be intact on the other side.

"Emilia..."

She turned, her eyebrows drawing together in a tight frown. I opened my mouth to continue, but the way she was watching me caused me to pause. "What's wrong?"

"You don't call me that anymore...or at least you haven't. You've been calling me Mia like everyone else."

"Oh. Yeah..."

"I liked it. I was wondering why you'd stopped."

I opened my mouth and then closed it. The reason I'd stopped calling her by her full name had everything to do with the reason I'd started. When we'd first met, it had been a way to verbally intimidate her. Then it had grown into a habit. Her name—her full name—was a term of endearment to me. The name that no one *but* me called her. I couldn't help but remember that every time I'd tried to claim her, to pull her into my orbit, I'd changed her life irrevocably...and not always for the better.

I took a deep breath. "I wasn't sure you liked it...you didn't, at first."

She looked at me, her face serious. "You're right. I didn't like it...at all." She turned and gazed out over the bay again, a small smile on her lips. "But I was determined I would *never* give you the satisfaction of letting you know that."

"But...that changed?"

She reached up and tucked her hand under her hat, rubbing her scalp. "Yeah...I started liking it. A lot. I think some time around the first night we spent on your yacht. It's not like I've ever hated my full name...it was just never...*me*. But that night..." She took a deep breath and then let it go shakily. "I began to realize it was the way *you* thought of me. Of who I was to you...the way you said my name sounded so right." She glanced at me shyly and then away, smiling.

That pride I'd felt earlier was morphing into something else—this muted joy of just being in her presence, of enjoying every moment with her. But we had things to discuss...

"So I was thinking that maybe we needed to talk," I began.

She turned to me, her eyebrows raised, and I patted the seat next to me. I couldn't move to her because I was seated behind the steering wheel of the boat. She frowned, scooting down the bench to sit beside me.

"We have been talking," she said, glancing up at me a little nervously.

"Sure...but I thought maybe...about last night?"

Her mouth fell open and she looked away. "What's to talk about?"

I drew in a long breath and then let it go. "Well, I get the feeling that you're not so keen on the 'going slow' plan."

She closed her mouth and then, without looking at me, shrugged. "I'm just not sure what it's supposed to accomplish."

I turned, suddenly uncomfortable, focusing on the polished wood of the steering wheel, running my thumb over the smooth surface. "It's not because I don't want to. You understand that, right?"

She looked down, clasping her hands together in her lap. "It's hard to understand what's going through your head regarding sex these days."

"I just want to do things right this time. I'm...I'm scared of screwing up again."

"I thought—" she said and cut herself off, shaking her head.

"What?" I prodded. "Tell me what you thought."

"I thought it was because you resented me."

I frowned, watching her. She still couldn't meet my eyes so I reached out, took her chin and lifted her eyes to mine. "I admit that...I still have some issues about your keeping this from me when it all started. It makes it hard..." My voice died out before I let myself complete the thought.

But she understood perfectly what I'd been getting at. "You don't trust me."

I swallowed. Yes, it was true. I didn't trust her—not fully, not after last time. But I was determined to find that trust again. And I would.

We still had a long road to her recovery—she had months more of chemo treatments in front of her. We had time. "I think we both need time...to learn to trust each other again. To learn how to be healthy—not just physically but in our relationship, too. I believe that we need to be slow and rational about this."

Her eyes looked slightly haunted as she nodded. "Rational. Right. So until we figure that out, we're just...roommates."

Navigating this conversation was beginning to feel like walking through a minefield. I took a deep breath, dropping my hand from her chin. "If being deeply in love with someone but not having sex with them counts as roommates..."

Her brow furrowed but a small smile played about her mouth. Something in what I'd said had pleased her. Perhaps it was the reassurance that I loved her. Perhaps that was what she sought whenever she pressed me for intimacy. I resolved to reassure her more often that I did love her. Very much.

"Come here," I said.

She leaned forward and I kissed her with no fear that she would attempt to pull me into something deeper like she'd often tried of late. I tasted her lips—with that hint of ginger chips—as always, just as sweet as I remembered. When I pulled away, she was smiling. That smile did amazing things to me—made me slightly disoriented. That magical moment, those few split seconds after our lips left each other, contained all of the thrill and excitement of those first days we had spent together, quickly—if reluctantly—falling in love.

I opened my mouth to tell her again that I loved her. But she held her hand up and turned her head away, looking as if she was trying to fend off a sneeze.

"Just a min," she said, her eyes half-closed, and then she let loose with the most violent chain of sneezes I'd ever heard from her. People in nearby boats looked over, shocked by the loud sounds coming from our boat.

At one point, I thought I'd have to grab her to prevent her from falling into the water. She'd sneezed a grand total of five times in a row and had to hold still afterward, convinced that she'd start again in seconds if not.

But she didn't, thank God. I handed her a wad of tissues and she blew her nose a few times before sitting back with relief on her flushed features. "Wow...where the hell did that come from?"

But I could only stare, because I just realized that something was very, very wrong. She frowned at me but only one of her eyebrows lowered—because the other one, it appeared, had been completely blown off by all the sneezing.

I didn't know whether to laugh or cry, to say something or allow her to keep the illusion for a short while longer—until her next glimpse in the mirror, anyway—that she still had her brows and lashes. Because it appeared that they were not long for the world. They'd finally succumbed to the chemo.

She looked like she was permanently raising her eyebrow at me, like Mr. Spock's freeze-face. I half expected her to turn to me and say, "That is illogical, Captain Kirk."

And I knew, under any other circumstance, Emilia would be laughing at this situation. But she was so delicate now, especially about her looks. I just didn't have the heart to laugh, or even break the news to her that she was now one eyebrow short of a good frown.

Without another word, I turned to the wheel of the boat and maneuvered us the short ride across to the slip beside my house, dodging the tiny ferry that went from the mainland to the Balboa peninsula and back multiple times every day.

When we got there, Katya was waiting for us, sunning her very pale Canadian skin on one of the lounges on our small beach. When she caught sight of us, she came running up, wearing big, white sunglasses and a huge smile.

When she saw Emilia, the smile dropped off her face. Before I could flag her and signal her to shut up with a finger slashed across my throat, she lifted her sunglasses and squinted at Emilia.

"Huh. What the hell happened to your eyebrow? It's gone!"

Ah, goddamn. So much for preserving Emilia's feelings. She ran straight into the house, demanding to look in the mirror. I gave Kat a long-suffering look.

"Yeah, you could have handled that better."

Her eyes widened in surprise and she threw up her hands. "What? Like you could have hidden it from her that she looks like she's permanently about to say something sarcastic. I mean, she's *her* and she's always saying something sarcastic, but damn. How long were you going to let her walk around with just one eyebrow?"

I sighed, giving up. When I saw Emilia about a half an hour later, she had no eyebrows and most of her eyelashes were gone, too. She'd either pulled them out or shaved them. I didn't have the heart to ask which. In fact, I never mentioned her lack of facial hair at all.

I resolved to get my hair bleached blond and dyed pink if her looks became a big issue for her. At least I'd be drawing the freak looks to me instead of her.

19
MIA

I WAS SURE THAT ADAM THOUGHT I COULDN'T HANDLE A LITTLE more hair loss. The truth was, I'd been expecting it. So I got a few different shades of eyebrow pencil and even a hypoallergenic Sharpie pen and practiced drawing in new eyebrows with Kat while we watched still more makeup tutorials online about eyebrows and eyelashes. With the swish of a pencil, I could go from appearing fierce and angry to permanently shocked, or even looking like a purely logical Vulcan. I could also draw in weird zigzags and symbols, like a rock star.

In short, I decided that I could either cry about it or laugh about it, and since there had been so much to cry about lately, I chose the latter. This whole situation was starting to teach me something about the nature of happiness.

And having Kat around to help me laugh at myself sure helped, too...

"Spock, Captain Kirk, Mr. Sulu," Kat said to me a few days later when I was thumbing through my notes on the secret DE quest in

186 | BRENNA AUBREY

order to prepare for another blog post. We were on the floor in my
room and I was using the bed like a desk.

"Hmm," I said, tapping my lip. "Original series or reboot movies?"

"The reboot. Duh."

"Let's see...Fuck Spock. Marry Sulu. Kill Kirk."

Kat raised a brow at me and we both laughed. "Yeah, I kinda want
to kill Kirk, too," she said. "Okay, my turn."

"The dudes from *The Big Bang Theory*," I said. "Leonard, Howard
and Raj."

"Dude, no!" She started laughing. "I want to kill all those guys."

I pinned her down. "The game is called Fuck, Marry, Kill. Not Kill,
Kill, Kill."

"That's brutal, Mia. Damn...uh. Fuck Leonard. Marry Raj. Kill
Howard." And then she shuddered.

I would have laughed, but I was already distracted by my notes.

"Are you obsessing over that quest again?" she asked.

"Yeah. I'm completely stuck. I'm *this* close to finding out where the
princess's prison is located, but every time I get near the location, I get
wiped out. I wish I had a healer."

Kat looked at me like I was crazy. "And what is Persephone,
chopped liver? I'm one of the best healers on the server."

I stared at her for a minute, a little shaken by having missed
something so obvious. If it had been a dog, it would have bitten me in
the ass. "Uh, yeah, I suppose I could do the quest with other
players...you think that's okay?"

She shrugged. "Uh, hell if I know. Ask your boyfriend."

"Oh no, he doesn't ever say a word about anything to do with the
quest."

Kat wagged her eyebrows at me. "You haven't tried to use sexual favors to bribe him?"

I looked away, laughing it off. It would be more like the other way around. It seemed these days that I wanted it more than he did.

"So, seriously, I'd need a tank, too," I said, referring to the common term for a character with a lot of life points who could stand in front of the "squishy" characters like me and Kat and take all the damage.

"Um, Fragged," Kat said. "Who else?"

"DPS." A character that could inflict the most damage per second on opponents.

"FallenOne."

I sighed. Why hadn't it even occurred to me that I could get my regular gaming group to help with the secret quest?

"Um. Gee...maybe you were meant to ask other people to help you, eh? Did that ever occur to you?"

I scratched my head with my pencil, peering over my notes. "No, it didn't."

I frowned, kind of shocked by my own stupidity. The next time we all had a gaming night, I'd ask for their help. And Adam would just have to sit there and keep his mouth shut and go along with what we were trying to do.

And that's exactly what I did...and that's exactly what he did. Over the course of the next little while, as we made slow but steady progress, my regular group of gaming friends helped me progress in the quest.

***

My life settled into a weird pattern. I'd go to the hospital for a new round, sometimes surrounded by my friends. Kat was there, and sometimes Heath, Alex and Jenna. William also showed when he could, but hospitals freaked him out so he wasn't terribly happy about it. Adam was always there, but he very seldom did much talking. He just kind of hovered near me, like a watchman.

Then we'd go home. Just him and me, and I'd be alone with him for days while I felt like I was being put on the rack for my many sins. Sometimes a nurse was there, too, on the first day, but Adam was there for every minute of it. And it occurred to me that he must be exhausted because he never stopped working during that time. Jordan or a messenger brought the work to the house, and he'd spend an hour or two away from me—almost always while I was sleeping anyway—and then be back by my side.

The moment I started feeling better, he'd pull twenty-hour days at the office until a few days before I was supposed to go in for another round. Then we'd do something special or different, or just go for a walk on the beach or take a boat trip around the harbor. Sometimes friends would come over and we'd play on the game and eat pizza.

My twenty-third birthday came and went. It happened to fall on one of the days when I was still sick from chemo. My mom was there to nurse me and later, when I was feeling better, Adam made it up to me by having our friends over. But I was in little mood to celebrate. Who knew how many birthdays would come after this one?

And who knew when things between Adam and me would go back to normal, if there even *was* a normal that we could go back to?

Nowadays, he spent almost every bit of every waking hour with me. But never the nights.

On one such day, a late morning with typically gorgeous weather, we sat on the back porch. Adam was reading the news on his tablet and I was flipping through some gamer magazines for ideas for my blog. Between all that was going on with me and the effects of chemo-brain on keeping me from thinking clearly, it was getting harder and harder to maintain a façade for the blog.

To say nothing of the awkwardness of blogging about DE. I'd gotten a lot of attention with my announcement about opening the quest. A lot of readers were following my vague progress reports and attempting to glean knowledge from them, but I was feeling more and more torn about the conflict of interest presented by my being with Adam and also blogging about his game.

As I paged through the magazine, I stopped at an article about the San Diego Comic-Con. Adam looked over when, about halfway through reading it, I huffed loudly.

"What's up?" he asked.

"Mmm. An opinion piece about how hard it is to get tickets for Comic-Con and how it's getting harder and harder every year. I've always wanted to go—someday..." I let my voice trail off without explaining the implication that, given my current condition, there was a chance that "someday" might never come. I glanced up at him and his dark eyes were somber.

These thoughts were constant gremlins that I mostly managed to shove to the back of my mind. Most people my age were completely unaware of their own mortality unless, like me, they were forced to face the possibility of their potential imminent death every day. But I also knew that, given Adam's personal history, he was all too aware of it. It haunted us like a poltergeist that we tried to ignore. Simple expressions that included the word "dying" took on new meaning for us. We were no longer "dying" to see a certain movie or even "dying" of laughter.

Because when you'd been given a fifteen percent chance of actually not making it to see your next birthday, it was no longer just a figure of speech. I cleared my throat and shoved the gremlins away again.

"I can hook you up with a pass to Comic-Con," he said. "But I'm surprised that you never applied for a press pass given your status as a blogger."

I laughed. "You overestimate my influence in the grand scheme of things."

"But GameGlomerate hasn't, apparently, because they want to buy you out."

I shrugged. "It's weird. I was never desperate to go, unlike Alex or my other friends. It was just on my 'things to do before I—things I really gotta do someday' list." I corrected myself midsentence and Adam's lips thinned.

"Well, then, I'll give you one of the tickets assigned to Draco. You can take the place of one of the interns. One less silly idiot I have to deal with on the trip."

"I shouldn't—" I sighed. I no longer worked for his company.

"What if I said I really want you to come?" He cracked a smile.

I smiled back. "In that case...why not? Life's too short."

He frowned and turned away. Ah, there it was—another gremlin had popped up to replace the one we'd cleverly avoided. I sighed. Instead of pretending not to notice his reaction, I moved to sit next to him, resting my head on his shoulder. "You hate it when I say that, don't you?"

He was silent, then glanced at me and kissed the top of my head. "Yeah, I do."

My arms slipped around his shoulders. "Then I won't say it anymore."

He pulled me against him, kissing me again. "Thank you."

We stayed like that for long moments. I wanted to kiss him so badly. We hadn't had a good kiss in a long time. How was it that we could be with each other every day, in each other's presence so often, and yet I'd never felt more distant from him?

I turned and kissed him on the lips. It was one of those kisses that an old married couple might give each other after fifty years together. Adam and I hadn't been a couple for even a year. But what a year it had been. Full of so many highs and so many lows. Had it caused our love to burn out?

I looked into his dark eyes as I kissed him again, feeling that familiar lurch in my heart. *My* feelings hadn't changed, but I was well aware that our past actions might have irreparably damaged that fledgling love. I pressed him for more, opening my mouth, but he didn't respond.

I pulled away, watching him. We stared into each other's eyes and I could hardly breathe. That same uncertainty, those same questions were squeezing my heart and whirring around my mind. His eyes were mirrors—but were they reflecting what he thought I wanted to see?

I took a deep breath. "It's my barf breath, isn't it? I have barf breath."

His mouth crinkled at the corners. "You don't have barf breath."

"You could tell me, you know. I can take it."

His mouth curved into a full-fledged smile. "You do *not* have barf breath. However, your eyebrows are disturbing me today."

I brushed my fingertips over the Sharpie-scribbled markings. "You don't like the magic symbols?"

"You look like a dark sorceress."

"I'll turn ya into a toad if you don't kiss me."

"That's backwards."

"Dark sorceresses swing that way."

He pulled me closer and kissed me again, presumably to ward off the toad curse. After a moment, the kiss grew into something more and with a sigh I rested against him, enjoying it. Adam always started every kiss with a soft touch—like a light taste. An amuse-bouche that left you craving more. It usually didn't last long. Soon that taste kindled a hunger that demanded fulfillment. From taste to indulgence, it invited complete immersion, a mutual relish. Then came the back and forth. I'd feed him, he'd feed me. We'd feast on each other and the more we did, the hungrier we became.

His hands were now on either side of my face, holding me still, holding me against his mouth. The kiss deepened and I found it hard to breathe, my heart racing like I'd just stepped off a treadmill. A cold thrill went through me. He was touching me like a lover again. Finally.

Pressing my mouth to his and opening it, I slid my tongue inside and I felt it—a sudden sharp intake of breath, the staccato of his heartbeat under my hand. I had no doubt in that brief moment that he wanted me. I wanted him, too. And the heat that was generating between us held a promise in it.

That was, until he pulled away—very gently and without warning. His face was flushed and I could easily tell he was aroused. But he ended it with another one of those goddamn kisses on my forehead— like a grandpa kissing his granddaughter. I sat back, exasperated.

"Adam—"

"Aren't you hungry? I'm starving."

I raised one of my drawn-in eyebrows. "Yeah, I'm hungry and so are you. But not for food."

He took a deep breath and let it go, sitting up and causing me to pull back from him.

"Why don't you want me anymore?"

He blinked. "Who said I didn't want you? It should be obvious that is not the case."

"Should it?"

He glanced down, indicating his ready erection. I moved a hand toward it, but he grabbed my wrist. "That's not going slow."

"You're making me crazy. It's been months..."

"Let's not argue about this, okay? You are going in for a new treatment tomorrow."

"That's tomorrow. And I have almost twenty-four hours until then."

He didn't say anything and I stared at him while he avoided my gaze.

"When, then?"

He shrugged. "When you are feeling better?"

"I have a month of chemo left."

"I know," he whispered. He pulled me against him. "I don't think we're ready yet."

But if not now, then when? And why not? What was fucking with his mind? Because it was obviously something. It was clear that he wanted it, that apparently the fact that I looked like Gollum from *The Lord of the Rings* had not completely repulsed him.

What was it then?

20
ADAM

I KNEW SHE HAD QUESTIONS THAT I COULDN'T—OR wouldn't—answer. I knew she needed to feel close to someone. I needed it, too. But we weren't ready. We were just getting our life back on the rails from the fucked-up mistakes we'd made.

She needed a friend right now and I was determined to be only that. Because the last time I'd touched her—well, we couldn't stand any more disasters. At least not until the debris from the current ones had cleared.

***

"Ugh. Okay, let's go again, I guess. Time for try number three hundred and sixty-two," Heath muttered. He may have thrown a dirty look in my direction, too.

With a long sigh, Emilia rubbed her forehead below the edge of the bandana wrapped around her head. "We must be missing something super obvious here. We've been at this for days and keep getting wiped out."

We were in the gaming room in my house, all sitting around a table with our laptops in front of us. Since we were all in the same room for once, we didn't need headsets. I stifled a yawn. They always got extra irritated when I appeared bored. What did they expect? I had to mentally sit on my hands and let them figure this out by themselves.

Kat straightened. "Okay, I've got all my spells back. We are good to go again."

"Shit. We have to do something different. I'm not just going to keep doing the same thing over and over again. This is bullshit. Seriously," Heath moaned.

Emilia was going over her notes again for the tenth time. "I agree that we are missing something...but what? We're at the right location. There's a fortress on top of the mountain and I'm ninety-nine percent sure that's where she's being held. The clues state there is a tunnel that leads to a secret underground entrance to the castle. In theory, that should be here, next to Sergeant What's-his-face. But every time we talk to him and he gives us the key, that horde of goblins pops up out of nowhere and wastes us."

"Maybe we aren't supposed to talk to him and just go to the entrance without him," Kat suggested.

Heath expelled a long-suffering sigh. "We need the key and the entrance doesn't even appear until we talk to him. So if we don't talk to him, there's no key and no entrance."

"But the minute we do, a fuckton of goblins jumps our asses," Kat said. "So either we are doing something wrong, or we need a *whole* lot more people here to help us."

"Dude, a raid of twenty-four players couldn't deal with that many high-level goblins!" Heath protested.

I sat with my chin in my hand, watching them all, silent as usual. They tended to forget I was here unless they needed to make a sarcastic remark about how frustrated they were. Then suddenly they'd become aware of me. They'd learned long ago not to try and wheedle any clues out of me.

I was actually pretty exhausted tonight, but God help me if I yawned. They'd jump down my throat in seconds.

"Let's just go again—maybe we'll learn something new this time," Emilia said.

Heath rolled his eyes. "That's what you've been saying for the last two dozen tries."

She raised her lightning bolt-shaped eyebrows at him. "Do you have a better idea?"

"Fuck, I don't know. I'm getting frustrated."

"Well, then, just talk to him and trigger the key and tunnel entrance."

Fragged approached the non-player character, Sergeant GriffonShield. Heath began typing furiously.

Fragged says, Hail, Sergeant GriffonShield.

Sergeant GriffonShield says, "Hail, traveler. What brings you to this forsaken part of the world?"

Fragged says, "I'm here to save the princess. She is imprisoned in the castle."

Sergeant GriffonShield says, "Some say that her prison is there, yes. The poor lass. I mourn her loss. If only a brave soul would help free her."

Fragged says, "Yeah, yeah, yeah, enough with your spiel, asswipe."

"That's not part of the script. He's not going to answer you," Kat said.

"I'm sick of this asshole. He's just going to rain goblin hell down on us in a minute if I type the correct line."

"So you are just going to swear at him? That will get you far."

Heath heaved a huge sigh. "Fine. I'll type the damn line. Sheesh."

Fragged says, "I want to free her."

Sergeant GriffonShield has offered Fragged a tarnished key.

Sergeant GriffonShield says, "Here, brave soul. Take this key and find the niche where it fits on yonder mountainside. It will take you to the passage you seek."

Fragged says, "Screw you, fucktard. Help us."

"Heath, just take the goddamn key," Emilia hissed.

Sergeant GriffonShield says, "Alas, I would love to help you, but I cannot leave my post until you gather my allies."

Three heads immediately jerked in my direction, eyes huge with surprise. I almost laughed at them. Almost. It figured that it would take Heath's exasperation for them to accidentally discover what they had to do.

I looked down, trying to appear very fascinated by something on my keyboard.

"Uh, what the fuck just happened?" Heath asked.

Nobody responded so I glanced up. They were all still staring at me. I cleared my throat. "I think he offered to help you. Can I yawn now?"

Heath grabbed a scrap of paper, balled it up and threw it at me. I batted it away with a laugh. "Wow, was that the doorbell? Let me go get that. You three can just...talk amongst yourselves."

I stood and, before leaving, caught Emilia's eye. She sent me a huge grin. I winked at her and left the room.

I returned about a half-hour later and declared myself—and Emilia—too tired to go on anymore tonight. She had another round of chemo in the morning and needed all the rest she could get.

At the top of the stairs, she turned and hooked her arms around my neck.

"Well, aren't you just full of surprises?"

"You're just realizing that now?"

She stood up on her tiptoes and kissed me. "No. Of course not. I'm dense but not that dense."

"You're not dense."

She stood perfectly still, hesitating.

"What?"

"Sleep with me tonight?"

I swallowed. It was getting harder and harder to say no. And harder and harder to deny that I really wanted it—wanted *her*. However, I slept in her bed. I folded her thin frame in my arms and pressed her against me. It was the most I could give her now. And I honestly had no idea when I could give her more.

21
MIA

SOMETHING WAS WRONG. I KNEW IT THE MOMENT THIS NEW medicine burned through my veins. It felt different and I was immediately swimming in a sea of weird delirium and constant nausea, which I fought—successfully, thanks to the antinausea medication I was on—to keep down most of the day. Given how things progressed later, it probably would have been better if I'd not fought to suppress that reaction while I was in the hospital under the watchful eyes of the nurses and doctors.

Because that night, I was in hell.

Adam always knew I had to head straight to bed on the first day of a round. I would be good for nothing but sleep and sickness for at least twenty-four hours, usually more.

But when I woke in darkness with the powerful urge to vomit—not even making it to the toilet on time—the sickness overcame me with such violence that I was projectile puking and peeing my pants at the same time. My body convulsed over and over. It felt as if every one of my cells was fighting the chemo. Every single inch of me ready to implode in rebellion against the poison merrily coursing through my veins.

I wanted to die.

And no, I wasn't exaggerating. I really, *really* wanted to die rather than endure this.

The craziest part was that I didn't hit the emergency button on the bathroom remote. I must have been mental or too damn fiercely independent, because in my weird psychotropic delirium, I actually *fought* the urge to call Adam for help.

Not until I was half passed out on the floor. By that time, when I went to reach for the intercom button, I found I didn't even have the energy to lift my arm in order to do it.

Instead, I turned my head, tears seeping from my eyes as my stomach continued to convulse long after there were any contents inside to empty out. Large blue spots in my vision and darkness at the edges indicated with only a split-second warning that I was about to black out.

22
ADAM

THANK GOD I CHECKED ON HER REGULARLY AFTER A NEW round. Because when I found her unconscious on the bathroom floor, I had no idea how long she'd been there.

"Fuck!" I said, kneeling beside her, pulling her into my arms. "Mia... Mia..." I jostled her and she immediately responded, muttering something under her breath that I couldn't understand.

"Sorry...so sorry. Should have told you..." she whispered.

"Are you okay? What the hell happened?"

She was shivering. "S-s-s-sssso cold."

"Come on." I pulled her up against me and she slid—almost fell really—but I caught her. She was scaring the hell out of me.

I put her thick bathrobe on her, but she continued to shiver. I wrapped her tightly in my arms. The violence of her reaction—the fact that the drugs she'd been administered were new—scared the living shit out of me. I needed to call the hospital immediately. But I wasn't going to leave her for a second to do it.

"I'm okay. I'm okay," she mumbled. "Get me to the bed."

So I picked her up and carried her to the bed. "Can I get you something? Water?"

She shuddered. I grabbed a blanket and tucked it around her. "I'm going to call your doctor—"

"No. No, stay here. I need you to write something down for me."

"What?"

She flopped her arm toward the nightstand, as if she no longer had control of her hand. "Get paper. I need to make a list."

"You can do that later."

"I'm fine. I need to make this list. Now. You need to write it down."

I grabbed a notebook off the nightstand and searched for her phone. It was nowhere to be seen. Mine was back in my room. I got up to go get it. She hooked her hand in my shirt.

"No, don't leave me. Please, you have to write this down."

I sat down with a huff. "Okay, quickly, because I need to call the hospital."

"Um. Okay." Her eyes rolled up toward her head as she sat, thinking. "Learn the tango. Kiss someone on the Eiffel Tower. See the *Venus de Milo*. Ahhh."

I scribbled them down quickly. "Okay. Got it. Now—"

She tugged on my shirt. "Not done yet. Keep writing. Sixty-nine, or sex in public."

"What?"

"Just write. This is my bucket list."

"You want to put sixty-nine on your bucket list?"

"Wish on a falling star. Knit a sweater. Volunteer medical work. Um...a sunrise, somewhere cool like on the Arctic Ocean. See the Northern Lights—"

"Okay, enough. You can work on this later. I'm calling the doctor now."

"I have to do those things. I want to before—before—"

I pulled her hand out of my shirt and ran back to my room for my cell phone. I had it up to my ear, having forgone talking to the after-hours urgent care and just called 911.

When I got back to her room, she was unconscious again.

Goddamn it.

I scooped her up in my arms, blanket and all, and shouted commands into the phone. There was no way the EMTs could bring an ambulance to the house, and I wasn't going to wait for them to wheel a gurney across Bay Island. Instead of taking the time to call the caretaker to meet me at the front door with a golf cart, I just carried her across the footbridge myself. And damn, she was so light that it was hardly a burden at all.

My gut twisted with fear and worry. She was stirring against my chest.

"It's okay, I'm going to get you to the doctor right away," I said.

She was mumbling so that I could hardly hear her. "I don't want to but...going to die. I deserve it, after what I did..."

Everything inside me dropped as if I'd suddenly shot up inside a fast-moving elevator. Nausea made my head swim, but I swallowed it and concentrated on what I had to do. In short minutes, I met the ambulance at the bridge that connected the island to the mainland and they spread her on the gurney, buckling her in. I squeezed into the back of the ambulance beside her and we sped away.

Hours later, I rubbed my sore eyes. It was four in the morning and she lay peacefully in a hospital room, IV fluid dripping into her arm. She was still and pale and hadn't stirred since we'd arrived. The doctor had said it was dehydration and exhaustion. She'd had a bad reaction to the new meds, and her oncologist had been notified and would be coming by to examine her first thing in the morning. For now, sedated and hydrated, she was safe and stable. And I was a wreck.

I deserve it after what I did. Her words rolled around and around in my mind. That ball of sickness hung in my gut like a boulder. Was she losing her will to live?

My face sank to my hands, the heels of my palms against my eyes. I was lost, with no idea what to do. Physically, for now, she was going to be okay. But her will was flagging. And if she lost her fight, who knew what would happen?

An hour later she stirred, her eyes cracking open. She turned her head to me. "Adam," she croaked.

I closed my hand over hers. "I'm here."

"I know," she whispered, a wan smile appearing on her cracked lips. "You're always here."

I didn't have anything to say to that so I just squeezed her hand.

"What happened? Why am I in the hospital?"

"You had a bad reaction to the new meds."

"God, my head is killing me."

"You got dehydrated. You don't remember anything?"

"Uh. I remember power-puking all over the bathroom and then passing out. That's about it. Is that how you found me?"

"Yep. Do me a favor next time and hit the goddamn button, please?"

She frowned. "I think I actually was trying to, but I thought about it too late. I was being stubborn."

"I'm shocked."

"Don't be sarcastic. It doesn't suit you. Now…you need to go home and get some sleep."

"I'm fine."

"You are not. Go and at least catch a nap."

"It's five…your doctor is going to be here in a few hours. I want to be here for that."

"You haven't gotten any sleep all night. Now who's being stubborn?"

I shrugged. "We're matched well, then, aren't we?"

She smiled and sighed. "I suppose you could say that."

I watched her, haunted again by the words she'd spoken in her delirium—words that apparently she had no idea she'd spoken.

"What's wrong?"

I shrugged. "Just worried about you."

"I'll be okay."

"Yeah? You *really* believe that?"

She tilted her head at me. "Did I say something to you?"

"You just seemed…it seemed like you were losing hope."

Her lips thinned. "I'm sorry. I don't remember saying that. But if I did say something, it's probably just borne from being so tired. I'm getting tired of the constant puking."

I nodded. "You made me write down a bucket list."

Her eyes widened. "Shit. I don't remember that at all. Like, what was on the list?"

"Sixty-nine."

"What?"

"You had sexual stuff on your bucket list."

She laughed and I thought I saw a little color creep into her cheeks. "You aren't bullshitting me, are you? Like weird stuff?"

"Not weird. Just...unusual. You aren't missing anything with the sixty-nine thing. It's not as fun as it sounds."

She tilted her head at me, suddenly very interested. "Oh?"

"Yeah...it's...well, there's just too much to multitask."

She frowned at me. "You're a computer programmer and you are complaining about multitasking?"

I shrugged. "It's kind of hard on the neck, too."

Now her eyes widened. "And how do you know all this?"

Oh, shit. Well, *this* was awkward. "Uh..." I looked away.

She laughed again. "It's okay. I'm just teasing. Though someday I'll kick the crap out of all those other chicks you did it with. Or at least in my mind, I will."

I smiled, heartened by her use of the word "someday." She'd had no idea about planning to die or wanting to make a bucket list or any of that, and I was relieved.

The doctor didn't arrive until almost noon and I was dragging ass, but all our friends had shown up by then so I could sit back and let her chat with them while I concentrated hard on staying conscious.

Liam arrived with a big bouquet of flowers. He'd managed to step foot in a hospital more times in the past few weeks than he had in his entire life. I was proud of him and impressed that his affection for Emilia had dragged him here.

"Thanks, William. They are beautiful. But the doctor is going to come in here and tell me I can go home. So I'll have Adam take them home and put them in a big vase for me, okay?"

Apparently, she didn't have the heart to tell Liam that she was restricted from having flowers or plants near her during her chemo treatments. Liam hardly seemed to be paying attention. He appeared transfixed by one of Emilia's friends—again. The quiet, studious

Jenna. I'd thought that infatuation had passed, but he was eyeing her in a pretty obvious way and she was pretending not to notice.

I grabbed the flowers and tucked them outside the door in the hallway on a tray.

Alex and Jenna had pulled out some dice game, and they were showing Emilia and Kat how to play it. Heath arrived late and then the doctor, who evicted us all from the room while he examined her.

Once he'd finished, I was allowed back inside while he made notes to her chart on his tablet. "She was down to her last three rounds when this happened, and her white blood count is far lower than I would like. So we are going to discontinue the chemotherapy."

Emilia threw a weak fist pump in the air. "Yesss!"

"Wait a minute," I interrupted. "Is that safe? I mean...if you originally determined twelve rounds and she's only had nine—"

"We were erring on the side of caution, Mr. Drake, given her circumstances. Her counts are down. She needs to rebuild her immunity. At this point, chemotherapy is no longer effective."

"Yeah, you heard him," Emilia said.

I ignored her. "I'm just—well, as you say, being cautious is best. But will the chemotherapy be as effective in the long run if it's been cut short?"

"We originally increased the dosage on her treatment plan for several reasons. Her age, first and foremost. And given the...the circumstances when she began the chemo..."

The doctor was rather delicately referring to the now-terminated pregnancy. I threw a glance at Emilia, who was resting against her pillow and watching the doctor, but her expression had not changed.

"I'm discharging her into your care today, but I'll be sending a nurse by every day to run a blood test on her. She needs rest and fluids."

He signed off on the chart and I suddenly felt the urge to argue with him. I wanted her to have those additional rounds of chemo. "What if you administered the old drug she was on for the additional rounds? So you could keep going—"

"Hell no," Emilia muttered.

The doctor had a long-suffering look on his face. "With her white blood count at the levels they are, she isn't going to be getting any chemo for a while. This last round wiped her out, and while it is an effective drug, the reaction she had to it could have seriously damaged her health. She needs to spend these next few weeks resting. But she's done with chemotherapy unless something is found in the full-body scan that indicates she should continue."

I opened my mouth again, but Emilia, recognizing that I was about to push the issue, interrupted. "Adam..."

I stepped back and took a deep breath. Emilia thanked the doctor and said goodbye. She then sat up in the bed and slowly slid off, walking to me.

"Are you okay?" she asked. "You're exhausted."

"I don't like this," I said, running a hand through my hair.

She slipped her arms around my waist and snuggled against me. "It will be okay. Can you take me home, please?"

So I waited while she changed into the clothes that my housekeeper had dropped off for her. Heath drove us back to the house, and I tried to disguise how utterly terrified I was. As long as she was undergoing therapy, we were doing something. The cancer was actively being fought.

But now we just had to wait and hope that it had been enough. The feeling of uncertainty was enough to gut me. But never, not in a million years, would I ever let Emilia see that.

23
MIA

"I CAN HELP YOU WITH ONE OF THOSE, YOU KNOW," ADAM SAID the next morning after we'd awoken and were lying in bed, talking. At my request he'd come to sleep beside me again. It had taken no effort at all to coax him. I think he was determined to keep an eye on me after the scare of the night before.

But after we'd slept in, both exhausted from little to no sleep the night before, I'd found the open notebook on my nightstand and had been looking over the list he'd scrawled down. Adam's writing was usually very even and neat, so the fact that I could barely read this spoke of the duress he'd been under when, apparently, I'd grabbed onto him and insisted he write down my bucket list.

"What did you have in mind to help me with? Sixty-nine or the sex in public?"

His mouth twisted. "Neither one of those. I was thinking the tango."

I checked out the top of the list. Number one, as a matter of fact. I wanted to dance the tango? I guess I had thought about it before, but it seemed an odd thing to put first.

"Don't tell me you know how to dance the tango, too..."

"I was my cousin Britt's practice partner by coercion. It wasn't just for the foxtrot."

"Mmm. Maybe you can help me knock out a few of these in the next little while." I waggled my eyebrows suggestively at him.

"Find someone else for sixty-nine."

I laughed at him. "Oh, so you're okay with that?"

"No. Did I say 'find someone else'? I meant 'cross it the hell off your list.'"

"I could find someone else. Someone into bald chicks. There's got to be *someone* out there who's got a cranial fetish."

He looked at me, reaching up to rub his thumb along my cheekbone. "All it would take is someone with a beautiful woman fetish, and there are too many out there with that." His eyes hardened. "I found mine. They can all go find their own."

I rewarded his sweet remark with a tight hug around the neck and then he coaxed me out of bed to eat a little something. For him, I managed to chew off a corner of toast, though the thought of anything more was still too much for me.

For the next few days, he insisted I stay in bed and I humored him because he was so worried about me. The rest of the gang logged in during every spare moment that they could to help me work on the secret quest. We'd spent time slowly gathering the Sergeant's allies by doing quests for them: finding the lost wedding ring for a lieutenant, sobering up an old, broken captain, busting a roguish type out of jail, and much to our surprise, going back to the beginning, to the original quest-giver, General SylvenWood. He wouldn't leave his spot at the city gate until we'd planted a garden of daffodils in honor of his lost love. Once the allies were gathered, we were ready to progress with breaching the castle.

With the help of the allies, we safely entered the tunnel while they kept the goblins at bay. Fortunately, we made our way into the castle, almost at our goal. But we found ourselves stuck once more.

Three days later, when I was back to feeling close to my old self again—my old "post chemo" self, anyway—it was time to teach Mia to dance the tango. I figured what the hell, I'd go with it.

"So you remember that the foxtrot is slow-slow, quick-quick—"

I shot Adam a sardonic look. "Amsterdam was over ten months ago. I don't remember that."

"Well, the tango is a lot like the foxtrot. Except the tango goes: slow-slow, quick-quick-slow. And it's kind of a slide. It's not hard to learn."

"I'm sure hearts are breaking all over the West that Adam Drake is dancing the tango with me."

He smiled at me. "It's a sexy dance. I'll be the first to admit it."

"Well, if it's sexy and it's with you, then I'm definitely in." I waggled my eyebrows suggestively at him. As usual, he didn't take the bait.

He kissed my forehead. "Britt's coming over to help me teach you."

And that's exactly what they did. In the dining room, with the long table shoved aside, we had tons of room, and even though I had to take a break once in a while to rest, I learned the basic steps to the tango.

This went on until right around noon, when Jordan showed up with a briefcase full of work to go over with Adam. He threw a quizzical glance around the room, raised a brow and said, "What's this, you're opening a dance studio?"

"Come on in, we'll show you how to do the polka!" exclaimed Adam's cousin, Britt.

Jordan glanced around and gave me a nod. "Hey, Mia, glad to see you're feeling better. Mind if I steal Adam for a bit?"

I smiled. "Be my guest. He's exhausting me, anyway!"

Adam left me with Britt and followed Jordan out to his office with an invitation for us all to sit down to lunch together afterward.

***

As we watched them go, Britt suggested we sit down in the living room with some ice water. I think my comment about being exhausted had concerned her. I gave her a smile. Britt asked after my mom, repeating how much she adored her and was certain she was the best thing that had happened to her father in a long time.

Then, after an awkward pause, she frowned and shifted in her seat to face me. "How are you feeling, Mia?"

I thought about that for a moment, mentally assessing my energy level. The achiness was gone, but I still became fatigued very easily. I answered with a vague shrug and reached up under my cap to scratch my sweaty scalp.

I glanced out the doorway through which Adam had left with Jordan. If Britt noticed, she didn't say anything. "So...I know everyone asks you how you are doing all the time. You must be getting tired of that. I am curious, though, about how Adam is doing."

I smiled. "I'm doing better, thanks. And Adam's..." I hesitated, looking at the doorway again. I shifted in my seat and fell back against the cushion.

"Intense, stressed out and distracted?"

I returned my gaze to Britt, confused for a second.

"It doesn't take someone with his IQ to figure that out after spending the morning with him." She smiled.

I shrugged, looking down. "I'm worried about him."

"He's worried about you."

I nodded and darted a glance at her, wondering how much she knew. It was unlikely that Peter or Adam or even my mom would have told her everything that had gone on earlier in the year.

She reached out and patted me on the leg. "It will be okay. It's his nature. He's always been the overprotective type."

"Somehow that doesn't surprise me."

Britt's mouth twisted. "In high school, he got into a lot of fights because of my brother."

I raised my brows—or *would* have raised them if I hadn't sweated them off already from the dance practice. I made a mental note to use the Sharpie next time I practiced. "That's...um...that's so surprising. Wasn't he a skinny weakling in high school?"

She laughed. "Adam was skinny, but he wasn't a weakling. He was an excellent runner. But Liam got picked on quite a bit. Kids are so cruel."

I nodded. "So Adam was defending his cousin?"

She shrugged. "Well, it started out that way. But the one big incident—he told you about that, right?"

He hadn't told me about it, no. But I *did* know from Heath, who had looked into Adam's background while doing research for the auction. Adam had been the victim of a particularly cruel bullying incident in high school. A group of boys had ganged up on him after a track meet and beaten him up, duct taped his arms and legs and mouth and shoved him into a locker, where he stayed until he was found the next morning. It had been so severe that he'd had to be hospitalized. He never returned to the classroom again, choosing to finish high school early via independent study.

"Uh, yeah, I know about that."

"Those kids started out by picking on my brother, but Adam deflected their attacks onto himself. Then he became the target."

I sat stunned for a moment. That was beyond awesome of him.

Britt straightened, perhaps realizing that she might be divulging sensitive information. She cleared her throat. "Anyway...it's just an example of how he is. He wants to be the big protector...and sometimes it really gets him into trouble."

I took a deep breath and nodded. She hadn't implied as much, but that same protectiveness had gotten him into trouble with *me*. His overprotectiveness combined with my stubborn independence had made a near-lethal combination for our relationship. I wondered if we could learn from that mistake and overcome those failings. Or were those shortcomings so inherent to our characters that we were doomed to fail regardless?

Britt must have seen the struggle on my face because she put a comforting hand over mine. "Adam is one hell of an awesome guy. And I don't just say that because he's family. I know you two have had a rocky road. And I know that this is probably putting a strain on your relationship, but you know what? I've never seen him happier, Mia, than since he's been with you. You two were clearly meant for each other."

I'd believed that, too—once. I blinked back the prickly tears that unexpectedly rose up. It was so frustrating. I was always shamefully close to tears and had been for months. It was almost as if my body and emotions were acting as if I was still pregnant. I bent my head and rubbed my forehead trying to think of something else so I wouldn't make a fool out of myself in front of her.

"I don't want to lose him..." The shaky words slipped out unexpectedly. I was angry with myself the moment they were out of my mouth. On some level, I almost felt like I deserved to lose him.

"You don't have to worry about that, and I think he'd be upset to find out that you were. I think he'd rather you concentrate on getting better."

He'd said as much—over and over again.

"In fact, you should make that your birthday present to him, since it's in a few weeks."

I smiled. "I'm working on it. And since I have no idea what to get him, I guess that's as good an idea as any."

She leaned forward and gave me a tight hug. "I think we'd all be delighted with that. Not just him."

And I wanted nothing more than to give that to all of them. But cancer was cancer. I had as much control in overcoming it as any other disease, like diabetes or polio or even the flu. It happened. Shit happened. And even though the feelings of unworthiness for all of my many flaws tended to weigh me down, I was slowly realizing that this hadn't happened to me because I'd been unworthy or hadn't deserved to be healthy.

The blame for other things still sat squarely on my shoulders, but the guilt for this was fading away and making things just a tiny bit lighter. And for that I was grateful.

24
ADAM

I SPENT ABOUT A HALF HOUR WITH JORDAN SIGNING paperwork and going over some details on our pet project when he finally stopped, sat back and rubbed his eyes. "Heard you had a scare the other day. She looks like she's doing a lot better now."

"She is, thanks."

"What's with the dance lessons? Trying to keep her mind off of things?"

"Ahh." I sat back, rubbing the back of my neck. "Actually, it has to do with her bucket list."

Jordan looked surprised. "She made a bucket list?"

I tightened my jaw and then released it. "Yeah, she wasn't doing very well at all. I think she thought she wasn't going to make it. She's been kind of down lately, so I thought this might be something to get her mind off of things."

He frowned. "So like, what else does she have on her list?"

I hesitated. There was no way in hell I'd discuss some of the things on the list, so I shrugged. "Oh, I don't know...something about the

Northern Lights and doing volunteer medical work and the Eiffel Tower."

"The Eiffel Tower?"

"Yeah, you know, the one in France?"

He gave me a look. "As opposed to all the other Eiffel Towers out there."

I shrugged and gave him a grin. I liked yanking Jordan's chain sometimes. Someone had to do it.

"So like, she's never been there? To France?"

"No. We hadn't gotten around to that yet."

"Yeah, I get it. Maybe soon, though?"

"When she's better...definitely."

"But if you wait 'til then, you might not be able to benefit from it. You said she's been pretty down lately. What if you took her in a private plane?"

I hesitated. I knew that he had his epic trip to Paris planned. He'd been working on it since the fall. "What, are you going to let us hitch a ride on your chartered Leer?" I said. It was a little bit insulting. I could afford the extravagance far easier than he could.

"No," he said, rubbing his goatee with a thumb. "No, I think you should just take the whole trip."

I laughed. "Good one. You almost had me there for a minute."

"I'm dead serious, Adam. Take it. Take her. All the plans are made. It's a great trip."

"I'm not going to take your trip."

"It's all planned. I've got the penthouse suite at the George V Hotel—the Four Seasons just off the Champs-Élysées. Even with all your money, you can't get reservations like that at the last minute. Just take the goddamn trip. It will be good for her."

I rubbed my jaw, studying him. He wasn't bullshitting me and I was stunned. Especially because Jordan had never been supportive of my relationship with Emilia. Or maybe he just didn't like her. I never knew exactly what it was. But his magnanimous offer now was nothing less than shocking.

"You haven't been able to shut up about this trip for months," I said. "I'm not going to take it from you."

"I'm not giving it to you, idiot. I'm giving it to her."

"Well, this is a bit surprising, I have to admit. I always got the impression that you didn't like her."

He shrugged. "I never had anything personal against her. I wasn't her biggest fan when you were going through all that bullshit with her, but...she's handled all of this with strength and grace and I admire her for it."

I clenched my teeth. In truth, he didn't know the half of what she'd been through. "It's very generous of you, but—"

"Goddamn it, Adam. Just stop arguing and take her. It will do her some good. She'll be able to cross another thing off her list."

"Two things, actually. She wants to see the *Venus de Milo*, too. That's in Paris."

"Good. Surprise her, then. The trip is in two weeks. Do you think you'd be ready?"

I blinked. "I'll call her doctor and ask."

Jordan looked supremely satisfied with himself after that. So I let him do his good deed. We spent nearly an hour going over his itinerary, and I made mental notes to modify it to suit our needs. I also made a note to make it up to him soon.

But for now I'd let him be the hero for the day. He seemed to be enjoying it.

I noted his secret smile when he hugged her goodbye. But it wasn't nearly as amusing as Emilia's shocked expression when he did it.

***

A few nights later, we were sharing a quiet dinner at my house with my Uncle Peter and Mia's mom, Kim. They had called, wanting to take us out, but Emilia had declined. She'd claimed she liked my chef's food better than anything a restaurant could make. Considering her dietary restrictions, I couldn't blame her, but I suspected it also had to do with her self-consciousness over looking like "something that'd been chewed up and spit out"—her words, which she'd refused to take back even when I gave her one of my stern looks.

Thinking it would be good for her to spend more time with her mom, I invited them over to our place instead. Nowadays, we ate dairy-free, gluten-free, probiotic and organic. It sounded worse than it actually was. But I did miss cheese.

Fortunately, my chef was amazingly brilliant and saw the restrictions as a challenge she was determined to overcome. So, in spite of it all, the meals were good. Not my first choice, but if Emilia could go through all she went through with minimal complaints, then I could put up with weird food for her. I just made sure to eat whatever I wanted when I was at work.

I should have known something was up with Peter and Kim based on their weird behavior. Peter, who is always quiet, was even quieter, and Kim's interactions with her daughter were stilted and a little strange.

So it was no surprise that over dessert and coffee, Emilia's mother turned to her and took her hand over the table. "So, uh...we had something we wanted to tell you. Um..." She flicked a glance in my direction. "It might be a little weird for you two, though."

Emilia and I shared a look and then she turned back to her mom expectantly.

"Peter and I have decided to get married."

Emilia immediately shot out of her seat and gave her a big hug, kissing her. "Mom, I'm so happy for you!"

Well...I was glad one of us was. I just felt like this was beyond bizarre, and I couldn't put my finger on why. I watched Emilia's overjoyed reaction. Apparently, she wasn't weirded out by this news. Maybe it was just me...

Because this would make Emilia the stepsister to Liam and Britt, my cousins.

Emilia was now hugging my Uncle Peter—her future stepfather. The thought of it was so surreal. I got up and hugged Kim and congratulated her. I hoped I was successful at hiding my reaction to their news. It had been coming, I supposed. I should have been preparing for it. They'd been dating for seven or eight months and getting along very well. And given both of their pasts, they deserved some happiness.

"When's the wedding?" Emilia asked.

"We're not doing anything fancy. Just something for the family and close friends, like Heath. I'd love to do something on the beach. But we don't have a date yet because..." Her voice died out when it shook with emotion.

Peter took her hand. "We're waiting until Mia's scan comes back negative. We'll figure out everything out then."

Kim let out a long breath and smiled at her daughter. Emilia hugged her again and reassured her that that would be soon. God, I hoped so.

Not too long after, we saw them to the door, where we hugged and congratulated them again. I was envious of their uncomplicated happiness. But it wasn't like they didn't deserve it. Peter's wife had left him when his kids were still young, and he'd had to raise them—and then me, later on—by himself. Kim had had her heart broken at a very young age by a worthless cheater and hadn't found someone to share her life with until now. I did wish them happiness, and I was certain I'd get over the ick factor—hopefully soon.

Once the door clicked closed and they were walking back across the island to their car, I turned back to Emilia, who was looking at me with a crooked smile on her face. I took a deep breath and smiled back.

She approached me slowly and put her arms around my neck. To avoid that always tense moment of "will we or won't we kiss?" I kissed her forehead and she blew out a sigh. I didn't trust myself to kiss her on the mouth again. Not after last time, when I'd almost been sucked into forgetting that we were still trying to take it slow.

"So, um…can I ask you something?"

"Yeah, sure. Anything," I answered.

"Aren't you a little…um…grossed out by that?" she said, making a face.

I exhaled in relief. "Totally."

She shuddered for a minute. "Um. So are you and I going to be cousins now?"

I shook my head. "Let's not talk about it."

"It's like...I had to jump out of that chair and hug her right away and not let myself think about it, but the whole time I was congratulating them, my brain was shouting, 'No! Ewwww!'"

We laughed and went to watch TV. She sat snuggled next to me in my recliner, her head on my shoulder. She smelled so amazing that I got a little bit of a high from the scent of her skin. I rested my hand on her waist, willing it to stay put. Fortunately, I was so exhausted I didn't have to remind myself too many times to keep my hands off of her.

25
MIA

TWO WEEKS LATER, THE NIGHT BEFORE ADAM'S TWENTY-seventh birthday, he got a car and driver for our first romantic night out in months. I would have liked to have been with him on the night of his birthday, but he cited an unavoidable event that would be taking him out of town for the next week. To be honest, I was nervous to be without him, but he gave me no details.

Strangely, we drove up to Los Angeles for dinner. We rarely ventured up into the City of Angels. Most residents of Orange County acted like they had a phobia of Los Angeles, which, I'd admit, was kind of silly. But everyone claimed to have the best of Southern California in their backyard, so LA became a necessary evil, only for things like transportation or big shows or the museums that just didn't quite cut it down south.

I dressed in a classic little black dress with a matching flapper-style hat, thanks to Sonia the shopper's impeccable taste. Adam had threatened to take me out for dancing—presumably the tango—

afterward, so I almost, *almost* donned a wig. I owned two—one of them with bright purple hair, much to Adam's dismay—but had never worn them for more than five minutes in the house before pulling them off in frustration. It felt fake to wear one and I knew that was a silly feeling...but it was there nonetheless.

The dress was short, showing off my now too-skinny legs, and had a high neckline—a requirement of my clothing these days. I never showed any cleavage at all, nor anything that drew attention to my chest. I was only worthy of dressing like a granny now. My body was no longer something to show off, to be proud of. It was a secret shame to shroud under layers of clothing.

Adam was as gorgeous as ever, wearing a dark blue evening suit with matching tie against a crème-colored shirt. I loved when he wore dark colors. It suited him, with his glossy black hair and dark eyes. It added to his alluring mystique. I used to feel beautiful beside him, like we complemented each other. We'd turned heads and I knew we were an unusually good-looking couple. But now it felt wonky, uneven. Like a teeter-totter overly weighted on one side so that it couldn't move. He was stunningly handsome, and I was a faded, insignificant, too-thin and sick-looking hanger-on at his side. We no longer looked like we belonged together. Quite possibly because in reality, we didn't.

I tried to push those thoughts aside as we slipped into the Beverly Hills restaurant together. As usual, Adam attracted a lot of female notice, which he either was unaware of or completely ignored for my sake. We had a quiet meal at the back, and I was proud that I was feeling so much better that I ate a normal amount of food and kept it down without one bit of nausea.

Someway, somehow, my body knew that it wasn't going to get any more poison and it was bouncing back. Reduced white blood cell count or no, I was starting, more than ever, to feel somewhat normal. Except for my faded looks.

But no matter. I was feeling good and Adam was ridiculously yummy all dressed up for his night on the town. I was going to try again and put the moves on him. He couldn't hold out forever.

"Is it dancing?" I asked when he wouldn't tell me what he had planned for after dinner.

"Nope." His dark eyes twinkled with mischief in the low light.

"Is it something on my bucket list?"

He smiled, my favorite dimple appearing just below his mouth. Sometimes when he did that, it stole my breath. "It might be."

"You're annoying," I said, folding my arms with mock irritation. "It's your birthday. *I'm* the one who is supposed to be surprising *you.*"

"Well, you know...control freaks don't take surprises very well."

My smile faltered and I wondered if he was referring, vaguely to the secrets I'd kept from him, and his reactions to them. There was a long pause before the waiter showed up and Adam made a point of telling him that we didn't need to order dessert.

Then he turned back to me. "Don't worry—this is something *I'm* going to enjoy, too. It will be your gift to me." He winked.

My hopes were soaring high when we slipped back into the town car, especially when Adam hit the button to raise the partition between the driver and us. I'd never listed limo sex specifically on the now-infamous bucket list, but maybe he'd decided to substitute that for the apparently awkward sixty-nine?

He bent to kiss me and my heartbeat raced. It was a light, affectionate kiss. It was playful, and there was something in his eyes that corroborated that feeling. A spark, a twinkle. It wasn't his usual look of passion or lust, but I'd take it. I was beginning to regret that

I'd worn panties under my dress but figured he'd resolve that situation easily enough with one of his famous panty-shredding maneuvers. My mouth went dry at the thought of it.

Then, he reached into the seat pocket in front of him and pulled out a scrap of black silk.

"What's that?" I asked.

"You'll see," he replied. Turning in one quick move, he slipped it over my head. A blindfold.

Oh, so we were going to get kinky? I sat up straight.

"I'm getting excited now," I said, reaching for him.

He pressed another long, lingering kiss on my mouth. "You should be," he whispered darkly and I shivered with anticipation.

The thought of his hands, his mouth on me made my entire body come to life, flushing with heat. Limo sex. Hmmm. When we got home, I'd quickly add this one to my bucket list and then just as merrily tick it off. The first time we'd be together in over four months. Oh yes, I was hotly anticipating it.

The next thing I knew, he slipped headphones on me. Big heavy ones. The kind that canceled out the noise outside. He lifted one of them and said, "I'm going to put some music on right now. No peeking until we get there."

"Get where?"

He laughed. "Nice try." The next thing I knew, I was being treated to the sounds of the eighties from Adam's playlist. "Sweet Dreams" by Eurythmics was the first song to play.

I sat back with a sigh and concentrated on the motions of the car. Adam didn't touch me. So much for the limo sex. I quietly hoped he had something even more exciting in mind. After getting my heart set on him and me together in the back of the car as it drove down the long stretch of Wilshire Boulevard, anything else was going to be a letdown.

A half hour later, the car was slowing, turning and parking. Adam's hand closed around mine and tugged me toward the car door as I felt him rise and get out. Like a wobbly newborn giraffe, I did the same and he steadied me against him. I raised my hand almost automatically to the blindfold, but he pulled it away, planting a kiss on my forehead. He wrapped a solid arm around my waist and pulled me along beside him. I tried to concentrate on any sounds that might escape the relentless beat of the Pet Shop Boys.

We walked on concrete and it was really windy. My skirt blew upward before Adam folded his coat around my shoulders. After a few hundred yards of walking, we made it to a set of stairs. I tentatively lifted my foot to rest it on the first step—textured metal to make it nonslip—but almost stumbled. Adam then lifted me and carried me up the rest of the way. I clamped my arms around his neck and we entered a building at the top of the stairs. When he put me back on my feet, I held a hand out to steady myself, landing against an upholstered wall.

Where the fuck were we, and why had it been necessary to blindfold me and muffle all the noise around me? Soon Adam was nudging me into a chair and settling beside me. It was wide and comfortable, like a couch, and the floor rumbled beneath us. My mind sifted through the possibilities.

Adam reached out for his music player, which hung around my neck, and turned down the volume.

"Do you know where you are?" he asked.

"Um. An airplane?"

He pulled off the earphones. "Good. Take off the blindfold."

I did and looked around. This was not like any airplane I'd ever been on before. It was a private jet and it was about to take off—very soon, if the rumble under the floor meant anything. The area where we sat had couches and lounge chairs grouped so that they were facing each other. The seats were comfortable, leather, padded, but they still came with seat belts. Wherever we were going, we would be traveling in style.

"A private jet? I thought you didn't use these on principle."

He grinned. "This is an exception."

I twisted my mouth. "So you weren't lying when you said you'd be out of town on your birthday. You just didn't inform me that I would be out of town, too. How typically you." I stuck my tongue out. It only seemed to increase his pleasure. "Where are we going?"

"You think after all the trouble I went through to get you on this plane blindfolded that I'm going to tell you that easily?"

"How long will we be flying, then?" I said, glancing behind us. I could see a sitting room and a bedroom through the doorway. A dim light emanated from the bedroom, with a bed all made up and looking as luxurious as any fine hotel room.

"We'll be flying through the night."

Holy crap. Then we *were* going far. Either the East Coast or even farther. Maybe we were going the other way and headed to Hawaii? Or perhaps we were headed back to St. Lucia, I thought with a sudden thrill. Wonderful things had happened between us in St. Lucia. I couldn't think of a better place for us to revitalize our relationship.

"I hope you packed my bathing suit and some suntan lotion." I grinned.

His smile deepened. "You're all packed up with everything you'll need, thanks to Sonia. Hopefully, you'll like what she picked out for you."

A flight attendant appeared, served us drinks and asked us to fasten our seatbelts, as we'd be taking off very soon. I sipped my mineral water and giggled, shooting a look at Adam. Maybe no limo sex, but what about mile-high sex? I could just as easily swap that out on my bucket list.

I decided to cheat and ask the flight attendant where we were headed. She smiled and glanced at Adam. "I was told that our destination is top secret. I can't divulge."

I sat back in a huff. "Okay, so how long are we flying for?"

"Eleven hours, forty-two minutes." She turned and left the cabin shortly thereafter.

Holy shit. I bounced up in the seat with a smile. "We're going to St. Lucia, aren't we?"

Adam shrugged and looked out the window.

"I'm excited to go back."

He turned back to me. "Yeah? Things didn't end well for us there."

I took a breath, wondering why he focused on the negative ending rather than all the wonderful things that happened before that. "Things started for us very, very well there. Don't you remember?"

He watched me, his mouth curving enigmatically. "I remember very, very well. Every moment of it."

I smiled. "Time for us to go back and make some new memories, huh?" I leaned in and kissed him.

He returned the long, lingering kiss before pulling back, his eyes moving over my face. "You're beautiful."

"Hmmph. You're a liar, but thank you."

He put a hand to my chin and looked into my eyes without blinking or turning away. In that clipped, no-bullshit tone of voice of his, he said, "I'm *not* lying."

26
ADAM

WE SLEPT IN THE BED TOGETHER AND I KNOW SHE WAS expecting more. It was getting harder to resist her than ever before. For the first time in months, she looked healthy. She was still thin and pale, but there was new life in her. Before this, when I'd felt like I wanted something, and especially when she'd made advances, I'd told myself she was just starved for affection. I'd tried to supply that in other ways. And I wasn't lying about being exhausted all the time. I was.

I made myself that way on purpose.

But tonight, well, it was different. It was like we were shedding our cares with each mile we put between home and ourselves. Like our problems were location-dependent, when I knew damn well that that wasn't the case.

I slept in my underwear and she was in a sexy black slip that she'd worn under her black dress. She had curled against me at once and tried to pull me into a kiss, but I'd held firm. I was proud of myself that I didn't succumb. She was vulnerable and I wasn't going to take advantage. She just wasn't ready, no matter what signals she was sending. *We* still weren't ready.

Maybe soon, but not now.

We landed at Charles de Gaulle Airport in the late afternoon, local time. She still had no idea that we were in Europe. And I hoped to hold out on that secret until the moment we hit a view with the Eiffel Tower in the background. Or maybe when we arrived at our hotel.

The weather was cold and wet when we walked from the plane to the waiting car. She screwed her head around, trying to look everywhere. But I hid most of what she could see with the umbrella that I'd been handed before we'd deplaned. We made it to the car before she could see enough to give her any clue as to where she was. And from what I could see, we could be in any nondescript US town for all she knew.

As it was, the jig was up the moment our driver made a phone call in French. The cold weather was the first clue that we weren't in the Caribbean. But the French was the second clue. She turned to me with saucer-shaped eyes. "You didn't."

I raised my brow to ask the question without saying a word.

"You didn't fly us to Paris..."

I didn't answer. I really wanted to smile, but I kept my face straight. She was in absolute shock. "There are other places in the world that speak French, you know."

"I've seen the bucket list that I supposedly dictated to you. You flew us to fucking Paris! Holy shit."

I finally cracked a smile. Her reaction was amusing. I loved doing stuff like this. Thanks to Jordan, I could.

We'd driven far enough into the city that the tower was now visible, so I indicated it behind her and she spun around. "No fucking way. We *are* in Paris!"

"We just might be."

She spun back to me. "How the hell did you do this? Does my doctor know I left the country? How the hell did we get through customs without my even knowing?"

I waggled my eyebrows. "I have ways. I am an international man of mystery."

"You are the coolest geek on the planet."

"Hmm. Flattery will get you everywhere."

She smirked at me. "That's what I'm counting on."

"Are you tired? Or do you want to do some sightseeing after we check in?"

"Umm. I do believe I have a few bucket list items to check off. How long are we here for?"

"Wait and see."

"Is this trip going to be all like this? With you just giving me no info?"

"Is it bothering you?"

She smiled. "No, it's actually kind of fun. I just won't bother to ask any questions then."

"Hmm. I should have thought of something like this long ago."

"Don't push your luck, bub. I wonder if bald women get a better rap in Paris? Maybe I could start a new fashion fad if I parade down the Champs-Élysées in front of the Chanel store."

"I think the most alluring models might just shave their heads, but—again—still won't be as hot as you."

Her eyes shone. "Well, aren't you just full of flattery yourself? It goes without saying that it will get you everywhere. Hell, as long as it's been, you needn't apply much flattery at all these days."

"Mmm. Then I'll save it for when it's needed."

She curled up a fist and playfully punched me in the arm as the limo slowed in the Avenue George V and the driver opened the door. This was going to be one of the highlights of our trip.

27
MIA

THE HOTEL WAS BREATHTAKING, AND FROM THE MOMENT WE entered, I couldn't stop gaping at everything around me. Quiet piano music played in the lobby. There were black and white marble floors decorated with tall black stone vases all arranged artistically in the hotel foyer, full of hundreds of fresh white flowers of all varieties. We were escorted to our own private elevator, given a special key card for access and whisked up to our room. The elevator opened right into our penthouse suite.

The place was amazing. It overlooked the city, with wraparound balconies on either side of the building providing a 360-degree view of the city. On one side, the Eiffel Tower loomed over the Seine, and on the other, the Arc de Triomphe stood immovable at the center of a sea of cars swarming around the Place Charles de Gaulle. I could hardly catch my breath as with each passing moment I got a view of yet another famous monument I'd seen only in pictures. This was surreal.

"So about that comment about being out of town for your birthday..."

He shrugged. "I wasn't lying."

I turned to him. "So what do I get the man who has everything?" I said, moving up beside him and slipping my arms around his taut waist.

He gave me another one of those exasperating forehead kisses. "You've already given me my present. You're getting better and stronger every day. I couldn't have asked for more."

I was thinking more along the lines of my naked body wrapped in a big red bow. That would be a present I could get behind—if I found a way to cover up the top half. Then again, maybe Kat was right...maybe all it would take would be a flash of some boob.

Because damn, if I didn't want to get under this man before, I sure as hell wanted it now.

"So do I get to know our plans for the night?"

"Hmm. First, we get dressed for dinner. Then, the car takes us to dinner. Then...we'll see."

"And where is dinner?"

He grinned again. "It might just be that we can eat dinner and hit one of your bucket list items all in one fell swoop."

My eyes widened. "We're eating dinner on the Eiffel Tower?"

"We're eating at Le Jules Verne on the Eiffel Tower, at a west-facing window table so we can watch the sunset.'"

"Then I'd better get ready!"

My bag had been unpacked and my things tucked away by the majordomo while we'd wandered around the suite that was bigger than most small homes and hung out on the balcony terrace.

I had no idea what had even been packed for me by Sonia. Who knew what sort of eveningwear she'd slipped in there?

I whipped open the armoire that had been appointed to me and gasped. In it, along with other clothing, hung one sexy black dress, one red dress and one crème-colored gown. They were completely different than the ones he had given me in Amsterdam but completely reminiscent of that first night we'd spent together.

I actually felt tears sting the backs of my eyes as I pulled them out and looked at them. Adam was in the shower and I took a moment to try each of them on. They were gorgeous, and I had no way of knowing if Sonia had picked them out or if Adam had. But each of them was cut lower in front than I would have liked. They weren't obscene but more like the necklines I used to wear. The red one was stunning, showing a lot of leg under a flared skirt and with a cutout in the back. When I heard the shower stop, I hurriedly tucked them back inside the closet, still unsure of what to do.

It was too much of a coincidence to ignore, and I decided, as I showered and did my makeup, that Adam had been behind the gowns, if nothing else. So I resolved to find the courage to wear one of them. If he wanted to see me wearing them, then I'd do it.

Maybe then he'd touch me.

God, I wanted him to touch me.

So during this preparation time, the seeds of Project Seduction were germinating. Because somehow, I knew if we could get over this hurdle—if he could stop seeing me as sick and fragile and helpless—that maybe we could be equals and both be present in this relationship again.

I spent extra time on my makeup because I had no hair to style. Though I did happily notice that my eyebrows were starting to sprout,

I carefully penciled them in like the video tutorials had shown me to do them. I also glued on fake eyelashes. Overall my makeup efforts succeeded in mostly hiding the sickly look I'd been sporting.

I'd found some stunning scarves and wraps in amongst the accessories so I experimented, tying a lovely black lace scarf around my head with a big knot at the back. It trailed over my shoulder, like a long shock of hair.

With the stunning red dress I'd chosen to wear, it actually made me look exotic and a little glamorous. For jewelry, I wore some big earrings, a gold bracelet and my compass. I always wore the compass—always.

I felt like a new person, like I was no longer faded and barely visible. Like there was actually some hope that I might get my looks back—or at least most of them. That my body hadn't permanently gone into premature menopause, and I wouldn't have the metabolism and skin of a woman over twice my age.

But those were things to hope for later. One thing this whole ordeal had taught me was to be present...to be in the moment. Enjoy what I had when I had it.

And tonight, I had the handsomest, most amazing man at my side, helping me into the limo, opening doors for me, holding my hand. Feasting on me with his eyes and complimenting me on my dress after casting long, slow looks down my form.

He wore a black suit and black tie with a white shirt. It really didn't matter what he wore, to be honest. He always looked great.

I shamelessly flirted with him and made sure my dress rode up my thighs in the car. He looked. I watched him with a suppressed grin. Project Seduction was in its early stages. I had no idea how it might progress. But hey, he was a healthy guy. He hadn't had sex in almost five months. It couldn't be that difficult, could it?

"The dinner at Le Jules Verne is wonderful. You're going to love it. You're also going to eat more food in this one meal than you have every day in the past month combined."

I snorted. My appetite was returning slowly, but it still wasn't what it had been—not by half.

"There are six courses, and they'll bring out a different wine for each course."

"Can't drink wine yet. Doc said not for another month or so. But you can have mine."

He helped me out of the car and that sparked an idea. Adam wasn't a drinker. I'd only seen him drunk once. He seldom drank anything stronger than beer or wine...but if he had *enough* wine, maybe that would help Project Seduction along.

Adam led us through the crowd that was lining up to get into the big elevators to take them up the tower and I looked straight up, gasping in delight.

We were at the base of the Eiffel Tower! It was a massive structure made of iron yet it actually looked like a delicate, dainty lady. It was lovely. But it was strong and unchanging. We made our way to a private elevator exclusive to restaurant guests, and after he showed the operator our reservations, we were ushered inside.

I grabbed his hand and squeezed. "We are on the Eiffel Tower! Holy crap!"

He smiled. "Yep. And you are stunning. My lady in red." He bent and kissed me on the cheek.

Damn it, I was getting sick of the cheek and forehead kisses. I looked at his handsome profile as we made the slanted climb to the first platform of the tower. My heart squeezed in my chest the way it always did when I just let myself look at him, be in his presence.

Moments like this, alone with him, consumed me—my thoughts, my feelings pulled relentlessly toward him like a sunflower in the sun. It used to scare me and make me wonder if I was obsessed or losing myself. Now, I accepted it. It was comforting. These feelings were reassurances that I was still alive. That cancer and its dubious cure might have eaten away at my body, but never my heart. Adam still owned that.

My throat tightened when he turned his head, most likely detecting my gaze. His dark eyes met mine and he smiled that devastatingly handsome smile and I was lost, finding it hard to catch my breath.

Shit. I was even more gone than the silly little Adam-groupie interns at Draco.

But that made sense, when I thought about it. They all were all dazzled by the exterior—rich, handsome, sure of himself, physically fit. He was the perfect package that made them all atwitter.

What made my heart surge whenever we were together? It was what they didn't see, what they had no idea existed—the Adam on the inside, who cast that outside Adam, as amazing as he was, into a very dark shadow. The man on the inside eclipsed everything around him. He wasn't perfect. But in every way that counted, he was perfect for me.

28
ADAM

I WAS ENJOYING THIS IMMENSELY. SHE WAS LIKE A LITTLE GIRL ON Christmas Day, all wide-eyed and full of wonder. And it felt good to see her looking so healthy and—finally—happy. We sat down to dinner and she made a respectable show of eating.

I kept track of every bite that went into her body, coaxed her to eat more than she probably would have on her own. She was too thin, of course. But now, three weeks out from her last chemo treatment, she was at least starting to get some of her color back—to say nothing of a little of her hair. I actually noticed that her eyebrows were starting to slowly grow back in.

She smiled—a lot. And when she smiled so much, I couldn't help but smile along with her.

"So is it true you are giving Kat her dream job of being a playtester?"

"If she makes it through all the HR screening, she's got the job."

Emilia's hand landed on top of mine, our fingers intertwining. "Thank you. It's been good to have her around."

I smiled. "It's been good to have everyone around."

Her mouth widened. "It's been good having *you* around. You are wonderful."

I tightened my fingers around hers. "I just do what I have to do."

Her golden-brown eyes seemed to search mine. "Oh..." she swallowed.

"Maybe that didn't come out right..."

She shook her head. "No, it's all right."

I frowned. "I meant that I did what I had to do...because I couldn't imagine doing anything less for you."

She took in a deep breath and tilted her head, watching me. "You know...I don't believe in former lives but if I did, I must have done something goddamn amazing in the last one to deserve you."

"Maybe we both did something amazing."

We shared a long look and time seemed to slow. There are moments that occur, that draw our memories that seem denser than the string of moments before and after them. Years later, in your mind, you are drawn to them by an offhand comment, a flash of color, a scent, a texture, a taste, a feeling. But seldom do you realize the importance at the time that you were experiencing them, the memory's equivalent of a bauble or souvenir.

This long string of seconds where we said nothing but looked into each other's eyes, seeing pure emotion but refusing to look away. I knew it right when it happened. This was one of the weighted moments, one of those memories I'd savor for years to come.

Finally, she looked away, a smile dancing on her lips. "You haven't finished your wine for the course. You're supposed to drink it and tell me how it is."

This was my third glass. I tipped it back and was finally starting to feel a bit of a buzz. Emilia watched me closely and then pushed her glass toward me. "Here's some more. Don't let it go to waste."

I threw her a questioning look and ignored the glass. The waiter cleared the glasses and plates in preparation for our next course. And with it, of course, came another glass of wine. Since this was the meat course, it was red. I did like a good glass of red wine.

"How is it?" Emilia asked, taking an inordinate interest in the wine.

I frowned. "It's good."

"Sorry," she said, suddenly self-conscious. "I haven't had any wine in a long time. Since before..." She cut herself off, shaking her head.

A dark feeling came over me. There was before and there was after. And it sat like an impassable valley in between our past and our future. Everything in me felt heavy with that realization. At times, I wondered if we'd ever be able to overcome this divide.

With a depressing sigh, I downed the rest of the red wine with one gulp, welcoming the warmth washing over me.

After dinner, we went up to the top level, crowding onto the high platform with everyone else. I had warned Emilia that even on the warmest days in summer, it got windy and cold up here so she had brought a jacket. The monuments of Paris spread out around us, lit up like jewels in a sea of black velvet. This city was unbelievably beautiful. And so was the woman beside me.

She watched everything with wide eyes, vivid excitement lighting up her features. The lacy wrap around her head was an elegant touch as the loose ends fluttered in the breeze. Soon she noticed the scattered padlocks clamped onto the cage-like safety grid over our heads.

"Oh, wow! Look at these. Love locks. I wish we'd thought of that."

I smiled, suddenly feeling very smug. I reached into my pocket and pulled out the heavy golden lock that I'd been carrying in my pocket all evening. "Fortunately, you brought the boy genius with you."

Her grin widened. "Yeah, fortunately I did!"

I handed her the lock, complete with key, and a permanent marker. "Here. Write something on it, and I'll lock it as high as I can get it."

Emilia grabbed the pen and began writing, then flipped it over and continued to write. "You aren't writing a manifesto on there, are you?"

She smirked. "No. Well, maybe just a short love manifesto."

She opened the lock, pulled out the key and handed it to me. I held it up to the light to read it: *E.K.S. + A.D.* I turned it over to read the back: *= Nat 20.* She'd used the gamer term from Dungeons and Dragons, which meant "instant, automatic success" by rolling a twenty on a twenty-sided die.

I laughed. "Now *this* is a manifesto I can agree with."

I jumped up and grabbed the cage above my head, pulling myself up and hanging with one arm while I used my other hand to loop the lock around the cage overhead and clamp the padlock closed. Then I dropped back to the platform, where Emilia promptly wrapped her arms around me and pressed her head against my chest. "That was awesome. Thank you." She held up the key and said, "And this is getting dropped into the Seine ASAP."

"Mmm. We still haven't hit your bucket list item yet."

"Yeah?"

"I believe it was to *kiss* someone on top of the Eiffel Tower."

"Hmm. I do believe you are right. Know anyone interested in helping me out?"

I ducked my head, pulling her closer to me, and landed my mouth squarely on hers. I'd been wanting to kiss her all night.

And if there was any sort of kiss to be had on the Eiffel Tower, it was this kiss. I touched my mouth to hers, tentatively. She angled her head to meet me. Then I locked my arms around her thin waist while she rose up to pull me deeper into the kiss. Her mouth opened to me, and my tongue slid inside to explore her. She gave out the most delicious little sigh, almost like a whimper, and my body came alive. My heart thumped and her hands came up my chest, and then my neck to settle on either side of my face, to hold me in place as if afraid I'd pull away.

I let her have her way with me—with this kiss, at least. She was starved, wanting more and more. Her tongue met mine and she was sighing and breathing hard. The more excited she got, the more enflamed it made me. And the more I realized that she wasn't the only starved animal here.

Minutes later, I pulled away slowly even though it was obvious she still wanted more. Her cheeks were flushed, her eyes bright, and when she looked at me, it was with so much love and trust in her eyes. I brought my hand up to touch her cheek—it was like touching an angel. Her eyes fluttered closed, her too-long fake eyelashes lying on her cheeks. I was reminded of that first night we spent together, on the balcony of our suite at the hotel in Amsterdam.

Something I'd inadvertently done had scared her and she'd been so vulnerable. But never fragile. She was strong. Like a warrior. She'd always been. Until lately. Until...

I sighed.

"You know what it's time for?" she asked.

"What?"

She pulled out her cell phone. "A top-of-the-Eiffel-Tower selfie!"

She moved up next to me and held the phone out, clicking on the reverse camera, and our faces appeared in the center of the screen.

Her hand wavered and when she pressed the button, our faces were cut off just under our noses in the photo. "Crap... I can't hold it still long enough. You try."

Someone approached us. "*Bonsoir*," the woman said. She had a glass of champagne in each hand. "*Pourrais-je prendre votre photo?*"

"*Bonsoir*," I answered with one of the half dozen words of French that I knew. Then, before she rattled off anything more, I used my favorite word in French. "*Anglais?*"

The young woman smiled. "Of course," she answered in clear, accented English. "May I take your photo for you?"

I handed her the cell phone and she indicated her full hands with the champagne. She handed us each a glass. She held up the phone and took our picture before giving us back the phone.

"I noticed you two from over there." She pointed at the champagne bar behind which she had been working. "And you looked so happy and in love that everyone around you was watching you and neither of you had any idea."

Emilia blushed and grinned, looking at me. She reached out and squeezed my hand.

"Take the champagne. Toast each other with my compliments."

Emilia glanced into the flute and I watched her until she looked up. "Top-of-the-Eiffel-Tower champagne. I think this is definitely worth a sip," she said.

I held my glass up next to hers. "What shall we toast to?"

"I am so not poetic. I think we should toast to all our tomorrows."

"To us," I said, clinking my glass to hers. "No greater love since Han and Leia."

She laughed and took a sip, watching me as I downed my glass. Then she handed hers to me and said, "Finish it."

So with a smile, I did. I'd call myself a lightweight, feeling the bubbles starting to go to my head, but I'd had almost five glasses of wine at dinner and this added to it.

By the time we set foot on the ground, our limo waiting to take us back to the hotel, I was feeling light-headed, pleasantly buzzed and one hundred percent into the gorgeous woman beside me.

"Are you getting tired?" I asked. I still had one more surprise in store for her tonight.

"No. I slept very nicely on the plane and it's only, what? Like three in the afternoon at home? I feel okay."

"Good. Because there's still one more thing I want to do."

She threw me a sidelong glance and a sly smile. "Oh?"

Our hotel had dancing in one of the grand ballrooms, complete with a huge polished stone floor, high columns, a private terrace and a live orchestra. And, thanks to my request, they were featuring the tango for part of the night.

When we arrived, Emilia threw me a look that was a mixture of surprise and terror.

"I don't know this well enough to do anything but make a complete fool of myself in public."

"You can be bald in public—you have the guts for anything. Besides, I know the steps. I'll lead you. Just trust me, okay?"

"Okay. I trust you not to let me make a fool out of myself."

I smiled. "Good. Just relax and let me lead you. 'There are no mistakes in the tango,'" I quoted. "'When you get all tangled up, you just tango on.'"

She squinted at me. "That's from a movie, isn't it?"

I smiled. "You know me so well. Al Pacino, *Scent of a Woman*."

I took her hand and led her to the floor. There were a few other couples out there, but many had sat down once the band began playing tango music. The steps I'd taught her were simple, and I could guide her easily enough through anything more complex.

We faced each other and she looked into my eyes. Her gaze then darted around the room and she took a deep breath. She was feeling self-conscious, either about the dance or about her looks. If I did my job right, she should forget about both.

"Put your left hand on my shoulder. Higher."

She complied, and I took her right hand in my left and curved my right arm around her to press firmly against the center of her back. "Relax your body. Try not to be stiff."

She grinned. "I'm having a weird déjà vu feeling."

I smiled. "Amsterdam?"

"Yep."

"You did beautifully then. You've got this."

She took a shaky breath and nodded. "Okay."

The music started up again and I stepped forward, guiding her to walk backward for three steps before gliding to the side. She fumbled for a moment, stepping forward just as I did.

"Sorry!" she gasped as she stomped on my foot.

"Let me lead you, Emilia. Do you trust me?"

She looked up at me and nodded. "Yeah."

"Then look in my eyes and stop watching our feet."

She took a deep breath and relaxed in my arms. And for the rest of that first song, she never looked down. Once she was more comfortable, I added a few more complex things, like a turn here and a dip there. The first time I dipped her, she let out a little squeak and laughed like crazy.

"My scarf is going to fall off and you are going to expose my chrome dome!"

Our bodies moved together. The tango was a sexy dance. Much like the sexual act itself, it was our bodies in close proximity, moving together, our hands holding each other, our eyes, fastened to one another. Our breath coming quicker. Our hearts beating faster.

Yeah, I'll admit it was turning me on. Between the alcohol, the kiss on the tower and now this dancing, it was going to be hard to resist her.

But then she pulled out the big guns—because I was well aware of what she'd been doing all night. She'd enacted a studied, careful campaign to seduce me. And I'd played dumb and let her do it.

"Don't twirl me so fast next time. My dress will fly up too high."

"What, you don't want the old goats in here to see your underwear?"

"I wouldn't care about them seeing my underwear, if I was wearing any," she said with an impish grin on her face. "Happy birthday."

I stumbled midstep. "You aren't wearing any underwear?"

She paused for a beat and I dipped her, holding her there until she answered me. She looked up at me, hooking a leg around mine as I bent into a deeper dip. "Nope. Not a stitch. Full commando."

Fuck me. I was hard immediately at the thought.

I pulled her up and stood absolutely still. "You are a very naughty girl."

Her gorgeous, puffy lips formed a pout and her eyes, all doe-like and innocent, grew wider as she said, "Mmm, hmmm. I should be punished."

I pulled her closer, her feminine body felt like heaven pressed to me. "You should," I whispered.

She pressed her face to my ear, took my lobe in her hot mouth and dragged her teeth over it. Hot lust streaked through me. God, she was a siren. And there was little holding her off tonight. My blood was on fire for her. She must have felt my erection pressing against her, because she undulated against it, eliciting a gasp of surprise from me.

And before we started doing anything indecent, like fucking right there in front of everyone, I grabbed her hand and pulled her off the dance floor. With a laugh swallowed in a gasp of surprise, she trotted along behind me as I strode with purpose to the elevator that led directly up to our suite. I wasn't even sure I'd make the elevator ride without committing some sort of lewd act.

The minute the door closed, she turned to me and I had my hands up her skirt, confirming the absence of her panties.

"You see? Nothing for you to rip off of me."

I pressed her against the wall of the elevator. "I'm going to push this dress up right now and fuck you."

She let out a breathy moan that cut right through me. "Yes, please."

"You want it," I said, my hand stroking up the inside of her silky thigh.

Her lids drooped. "Yes, I do."

"But I shouldn't give you what you want, naughty girl. I should punish you."

When the elevator dinged and the door slid open to the suite, I gave her a light push out in front of me, turning back to press the lock button on the elevator so we wouldn't be interrupted. She cast a wary glance up at me and then turned away from me, facing the wall.

"Punish me, then."

29
MIA

PROJECT SEDUCTION WAS ABOUT TO CASH IN. WITH BREATHY anticipation, I waited as he moved behind me. He stopped, standing very close without touching me. I stood perfectly still, even holding my breath.

Adam grabbed my wrists and pulled my hands up by my head as he pushed me forward. His hips pinned my body to the cold marble wall.

"I need to fuck you," he said. And he began to kiss me. His mouth slipped across the back of my neck, my shoulders, my ears, my jaw, his kisses sizzling on my skin like icy raindrops on a steaming hot street. I tingled with his touch, his hands braceleted around my wrists. He took his time tasting every inch of me and I could feel or think of nothing besides his mouth, his hot breath on my skin. I shivered and his hands tightened around my wrists, his breath faltering where his mouth devoured my earlobe.

"Adam, please," I whimpered.

He pressed my hands on the wall beside my head and dropped his hold to fumble with the fastening on my dress, unhooking and unzipping it in two quick movements.

"My God, you are beautiful," he said in a tight voice. Everything in me hummed to the vibrations of his uttered words. I swallowed, still fearful for him to see me. If he stripped off my dress, he'd still find my serviceable, unattractive bra hiding my disfigurement. I'd just ask him not to take it off.

And I could brag to Kat that I was so good, I didn't even have to show him the girls to get into his pants.

His hands slid inside the dress, tracing my spine from the small of my back to the base of my neck, and then his hot, wet mouth replaced the touch there while his hands went to cup my hips. The sensations were stunning, overwhelming, and I was certain that if I hadn't been propped up against the wall, I might have swooned like an old-fashioned lady in a too-tight corset.

Inside my dress, his hands moved from my hips, over my stomach, one settling between my legs. He traced his finger there, pressing his mouth to my ear. "You're so wet for me."

I leaned my head back on his shoulder and barely managed to answer with a hoarse whisper. "Yes."

"I think my naughty girl needs to come," he said, stroking me again. I gasped. *Oh yes, she really, really needs to come.*

"I think the birthday boy needs to come, too," I replied.

Suddenly, his hands were everywhere, moving over my thighs, over my stomach. He moved them so fast it was like he was trying to make up for lost time in minutes, like he didn't know where he wanted to touch next. I was the air he needed to breathe, the water he needed to drink.

Those hands came up to my breasts and cupped them over the thick material of my bra. I took a deep breath and fought the urge to push his hands away. He rested them there, as if testing me to see what I would do. So against my instinct, I relaxed against him, my heart racing in fear mixed with anticipation. He moved his thumbs across my nipples and they immediately responded. I cried out, the feeling shooting through me so intense. Too intense. I arched against his broad chest and his hot breath scorched my neck.

He was flame and I was paper. His touch immolated me and I felt light, like the fiery embers of paper ashes carried away on the wind. I wanted him—needed to accept him into my body, feel him move inside me, touch every corner and every hidden alcove, empty himself into me.

We two needed to be one. One in desire, one in purpose, one in life.

I backed against him, moving my butt against his erection. He sucked in a sharp breath. "I should spank that naughty little ass."

A dark feeling clutched at my throat. His words reminded me of the night we'd been together in Vegas—the last night we'd had sex, over five months ago. He'd spanked me then. But it had been out of anger, frustration. I'd broken up with him without explaining anything to him. Guilt clutched at my throat. He'd hated me for it.

Did he still hate me? Deep down? For everything I'd put him through?

Could we just enjoy each other tonight and shove away the baggage? Could I make it up to him?

I was determined to try.

I turned my face to the side so he could hear me. "You can do anything you want. I'm yours."

His voice was a growl against my ear. "Say it again."

"I'm yours, Adam. Always."

His hands tightened on me and before I could check myself, I yelped in surprise. He immediately yanked them away from my breasts.

"Shit, did I hurt you? I'm sorry!"

I stifled a groan of frustration. "I'm fine. I'm okay."

He reached out and took the edges of my dress in his hands. My heart lurched. He was going to slip it off. I could barely contain my excitement, closing my eyes and tipping my head back. I was ready to lie back and enjoy the feel of his magical hands on me.

Instead, he zipped the dress back up.

Um.

Fuck.

I turned around and looked at him, frowning.

We held each other's gazes for a long, tense moment.

"I'm sorry," he repeated, backing away.

"You didn't hurt me. You just surprised me. I—It must be all the procedures and stuff. I feel very—clinical about my chest."

He nodded and ran a hand through his hair. "I got carried away. It didn't even occur to me." His mouth pursed in thought.

I approached him and slipped my arms around his waist. "It's okay. I'm fine. I—I really want to be with you tonight."

He hesitated, watching me. His eyes weren't mirrors, they were vault doors, shut and locked tight to me. He frowned. "We probably shouldn't. You aren't—"

I wanted to stomp in frustration. "I'm fine. The doctor says it's fine as long as I'm feeling like it. Everything is fine. Adam, I want to be with you. I want us to make love. I know you want it, too."

He blew out a long breath, the furrows not disappearing from his forehead. He shook his head.

So I took action. I stroked along his jawline, gently angling his head so I could kiss him. Pushing my tongue into his mouth, I felt his breath quicken, his hands coming up to cradle the small of my back.

"I know you want it," I whispered again. "Please."

And then I ran my hand down over his hard stomach and lower, fondling him through his slacks. Yeah, he was still hard. His brain was saying 'no' but his body was saying 'yes' and I was hoping that would be enough to persuade him. He sucked in his breath. I unbuttoned his pants and he put a hand on top of mine as if to stop me.

But I didn't stop and he didn't say no. I unzipped him slowly while I kissed his neck. "Let me...please?" I sank to my knees in front of him, and he exhaled sharply when he saw what I was going to do.

I took him into my mouth, opening for him and taking it in deep while I caressed him with my tongue. He groaned, putting one hand on my head, then the other. He didn't pull or push me, but he slid his hands down to my neck, my shoulders. The lace scarf slipped off my head as I moved back and forth, my heart racing with his every heated gasp and groan.

"Emilia..." he ground out. "Fuck."

I continued the rhythm I was building, closing my eyes, concentrating on sucking and licking in all the right places. He put his hand on the top of my head and gently pulled away.

Then he bent and picked me up, pressed me against him. My legs went around his hips and only the thin layer of my dress separated us as I felt his hardness rubbing against me. My arms locked around his neck and his mouth sealed on mine. He was carrying me to the bedroom. I closed my eyes and concentrated on the taste of his mouth, his tongue. I couldn't get enough of him. My heartbeat was thready and rushed, and I could hardly catch my next breath.

He stopped us at the edge of the bed, locked together at our mouths and hips. I couldn't wait another second for us to be together. His hands were on my ass, tight and insistent again. Then he dropped us to the bed.

If I'd been expecting it—and had prepared myself—his weight landing on me like that would have been no big deal. Hadn't I been longing to feel his weight on top of me for months? But instead, it knocked the wind right out of me and I had to gasp to suck in air.

Adam scrambled to the side as I fought black spots at the edge of my vision, unable to move. "Shit! Emilia..."

I turned my head and opened my mouth once or twice before I was able to get my breath back. Blinking, I coughed. "I'm fine. I'm okay."

But he was pale and his forehead was beading with sweat. "I squashed the hell out of you. I'm so sorry."

I extended my hand to grasp his, but it was out of my reach. "It's okay. Everything's fine."

He reached out and cupped my cheek with a shaky hand. "Fuck. I'm so sorry. What the hell is wrong with me?"

"Come here. Kiss me," I said, trying to distract him. He looked like he was about to freak out.

Instead, he rose from the bed and looked down at me, eyes still wide with concern

We looked at each other for a long time. And I knew that our moment was over. We weren't going to make love tonight. I sucked in a shivery breath and blinked back tears, pulling myself to a sitting position.

Adam knelt in front of me, putting his hands on my waist as if he were checking for broken bones. When he gazed up into my face, he saw the tears that were leaking out. I felt like a miserable failure.

"Please don't cry," he murmured, kissing me.

"What's wrong with us?" I asked in a squeaky voice. "We're broken."

He sucked in a quick breath and shook his head. "No. No...it's just—I'm worried about you. I don't want to hurt you again."

"You're not going to, Adam. I swear that I'm fine."

"When you are healthy... When we get home and you get the scan—"

I pulled away from him in frustration, scrubbing the back of my hand over my cheeks. I stood and went into the bathroom. He followed me.

"It's how I look, isn't it?"

His mouth thinned. "No. You are beautiful."

I turned on the faucet and splashed water on my face. "You can be honest with me, you know. I can take it. You don't have to spare me."

I blotted my face with a soft white towel while he watched me in the mirror. When I turned to go, he stepped in my way, wrapping his hands around my forearms so I wouldn't move away. "You. Are. Beautiful. A head of hair doesn't change that one bit."

I sighed and looked into his eyes. "I'm worried about us."

He smoothed my cheek and smiled faintly. "Don't be. I love you more than ever, Emilia. I mean that."

I swallowed a lump in my throat. There was something he wasn't saying. I was certain of it. But I didn't want to fight, and I didn't want to force something from him before he was ready to tell me. Maybe he was just worried about my health. God, I hoped it was something as simple as that. Because the moment that scan came back clean, I was jumping his bones.

I took in a deep breath and expelled it. "I'm so tired all of a sudden."

He relaxed a little. Relieved, apparently. "Me, too. I'm about to keel over onto the nearest bed."

I frowned. There were three bedrooms in this huge suite, all of them equally amazing and luxurious. "Please don't say we need to sleep in separate beds."

He pulled me into a gentle hug. "I'm not going to say that. I want you in my arms tonight."

He wanted me in his arms. *Sleeping*. Nothing more.

Project Seduction was dead in the water. Mission failed.

30
ADAM

I FOLDED HER IN MY ARMS, HELD HER TIGHTLY—LIKE SHE
sometimes asked me to do. I noticed those were the times when
she was feeling the most lost, insecure. And I cursed myself for
not having sex with her tonight. It would have done good things for
her self-esteem and body image.

I'd certainly wanted her, too. But that moment of hurting her had
snapped me back to reality, back to all the problems and doubts and
worries. There was so much that needed to be covered first. What
about birth control? I hadn't brought condoms with me—though
they'd have been easy to get here. But I hadn't planned that far ahead,
just assuming that things wouldn't progress that quickly between us.
I was still thinking of her as ill, weak, that semiconscious sick woman
in my arms declaring she deserved to die...

In the silence, I listened. She had long since started that slow,
measured breathing of sleep, and I kissed her, laying my cheek against
hers. I closed my eyes, replaying everything in my mind again—
thinking about my colossal fuck-up and how it had only served to hurt

her more. As if in that one split second, all the good of the night had been erased.

But I couldn't risk hurting her again. Not even the smallest hint of a risk. I fell asleep like that, with me wrapped around her. Like I was her coat of armor, protecting her. And I wished it could be as simple as that. But the truth was that sometimes I was her greatest threat instead of her protection.

***

The next few days in Paris were wonderful. We took a long walk down our street, Avenue George V, with its iconic cafes, exclusive boutiques and stunning cars parked along the curb. I even suffered through a little her shopping on the Champs-Élysées, but since Emilia wasn't a big shopper, I didn't have to suffer long.

We spent most of one day in the Louvre, where she got to study the *Venus de Milo* up close and in person. I'd been to the museum several times before, but what I found most enjoyable about this trip was that I got to watch her react to the priceless, famous works of art hanging on the walls before her. Emilia looked at the canvases, spending time getting perspective, sometimes taking steps back to look at them from another angle. And I spent that time watching her.

They say that a person should visit Paris three times in their life— once when they are young, once when they have the money to truly enjoy it, and once when they are in love. I'd already checked the first two off my list. This time, it was like a whole new city to me, because I was seeing it through her eyes, and through the eyes of love.

A sappy, sentimental thought so uncharacteristic of me. But one thing I'd learned in the previous few months of utter tribulation that we had gone through—happiness and love were fragile things. And we should be thankful for what we have when we have it.

And to say I was grateful for having her in my life was an understatement.

We spent one afternoon on a park bench in the Tuileries gardens, sharing a baguette and some cheese between us.

"So, we have two more days here," she said, munching the last of the baguette and murmuring regrets that it was gone.

"Yep. We've ticked off your bucket list items. Anything else you can think of?"

"Mmm. No. Not really. I'm just enjoying soaking up the ambiance of this place. I can see why they call it the 'City of Love'. I still can't get over how you ninja'd this trip on me. That was amazing."

"Well, Jordan helped."

She shot me a puzzled look. "Jordan? Really?"

"He'd been planning the trip for a while. When he heard about you getting so sick from the reaction to those meds, he insisted I take over his plane and hotel reservations."

Her faint brows rose. "So we are on Jordan's trip?"

"Well, kind of. I did a lot of tweaking to his plans but, yeah, more or less."

She expelled a long breath and looked out over the park. "I always thought he hated me."

"I think he hated the idea that I wasn't going to be his wingman anymore."

"He sure tried to rope you back again...when we were broken up..."

I shrugged. "I think he feels worse about that than I do, if that's possible."

She turned to me, frowning. "Why do you feel bad about it? We were broken up. You went out on a date with someone else. You didn't do anything wrong."

I shifted, suddenly feeling uncomfortable. I wanted to change the subject and opened my mouth to do just that when I realized that this was something we *should* talk about. We couldn't avoid the subject of that dark time in our relationship forever.

"It felt wrong," I said.

She watched me and I focused on the water basins, where laughing children were launching toy sailboats. "We both made a lot of mistakes," came her soft reply.

I took a deep breath, forcing myself to continue when I just wanted to shut this down. "I was angry. I went out on that date because I was just so pissed off at you. So clearly for the wrong reasons."

"I did stupid things because I was angry, too. I shouldn't have broken up with you. I just—" She sucked in a breath suddenly, and I could tell she was getting emotional, but I didn't stop it. This needed to come out and I had no idea how I knew that. Instinct, maybe? "I felt like you were being so demanding and unyielding, and it made me want to do the same thing. I thought that if I gave in...well, at the time it seemed all-important. Now, looking back, after everything, it was trivial bullshit that we could have worked out if we'd kept level heads and just talked."

I reached for her hand, closed it in my own. "We're talking now."

"Yeah, I guess we aren't complete idiots if we can actually learn from our mistakes, right?"

I raised her hand to my mouth and kissed it. "What's important is that we can learn from them and also move past them."

She looked away and I saw her visibly swallow. Her hand tightened around mine. "So you don't think it's too late?"

"Would I be here if I did?"

She shook her head, closed her eyes.

"And you? Do you think it's too late?"

"I hope it's not. I don't trust what I think anymore because my judgment hasn't been good for me up to this point."

"Hey." I gently tugged her hand to get her to look at me. "We had a deal. No recriminations, self or otherwise. We move forward and we only look back to learn from our mistakes."

"Okay." She nodded, the ghost of a smile hovering on her lips. "And when we get home…?"

I inhaled a breath and held it. "When you're better, and we know for sure you are healthy, then we'll cross the other bridge when we come to it."

She looked at me with that same enigmatic smile that might have put the *Mona Lisa* to shame. "I'm really, *really* looking forward to crossing that bridge."

I grinned, a laugh slipping past my lips. "Me, too."

With that, we stood, discarded our garbage and walked back to the hotel, enjoying each other every step of the way.

31
MIA

THE NIGHT BEFORE WE WERE TO FLY HOME, I FOUND THE courage to take a bubble bath in the enormous bathtub in our penthouse bathroom. It had a full window in front of it from which I could watch Paris below me. So I dumped a ton of bubble bath into the tub and let the bubbles rise up. I didn't lock the door. I'd built up a wall of bubbles all around me so that if Adam came in, he wouldn't see my ugly scars and tattoo marks. He'd just see a naked woman sitting in his tub. If I got lucky, he'd volunteer to join me.

They had a special mechanism in the tub that kept the water warm so I could soak in there as long as I wanted. After spending over half an hour with my eyes closed, my head resting against a waterproof cushion, I heard steps in the doorway.

"Have you shriveled up like an old lady yet?"

"You should try it before you knock it."

"Hmm. So many things I could do with that."

"When was the last time you took a bath?"

"I have no idea. I can't even think of a time I've taken a bath since I was a little kid."

I turned around and looked at him. "Are you shitting me? Seriously?"

"I'm seriously not shitting you."

"Then strip and get in here."

"Hmm. How do I know you aren't just using this bath as an excuse to get me naked?"

I laughed. I was extremely transparent these days, apparently. It had been way too long since I had seen him naked, goddamn it. And I didn't want to leave the City of Love without a glimpse of my favorite six-pack and those muscular thighs—to say nothing of his butt. "Well, that's not beyond the realm of plausibility. But until you've enjoyed the true luxury of soaking in bubbles, you can never understand."

"I'm just having a lot of fun standing here watching you enjoy it."

"Hmm. That sounds kinda pervy. I like that."

"I do have a pervy streak."

"I already knew that. Well, get over here and make yourself useful, then. I need my back scrubbed."

He took a step forward and I glanced down, noting that the bubbles had mostly flattened after I'd been in the tub so long and, thus, were no longer covering my breasts.

"Wait! Turn around, please."

He froze. I could see his surprised profile in the mirror as I reached out, grabbed a small hand towel and draped it over the upper half of my body. He turned around, his features blank.

"Okay, I'm good," I said, leaning forward. With a little hesitation, he approached again.

"There's some soap over there, and a washcloth."

"As you wish, my lady."

I laughed, amused by the *Princess Bride* reference. I adjusted the towel against me and said in my best imitation of an English accent. "Farm boy, wet the cloth and wash my back. Every bit of it—please."

He did as I asked with a quiet, "As you wish."

He used the towel at first, and then his hands were on my back, sliding over my soapy skin. I let out a long breath, tantalized by the feel of his hands on me, even if just to clean me. After massaging my shoulder blades, along my spine and down to the small of my back below the waterline, he rinsed the washcloth and rubbed it over me again.

"Farm boy, don't forget my neck."

"As you wish," he repeated, but instead of washing it, he kissed it. I tilted my head, giving him access to more as tingling energy sluiced through me. My body was alive and coursing with lust from his touch in under five short minutes. When would it be time to cross that goddamn bridge again? Oh yeah, we hadn't come to it yet.

"So...you want me to wash your hair, too?"

I opened my eyes. "Shut it."

"No, you have little teeny weensy hairs here. I see a couple. I could wash them. I think I could spare one or two drops of shampoo."

I blew out a breath between my lips and instead of retorting, I splashed him.

"Hey!" He jumped back, but I scooped up more water and got him right in the middle of his chest. His shirt was now clinging to the muscles underneath. Oh, yummy. I should have done that a half hour ago.

"Brat."

"Dickhead." I splashed him again. "You're wet now. Might as well get in here." I punctuated this statement with another big splash.

He stepped back and slipped on the floor, only barely recovering his footing before he fell. He pulled a couple towels off the rack and laid them on the floor, then fixed me with a grim look before his mouth turned up in a smile. He reached up and pulled off his T-shirt. *Hell yeah.*

I wasn't coy about watching him strip, either. His body was solid, muscular and beautiful. I sighed with just a little too much longing when he finally pulled off his jeans and boxers.

"You're quite enjoying yourself, aren't you?" he said as he placed his clothes on a nearby chair.

"It's an amazing view. And I'm not talking about the Eiffel Tower all lit up outside my window."

He came over to the tub, and I reached up and lightly stroked his washboard abs. I'd missed that hard, flat stomach. He stepped over the side of the tub and sank down opposite me. I grabbed some more bubble bath, dumped it into the water between us and said, "You need some more bubbles to truly enjoy the bubble bath experience." I opened the faucet, letting more hot water into the tub.

I had to bend over him to reach it, but I made sure to keep my towel pinned securely to me. Adam's dark eyes followed me and I leaned over him until the tub had refilled adequately, then turned off the water. Before I could lean back, he caught my arm and pulled me toward him and my mouth landed on his.

I moaned as he plunged his tongue into my mouth. I fell against his chest, returning the kiss with about twice the passion he put into his—which was saying something because his kiss was far from chaste.

But I was starved for him, and I wasn't going to let him out of the tub without letting him know that.

He reached up and put one hand on my back, the other against the towel I held to my chest. When we finally came up for air, he looked up at me and swallowed hard. "This isn't easy," he murmured.

I shook my head. "Nope. It's not."

The hand on my chest moved slightly to the side, as if he wanted to slide it under the towel. I pulled it tighter to me. Our eyes locked and I could tell he wanted it as badly as I did.

"I want to touch you. I want to see you," he said.

I hesitated, freezing in sudden terror. I couldn't let him see me. I was ugly, scarred. It would disgust him. He'd never want me. I swallowed the fear, but it rose up again immediately. Finally, I gently shook my head.

He looked away for a stretch of minutes and sighed heavily. "Okay. I'm not going to make you do something you don't want to do. But eventually..."

I sat back, putting a little distance between us. "Eventually, I'll get some reconstruction."

His eyes flew back to mine. "So I don't get to see you until after that?"

I didn't answer. I had no answer. It wasn't fair of me. I did want him to touch my breasts. But the fear was too strong.

"What are you scared of, Emilia?"

I took a shaky breath. "You have no idea what it's like to go out in public at your side. You are perfect. Everyone looks at you and they wonder what the hell you're doing with me."

He frowned. "You think that if I see you, I won't want you."

I nodded. "Yes. That's exactly what I think."

"Yesterday at the park you said you don't trust what you think anymore because you question your judgment. That's about right because with this, you're absolutely wrong. If I just loved the outside of you, then, you're right, I probably still wouldn't be here. I'd see only that your beautiful hair was gone or that you were sick all the time."

I lowered my gaze to the surface of the bubbles, his words stinging me. They were honest but they hurt.

"But I don't just love your hair or your beautiful skin, your breasts or your eyes, your body. Those are the bonuses and they will come back. I love *you*, Emilia. I love your heart, which is worried about me even when *you* are the one hurting. I love your brain—that we can have long conversations about things and you *get* it. You get *me*. I love your soul, which feels, sometimes, like it's mine, only in your body."

It hurt to breathe as I sat there absorbing his words, the simple beauty of them stunning me to silence. For a moment, my mouth worked and then I began sobbing on the spot. His words were so honest—so unexpected. He moved forward and pulled me into his arms. I wept against his hard, naked chest, his warm skin against my cheek.

But I still held that damn towel to me as tight as ever. I wasn't brave enough yet. It was too scary. His arms tightened around me. He said he loved my soul, but he had no idea of the darkness lurking down in the depths. The wretched, horrid thoughts I forced down on a daily basis. The self-loathing.

Yes, I was alive. But at what cost? Had it been worth it? I swallowed the sting of that hurt yet again and then turned and kissed his neck, his shoulder, his chest. I showered him with my love. The kisses weren't meant to seduce or arouse, but to show him without words that I loved him, too.

"I love you—so, so much," I said. It wasn't nearly as poetic or romantic as what he had said to me, but it was all I could choke out between whimpers and sobs. He held me to him until I stopped crying and for a long time after, the only sound the crackling of the bubbles and the movement of the water around us, echoing in the white marbled bathroom.

I pressed my teary cheek to the damp skin of his shoulder and I felt calm, peaceful. When I spoke, it was with a quiet voice. "I'm scared to go home."

"Why?"

"Because it's been so magical here. Like a fantasy. Here, I have you all to myself. I don't have to share you. I'm selfish, but I've loved every minute of it."

"You have all of me, all of the time."

No, that wasn't true and he knew it. There, I competed with the job, the friends, all the perfect-looking women around him, co-workers, acquaintances. There, I had the constant fear that I would lose him.

"You have me, too," I said. "Always. Forever." For as long as that happened to last.

He kissed my neck and breathed against my cheek. "I need to tell you that I'm scared, too," he said suddenly.

I swallowed. "About the scan?"

"Yes."

"I guess it's easy for me to say 'forever' when that might not mean a very long time."

He pulled back and looked into my eyes. "None of us know when forever will end. It's not just you. We never know. What makes forever worth it is each day we live and enjoy being with each other. Each day we make each other's lives better."

My eyes dropped and he trailed the tears on my cheeks with his thumb, outlined my lips. I kissed his fingers as he moved them over my mouth.

"So you know that my love for you is not about your looks anymore than yours is for me...right? Or do you love me just for how I look?"

I smiled, almost wishing I could make a joke, but I didn't want to spoil the moment. "Hmm. I love the man who makes breakfast for me even when he can't make toast without burning it." He laughed, continued to trace his fingers over my mouth, my jaw. I closed my eyes, relishing the feel.

"I love the man who signs his notes to me with a lopsided heart. I love the man who listens to songs only old people and hipsters know." He barked out another laugh. I smiled. "I love the man who was there for me...all the time, even when I wasn't there."

Silence again and the bubbles fizzed around us.

Minutes later, muttering that I was turning into a prune, I carefully got out of the tub. He lay back and watched me cinch a fluffy terry cloth robe around me before finally dropping the now-soaked towel. I snagged the other bathrobe and laid it near, where he could grab it when he got out.

"Hey, farm girl, what about me? Do I get my back washed?"

I sent him a crooked grin and ducked my head. "As you wish."

But it was hard—damn hard, rubbing the soapy washcloth over his muscular back, down his trapezius muscles to his lower back along his latissimus dorsi, to his narrow waist. Oh God, he was just too sexy for his own good. And touching him had riled me up again. It wasn't fair.

I was healthy enough to have an over-the-top sex drive, but apparently not healthy enough for him until that clean scan came back. I sat back with a sigh of sexual frustration.

"There. And now, I'll be in my bunk," I said.

Adam laughed. *Firefly* was one of his favorite shows.

I got up and went into the bedroom, where I sat in the dark and listened to him in the bathtub. The real reason I'd gotten out of the tub was that it hurt too much to keep hiding myself from him. I knew he'd wanted me to drop the towel and stop covering myself. I *was* hiding from him, in so many ways. Hiding from myself, too.

I lay down on the bed and relived those beautiful moments with him where we sat together, where he told me *I want to see you. I want to touch you.* My daydreaming self was much braver than my real self, so in my fantasy I dropped the towel and he looked at me. And instead of the disgust I feared in his eyes, I only saw desire. Hot desire. When Adam was turned on, his dark eyes glowed with it. They were luminous, beautiful. Like smoldering coals.

I swallowed, my throat suddenly tight, my heart racing with my own desire. I pictured Adam's hands sliding up my waist, moving over my breasts. I remembered how it had felt the other night, his thumbs rubbing over my nipples repeatedly. Lust arced through me and despite the irony of joking that I'd be in my bunk, my hand went between my legs because the tension that had been building in me since arrival was now full to bursting and I couldn't take it anymore. He wasn't going to touch me until we knew for sure I was better. But I couldn't wait any longer.

I let out a little moan. It was my hand but I imagined it was his, and in the middle of my fantasy, I felt a weight sag the bed. I stopped, opening my eyes and looking up. Adam sat on the bed beside me, watching me. He'd never caught me in the act before, and in my daze I realized I should probably be embarrassed, but I was just too turned on to be. And the fact that he was sitting there, watching me, turned me on even more.

He bent down and kissed me, took my hand and put it back where it had been, rubbing against my clitoris. His hand settled on top of mine, pressing it down. He began penetrating me, his tongue in my mouth and his fingers inside me. I cried out, but it was muffled by his mouth.

When he pulled his mouth away, he was whispering things that made the nerve endings dance all over the surface of my skin. "You are so sexy, Emilia. My sexy, naughty girl. I want to watch you come. I want to hear you."

I gasped again. "I'm imagining you on top of me. Inside me."

He groaned and kissed me again, my mouth, my neck, my ears. He lay down beside me, his robe falling open, and I could see the corded muscles of his chest, the edge of his tattoo peeking out from under the snowy white. "I wish you could fuck me, Adam. I want you so much."

"I want you, too. I want to pleasure you. I want to make you feel good. Do you feel good?"

"Yes, yes, I feel good."

He moved again, pushing my legs open, and placing himself between them. My thighs pressed against his sturdy shoulders and he was licking me. I yelped and grabbed the headboard behind me, my eyes rolling back. It felt—So. Damn. Good. Every part of me was on fire and I was breathing so fast I couldn't catch my breath. All I could feel was that point of my body where Adam's mouth connected to me, his tongue penetrating, his mouth sucking. My back arched and I came so violently that my hips bucked off the bed and collided with his head. He jerked back and held me down, then put his mouth against me again, refusing to let up until the powerful convulsions had stopped and I was whimpering, begging for him to take his mouth away because the feelings were so intense they now hurt.

My body was plunged into lassitude, every bit of tension wrung from it like a damp rag. I could only lie there and relish that stunning afterglow that had me flying so high. Adam straightened and looked at me, then ran a hand over my stomach before moving up to lie beside me. We lay like that for a long time, the tops of our heads pressed together but no other part of us touching. I reached out and grabbed his hand, lacing my fingers around his.

Then he turned and said the most wonderful thing of all. "Don't let that shitty voice inside your head tell you that you aren't sexy. *Ever.* Because you are burning a hole right through me. And I love it."

32
ADAM

TWO DAYS AFTER WE RETURNED HOME, EMILIA WENT IN for her scan. I could hardly breathe at all the entire day. And I had to sit in a waiting room in the hospital while she was gone for hours, much of the time locked inside a giant machine, keeping absolutely still. At least that's how they'd explained it would happen.

Since waking up that morning and getting ready, she'd been unusually quiet. Just before being called back, she had taken off the compass I'd given her—probably one of the few times it was ever off of her body, but she had been prohibited to wear or hold it during the scan. She'd pressed it into my palm and made me swear to keep it safe. I looked down into my palm now, studying the dark blue surface, the constellation outlined in diamonds. My throat closed with emotion and I stuffed it in my shirt pocket.

I glanced across from me where Kim sat, paging jerkily through a magazine without reading it. My Uncle Peter had a hand on her leg, watching her with concerned eyes. My leg bounced up and down repeatedly.

She was going to be okay. I'd repeated that phrase in my head a thousand times since waking up. It was my mantra today. The scans would come back clean and we'd be able to breathe again. If all it took was sheer thought power on my part, we'd have this in the bag. Because I'd dedicated every spare thought and feeling to this outcome for weeks.

Peter looked up and we shared a glance, and then I shot out of my seat and went to the water cooler down the hall for what seemed like the twentieth time. Peter was beside me a minute later.

"You okay?" he asked quietly.

"Trying to be," I answered.

He put a hand on my shoulder. "You know you can talk to me whenever you need to."

I nodded.

"Don't try to be the strong, silent type here. I know it's your personality. You're just like your dad in that respect."

I shrugged and took a sip of water. "If you say so."

"Adam, I know we don't like to talk about these things much. I know you and I have had some kind of silent understanding since you came to live under our roof, but—I just need to say this. As far as I'm concerned, you're my son. I've loved you since you were born, and I was glad and fortunate to have been able to help raise you. Your dad was my favorite brother."

I laughed. "My dad was your only brother."

He grinned. "Details. But he wasn't just my brother, he was my best friend. It was hard to lose him, but having you here, in my life...it's like having him still. And I want you to know that I'm here for you. If you ever need to talk or...for whatever."

I set the cup down and looked at him. This was weird. Peter rarely talked to me like this. We'd always had a good relationship, but it had never involved much talking. I always knew that Peter got me on a deeper level than words ever could. He was the father I never knew. I smiled. "Thanks. I love you, too." I reached out and clasped his shoulder.

And to my surprise, he pulled me into a hug. Weirder and weirder. It was an awkward man-hug sort of thing, which involved some backslapping. Just when I deemed it appropriate to pull away, he turned his head and said quietly, "She's going to be okay."

My breath froze and I stepped back. I looked away and nodded. I wasn't the only one fixated on that hope, apparently.

An hour later, she came out, fully dressed. She looked exhausted, with circles under her eyes, and I thought my eyes deceived me but she looked pale, too. She immediately asked me for her compass back. I pulled it out and slipped it over her head.

Kim and Peter said something about going out to get some lunch, but Emilia quietly shook her head and tucked herself under my arm, asking me to take her home.

So I did.

The next twenty-four hours were hell. This was the time it took to get her doctors to go over her scans in minute detail and determine whether or not the cancer was still in her, and God forbid, whether or not it had spread to other parts of her body.

We spoke little. Watched a lot of television together. We made it through the entire fourth—and final—season of *Farscape*. We sat in the same lounge chair, my arms around her waist, her head on my shoulder.

The next day when her phone finally rang, we both jumped. It was her doctor's office. With a look of no small terror, Emilia answered.

"Hey, Dr. Rivera," she said, sounding completely normal, if a little breathy. Her hand reached out and clamped fiercely around mine. I sat beside where she stood and looked up in her face, hoping to be able to tell what the news would be.

"Okay," she said, darting a glance at me and then looking away. "Should I come in?"

Another long pause. Her face showed nothing. She took a deep breath and the hand around mine squeezed tighter. I had no idea what that meant.

"Thank you. Yes. Next week, then. Yeah—I'll do that right away. Thanks."

She immediately clicked off the phone and I stared at her expectantly.

Her mouth turned up. "No evidence of disease," she said in a trembling voice.

I shot up and pulled her into my arms, squeezing her tight. The air rushed out of me in dizzying relief. "Oh, thank God. Thank God." I lifted her off the ground and twirled her around me.

She laughed, her arms tightening around my neck. I kissed her cheek, her neck, her face, her ear. Wherever I could reach her, I kissed her. She laughed even harder.

"You have to put me down," she finally said.

"I don't want to put you down."

She laughed, turning her face to mine and planting a solid kiss on my mouth. "If you don't put me down and I don't call my mom in the next five minutes, she'll come after you with a spoon to dig your heart out."

"Mmm." I tilted my head to the side as if considering the risk versus the reward. "I guess I can let you down for a few minutes."

"I think we both need to make a lot of phone calls." She walked over to her nightstand, grabbed up a slip of paper and then tore it in half longwise. "You take this half of the list and I'll take the other. Let's get this done quickly or we are going to be up until midnight."

I pulled out my phone and as silly as it was, we sat on her bed, side by side and made it through the list in just a few hours.

When we were done, I sighed and flopped back on the bed. "We've got that Bay Island charity house tour thing tomorrow, but after that we need to do something special to celebrate."

She seemed to deflate at the mention of the benefit. I turned, propping my head up on my hand to watch her. "I hope you don't mind. I bought some tickets for our friends. So there will be people that you know there—Jenna, Alex, Heath, Kat, my cousins..."

She threw me a slanted smile. "We don't need to crash your charity thingy with my nerd herd."

I laughed. "I thought you might be more comfortable if they were there."

Her lips pursed. "Actually, I was going to bow out of that, if that's okay with you."

I didn't say anything and she scrutinized my face.

"It bothers you, doesn't it?"

"I'd like you to go—to be by my side."

She hesitated and looked down for a long moment, then squared her shoulders. "Okay. I can do it for you. I'm sorry. That hadn't even occurred to me."

I *did* want her to go. But it was more for her good than for mine. She'd have to get used to being seen in public again. It had been easier for her in Paris, where everyone was a stranger. But work acquaintances and friends, apparently, were a much tougher crowd for her.

I called up Sonia and asked her to come over, bring us a new batch of clothes and arrange for a makeup artist to come on the day of the benefit. The better Emilia felt about her looks, the easier it would be for her.

33
MIA

I WAS DOING THIS FOR ADAM. HE WANTED ME THERE. I HAD TO repeat that to myself several times the next morning when I wanted to hyperventilate and back down, the fear so strong it threatened to steal my breath.

Hanging out with my friends in small groups was one thing. Even in public where the public was at a distance—like in Paris—that was fine. But here at his house, it was different.

There would be people I'd worked with at Draco, and some of Adam's rich and important friends. I'd decided to chicken out when the makeup artist had finished with my face. She'd done my eyebrows realistically and applied some lovely fake eyelashes—though my natural ones were almost all the way in. But nothing could account for the tiny bit of fuzz covering my scalp. We tried on three or four different wigs, but none of them looked right. I settled on one with a short bob cut, the hair similar to my own natural color.

I was wearing a colorful dress that fit my standards—a high, scooped neckline. There was little to complain about, really, with my looks. Yes, I looked different, but I now looked better than I had in months.

I clamped my hands over my knees, rocking back and forth. I didn't want to go and there was no way I could force myself to do it. Not even with the lure of my friends, who had all been invited. I was going to cower in the house until the last possible minute and hope that eventually, they'd come inside and hang out with me while we watched the hoity-toity charity-giving crowd mill around the gardens, board the yacht and schmooze with Adam.

There would be drinks and hors d'oeuvres on the lawn, and then the group would progress to a dinner at a nearby exclusive restaurant. Partygoers would tour the grounds and homes of Bay Island, including the downstairs of Adam's house and his yacht. If I hid up in my room and locked the door, I wouldn't have to worry about a thing.

Except disappointing Adam. And he was somewhere in the house, getting ready and totally unaware of the inner war I was fighting. I was terrified and I didn't want the pity looks, or worse, the "why is *he* with *her?*" questions. And every time I thought about it, it made my throat close up more.

When he came to get me, I didn't move.

"I'm sorry," I said, yanking off the wig. "I can't do this."

He sat down on the bed and looked at me. He was absolutely stunning in dark jeans, a white button-down shirt and a black blazer. His beauty took my breath away. How could I stand next to that?

I used to be able to do it, confidently. But not anymore. People would think I was his mother—or grandmother.

"I'm sorry," I repeated when he sat there, quietly watching me.

"I was going to say that you look amazing. It would be an honor to stand beside you."

I rubbed my hand across my now fuzzy scalp. "I'm sorry. I just don't—I—"

"And all your friends? Heath, Kat and Jenna...I even convinced Liam to come by saying you'd like to see him."

"I *would* like to see him. Maybe they can come up here and hang out with me?"

Adam clenched his jaw and put his hands on his knees but didn't appear upset. "You're going to have to jump back into the land of the living sometime, you know."

I looked away. "I know. It will be easier to do that when I have hair and a little excess weight on my body."

He sighed and stood up. "Okay. It goes without saying that I would like you to be down there with me, but I'm not going to make you do something you don't want to do."

I looked down, my face flaming with shame. "I'm sorry."

He bent and kissed the top of my head. "Don't be. But if you are feeling better later, please come down?"

"Okay."

He smoothed a hand over my cheek, smiled and was gone. And it felt like my heart was following him out the door because it suddenly hurt. I knew I was disappointing him, but I just wasn't ready for this.

As people started to arrive and progress through the homes, I had a prime 180-degree view of the garden from my windows, and I'd even adjusted them so that I could see outside without them being able to see in. Smart windows indeed! I sat in my window seat and saw faces—more I didn't recognize than those that I did—of the people on the charity tour. Adam greeted every single one, shaking their hands, handing them off to the party planners, caterers or tour guides.

In all, there were several hundred people in attendance. Jordan showed up with a gorgeous woman on each arm. One was a dark-haired, mocha-skinned beauty, and the other a voluptuous redhead in a tight dress. Two? Really? Typical Jordan.

Kat arrived with Heath and Connor, all nicely dressed. I got excited, hoping that that they would come into the house and hang out with me. Instead, they all hightailed it to the open bar and got drinks. *Sheesh.* Nice to see I rated lower than a free cocktail.

I pulled out my phone and texted Heath, but he never even checked his phone. He just sat with Kat at a table under the awning, just at the edge where I could see them, and they were soon joined by Jenna, Alex and eventually Adam's cousin William.

Soon I was aching with loneliness, up here all alone. But what the hell had I expected? I had chosen to exclude myself. I was like a little girl, pouting, sequestering myself, wanting to be a part of the party but not willing to do what it took.

I had my face pressed against the glass when suddenly there was a knock at the door. I jumped up, hoping it was Kat. Looking down, I saw her shock of dark red hair next to Heath and knew it must not be her. Who, then? Had Mom and Peter slipped by without me noticing?

I got up and opened the door and almost fell over in shock. Jordan stood alone with a drink in either hand. He held one out to me while he sipped at the other.

"It's mineral water," he said. "You thirsty?"

I reached out and took the cold glass with a shaky hand. "Yeah. Thanks."

"Can I come in?"

"Aren't you busy enough tending to your harem?" I said with a smile.

He laughed. "Ah, you saw me arrive with two women. Nice. I hope everyone else thinks that, too."

I stepped back and let him into the room, sipping at the fizzy water he'd brought me and trying not to show my puzzlement that he was here. "Hey, uh, I wanted to thank you for the trip—"

He held up his hand. "Do not say another word, okay? Adam footed the whole bill. He just took over my reservations. I was probably in over my head with that anyway. He did me a favor."

I nodded. "Okay, I won't say another word. Except thank you, and that was incredibly sweet of you."

He threw me a look of exasperation and then went to the window to look out over the lawn. "Well, at least you've got a nice view from up here."

"Yeah, I'm hiding out. How did you know to find me here?"

He looked at me out of the corner of his eye. "Adam, how else?"

I raised my brows. "Did he send you up?"

Jordan laughed. "Hell no. He knows better than that. I came up because...well, I feel bad."

"What about?"

He motioned me over to the window and pointed down into the yard. My gaze followed his hand and I saw Adam talking to the redhead in the tight dress, one of the two women that Jordan had arrived with. She was stunningly beautiful, standing very close to him and gazing up into his eyes adoringly.

Something tight and visceral clamped around my throat. *Back off, bitch.* And the thought startled me so much that I almost laughed. "Why is your date flirting with Adam?"

"Hmm. She's not really my date. I've been seeing the other one, her roommate, off and on. This one bought the tickets for the benefit months ago. Back when…well…let's just say during those brief weeks when Adam was single."

I swallowed a huge lump in my throat. "That's the woman he went out with, isn't it?"

Jordan shifted in his place. "Uh, yeah. I don't think Adam even realized she was coming today."

My entire body tensed up. Sure, it was one thing to live with the idea that he'd gone out with someone else when I'd broken up with him during my emotional freak-out. It really hadn't been wrong of him to go out with her.

But to see her here, looking like *that*, and flirting with him like he was still available? No. Just no. That was not happening.

"So, uh. I'm sorry about this. I just wanted to explain that. And you shouldn't get mad at him."

I folded my arms over my chest, turned my back on the scene and sank onto the window seat, rocking back and forth, thinking. Jordan stepped back, watching me.

"You okay?"

"Not really," I said through tight lips.

"You sure you don't want to go down there?"

My jaw clamped shut. "Not looking like a circus freak show, no."

"Carisa's a nice girl and pretty gorgeous, but I wouldn't worry about it."

"Oh? Why shouldn't I worry about it?"

"Because he was never the least bit interested in her. I'm sure he's even less interested now, if that's possible."

I breathed in and out slowly. It was so weird even to be having this conversation with Jordan. The only reason I could think of was that he felt sorry for me. That kind of ticked me off.

"So did you come up here because you were taking pity on me?"

Jordan looked at me, his hazel eyes full of something—not pity. If I didn't know better, I would have thought admiration. What the hell did he have to admire?

"No. I told you. I just feel bad. That you are up here all by yourself. That I even brought her. I figured you might be able to see and I wanted you to know that it doesn't mean anything."

I turned and looked outside again. They hadn't moved. She was still standing inches away from him, right at his arm. Apparently, they had *something* to talk about.

"Feel bad for Adam. His girlfriend is a coward."

"Hmm." He took a long pull from his beer and glanced out the window again. "I haven't seen anything cowardly from you for months. Quite the opposite, actually." I was silent and Jordan turned back to me. "Besides...you could totally take her. I'd pay good money to watch that."

I burst out laughing. "You're such an ass."

"Yeah. But I'm a loveable ass."

I nodded, agreeing.

"Well, Marta's going to be wondering where I disappeared to. I just wanted to make sure you were okay."

I rubbed my temples with my fingertips, looking down at my pretty dress.

"And stop thinking you are a coward. I'm sure everyone understands."

I looked up and actually felt a prick of anger at those words. Jordan's gaze locked on mine, his mouth turned up at the corner. It was almost as if he *knew* that would piss me off, too. I clenched my jaw and narrowed my gaze at him, and he only smiled wider.

"See you later, Mia." And without waiting for me to reply, he turned and left the room.

Fuck you and the horse you rode in on, I thought. I stood up and paced for a minute, then stopped and looked down through the window again. This woman—Carisa, apparently—was standing even *closer* to Adam and there were a few others in the group now, too. But Adam was still talking to her and practically ignoring all his other guests.

Blowing out a breath of frustration, I walked over to the closet and pulled out a couple of boxes and some hangers full of scarves and threw them all on the bed and began rummaging. I was already decked out in this lovely floral dress—just perfect for a garden party—and I'd had my makeup professionally done. I just had to figure out what to do about this bald head.

A wig? It would be the easiest solution, though the thought of sweating under it made me nauseous. A hat? On a whim, I had purchased a big floppy hat that, I guess, was fashionable. But it just wasn't me.

In the end, I grabbed a scarf that complemented the colors of my dress, went to the mirror and tied it in one of the ways that Sonia had showed me. It was what she had called a tichel knot, used by Orthodox Jewish women to cover their heads for religious reasons. It looked glamorous when done right and I'd practiced it enough. It looked almost as good as that black lace scarf I'd worn on that magical first night in Paris.

I studied myself in the full-length mirror in the bathroom. Okay, I didn't look *terrible.* But I did look like a bald woman who was hiding her baldness under a scarf. I fisted my hands at my sides, staring at my reflection. "You've got this," I said. It felt ridiculous to say that aloud, but it also gave me some courage. I slipped on my shoes and before I could have any second thoughts, I went down the stairs and plunged myself into public sight as quickly as I could. The sooner I was seen, the sooner that whole awkwardness would be over with.

There were a few people inside downstairs, ambling through the rooms, but no one whom I recognized. So I slipped out the back door toward the beach side of the house where Adam had been standing with the redhead—*still*—the last time I'd checked.

My first obstacle proved to be a difficult one. A cluster of the dreaded interns from Draco—okay, there were only two, the two who had rich enough daddies to buy them the pricy tickets to the charity function. They drove BMWs to work and wore designer clothes and were only there to finish their internships for their résumés. Cari and April were two of my biggest nemeses in the marketing department, where I'd worked for months before quitting that awful day of the pregnancy test in Adam's office.

While I'd worked with them, they'd had no idea that I was in a relationship with "the boss." They had proceeded to openly gossip and drool over Adam during every spare minute of their time. They even had a scale where they rated how good he looked on any given day based on what he was wearing. It was usually a nine or ten or even a ten-plus.

Ugh. I hated them.

And right now, they were on the porch staring at Adam, who was *still* chatting with the redhead, their heads pushed together. I halted, putting a big potted tree between them and me, trying to sum up my courage to walk past them.

Standing this close, I couldn't help but overhear what they were saying. Surprise, surprise. They were gossiping about Adam. "Oh,

God," Cari said. "If he looks over here again with those sultry dark eyes, I think I'm going to spontaneously orgasm."

"He's *so* hot," April concurred. "That chick he's talking to is a *Sports Illustrated* swimsuit model."

"Well, considering that his girlfriend now resembles the walking dead, I don't blame him. But—shit—I need to find a way to get under that man. Now that I've seen his house, I think I'll die if I don't get into his boxers."

"He's very lickable but also pretty loyal. They *are* still together."

"*Loyal*," Cari snorted. "For now. A dog is loyal. A young, hot man like that? He'll want a woman who can suck the paint off a—"

"Maybe that's why he keeps her around—like maybe she's just *really* good in bed."

Okay, I'd been mortified before, but *now* I was just downright pissed off. With a deep breath and my hands fisting at my sides, I moved out from behind the tree.

"Hey, Cari, hey, April."

They spun, both sets of eyes widening and both mouths dropping at the same time. Cari nervously twitched her huge mane of blond hair over her shoulders and glanced at April. "Hey, Mia! You're here. We were wondering where you were."

April had the decency to just stand there and look completely mortified.

"Uh-huh," I said, then pretended to inspect my nails, which looked half-decent, considering they hadn't grown in forever, but I'd had an expensive manicure recently.

I turned and glanced in Adam's direction. "Ten-plus today, I think. Of course, I think that every day." Then I threw them a wide shit-eating grin. "Maybe it's 'cause I have the advantage of getting to see him naked."

They exchanged uncomfortable glances and Cari was about to say something when I interrupted her again.

"Oh, and with regards to what you were just discussing…I do more than blow a guy's dick, girls. I blow his mind." I gave them the once-over. "Excuse me. The walking dead like to feast on the brains of the living and there doesn't seem to be much of a supply of those here, so…ta-ta." I threw them a smirk and a mock salute, and April's face went scarlet.

I was feeling immensely proud of myself with each step I took away from them, but also increasingly self-conscious with each step I took toward Adam. He was once again alone with the chesty swimsuit model. She now had her hand on his arm and he didn't move it away. So as with the two idiot interns, I pushed through my self-consciousness, fueled by my anger.

I came up next to Adam on the opposite side of Ms. Tight Dress and bumped his arm with mine. "Hey," I said quietly.

His head jerked in my direction, his eyes widening and his even, white teeth gleaming from the huge smile on his handsome face. He pulled me into a hug and kissed me on the cheek. I took the opportunity to throw a curious glance at Jordan's model friend over his shoulder. She was regarding me with equal curiosity. Adam whispered in my ear, "I'm so glad you're here."

I turned and kissed him on his cheek and Adam straightened, turning to make introductions. "This is Carisa. We were just talking about you. Carisa, this is Mia."

Her mouth curved into a half smile. She looked like one of those people standing on the podium at the Olympics with a bronze medal around their neck, trying to look gracious while masking their disappointment and not quite succeeding. "Hey, Mia, nice to meet you."

"It's good to meet you, too," I lied. "So you came with Jordan?"

"Yes, yes, I did. He's been seeing my roommate for a while." She and Adam exchanged a look, and then she glanced away with a smile that made my blood boil. I nestled myself closer into Adam's side and he tightened his arm around me.

I decided the best recourse was to ignore it because making a scene would just make everything worse. I turned to Adam. "How's the tour going so far?"

"Good. Better now." He smiled.

I grinned back at him. "Well, I'm glad I came down, then."

Carisa excused herself a few minutes later, claiming she was thirsty. I let out a breath of relief. Adam watched me watch her go. "So I take it Jordan told you," he said in a flat voice.

I shrugged. "I guess I needed some motivation to come down."

He smiled. "That was very brave of you."

"I was getting sick of being a coward."

He kissed me on the temple. "That's my girl."

I turned to him, gripping the lapels of his blazer in each hand. "I was thinking...you know it's been over twenty-four hours since I've been declared NED. Do you think we can...cross a bridge tonight?"

He immediately understood my meaning. With that delicious dimple that sometimes appeared at the side of his mouth when he smiled and a gleam in his eye, he looked out over the lawn and said, "I think that could be—very enthusiastically—arranged."

I grabbed his hand and squeezed it. "Good."

"Do you want something to eat or drink?"

"I was going to wander over and say 'hi' to the friends. They were at a table, last I saw."

"Actually, I think they are hanging out on the yacht. I saw them go that way just before you came up."

I looked over at the boat. There were people on the deck. "Oh, really? Maybe I'll take a look there, then."

"I think they'd be very happy to see you. The tour organizer wanted to speak with me briefly, but I'll come over in a few."

I turned and planted a long kiss on his mouth and he pulled me tight against him. I sighed. It felt good. I'd wanted it. And a little public display of affection never hurt when there were hungry little interns or a swimsuit model waiting in the wings, ready to pounce. If I were a dog, I'd be peeing all over my tree to mark my territory.

With that less-than-sexy image, I turned from him, a smile on my lips. It felt freeing to have fought my way through the fear of exposing myself because of my looks. The way that Adam looked at me, held me, kissed me in the middle of the crowd at his house party made me feel like the most beautiful, desired woman in the universe. And on the back of that triumph, I grinned and strutted my way over to the slip where Adam's yacht was moored.

We hadn't been out on it in a long time because we'd feared that my nausea would only worsen out on the ocean. But I was looking forward to when we could go again. Maybe even take a long trip down to Cabo or over to Hawaii. The thought of it made my blood sing with joy. Weeks alone on a boat with Adam. I could go for that any day of the week and twice on Tuesdays.

I found my crowd of friends all huddled around a board game at a table in the lounge. They were in the middle of a heated discussion over the rules when I slipped through the doorway. "I'm here to take your drink order."

Everyone looked up and Heath leapt to his feet. "Hey, hey, hey! Look who finally decided to make an appearance!"

Alex bounced up on the other side of me. "She was just being fashionably late, Heath. And look at how fashionable she *is*."

Jenna and William hardly even seemed to notice that I'd arrived. They seemed embroiled in some kind of dispute over the rules.

"I don't see what the harm is. House rules can be a lot of fun," Jenna said.

"House rules are not allowed in the listed rules. Monopoly has been playtested and balanced in such a way as to provide the optimum game experience."

"Yes, that's why they are called 'house rules.' And they can be a lot of fun! You really should—"

"House rules disrupt the balance of the game and prolong it, especially that one you propose, about the money under Free Parking."

Jenna smiled wryly. "Why, William, I can't believe that you have no interest in prolonging your pleasure."

Kat bust out laughing.

Connor stood up and gave me a hug, kissing my cheek. "How are you, Mia, darling?"

"Darling?" Heath said, throwing him a cutting look. "How come you never call me that?"

He shrugged. "She's prettier than you are."

I giggled. "I hope to God I'm prettier than Heath, even without my hair."

"Is it growing back in yet?" Alex said, trying to peek under my scarf.

"Hey! It took me a long time to tie that just right."

"I was telling everyone that I know how to do *frenología*— phrenology. My grandma was from Argentina. She showed me how to read head bumps."

"What the what?" I said. "No one's reading my bumps."

"Except for Adam," snorted Kat.

I stuck my tongue out at her.

"No, seriously, Mia. I could totally tell your fortune by looking at your head."

"Why not just use a crystal ball?"

"Is there a big difference between your head and a crystal ball these days?" said Heath. I elbowed him in the stomach and he feigned doubling over.

"Come on, Mia. Let me try it. We've all seen you bald, and since your hair is growing back, we might not have this chance again."

I sank into a chair between Jenna and Kat and looked across at William, who was meticulously packing up the gaming pieces and ignoring everyone else around him. "Hey, William. You okay?"

He shrugged.

Jenna leaned into me. "I've pissed him off, apparently."

"Don't be mean, Jenna."

"She's not mean," William said without looking up.

I scratched my head through my scarf.

"Just take it off and let me read your bumps."

I sighed. "Jeez, Alex."

"Come on. I can tell you your future."

"She already knows her future," Heath said. "Her hair's going to grow back. She's going to go to med school in the fall. In four years, she's going to be Dr. Mia Strong."

"Not Dr. Mia Drake?" Alex said.

I frowned. "Um, guys, you don't need to talk about me like I'm not here."

"Hmm. What about Dr. Strong-Drake?" Heath said.

Alex and Kat laughed. "That sounds ridiculous."

"You guys are all idiots," I said. "Maybe I'll just go by my first name, like Beyoncé or Adele. I'll just be that awesome."

"Dr. Mia," Alex said. "Let me read your bumps."

"Promise you'll stop bugging me if I take this scarf off?"

She nodded ferociously. "Yes. Yes. I promise not to be a pain in the ass."

"Too late," said Heath.

Alex flipped him her middle finger. Jenna's eyes widened. "Holy crap, do *not* irritate the Latina. You'll regret it, Heath."

Heath shrugged and everyone sat again. With a long-suffering sigh, I slipped my scarf off my head and let Alex look at it.

"Oooh, how cute, you have little fuzzy hair coming in. It's like baby chick feathers."

"Just read the bumps, for chrissakes."

"Okay, okay. I need to touch your head. Can I do that?"

"Whatever. Just tell me my fortune."

"Hmmm." Her fingers flitted over my scalp and it tickled a little bit. I giggled when she placed a thumb on either side of my temple, then spread her fingers across my naked pate. Then, she stroked me as if she was petting a dog. Heath started to chuckle under his breath and Kat shushed him.

"This part of your head here at the crown talks about your academic and career success. Yours rises very sharply, which says you will have a very long and prosperous career. You will be very dedicated to your profession."

"Wow, sounds like hard science to me," Heath cracked, and now it was me who shushed him because I didn't want Alex's feelings to get hurt.

"And this part, the widest part of the front of your skull, in between your temples, is about your love life. You will have a long-lasting pairing with the love of your life. Hmm. One marriage."

"We already know all this stuff," said Kat. "We get it. She and Adam are mated for life. Now tell us something useful, like how many kids they will have or something."

My throat closed at Kat's words. "That's not—"

"Oh! That's right here at the base of the skull." She ran her fingers along the top of my neck at the part of my head that formed the edge of my cranium. "Hmm. Two? Nope...one. Only one baby."

I jerked away from her, unexpected emotion suddenly slamming me against my chest. It was hard to breathe.

"Okay, all done," I said in a trembling voice.

"But I haven't—"

"She's done, Alex," Heath said, watching me with concerned eyes.

"I—uh—I gotta go find the bathroom," I said, stumbling to my feet. I turned toward the doorway and saw Adam standing there, leaning up against the frame, watching me with his dark, serious eyes.

Tears prickled the backs of mine and I swallowed fiercely. "Excuse me," I whispered as I squeezed by him. Instead of heading all the way to the nearest bathroom, I jumped up the stairs and turned into one of the cabins, tucking in as the tears suddenly breached my eyes. I closed the door and sank onto the bed.

Only one baby. I bent over, pressing the heels of my hands to my eyes. I would not cry. I could not cry. I had to get over this. But how could I, when I'd vowed never to forgive myself? Long-suppressed grief clamped down on me. Grief I'd stuffed down so deep, hidden like bits of dust and grunge tucked so far under the furniture that they were never cleaned out, never saw the light of day. But it was there, self-hatred, self-judgment. I could have done things differently. I could have...

Now, I had no idea if I would ever be a mother. Ever hold a child. But Alex, with her drummed-up fortune, seemed to confirm those doubts. That my chance—*our* chance—had come and gone.

A minute later the door opened and I knew who it was, so I didn't bother to look up. Adam sank down on the bed beside me and hooked an arm around my shoulders.

He didn't speak, just pulled me against him. I wouldn't weep. I wouldn't. I couldn't. I wouldn't allow it. I'd stifle it, refuse to let it out. I could be strong. I couldn't let him see this.

I would ignore the fact that I absolutely loathed myself in this moment—and probably always would.

34
ADAM

"**D**O YOU WANT TO TALK?" I WHISPERED.

She shook her head. She was shaking in my arms but she didn't cry. That was a good sign, at least. Wasn't it?

"Tighter," she whispered.

I lowered my arms around her waist and tightened my hold around her torso.

"Talk to me," I urged quietly.

She shook her head. "I'll be okay. She just caught me by surprise."

"Emilia—"

"I'm fine," she countered. "See?" She pulled out of my arms, running the backs of her hands over her eyes—and in the process smearing her mascara. Leaning back, she looked into my eyes. She wasn't crying. But the pain was there, deep and lurking behind the fake smile hovering on her mouth.

I rubbed my hand along her back. "Have you thought about...finding someone to talk with about all this? Like your oncologist suggested?"

She stiffened, staring at the ground, and I saw the color wash out of her face. "No."

I swallowed, suddenly clueless and afraid of how to proceed. "But it might help—"

"Do you think I'm screwed up?"

My jaw tensed and then I relaxed it with a deep breath. "I think you've been through a lot in a very short amount of time."

She turned and looked at me. "I can handle it. I'm tough. I've been through shit before. I'll bounce back."

Something dark and heavy weighed down on my chest. I wished I could be as optimistic. But I had no reply for her. I couldn't force her to get help. I hoped in vain that she was right about bouncing back. She didn't remember it, but I did—that firm declaration that she deserved to die because of what she'd done.

Every single time I thought about that moment, it gutted me, rendering me powerless. I watched her carefully.

She was dabbing at her eyes again. "I just need a little time."

"Okay." I swallowed. It was easy to see that she had herself tied up in knots emotionally and I had no idea whatsoever how to help her. This didn't bode well. She was physically healthy again, but in all the time we had concentrated on her healing from the cancer, had we neglected some other important components along the way?

"It will be okay. We'll be okay," she said in such a way that it sounded as if she was convincing herself as well as me.

I smoothed my hand along her cold cheek. Deep down it felt wrong, shoving this aside again, as we had for months and months.

This was wrong.

"Mia, at least talk to me. Tell me what you are feeling."

She shook her head again. "I'm okay. I promise…it was just a brief thing that I wasn't prepared for. Next time…" Her voice died out as if she realized how ridiculous her words sounded.

"There will be a next time, and one after that. This won't go away if we just ignore it."

She nodded, avoiding my eyes. "You're right. We shouldn't do that. But let's just give it a little…time?" Abruptly, she stood and went into the cabin's bathroom. She spent a few minutes wiping off her smeared mascara from the suppressed tears. Because that's what she was doing—suppressing her pain. Burying it under a brave face.

I was one hundred percent certain that this was going to bite us in the ass. And I had no fucking idea how to deal with it. Or even if there *was* a way to deal with it.

When she came out, she was looking a little paler than normal but otherwise fine and acting like nothing had happened. This did *not* reassure me.

"I'm so pissed I left my scarf behind."

I pulled it out of my jacket pocket. "I grabbed it for you."

She grinned a grin that didn't reach her eyes, bending to kiss me on the cheek. "Now I know why I keep you around, boy genius."

She tied her scarf back on and stuck by my side for the rest of the party. At the end of the event, we stood at the end of the footbridge with the other homeowners, bidding everyone goodbye as they went off to the charity dinner. It was getting dark when we walked back to the house together. She held my hand, firmly lacing her fingers between mine.

I remembered that she'd intimated that she wanted us to be together tonight, and I stole a glance at her bowed head as she picked her way back in the dim light. I was feeling tired, as usual, but if I put her off, she'd get insecure about it and take it as a personal rejection.

Maybe the encounter with our friends had changed her mind? She'd seemed quieter than normal since it had happened.

We came upstairs and there was an awkward moment at the top when we hesitated near the doorway to her room. She turned and looked at it and then looked back at me. She swallowed. "How much longer are we going to do this, do you think?"

"Do what?" I asked.

"The separate bedrooms."

I ran a hand over my jaw. "You want me to come sleep with you tonight?"

She turned and wrapped her arms around my waist. "I want to do more than sleep."

I almost made up an excuse. I was still so worried about her, but then she was kissing me on the neck and it felt so damn good. And for God's sake, it had been five months since we'd had sex. My starved body was responding instantly. I'd probably have to have been half-dead not to respond to her.

She stepped back from me and said, "Meet me back here in ten minutes? I want to change into something."

"Come find me in my room, then," I said. "I'm going to take a shower."

She smiled. "Okay."

My mind raced the entire time I was in the shower. Certainly, most of it was dedicated to the happy thoughts that I was going to have sex again after such a long dry spell, but the small part of my brain that could still think rationally was worried. Was she ready? She'd insisted over and over again that she was. Physically, maybe. But what about emotionally?

And she still felt so frail in my arms, the thought of being on top of her scared the shit out of me, like I'd break her in half or something. But I was desperate to find a way to make this work because I knew when I got out of that shower, she was going to be there. I had to think fast.

I came out of the bathroom with my towel around my hips. The lights in the bedroom had been dimmed—her doing, because they had been perfectly normal when I'd gone into the bathroom. She was on the bed, laying crossways with her elbows on the mattress, her head in her hands, watching me.

She had on a silky blue nightshirt edged with lace. It completely covered her on the top but ended right below her hip, showing every delicious inch of her long, lithe legs. And she had a matching beret on her head to cover the baldness—not that she needed to. She usually didn't bother to cover her head when it was just us at home, but if it made her feel sexier, then I guess whatever worked.

"Hey, gorgeous," she said, her eyes running down my chest with open admiration. "You come here often?"

I stopped in front of her and smiled. Those long, silky legs, bent at the knee with her feet up, that beautiful smile and that open look of lust in her eyes as she watched me was enough to turn me on. Hell, a stiff breeze would probably turn me on these days.

"Hey, beautiful, I'll come here often—with you."

She wrinkled her nose at me and laughed. "That was baaaaaad."

I sat down on the bed beside her and ran a hand over the silky material on her back. "I know."

She angled her head around and started kissing me on the chest. My heart started to race. I closed my eyes. Her touch burned me and it felt so damn good. She sat up, her face even with mine. "I picked this out myself. Your favorite color."

Our gazes locked. "Yes, I noticed. Very, very nice."

She leaned forward and kissed me and I reached out, holding her mouth to mine. Soon my cock was straining against the towel with a painfully aching hard-on. My body was one hundred percent on board with the idea of sex tonight, but as I held her to me, I couldn't help but continue to worry about how this would work. I feared hurting her again like I had in Paris, not even realizing that in my desperation to have her, I was holding her too tight—or worse, crushing her.

In the shower, I'd thought of a solution for tonight, but I didn't know what she'd think of the idea. I pulled back from her and she looked up at me, an expectant smile on her luscious mouth.

"I was thinking of maybe trying something a little different tonight." I began.

She raised her thin eyebrows. "Oh? Our first sex in almost half a year and you want to do something different?"

I had to do this carefully, so she wouldn't get self-conscious. "That night in Paris, I hurt you completely unintentionally—"

She put a hand on my cheek. "You need to stop worrying about that."

"I'm not going to stop worrying about it. You're lighter than you were. I'm just... I don't want to get rough with you. I think it might be best—and even fun—if you are on top."

She laughed. "That sounds great, but it's not like that's new for us."

"Well, what's new is I was thinking you could tie me up."

She paused. "Say what?"

"You could tie my hands to the headboard."

Her mouth dropped open. "Why do you want me to do that?"

"You don't think it might be fun?"

"I'm not saying I don't think it will be fun, but..."

"Well, if I'm tied up, then I won't get...overenthusiastic."

She took a deep breath and sighed. "You are really *that* worried about hurting me?"

"Yes."

She blinked. "Okay. I'll tie you up. To be honest, that is more than a little hot. And then sometime soon you can do the same to me."

"That's more than a *lot* hot," I leered at her. She stood up and her legs were so sexy in that short nightie. I was already envisioning them wrapped around me as she rode on top of me. Shit, this hard-on was starting to hurt.

She turned back to me. "You have handcuffs or something?"

I shot her a weird look. "No. Use one of my ties. In the closet."

"You want me to tie you to the bed with a five-hundred-dollar tie?"

"The sacrifice won't be in vain."

She laughed and shrugged, disappearing into the closet and coming out with three ties in her hands. I raised my brows. "Just how overenthusiastic do you think I'm going to be?"

"You could be like some sort of sexual Hulk, turn green and break out of your bonds and chase me down."

"I have a feeling you aren't going to run far."

"Nope, probably not."

She tied a loop with the skinny end of one of the ties and asked for my wrist, which I gave her. She put it into the loop and then pulled my arm back toward the headboard. "So do I tie your wrists together or apart?"

"I don't care."

"You know, figuring out the logistics of this should probably be killing the mood, but it's just making me hotter." She pulled the other end of the tie to the headboard, above my head. I lay down and she tightened it, so that my arm was extended above my head. She grabbed another tie and did something similar with my other arm. By the time she was done with that, she was flushed and breathing fast and I was more than a little turned on myself.

She ran her hand down my arms. "I love your arms. Sometimes I get turned on when you are fully dressed but you have your sleeves rolled up. Your forearms are so sexy."

I laughed. "My forearms? Really?"

She ran her hand over them appreciatively again, as if admiring artwork or craftsmanship. "I love your body. And your arms are amazing. Strong forearms, your biceps...firm, powerful, but not bulky."

"You've given this a lot of thought, haven't you?" I said, my eyes half-closed, utterly relishing the feel of her hot hands on me.

"Oh, I have. I do. Early and often."

She bent over me, checking the tightness of the knots holding my arms above my head, and her breast grazed against my cheek. On instinct and out of pure lust, I turned and caught her nipple in my mouth, sucking it through the thin silk of her shirt. She let out a loud gasp and froze. I didn't release my hold and she didn't pull away. With my tongue, I traced her nipple, sucking more of it into my mouth. It hardened to a tight point.

Panting on top of me, she pulled back and straddled me. Then she bent to kiss me first on my mouth, then my neck and chest. She ran her hands over every inch of my chest and stomach. "You are so incredibly sexy. It pisses me off when women look at you, but how the hell can they help themselves?"

I laughed. "You're going to give me a big head."

She snorted, her hand gliding over the towel still knotted around my waist. "I think I already did," she said, fondling me. I closed my eyes, and as if she were reading my mind, she slipped her hand under the towel and grasped me, stroking with her fingers. Electric pleasure crackled down my spine.

I wanted this so badly I could hardly breathe. I opened my eyes and looked up at her. "Kiss me," I said.

35
MIA

I UNDID THE TOWEL FROM HIS WAIST, THEN EXPLORED HIM everywhere with my hands before taking his silky-smooth length in my hand again. Firmly I stroked him, relishing the sound of his hoarse gasps. His eyes tightened again. "Kiss me, Emilia," he demanded again.

Trust Adam to try to take over even when he was tied up and I was on top of him. I decided to torment him with my hands for a little while longer before finally leaning forward. He pulled his head up and caught my mouth with his, groaning. His tongue plunged into my mouth urgently, moving in and out quickly as if showing me how he wanted to penetrate me in other ways. My body sang in response, completely aroused and ready for him.

And since he was under me and totally at my mercy—and quite obviously ready—there was no time like the present. I scooted down over him so that our hips were even with each other, thinking we could start with a little rubbing—

He stiffened and pulled his mouth away from mine. "Stop!" he almost shouted.

It startled me so I sat back and looked at him. His eyes were wide. "Am I hurting you?"

"No," he said and took a long breath before letting it go tightly. "We need a condom."

"Oh...yeah. Shit. Yeah, we do." We'd never used them before, but for obvious reasons that was no longer going to be the case. For the rest of my life, I was banned from using any sort of hormonal birth control.

He looked at me, exasperated and a little angry.

"I'm sorry, it didn't even occur to me. That was dumb. I didn't buy any."

His mouth thinned. "Under the sink in the bathroom."

I did not want to know why he had condoms in the house. I'd seen the box there before when I lived here and assumed they'd been from his swinging single days. He'd told me he hadn't been with any other women since before we got together, but sometimes the uncertainty of those days when we were apart got to me. Adam had never lied to me and I trusted him. But often it was easy to let my own insecurity whisper doubts into my ear.

I slumped, got off the bed, went to the cabinet he referred to and saw the box. It was one of those jumbo packs with a hundred or more inside. And it was half-empty. Shit.

Don't think about it, Mia. Don't think about all the women he's been with before—about how much prettier and healthier and more experienced they were.

Adam hadn't been with another woman in over a year. Why should I still care? The thought still stung, but I willed myself to build a bridge and get over it. I plunged my hand into the box, grabbed a handful and came back. It occurred to me that I'd never used one— never learned how to use one—and his hands were tied up.

I put the handful on the night table and grabbed one of them. Glancing down, I saw that he was still erect. I bent over and kissed his mouth. He enthusiastically returned the kiss. I peppered some more kisses on his chest and leaned back, tearing at the foil wrapper. "Here goes nothing..." I murmured and he watched me carefully.

I pulled out the condom and put the wrapper back on the nightstand. "Wait—" he said. "What does the date say? That box is at least two years old. Are they still good?"

"Do condoms come with an expiration date?" I said, and he only answered me with a glare so I shrugged and looked at the wrapper. The date on it was sometime next year. "Yep, we're still good."

"Let me see it."

Puzzled, I held out the wrapper for him to see. Apparently he didn't trust me to read the date? I'll admit that sometimes I forgot things or said stupid things due to chemo-brain, but I wasn't *that* far gone.

"Okay," he finally muttered. He didn't look happy. I frowned at him. The look in his eyes could only be described as intensity tinged with a little fear. What on earth did he have to be afraid of?

I took the condom and placed it against the tip of his cock, hoping the thing would unroll easily because doing this now was turning me on again and I really wanted to get to it. Adam watched every move I made like a hawk, though not with an expression of arousal but as if he was afraid I'd make a mistake.

I was aware of my first mistake when it wouldn't unroll as easily as I thought it should. I put my other hand to the task. Many couples didn't like using these things. They certainly killed the mood and the spontaneity of being together. Sighing, I began to feel frustrated.

"You've got it upside down," Adam observed. "Flip it over."

I did as he asked and it unrolled easily, I pulled it down, all the way against the base of him. Then I ran my hand up and down his length. I could tell it turned him on, but he didn't take his eyes off what I was doing. "Be careful, you don't want to tear it."

"Do they tear that easily? What's the point if they do?" I got up to swing my leg over him again when he moved his hips away. "Wait..."

"What now?"

"I don't want to take a chance with that one tearing. Put another one on top of it."

I paused. I'd never heard of that before. Then again, I'd only ever had sex with Adam, so what the hell did I know? Apparently, he was all kinds of experienced—even with some of the kinkier stuff, too. My pointless jealousy rose up again. This was starting to piss me off.

"Will that work all right?" I said, reaching for another condom and pulling it out of its wrapper.

"If one tears, the other will hold. The odds of them both tearing are much less."

"But...won't they just rub against each other and cause more friction?"

He started to tug against the ties holding his arms. "Untie me. Let me do it." He gave another jerk, almost frantic to be untied.

"Hold on...wait. Let me get it."

But he was yanking again, almost panicked now.

"Wait, Adam. Let me untie it. Hold still."

He visibly swallowed as he watched me, and it was the first moment where I realized that it was more than that small fear I had detected in his eyes earlier. He was downright terrified.

I untied him and he sat up, rubbing his wrists. Judging from the marks around them, he had pulled pretty damn hard to get out of his bonds. I sat back, suddenly too worried about him to care that we probably weren't going to go through with this now.

He pulled off the condom and wrapped the towel around himself again. Tears clogged in my throat. "I'm sorry…I screwed that up, didn't I?" I said in a quiet voice.

He shook his head. "No." He leaned forward and put his face in his hands, and I watched him for long, silent, tension-filled stretch of minutes.

"What the hell just happened?" I asked, my throat tight.

He didn't answer, just ran a hand through his dark hair while focusing intently on some spot in front of him on the bedspread.

He'd actually been afraid, panicked, terrified of something. I thought back through it all. His reaction when he'd thought I was going to proceed without a condom. The insistence on looking at the date to see if they were still good. Then the suggestion to double the layers. I sucked in a long and painful breath.

When I spoke, my voice was trembling. "You're afraid I'm going to get pregnant again."

He abruptly stood up from the bed and went into his closet. When he came out, he was dressed in pajama pants and a T-shirt. I hadn't moved. And when we looked at each other, I knew that I had hit the nail right on the head. He didn't deny it.

My breath rushed out of my lungs and I wasn't certain I'd be able to draw another.

36
ADAM

I WATCHED AS HER FACE CLOUDED, LIKE A STORM SUDDENLY sweeping overland. Her eyes filled with tears and she blinked. But I had no words. And even if I had them, what could I say? She was absolutely right. I was fucking terrified to touch her. The thought that I might get her pregnant again not only petrified me, it made me nauseous.

Finally, I looked away. I couldn't watch as her heart broke, knowing that I was the cause, however unconsciously.

The silence in the room was deafening—like a distant ringing that buzzed in my ears. I looked back at her. Her eyes were damp, focused somewhere between us. I clenched my jaw. There was nothing I could say right now to comfort her. And part of me didn't even want to. This was the harsh reality of what she had tried to avoid earlier—when she'd insisted over and over again that she was fine, that she was tough, that she could get over this by herself.

It was best this came out now. But I honestly had no idea how we could possibly resolve it.

Suddenly she stiffened, as if she was tired of waiting for me to say something. Biting her lip, she stood up. "I'll go sleep in my room," she said in a shaky, quiet voice.

I watched her go and I didn't move a muscle.

The minute she disappeared into her bedroom, I ran a hand through my hair and began to pace. My mind whirred through everything that had just happened, every thought that had gone through my head. The moment that everything had snapped for me was the minute when I'd thought she was going to initiate sex without even a thought about the lack of birth control.

Things slipped her mind a lot these days. She'd forget things or do things she'd just done over again without realizing it. It was a side effect of the drugs she'd been on. I could have just as easily attributed that to this—her almost starting sex without thinking about a condom.

But it had been reckless, dangerous. It could have killed her.

I could have killed her. Or brought her cancer back. Just by having sex with her. Just by getting her pregnant again.

I buried my face in my hands, a sense of helplessness smothering me. Then, I heard her walk down the hallway toward the stairs. I could let her go, or we could talk this out. I could convince her that she needed to talk to someone.

And who knows, maybe I did, too.

Because *goddamn.* The weight of our baggage was finally beginning to bury me, and I could see no way out except to suffocate under it.

I moved to the stairs, half the length of the stairway behind her, calmly following her. She had changed from the silky nightshirt into some yoga pants and a T-shirt. Turning her head slightly, she seemed aware that I was behind her but did not speed up to avoid me as she moved to the side door, opening it and leaving it ajar for me to follow her.

As I was still approaching the water's edge, I saw her sit down in the sand and hug her knees to her, burying her face against them. When I got closer, I could hear her quiet, weak sobs. Each one sliced right through me. I stood inches from the spot where, a few months ago, I'd kissed her so tenderly...where she'd questioned our future. I had silenced her then, so intent on one thing and one thing only—her survival.

Perhaps that moment had cost us *our* survival as a couple. I swallowed, my throat suddenly feeling thick. I had no idea what I could say to her. So I let her cry until she calmed down. I slowly sank to the sand a short distance from her.

Finally, after an endless period of sobbing, she quieted, rubbing her cheeks against her pant legs. Wearily, she lifted her head and with a sniff and a hiccup, she spoke in a quiet voice. "I should go," she said. "I should let you get on with your life."

That tightness in my throat threatened to strangle me. Because I was beginning to think that maybe this was the only solution.

37
MIA

I WAITED AMID THE THICK TENSION BETWEEN US FOR HIM TO respond. And as each second stretched on, it became more likely that he'd agree with me—that I should go. That this was the only option for us. And that scared me most of all.

I'd finally had the cry that I'd been craving since that afternoon—since Alex's pronouncement that Adam and I would have one child and one child only. Because I knew—and he knew—that we'd already endured that secret, shameful loss. All I could feel was this void, like my chest had been ripped open, my eyes sore and my head aching. I breathed again, those painful, shallow breaths. *I should let you get on with your life...*

He took in a shaky breath. "What makes you think I have a chance in hell of doing that without you?"

I gulped in air around a hiccup. "I'm starting to think we might be broken beyond repair."

He shifted beside me. "Sometimes I feel like there hasn't been better communication between us than there is now. We talk about everything. We don't keep secrets. Except the one."

"I'm not keeping a secret from you," I said.

"You are. Maybe you're also keeping it from yourself."

I turned and looked at him. He was looking out over the water, his hand sifting absently through the sand. "I have nothing to hide."

He tensed, jerked his head toward me. "Really? No self-loathing? All the blame you've taken on yourself. The guilt you've buried so deep it almost threatened your life—"

I stood up in a huff and looked down at him. "You're projecting, Adam. I'm fine."

He didn't move, kept his gaze out over the water while I stood looking down at him in the dim light. I crossed my arms over my chest. The cool sea breeze ruffled over my bald scalp, making me regret not having pulled on a sweatshirt. I clasped my upper arms tightly, growing impatient.

"You were practically catatonic—for *days*. No talking...you turned your face to the wall, hardly ate a thing..."

"How can you blame me for that? It was a shitty time—"

"I agree. But you wouldn't let anyone in to help you. You deliberately increased your own suffering. You refused the pain medications. Why did you do that?"

My breath squeezed out of me like I'd just been punched in the gut. Suddenly, I was shaking. I sank into the sand beside him again. I didn't have an answer for him that he didn't already know. I'd insisted on feeling every cramp, every ache, every bit of the pain. It had been my way of acknowledging the potential life that I was ending.

But Adam wasn't about to let me off the hook. After minutes of silence, he turned and pinned me down with his black eyes. "*Why,* Emilia? Tell me."

"You already know why, apparently."

"Do *you?*"

I leaned away from him. "That was months ago and I was going through hell."

He looked away. "We both were, but that gets lost in the shuffle."

I reached out and touched his solid arm on which he was leaning. My hand closed over it. "I never want you to think I don't acknowledge that this was your loss, too."

"What about the blame?"

My jaw dropped and my mouth worked. His eyes were hard, accusing. "I—I'm sorry I got pregnant. It was my fault—"

"Wrong."

I breathed in, a vice tightening around my chest. That pain was back and increasing. "I don't blame you—you didn't know I'd gone off birth control. I didn't tell you. It *is* my fault. Everything is my fault."

"Why not blame yourself for getting cancer, too, while you're at it? You're going to punish yourself. Like refusing the meds, you're going to keep this poison and darkness inside and never let anyone help you—because you *never* let anyone help you. You're going to hide yourself from everyone—from me. Like the scars on your chest."

Tears sprang from my eyes and I shook my head. "You're not being fair."

"Neither are you. It takes two people to conceive a child, Emilia. *I* was there, too. *I* put you in that situation. And I know about the guilt and self-loathing you feel because I feel it, too."

I put my head in my hands, resting my elbows on my knees. Adam made no move to comfort me, and I couldn't tell if he was angry, frustrated or just scared.

"I'm sorry..."

"No. Stop it. I don't want to hear that from you. Life happened. Shit happened. You made the decision that saved your life and now you torment yourself for it. You've built a prison for yourself and I'm afraid that you'll never let anyone in to break you free."

I shook my head, denying his words.

"You *have*. You told me as much, that night you went to the hospital—" He cut himself off, as if he'd said something he instantly regretted. He jerked his head back and turned to look out over the water again.

"What did I say?"

He closed his eyes, squeezed them tight and then took in a shivery breath. He looked as if he was moments away from breaking down himself.

"Please...tell me."

His jaw tensed and he didn't look at me. "You said that...that you didn't want to die but you were probably going to...that—" He straightened, tensing, as if fighting his own grief with everything that was in him. "That you deserved to die because of what you did..." His voice trailed off, swallowed in emotion. He reached up and angrily swiped the back of his hand across his eyes and I sat back, flabbergasted.

I'd said that? I stared at him, utterly overwhelmed at what he must have gone through then. The feelings he must have felt—the thoughts that must have run through his mind when I'd said it. He'd been in fear for my life, carrying me, barely conscious, to the ambulance, staying up with me all night in the hospital with my words running through his mind on repeat.

"Adam, I shouldn't have said that. I'm so sor—"

"Stop it!" he practically shouted in my face and I jumped, pulling back. His fist slammed down in the sand. "Goddamn it, Emilia, if you say you are sorry one more time..."

I held my hand up. "I'm afraid...how about that? I'm afraid about what this has done to us. I'm afraid we don't know how to fix this."

"I'm afraid to touch you."

That hung in the air, thickening it with tension. My mouth opened to reply but nothing came out.

He shook his head and eventually continued. "I can't go through that again. I can't watch *you* go through that again. Every time I touch you—every time I want you, I'm scared shitless that I'm going to put another baby in you and it's all going to happen again."

"It doesn't have to happen again. We'll be careful..."

"We need help. *You* need help. Professional help."

I sat back on my haunches and looked at him. "I'm not—"

"You said you didn't deserve to live. You need help that I can't give you."

"Will that make a difference?" I asked in a tiny voice. "Will it even begin to eliminate the baggage we are carrying?"

He looked away and shrugged. And that shrug did more to me than any of his words previously had done. My gut sank. I felt like I was suffocating. Adam had lost hope. He no longer believed that we could be fixed.

This realization shook me harder than anything because, since the beginning, he had always believed in us. Long before I had ever thought it possible, he'd believed. He'd pursued this relationship because he'd known we were right for each other. He'd known what he wanted. He'd always been so sure of us.

But, apparently, not anymore.

"You've lost hope," I said quietly.

"I don't know. Maybe. I just feel empty right now. We're human. We can only take so much. And we've had more than our fair share."

"You said that life isn't fair. That we don't get to have everything. But does that mean we don't get to have *anything*—that we've gone through all that together not to deserve to be happy together?"

He shrugged, shaking his head.

I wanted to cry again. I felt lost, cut adrift. My hand wandered to the compass around my neck, my fist closing around it. We'd lost our way. We were drifting aimlessly.

I watched him and he didn't move, his hands fisted in the sand, leaning back on stiff arms, staring out over the black water. The water lapped against the shore. I could hear the song of frogs coming down from the wetlands. People were talking out on their patios on the other side of the Back Bay. But between us? Dead silence.

Void. Emptiness.

"Adam. I still believe in us," I whispered. It hurt to put that out there with no idea of how he'd react, but the silence between us had hurt worse.

After a long silence he said, "I wish I could say the same. More than anything I wish it."

Grief seized me then but I didn't cry. I'd traveled past that stage into a desolate wasteland that was beyond tears. It was dry, empty and lonely, this wasteland. It was a place of my own making and I had no idea how to find my way out. I fingered the compass.

"More than anything, I wish that I had the words to tell you how I feel...about you, about this," I said.

"But you don't. And that's the problem. Because I don't have those words either."

Space and time seemed torn and shredded between us. Ripped. An impassible barrier. My throat constricted. "What should we do?"

He turned to me, watched me. "I don't know. I have to think. You have to think. I'm tired and it's late and we should sleep."

I knew damn well I wasn't going to sleep. I'd be up all night worrying about it, running the past few hours through my mind over and over again—running the past months through my mind, whether I wanted to or not.

Why did love hurt so much?

Without another word, I stood and then watched him get up and brush sand off his pants. Slowly, together but apart, we walked back to the house. He paused to let me enter first and I glanced up into his eyes. Not mirrors. Not shutters. They were pools of black emptiness, suffering, hurt.

I'd done that to him. I fought for another breath, moved through the door up the stairs and into my room without stopping. We never spoke another word to each other. Not even good night.

I closed my door and flipped off the lights. In the blackness, my back up against the wall, I slid down to sit on the floor and for hours, long after I had any feeling left in my legs and butt, I sat and stared. And thought.

And felt. And ached.

And then went numb.

38
ADAM

I WAS UP ALL NIGHT. I DIDN'T EVEN TRY TO SLEEP. PART OF IT WAS spent pacing in my office, another part on my laptop in bed— despite Emilia's efforts to break me of that habit. At one point I found myself typing out exactly what I wanted to say to her. Despite the emotionally painful confrontation on the beach the night before, there were plenty of logical facts and reasons for deciding how to proceed. I agonized over them. We were both burying ourselves under mounds of grief and guilt and pretending we could make it go away without having to deal with it.

We were both good at doing that.

I didn't want my words to be delivered from some impersonal email, so instead I memorized the main points of what I wanted to get across and called it even. At six a.m. I changed into my shorts and running shoes and went down to work out in the exercise room.

I'd already run ten kilometers on the treadmill and was getting a drink before going back to do some weights when Emilia came down for breakfast. She was fully dressed in jeans and T-shirt, a bandana tied around her head. And she was pale, drawn, with dark circles under her eyes.

She'd slept about as well as I had, apparently.

I was refilling my water bottle when she came to stand beside me at the fridge. I took a deep breath and said, "Good morning."

A faint smile ghosted her lips before vanishing. "Hey."

"I'd ask how you're feeling but...well, I think I already know."

She looked into my eyes then. "Yeah. Best not to ask that."

I screwed the top back on my water bottle and turned from her when her hand darted out to stop me. "Can we talk now? Please?"

I froze and turned back to her, my insides constricting. I hadn't wanted to do this now. I'd wanted to wait a little while, until lunch maybe, or the afternoon. Because I knew exactly what I wanted to say to her, but I wasn't ready for how she was going to take it. I'd need a few more hours to get the courage to break her heart.

Despite that thought, I said, "Sure."

I moved to the kitchen table and sat down, and she sank into a chair across from me. I set my water bottle aside.

"That was a pretty gigantic can of worms we opened last night," she began.

I fell back against my seat, watching her carefully. "Yes."

She stared at her hands, laced on the table in front of her. "And I've been up all night trying to think my way through it. I think between the two of us, there's a lot of brainpower here, and I know there has to be a way through this for us."

I envied her that hope. Because I just didn't feel it. I studied her delicate, feminine features, the way she fidgeted with the woodwork on the table, tracing the pattern with her finger, the way she bounced one knee up and down.

The love. That pure, strong, unquestionable emotion. It was there, like always, but dampened, muted. Drowned out by a howling ocean of pain.

Before I let her travel any further down that road of hope, I knew I had to get this out quickly, like the proverbial ripping off a bandage. I swallowed. "Emilia..."

Her eyes shot to mine and I saw the fear there. She knew and she was trying to avoid the inevitable.

She shook where she sat. "Please don't say it," she murmured.

I said it anyway—could barely get it out, but I said it. "We need to be apart for a while."

She inhaled and the noise that came from the back of her throat sounded like a sob. She sat back as if I'd slapped her. She took in another long breath, as if it might be her last, and shook her head. Her fist closed on the tabletop and her features flushed.

"You don't get to do this, Adam. You don't get to give up."

"I'm not giving up—"

"Bullshit!" she said, standing up so fast the chair behind her scraped across the floor. "This is bullshit—" Her fist pounded on the table. "After what I did for you—" Her voice cut off again in a strangled sob.

I sat, fighting the emotion rising up, clenching my own fist at my side, willing myself to calm down when I wanted to stand up and start shouting, too.

"Sit down," I said quietly.

She folded her arms across her chest and didn't move. Our gazes met and the betrayal I saw there—it sucked all of the fight right out of me. I pulled my eyes away, leaned forward, put my head in my hand.

"Did you just hear yourself?" I said, my own voice shaking with emotion. "After what you did—you think you did it for me, for your mom, for your friends. Because somewhere inside of you, you can't let yourself believe you are worth putting yourself first for your own sake."

Emilia turned for a moment, her back to me, then reached out for the chair, and instead of pulling it back to the table so she could sit down, she pushed it over. It clattered across the stone floor and she had her face in her hands.

"This fucking sucks!" she said, and then, with a kick that might have done more damage to her than the chair had she connected with more than a glancing blow, she lashed out again. "So now...I get to live—hooray!" She threw her arms up in a mock cheer, but her eyes and cheeks were drenched with tears. "But I don't have you. And I don't have a baby."

"Emilia—"

"No, you don't understand."

I swallowed. "You're right. I don't."

Our eyes locked and the minutes stretched out into what felt like an eternity when I couldn't breathe. "You need help. I can't help you. And you are incapable of asking for help. Therefore, this situation is impossible."

"What about *you*?" she hissed. "Is everything so perfect in there?" She pointed at my head.

"No, it's pretty fucked up in here, too."

Then she really started to sob, so much that she couldn't even stand up straight. She doubled over as if in physical agony and seemed to be gasping for breath. I was worried she was going to lose her balance and fall over.

I shot out of my chair and went to her, pulling her into my arms. "Breathe," I said.

But she was gasping so quickly that I thought she might pass out, her face buried in her closed fists. On instinct, I tightened my hold around her and miraculously she almost immediately calmed down. Her breaths came at a more measured pace and her sobs slowed until, minutes later, there was just congested breathing punctuated with a quiet whimper. My shirt was now drenched with her tears.

Finally she spoke, her face pressed against my shoulder. "I can't believe that it ends like this. Is that life's way of playing a sick, cruel joke?"

"It's not the end, Mia," I said.

"Then what is it?"

"I don't know. It's just...time...time we need to take to get our shit together."

"Why can't we do that together?"

"Because we're both pretty messed up in our heads right now. I think we have to work on ourselves first."

Another period of silence, and then she stiffened in my arms and gently pulled away. I let my arms fall slack and she took a step back. Yanking off her bandana, she mopped her face with it, avoiding my eyes.

She cleared her throat and when she spoke, her voice was calm. "How long?"

I took a deep breath. "I think you should go home to Anza. Spend some time with your mom before her wedding...maybe go talk to your old therapist."

"And you'll stay here and work? How will that be working on things?"

"I haven't thought all that through yet, but I have some ideas."

I met her gaze and wished I hadn't. Her eyes were stricken, haunted. I wanted to abandon this plan. I was hurting her. Too much.

"And then what?" she asked.

"There's the wedding in June. We'll see each other then."

"That's two months from now," she rasped. "You honestly think that the best way for us to communicate with each other about our issues is to...not see each other?"

"Emilia, we've been put through a lot of shit in a short period of time. We need to try to heal from it."

She shook her head. "I hope to God you know what you are doing, Adam, because I think this is a really bad idea." Then she pressed her hand to her forehead and closed her eyes as if to will the tears to stop.

Mine were minutes away from starting. But I had to show her the brave face—what I definitely *wasn't* feeling—that I was confident this was a good idea.

I cleared my throat. "I think it will be good...for both of us. I couldn't let you go, before...when you wanted space. I kept trying to force the issue and I made things worse with us. I think I've learned now."

She sucked in a painful breath but didn't speak until she finally stuffed her bandana in her pocket and straightened. "I'll go pack, then. I need to get my car back from Kat."

"I'd rather you didn't drive there today...in this condition."

She turned to me, her eyes clear but full of pain. "It will be a lot easier for me to drive than it will be for me to stay here another night like this."

I frowned, running my hand across the morning beard on my jaw. "Okay. Then at least take the Tesla. I want you in a safe car. I've been driving the Porsche everywhere, anyway."

She turned and left on shaky legs. I watched her go, running a hand over my face.

This was so hard. I wanted her more than anything. I wanted her here, in my life, by my side, but we were both so wounded I had no idea how we could be together until we healed. Until we figured out where our heads were—where our hearts were.

I loved her with everything that was in me.

But sometimes love just wasn't enough.

39
MIA

FULL CIRCLE. THAT'S WHAT THIS WAS. ELEVEN MONTHS AGO, I'D made this same drive with an injured heart and emotions like tropical storms swirling inside me. And here I was back where I was then, making this same drive. Like my life was on some kind of sick, endlessly repeating loop.

Only this time, I'd left my heart behind. Battle-wounded and bloody and left for dead. I fought fresh tears every stretch of that two-hour drive until...until I was about fifteen minutes from pulling into the driveway of the ranch. Passing through the old familiar sights of town—the convenience store on the corner, the little rustic café where I'd hung out sometimes, the small high school, some of my old friends' houses, a weird sort of peace came over me. I had no idea what it meant. Just that I hoped it would be okay. That I still had any hope at all inside me was a miracle.

Mom greeted me with concern in her eyes, pulling me into her tight hug. When I'd called her and told her I was coming to stay for a while, I hadn't given her details. But I'm sure she'd concluded a lot.

346 | BRENNA AUBREY

"I'm glad you're here, baby."

I wished I could say the same. I had no idea what I'd accomplish here for the next eight weeks. Going back to Anza was going backward, I'd once told Heath. But sometimes no matter how old a person got, they needed their mom. And thank God she was here.

"Mom," I said, pulling back from her and looking her in the eyes. I'm sure she could see from the swelling in mine that I'd been crying— a lot. "I want you to know that I'm so completely happy for you and Peter. And—whatever happens between me and Adam won't change that."

She nodded. Taking my bag off my shoulder, she turned to take it into the family wing of our bed-and-breakfast home. "You don't have to talk to me about this at all. But as far as I'm concerned, you are here to heal your body and your heart." She turned to me and smiled, putting a hand to my head. "Your hair is growing back! It's coming in darker than it was before."

I put a self-conscious hand to the fuzz on my head.

"You're going to have respectable coverage by the time the wedding rolls around."

"Yeah? It grows that fast?"

She grinned. "Yeah. It will be back in no time. Thick and glossy. And the rest of your body will bounce back, too. You'll see. I'm on a mission to fatten you up."

"Not sure I feel much like eating these days, even if I'm not nauseous anymore."

"Well, you have no choice in the matter. We need to put some weight back on these bones. And I'm fixing your favorite stuff every day. I just made a whole fresh batch of baklava. We're healing body and heart. Okay?"

I nodded.

Mom left me and I immediately went to my desk, rifled through my drawers and found an old blank notebook that I'd been saving until I had something important enough to write in it because it was just so pretty. It had an imprint of illuminations from the medieval Book of Kells with Celtic knotwork design and gold embossing. I ran a hand over the cover and pulled it open to gaze at the creamy blank pages within.

Without realizing what I was doing, I grabbed a pen and began writing. Those first few entries might have contained more than a little anger. There might have been smudges staining the pages with my tears. But I began to feel better because I had my own place to let it all out.

I wrote in it every day.

And I went to see Dr. Marbrow, my psychotherapist. I was determined to do this thing. I was determined that when I saw Adam again, I would be healthy enough in body, mind and spirit to look him in the eye and tell him how much I wanted him—how much I needed him in my life. And I could only hope that he felt the same way.

So with that goal to fuel my courage, I faced my demons.

***

After some weeks in Anza, Heath and Kat came up to spend a long weekend with me. I think Heath was really worried about me because he kept giving me that concerned look over dinner—homemade gyros and fresh Caesar salad from Mom's garden. Of all the delicious things my mom made, this dish was his favorite, but he barely paid attention to it.

After dinner, I was getting the horses ready to take them on a sunset ride when he came out into the barn alone.

"Where's Kat?" I said as I brushed the dust out of Snowball's coat.

"She'll be along. I wanted to talk to you."

"Okay...hey, do you want to ride Whiskey or Tate tonight?"

He made a face. "Tate's an asshole. He threw me repeatedly in high school. Put me on Whiskey. Damn, I haven't ridden in years."

I smiled. "I know."

"How are you *really* doing, Mia?"

I blinked. "I thought I was looking better...maybe not."

"You don't know how badly I want to go beat the shit out of Drake right now."

I burst out laughing. "He's back to being Drake to you, huh?"

"I can't believe he broke up with you when you have fucking cancer."

"I *don't* have fucking cancer anymore and he didn't break up with me."

Heath glowered.

"No. Stop it, okay? Adam is your friend, too. I don't want you to take sides. There are no sides to take."

Heath folded his arms and shoved his shoulder up against the barn. "You two didn't break up?"

"You're nosey," I retorted.

"I'm pissed. If you two don't make it, then there's no hope for the rest of us."

I dropped the soft brush into the plastic tote and grabbed Snowball's saddle and pad from the tack room—Heath insisted on carrying it over for me even though I was sure I could do it myself. He rested them on Snowball's back and I adjusted the pad, stooping to grab the girth to begin cinching it up.

"I think I'll put Kat on my boy Snowball here."

"Mia—"

"Heath, you of all people know the most about what we are dealing with. What we are going through. The losses we've had to face. I can't wave a magic wand and wish it away. We have shit to work through."

"Then why aren't you down there going to counseling with him? A good couples' counselor—"

"That's not Adam's style. He's going to find his own way to deal with his shit. And I'm finding a way to deal with mine."

"That's the problem. You aren't dealing with it together."

"Hmm. Maybe it's not time for us to do that yet. Maybe in order to be a healthy couple, we need to be healthy individuals first." I said the words and this time I believed them, though I'd doubted their wisdom when Adam had said them to me.

He was silent so I went to the stall where Whiskey was poking his head out, eyeing me expectantly. I scratched his head under his forelock. "Who's my good boy?" I slipped a halter over his head and pulled him out of his stall. "You're going to be a good boy for Heath, aren't you?"

"Yeah, or Heath's going to kick your ass. Ask your buddy Tate," Heath said. He turned back to me. "This was his idea, wasn't it? For you to separate, to come back here."

I didn't answer, bending over to use the hoof pick to clean out Whiskey's hooves.

"That's what I thought."

I straightened and blew out a breath. "I'm not going to judge him for how he's dealing with this. He needs time alone. I'm going to give it to him. I'd be a hypocrite to judge him when I didn't exactly handle things the best way possible between us last time."

Heath looked away. "Don't be so hard on yourself. You are only human." He sighed. "This relationship shit is so hard. Sometimes I wonder if it's even worth it."

I grabbed the currycomb to give Whiskey a quick once-over on his dusty coat. "Things okay with you and Connor?"

"Better than with you and Adam," he replied.

"That's not saying much."

"Can I go talk to him, at least?"

My hand froze. Heath was one of precious few people who knew all that Adam and I had endured. Maybe it would help him to have a sympathetic ear...if, indeed, Heath's ear was sympathetic.

"He'll think I sent you to talk to him."

"You just said yourself that he's my friend, too. And who else is he going to talk to about the—about everything."

I swallowed, focusing on the dust I was stirring up on the surface of Whiskey's coat. "You can say it, you know. You don't have to spare my feelings."

Heath sighed. "This is reminding me way too much of that shit that happened to you in high school, and that thought is making me *physically* ill."

My brush froze midstroke, but I didn't look at Heath.

I knew exactly what he was referring to—that night that Zack, my high school boyfriend, had gotten drunk and assaulted me.

"You blamed yourself for that shit, too, or have you forgotten?"

I flung the brush into the tote and both horses jerked their heads up, startled. I quieted them by reassuring them and stroking their necks.

Heath came up to stand beside me and took the arm that I was using to stroke Whiskey's neck. "Don't be pissed at me, Mia. But I'm calling you on this bullshit. What happened to you—getting cancer, getting pregnant, losing the baby—was no more your fault than that bullshit in high school was. It *happened* to you. Don't punish yourself for it."

Tears started to sting my throat and I blinked, gently pulling out of his hold. I cleared my throat furiously, blinked again and looked away.

"Does *he* blame you? Is that what all this is about?"

I waved him off. "Put the boxing gloves away, Sugar Ray. He doesn't blame me. He says he can't deal with how much I'm blaming myself."

Heath folded his brawny arms across his chest. "Well, that makes two of us. I can't deal with it, either. I see it in your eyes all the time. I saw what that innocent comment from Alex did to you."

I curled in on myself, putting my forehead in my hands. Tears were threatening again. I turned and tilted away from him, but he grabbed me, pulled me close and hugged me. "Shh. I'm sorry. I didn't mean to upset you."

His arms were comforting, but they weren't the arms I wanted around me.

***

"So, to repeat your words back to you—you believe that if you let him see your scars, that will cause him to stop loving you?" Dr. Marbrow said, leaning forward.

I shifted against the sleek couch in her office, the leather squeaking underneath my fidgeting. "It sounds ridiculous coming out of your mouth but makes perfect sense in here," I said, pointing to my head.

She tilted her head, a smile hinting at her lips. "That voice in there may be the most illogical thing you'll ever hear, but it will always sound right to you. It's human nature. We give that voice a lot of power. Thus, sometimes the solution is to change that voice, change what it is saying to us."

I shook inside. "I don't want to. I mean...that voice is making me miserable inside, but I don't want to let it go."

"Of course not." She leaned back and crossed her legs. "How else would you torment yourself if that voice was gone?"

Suddenly, it was hard to breathe. I fiddled with my hands in my lap, staring at them. The backs of my legs were sweating and, since I was wearing shorts, sticking to the leather couch. I had no reply to that. I *had* been tormenting myself. Because everything in me believed that I deserved it. Dr. Marbrow noted something on the legal pad in front of her and then watched me before determining that I wasn't going to answer her.

She tucked a long strand of blond hair behind her ear and began in a quiet voice, "Will the scars on your chest truly cause him to leave?"

I shook my head slowly.

"But you do fear you'll lose him."

If I hadn't already. I closed my eyes and nodded.

"What will make him leave, do you think?"

I inhaled sharply through my nose and exhaled shakily.

"It's what the scars represent..." My voice faded and I cleared my throat, placing a hand over my heart. "The scars in here. The ones that make me feel so ugly on the inside."

She nodded. "That's the definition of love, you know. That the person is with you and stays by your side in spite of the ugliness—and that you do the same. *He's* not perfect, either, as I'm sure you are well aware."

I shook my head. "I did terrible things to him."

"Such as...?" She raised her brow.

My breath faltered. "I left him. I was angry—I—I didn't know how to deal with how he was acting. So I didn't tell him about the cancer— I thought I was protecting him, but it was just easier that way. Easier for me to stay inside myself, to not have to rely on anyone."

"But you can't be sick and not rely on those closest to you. You had to accept help."

I rubbed my temples. "The craziest part is that I had to force myself—even at my sickest. I have all these people around me who love me, who *want* to help me, and yet I refuse to let them. And because of that..."

"You made some bad choices. So did he."

I put my face in my hands. "But it's all my fault."

"You see what you are doing there, don't you? You won't even let people in on their share of the blame. It's rather narcissistic when you think about it, to assume that all that has happened to you was caused by your actions alone. But that's human nature, too. Because in taking blame for something, we are deluding ourselves that we have some control over the chaotic events in our lives we just can't control."

"I haven't had control—" My words cut off in a sob.

"It's no wonder that Heath compared your reaction to this to what happened to you in high school. That was another instance where you had no control over what was happening to your body. Now this, the cancer, the chemo, the pregnancy, the abortion..."

My breath left me and I sat back, dazed. "I had a choice. I ended it."

"Was it really a choice, though? You did what you *had* to do to survive."

I shook. "I don't think our relationship can withstand something like this." There was a long pause while she just looked at me, obviously expecting me to go on. I took a deep breath. "I don't understand how he could love me anymore," I said in a tiny voice.

"He loves you because he doesn't blame you."

"He said he's afraid to touch me."

She nodded. "Sounds like he's indulging in his share of the blame game, too. And your job is going to be to help him understand that— once you get over your own guilt."

I looked at her through a shaky, tear-stained smile. "Can I put you in my pocket and keep you with me for a while?"

She smiled. "What you can do is bring him up to meet me some day. If he's okay with that."

***

Days later, out in the paddock, I had my own sort of epiphany as I watched Rusty with her three-month-old colt, Silver. I studied them together. Trotting around, side by side. Sometimes he'd dart out in front of her, head high and proud of his independence but always casting an eye back at his mama. And Rusty never let him get too far, sometimes scolding him with a light nip or flick of her tail.

My throat tightened as I watched them and I let myself feel what I hadn't allowed myself to feel in months—the mourning, the loss, what could have been. The tears came and I didn't stop them. Not this time. I couldn't shove those feelings away any longer.

I wrote in my journal every day. I poured out every thought, every emotion. More often than not, I wrote in it more than once a day, going back to it when a stray thought flitted through my mind. It felt freeing to let out everything that I'd been keeping inside.

I also Skyped with my friends. Jenna and Alex filled me in on the goings-on from the South Coast. Heath called me every few days to check up on me and I had a chance to videoconference with Kat.

"So we all went out for pizza the other night..."

"Really? Did you have fun?"

"Hmm. Well, it was a big group. Most of us had fun. Jenna and William were at each other's throats again about some obscure game I'd never even heard of before. Those two just need to fuck and get it over with. And then Heath and Adam wandered off somewhere for an hour."

I tensed at the mention of Adam and she noticed. "Oh—yeah, sorry I forgot to tell you that. Heath and I twisted his arm to come out with us. We had to go get him at his office and force him under threat of exposing game secrets to the world."

"You didn't! You held the secret quest hostage?"

Her smile grew devious. "I know how to get what I want. He wasn't budging so I threatened."

I paused for a minute, looked away from the screen and fiddled with some things on my desk. "How is he?"

She knew I wasn't asking about Heath.

She nodded. "He's fine. He's his typical grim, intense self."

I laughed. "He's not always that way."

She gave me a weird look. "Fallen has been intense for as long as I've known him. I just never knew why until now. But now that I know his real self, it's understandable. He's just that type of guy." She threw me a mischievous look. "It's a good thing he's so pretty to make up for it."

I rolled my eyes and then laughed, quickly changing the subject. She groused about my lack of playing time, and I didn't want to tell her that the thought of playing the game right now was a little too painful. Between all that was—or wasn't—going on between Adam and me and the increasing conflict I was feeling over blogging on the subject of the secret quest, I felt torn about DE. I missed it, but I knew I needed a break from it as well.

Every day, I hiked to my special spot up on the valley rim near my mom's house. I would arrive just at sunset, when the early summer evenings were painted in oranges and deep, deep purple. Where the heat of the sunbaked rocks seeped through my clothing, where the dry smells of white desert sage and the sound of cricket chirps assailed my senses.

I took this time to close my eyes, to think, to breathe in the ways that Dr. Marbrow had showed me. I focused on color and light and tried to think about all that I had to be thankful for. I'd seen a lot of heartache in my short twenty-three years of life, but the things I'd done, the places I'd been, the people I'd known. The love I'd felt...

All those had made the pain worth it. And just a little bit more each day, I began to realize that.

On one of my last nights in Anza, I was outside at night, enjoying the darkness and the primal beauty of the dome of stars above my head. There were few night lights up here and no light pollution, unlike down on the coast around the big cities.

Like every other evening, I found my eyes wandering up toward the constellation Draco while fingering the ever-present compass around my neck. *It's always there,* he'd said, *no matter what time of night, no matter what season.*

I was now familiar with the main points in this long, snakelike configuration of stars. My eyes traced the outline of it in the sky. *True north.* What was that? How could I find the direction? I thought of the figurines William had made for me, particularly the Guide, who was like a compass, to show me the way in troubled times.

If these weren't troubled times, I didn't know what were. I stared long and hard at those stars, fixed right between the Big and Little Dippers. And after a long stretch of nothing but the quiet sounds of night in my ears, a streak of fire appeared from nowhere and cut its way directly across Draco.

Wish on a falling star. It had been noted in that now-dubious bucket list that I'd wanted to wish on a falling star. Growing up here, I'd seen a lot of them, but had never had a wish that I'd wanted so much I'd wish it on a meteor.

But tonight I did. I closed my eyes and pictured my arms around Adam, his arms around me. I wished us together. I wished us happy. I wished us strong enough to fight our way through our own messed-up emotions and doubtful thoughts to be together again. Each beat of my heart thrummed through my chest and it hurt. I swallowed and instead of suppressing the tears, I let them flow down my cheeks. There was no one here to reprimand me, no one here for me to reprimand. There was no reason to keep the tears at bay.

It felt good to let them out. But they weren't just tears of sadness or loss, tears of loneliness; they were also tears of gratitude. I silently thanked the Universe for all that I had to be thankful for: my health, my future, the fact that I had known true love. It didn't matter what the future held, because those short moments of love that I'd experienced had taught me that, thorns and all, life was worth it. And that for me, happiness was a choice.

That night, my face wet, my eyes sore, my heart full, I made that choice.

***

I maintained the blog, but my heart wasn't in it anymore. I'd already resigned myself to the fact that I wasn't going to be able to continue it. With Adam and me together, the blog was going to come between us eventually. Either I'd solve the quest and feel obligated to pass those clues on to the readership, or Draco Multimedia would implement some game change that would irk me and I'd need to rant about it. Or—and my stomach dropped to contemplate that possibility—Adam and I would have broken up and it would hurt too much to continue playing Dragon Epoch.

Whatever the reason, the possibility of beginning medical school in a few short months dictated that I was going to have different priorities on my time. So I spent days drafting long emails—one to Johns Hopkins University's Dean of the College of Medicine, some to other schools, some to my key readers and contacts in the blog world and to the original company that had made an offer on my blog.

Because I had a plan.

About a week before the wedding, we drove down to Orange County to pick up Mom's dress for the final fitting. The wedding was not going to be a gala affair. The bride and groom had invited family only and they'd chosen to tie the knot at one of their favorite places, the beach at Crystal Cove State Park.

But I had other errands to run while we were there. I borrowed the car from my mom and told her I'd be back in a few hours after dropping her at Peter's. Mom assumed it meant I didn't want to chance running into Adam there. I figured that was as good an excuse as any. But I had other business to attend to.

There was a week left, and as my mom's giddiness grew, there were feelings bubbling inside me, too. I couldn't wait to see Adam again. It had been over two months. I wondered how his journey had gone. Had he made any interesting self-discoveries? Had he found he couldn't live without me, or did he think it best we walked away while our souls were still intact?

I had no idea.

And the waiting was starting to kill me.

I had my bags packed two full days before the wedding. The happy couple and their children and close friends would gather for dinner the night before the wedding day. For hours before that, I paced, chose and then discarded no less than five different outfits. Could not sit still more than five minutes to the point where my ever-patient mother had ordered me out of the room to go for a walk.

Because in just a few minutes, I'd see Adam again. And sometime in the next twenty-four hours, I'd know if there was hope for us to move forward together—or if that hope was lost forever.

40
ADAM

I DREAMT ABOUT HER EVERY NIGHT SHE WAS GONE. SINCE I'D loaded her bags up in the Tesla and watched her pull away, my thoughts had never been far from her. She'd texted me a few hours later when she arrived at her mom's house and that was it. Radio silence.

It was better that way. This would be my forty days of trial in the desert. A long stretch of time without her where I figured out what the hell was going on in my own brain. Since that horrible couple days where I'd found out about the pregnancy and her cancer, I'd barely had time to think about anything else but the one prime imperative— her survival.

I spent long days working, of course. It was always my primary method of coping. I spent my nights in solitude—running along the beach at Newport, mostly. Or just spending long periods sitting on the sandy beach, watching the relentless tide come in, the thunder of the waves sounding over and over again—a rhythm so ancient and primal—until it meshed with the beating of my heart. My mind was always working, always trying to find ways around the problems that cropped up. I was, by nature, a problem-solver. So to spend long periods just losing myself in the beat of the waves on the shore with no thought to anything else was like meditation.

Because oftentimes the quiet mind could see and hear things the busy mind could not.

I also spent far more time sleeping than I had in months. There were months and weeks of pure exhaustion to recover from. When she'd needed me to be there for her, I hadn't let myself rest. With her gone, that pressure was removed. And with the sleep and rest came rejuvenation.

Taking care of myself physically was key to recovering my mental health. And eventually I found myself in circumstances where I could seek help from others—in some of the unlikeliest places of all.

One night, about a month after Emilia had left, I was at work after hours. Someone knocked at the door to my office and since my secretary had already gone home, I called to the person to come in.

The door opened and Katya's red head poked around it. "Well, hello there, boss!"

I sat back with a grin. "Well, well. If it isn't my newest playtester."

She strutted inside, pumping a fist. "Best job ever, by the way. You are my new favorite person."

"Glad you like it," I said, reaching back to rub my aching neck.

"Yes. So I know you don't fraternize with your employees and all that, but we're going out for pizza tonight and I'm kidnapping you and bringing you along."

"I'd like to but I have a ton of shit to get done."

Her brows rose and she folded her arms across her chest, sinking into the chair across from me. "Listen up, dude. I'm the fun police and you're about to get arrested for the serious lack of fun in your life right now."

I chuckled but didn't say a word. She narrowed her eyes at me.

"I even brought some muscle, should you foolishly refuse this opportunity to rehabilitate." She raised two fingers to her lips and let out a loud, sharp-pitched whistle. Heath came through the door.

"Well, there goes the neighborhood," I said.

"So do you come along with us peacefully or am I going to have to twist your arm?" Heath said, cracking his knuckles.

"Hmm. You are making this *such* a tempting offer of 'fun,'" I drawled.

"I have a whole army out there, including your cousin, so you better come along with us peacefully."

"Yeah, don't make me beat the shit out of you again," Heath said.

"Again? That would imply a first time." Perhaps he was obliquely referring to the cheap shot he'd gotten in when he'd been as overcome by his shock about Emilia's condition as I had. We shared a long look. "Maybe you've been thinking those wet dreams are reality again?"

Instead of looking angry, Heath only grinned. "Pizza and video games, dude. Relive your adolescence."

"Some of us never left it in order to relive it," Kat quipped, shooting out of her chair. "Come on. Grab your keys, let's go. I call shotgun in your car, *boss*."

With a sigh of surrender, I got up, packed up my stuff in my computer bag and left with them.

The pizza was terrible, but the company great. We were joined by Connor, Alex, Jenna and my cousin, Liam. And sometimes people wandered off with their hands full of tokens to play games, then wandered back for some more beer and gross pizza. I'd set my mind to stay an hour and then find an excuse to wander home. Because as fun as they were to hang with, their presence only emphasized the lack of *her*. And that lack was like a giant, painful hole right now.

I finished up my one and only glass of beer and was about to stand up when I felt a hand slap my shoulder. I looked over. Heath grinned. "Can I have some more tokens, Dad?"

I raised a brow at him. "You don't get any more allowance 'til next week." I stood up. "I think I'm gonna get going."

"I'll walk you out," Heath said, popping up and giving me no say in the matter. Okay, it was obvious he wanted to talk. I knew that he'd been up in Anza visiting Emilia the weekend before. I'd resolved not to ask him about her, no matter how badly I wanted to.

I said goodbye to the rest of the group, who all seemed disappointed I was leaving so soon, but once they realized Heath was going out the door with me, none of them said much—as if they all knew we had things to talk about. As torn as I felt about talking to him, I couldn't see a way to avoid it.

It was quiet out in the parking lot of the strip mall where the pizza joint was. As it was ten o'clock on a weeknight in the somewhat sleepy city of Orange, it was peaceful. I clicked my car unlocked and turned, leaning up against the door to face Heath. "That was shit pizza," I said by way of breaking the weird awkwardness between us.

"The games are good. What place do you know of around here that still has a working version of Tempest, Galaga *and* Asteroids?"

I shrugged, then glanced out over the street where the occasional car sped by. "With a day's warning, I could have all of those set up in my arcade room at home."

"Or you could just program your own."

"I got my own game to work on."

"How's everything, anyway?"

"With the game? Great. We're getting ready to unveil the preview of the new expansion at E3 next week. And then there's Comic-Con in July."

"Great." He nodded, looking down at his feet and then shifting uncomfortably again. "And—and personally? You okay?"

I was silent, unsure exactly what I wanted to share with Heath. We'd been friends for a long time, but lately there had been tension between us, mostly over the way I'd handled things in my relationship with Emilia, whom he'd claimed over and over was as good as a sister to him.

"I'll live," I said.

Heath nodded. "There's something I wanted to say to you...and I know things have been tense between us since Mia got sick..."

I folded my arms across my chest, leaned back against my car and nodded. "Right," I said in a neutral tone of voice.

"Adam, I said some shit that I really regret now. I blamed you for what happened and I shouldn't have done that."

I shrugged. "You weren't wrong."

His eyes narrowed. "Yes. Yes, I was wrong. I want you to understand where my head was at during all that. She..." He hesitated and then took a deep breath. "She was falling apart. You two had just broken up and then she found out about the cancer and she swore me to secrecy. I blame myself every day for keeping a secret I had no right to keep."

My jaw tightened and then I relaxed it enough to speak. "You were being loyal. You were doing what she wanted."

He shook his head. "She wasn't rational. I shouldn't have agreed. But I did and I blame myself for that."

"There's too many of us assuming blame for things that we shouldn't be."

He studied me, scratching the side of his mouth with the back of his hand. "Yeah...so about that. I'm just saying—that day I took a swing at you and those weeks afterward when I wasn't very kind...I was wrong. I was stressed out beyond words and worried out of my mind about her. And you were an easy target to focus all of that on."

"Well, like I said before, thanks for being there for her when she needed someone." I shifted, trying to power through this very uncomfortable conversation.

He looked away and then, when I turned as if I would open my car door to move this along, he put a hand on my shoulder. "Adam, don't give up on her."

My shoulders sagged. "It's not a matter of giving up on her."

"Man, I know what you are thinking. I know you can't take what she's doing to herself. She just needs the time to heal from all of this. It's been a shitty year for both of you. But from her point of view, she had to make a gut-wrenching choice and we both know she made the best choice. But I don't think she's realized that yet."

I shook my head. "She's in hell and it's not a hell of her own making. I put her in that situation—"

Heath's hand slipped off my shoulder and he nodded. "Hmm. Somehow I knew that was at the bottom of all this. That she wasn't the only one wrapped up in her own irrationality. Given her emotional state these last few months, I'd expect that of her. But from you, I thought I'd get much more logical reasoning."

"What's more logical than she had to end a pregnancy that I caused in the first place?"

"Shit happens. You aren't the first guy who got his girlfriend pregnant. It's not like you invented that. Thank God I'll never have to face that problem. Gay guys have plenty of issues of their own. But for God's sake, man up and realize that shit happens. It happened and it might happen again. Or it might not. You never know with life. But it's not like you set out to do that to her. Any more than she set out to have it happen to her."

I took a pained breath and let it out. He was right, of course, but I wasn't ready to admit that.

Heath spoke again. "I talked to her the other night."

"She's okay?" I asked between clenched teeth.

"She's hopeful. She's still very hopeful about the two of you. But she's worried about you."

I sighed. "I'm not so hopeful. That's why she's worried."

"Well, you've got some questions to ask yourself, then. You need to figure out whether or not you're willing to go forward without her. Because that's what it's going to be. You either do what's necessary to have her in your life or you back away, declare it too hard and not worth it and live without her."

"Thinking like a programmer. How very black and white of you..."

"Adam, you're a problem-solver. You have a problem. You need to figure out a way to solve it. Put that genius brain to work."

"I am. I have been."

"Well, whatever the resolution you come to, I hope it's the one that makes you happy."

Happy. What was that? An elusive state of mind? A destination? Or a decision?

Days went by and I pondered over that. I occupied myself with some odd things that had nothing to do with work. I was struggling to find a way to communicate with her while we were on radio silence from each other. I had an alert set up that would let me know if she were to log in to the game. She never did. I wasn't surprised. Either she was avoiding it or she was working hard at the task of finding herself.

It was on the way back from the last day of the E3 convention in Los Angeles, in bumper-to-bumper traffic on the 110 freeway,that Jordan, finding me his captive audience for the hour or hours it would take, laid into me.

He looked up after having fiddled with his phone for the first fifteen minutes. "Goddamn. We should just pull off and go sit somewhere for a few hours until this blows over. This traffic sucks shit."

"Whether we sit at a bar for hours or just power through the traffic isn't going to make a difference in how soon we get home."

"We should have ordered a car and driver so at least we could do some work while sitting in this crap. Or maybe even knock back a beer."

I shrugged.

Jordan readjusted his sunglasses and set down the phone. It was a warm day. We'd both shed our business attire and the top was down, a cool breeze blowing in from the coast as we motored along at five miles per hour.

"So I gotta ask how Mia's doing...I haven't seen her around much."

"She's up at her mom's for a while."

He jerked his head to glance at me. "'A while' sounds like a long time."

I didn't reply, checked my mirror and changed lanes.

"You guys okay?"

"Not really."

"What the fuck do you mean 'not really' and why am I only hearing about this now?"

I darted him a quizzical look before jerking my eyes back to the road. "I didn't realize that I owe you a 'state of the relationship' address."

"Damn right you do. After I gave up my trip to Paris for you guys—"

"I thought you did that for her."

"I did. But that means you don't fucking dump your sick girlfriend. What the hell is wrong with you?"

I white-knuckled the steering wheel. "I didn't dump her and she's not sick anymore, so calm the fuck down. Jeez, what the hell happened to you? Someone cut off your balls or something?"

He flipped me the bird. "Don't be an ass, Adam. What's going on? You need to talk to someone."

"It's complicated."

"It usually is."

I let out a long breath and then changed lanes again. Not such a great idea. Some jerk-off honked at me and Jordan sent the driver his middle finger.

"Jesus, you're gonna start a road rage incident. Put that thing away."

"So how is it more complicated than any other relationship out there?"

"We have…issues."

"What issues do you have with Mia?"

"Oh, so you like her all of a sudden, huh?"

He shrugged. "I think she's a nice girl."

"She is a nice girl." A nice girl with a lot of problems.

"So what's the deal? Is there, like, someone else? Did you fuck around on her? Don't tell me it was Carisa, because—"

"I didn't cheat on her."

"Well?"

"We're taking a little time off from each other. We have some shit to deal with."

"And you're not going to tell me what it is."

"I would, if I thought you'd take it seriously and not be an ass about it."

He pulled off his sunglasses and tucked them into his shirt. "Do I look like I'm going to stab you in the back?"

I swallowed. "No."

"Lay it on me. What happened?"

"I don't trust her."

"She fucked around on you?"

"God, nobody fucked around on anybody. Let me just get it out, okay?"

He held up a hand as if to stave off my irritation. "Okay, okay."

"We broke up because—well, because of stupid shit, really. But while we were broken up, she found out about the cancer and didn't tell me."

"Okay."

"And then in Vegas—"

"Yeah, yeah. I know all about what happened with you and her in Vegas."

"I have no idea how you know that and it's kind of creepy. However, what you don't know is that she got pregnant."

There was a long silence from the other side of the car. I focused on the traffic and when I finally glanced over at him, he looked pale. He reached into his pocket, grabbed his sunglasses and stuck them back on his face.

"I think I can guess what happened since she has just gone through chemo and is obviously no longer pregnant. That's, uh...that's some heavy shit."

I didn't answer. The silence lasted for a few more miles—which took almost a half hour in this damn traffic. Finally, Jordan cleared his throat. "So you said you don't trust her. This must mean you blame her for it...and if that's—"

"I don't blame her. But yeah, I don't trust her. It's more...general. I don't trust that she's not going to shred me again. That she believes in this enough to—"

He laughed—*laughed*—at me. "Damn, Adam, that's such a pussy thing to say."

I clenched my jaw, gripped the steering wheel and ran my mind over the last few things I'd just said. "Adam's afwaid he's gonna get huwt. Poow widdle Adam."

"Do you need me to let you out here? I think you can thumb a ride home with a serial killer or something," I ground out.

"I don't mean to be a dick but—"

"Too late—"

"You need to sac up, dude. Whenever you put yourself in a serious relationship, you run the risk of getting hurt. It's how it works."

"But usually you trust the other person not to do it."

He shrugged. "Yeah. And what makes you think she will? Because of last time? You mean when she was scared out of her mind with a life-or-death diagnosis right after breaking up with her boyfriend?

You really think that's a time to judge how someone's going to act under more normal circumstances?"

I swallowed, suddenly feeling like a dick myself.

"Here's the deal...and you can consider the source and shitcan this advice if you want, but here's Uncle Jordan's take on things. It doesn't matter who the person is, when you make a commitment like being in a relationship, you are always going to open yourself up to be shredded. It's the nature of the beast."

I turned and looked at him but didn't reply, adjusting my sunglasses. The traffic was starting to loosen up and we'd made it up to about twenty miles per hour with not a brake light in sight.

"She hurt you before. I get it. You hurt her, too, right?"

I nodded.

"I'm your money guy so I'm going to put this in terms that are familiar to me. You need to look at this like a cost versus value decision. Is the risk you take of getting hurt worth the benefit of what you get from having her in your life? If yes, then stay with her, be with her and try to make it work. If no, then end it."

"I guess that's what I have to figure out."

"Yeah. But for what it's worth, I thought you two were good together, for all that it irritated me."

The rest of our trip devolved into bouts of silence or small talk and I was relieved. Jordan's words were abrasive but not unwelcome. I wasn't above admitting that sometimes I needed to be called on my shit. And I was sick of licking my wounds in silence.

So to get over the bouts of loneliness—especially on the weekends—I went over to my uncle's house for Sunday dinner. They all knew about Emilia being up in Anza with Kim, of course, so no one asked after her—not even Britt's kids, so I had to give props to their mom for schooling them beforehand on that.

After dinner, we sat on the couch, one boy on either side of me while we played Mario Kart on the console. They thought it was hilarious to play teams and gang up on me. After my second victory—this one by the skin of my teeth—they gave up.

I put a hand on each of their heads as they tried to wrestle me down. They lost at that game, too. I loved those kids—even when DJ was trying unsuccessfully to shove his fingers up my nose. Given the state I was in lately, I sat back and quietly watched them get involved in game of checkers. I let myself think about the fact that at this time, I might have been an expectant father in other circumstances.

I'd never given myself the chance to even consider that possibility. The situation had been so dire. My every thought and goal had been toward Emilia's survival. And when she'd been around, I'd never let myself go there, even after we knew she was healthy. Was it fair, now, to regret what I might never have after urging her to do what she did? When I gave them their hugs goodbye, I couldn't ignore that little pinch that reminded me of my own loss. And that date—that date that Emilia had recited in the doctor's office on that bleak morning: August 18. The due date.

I hung around after Britt and the kids left. Liam had already taken off and I think Peter could tell that I wanted to talk because he went to the fridge without saying a word, pulled out two beers, opened them and sat next to me on a stool at the kitchen counter. We sipped in awkward silence for the first few minutes before I cleared my throat.

"How go the wedding plans?"

He smiled. "Great, for me. I don't have to do anything. Britt's handling stuff on this end and Kim and Mia are doing the other stuff from theirs. I just have to show up with a wedding gift and a ring."

"Sounds like a great deal to me."

Peter cast a sidelong glance at me as he sipped again. "You doing okay?"

I put the beer down, resting my elbows on the counter. "Kinda."

"So...I know things are delicate right now with you two. Kim and I are a little worried."

I knew what that meant. They were a *lot* worried. In a lot of ways, their future happiness as a married couple was dependent upon how well Emilia and I could manage our relationship. Things could get messy for them very quickly if the two of us couldn't get along, considering how close our family relationships were now.

"That makes a lot of worried people, then," I said.

"I've also been worried about you. I know in cases like these, the person with the medical problems gets most of the attention—and rightly so. But sometimes it's hard to be the silent partner who has to keep it all together for the sick one."

I shrugged. "I didn't mind that. It's one of the rare times she actually accepted any help from anyone." And I cut myself off after that sentence, punctuating it with a long pull of beer because I hated the acid tone of my voice when it came out. It was getting harder and harder to hide the bitterness.

But he'd heard it and, like the sharp man that I knew he was, zeroed in on it like I was a witness he was cross-examining in court. "That's the other difficulty...to deal with and stockpile the rightful resentment you've felt all these months. And you can't express the anger when the person you are angry with is so sick."

I cleared my throat. It felt tight with my own shame. I looked straight ahead, my hand opening and closing on the table in front of me.

He put a hand on my shoulder. "Don't be so hard on yourself for feeling that way. You're human. Your feelings were hurt pretty badly. You have a right to those feelings whether she's sick or not."

"How were you and Kim able to figure it all out so quickly?" I said finally, mostly to take the heat off of me a little, but also because I was genuinely curious.

He laughed. "Quickly? She's forty-three and I'm almost a decade older than her. I wish I'd found her when I was your age. But life doesn't work that way. I'm just glad I found her now." He shrugged. "And when I knew she was the one for me—well, I wasn't about to waste any more time being alone."

I nodded. His words ran through my mind over and over again during the drive home and the rest of the evening. That night, I refused to go in my office and drown out my thoughts with work when I seemed to have come upon something valuable to think about.

Instead, when I hit the top of the stairs, I went into her room— that private sanctuary that I'd made for her. I sat on her window seat and watched the lights on the dark water, my throat tight, my head aching and heavy with thoughts. Glancing over, I saw a well-worn blue bandana on the night table. Picking it up and not knowing why, I brought it to my face, smelling it. Smelling *her*.

The scent washed over me and I closed my eyes, overwhelmed by feelings that I'd been steadily attempting to block out. The feel of her slight body pressing against mine for a hug, for reassurance, tucking her head under my chin. The way I'd lie next to her, my hand on her back to make sure she was still breathing. The shine in her beautiful golden-brown eyes when she was being particularly witty or funny. The pout of her luscious lips right before I kissed them. The sound of her heartbeat when I laid my head on her chest. The taste of her tears when I comforted her.

These feelings gripped me, held me hostage in this one point in time, assailing me with every memory from the moment I'd logged in to Dragon Epoch and first met her online as FallenOne to the last time I'd seen her, slowly, sadly tucking herself behind the wheel of my car and driving away. My eyes stung with unshed tears and I actually wept into that damn bandana. I missed her. I needed her. But I was still unsure of her.

And I had no idea if I ever could be.

***

The night before Peter and Kim's wedding, we met at a nearby restaurant to share a quiet dinner as a family. I knew I'd see Emilia there for the first time in eight weeks, and I was both excited and nervous to see her. I had no idea what she had gone through during her time away. I only knew how difficult my own journey had been.

I hoped that we could sit down and talk calmly like adults. I hoped that we could find our way through this in a way that left us both able to face the future.

I met Peter out in the parking lot. My cousin had already gone inside but Peter, catching sight of me, stopped and hung back. I walked up with my gift in hand. "Hey! How's the happy groom-to-be?"

Peter clapped his hand on my shoulder. "Nervous as hell."

"Ah. What's there to be nervous about? You've found yourself an amazing woman."

He grinned and nodded. "It's not her I'm nervous about. It's living up to deserving her that makes me think twice. It's a tall order."

I hesitated, smiled and congratulated him, a sudden inexplicable knot of emotion in my throat. Why had that simple statement of anxiety choked me up?

I followed my uncle in and glanced over his shoulder at the party that was already partially seated at the table in the private room they had rented to us. When we arrived, everyone stood up. My eyes were sifting through the group of people—Britt, Rik and their kids, Heath, Liam—when a hand grasped my arm and I turned.

"Adam," Kim said, smiling up at me, and then taking me in a tight hug.

I hugged her back. "Congratulations to the lovely bride."

"Thank you. And...there's someone here who I think you might like to see?"

I smiled to cover the nervous jitters inside, pulling back from the hug. "I think you're absolutely right."

Kim gave me an encouraging smile. "She just went to the bathroom. She'll be right back."

I let out a tight breath and turned around to watch the entryway. She was standing there, frozen in her spot, staring at me. I stood still, taking her in.

She wore dark colors, black jeans and a dark grey shirt. But nothing on her head because it was covered with a thick layer of her own hair. It was short, but it looked almost as if she'd cut it that way. Her natural eyebrows, although thinner, were back. And her skin...it glowed with healthy color.

She took a hesitant step toward me, a shy smile on her mouth.

I stepped toward her at the same time she stepped toward me and we met in the middle. "Hey," she said, and she leaned forward as if to hug me, but when I didn't reach out to hug her, she swayed back, a question in her eyes.

"Hey," I said, throwing a glance at the table and the eight pairs of eyes all fixed on us.

Emilia's gaze followed mine and she laughed. "Wow, it's like we are a reality show or something."

With her thus distracted, I leaned down and gave her a peck on the cheek before turning to sit at the table. Without a word, she sat across from me. We spent most of that meal engaged in a full table conversation about the upcoming nuptials, teasing the bride and groom, discussing various memories. Kim told some stories from Emilia's childhood and I found out some new things about her. My cousins got revenge on me for some of the things I'd said by sharing some embarrassing facts about me.

We laughed. It was fun.

But Emilia and I never had a chance to talk like I'm sure we were both hoping to. When it was time to get up and leave, it was after ten o'clock and there were things to do in the morning. Emilia had to help her mom. I stood beside her in front of the restaurant and people filed past us, giving us a wide berth to afford privacy.

Emilia looked up at me a little nervously. "I hope you're doing okay. But I hope it wasn't too okay without me."

"I'm okay. But not too okay. And you?"

"Somewhat okay," she said with a short nod. Then she came forward and, pulling herself up on her tiptoes, slipped her arms around my shoulders and kissed me on the cheek. "I missed you like crazy," she whispered before pulling back. Then she reached into her bag and pulled out what looked like a gift, wrapped in tissue paper. "Open this when you get home tonight, please?"

I reached into my pocket and pulled out something I had for her. "You brought your laptop with you?" At her nod, I placed the flash drive in her hand. "Use this when you get back to your room tonight." She looked down at it, frowning, and then nodded.

I leaned down and kissed her, this time on the mouth, but it was short, sweet. "Good night."

Emilia stepped back and slowly made it to the car, looking down at her hand and then back at me before stumbling.

I went to my car and immediately tore the tissue off her gift. Holding it up to the dim light in the parking lot, I saw that it was a journal with a beautiful gold-embossed cover made to resemble an illuminated book from the middle ages.

I flipped it open, astonished to see that every page was covered with her writing. She'd written an entry in it every day, like a journal, except at the top of each day she'd started out her entry *Dear Adam...*

I laid the book down on the passenger seat, started the car and headed home. I had the distinct feeling that I wouldn't be sleeping much tonight.

41
MIA

THE HOTEL ROOM IN WHICH WE WERE STAYING FOR THE wedding was only a few blocks away from the beach, and I was sharing a room with my mom. When we got back and she came out of the bathroom ready for bed, she paused. I'd set up at the desk with my laptop open and my headset plugged in. I was just about to put Adam's flash drive in the USB port. Mom watched me and I froze.

"You going to be up playing a game tonight?"

I swallowed and held up the flash drive. "Will it bother you? I don't know what this is. Adam gave it to me and asked me to plug it in and look at it tonight."

Her brows rose. "Ah, okay. And, um, how were things with him tonight?"

I looked down and shrugged. It had been cold, distant and awkward. I pretty much figured everyone present could detect that.

Mom sank onto the bed and folded her arms across her chest, watching me. "You need time. And so does he."

I blinked. "That's what these past couple months were all about. Giving us time."

Mom nodded. "You two have been through more than your share of sadness, together and apart."

I fiddled with the edge of the desk for a moment, avoiding her gaze. It was a delicate situation, to address things like this to a person who was about to begin a new life with the person she loved. "Who's to say that the sadness is over with?" I said.

"You never know, do you? Life is so uncertain. You've learned that lesson this year. There's never the perfect time to choose to be with the one you love. It's a commitment that you'll be there in the good times and the bad. That you'll hold each other's hand and do it together."

I nodded. "Thanks, Mom. And I want you to know that I'm really happy for you." No matter how weird it made things with Adam and me. Step-relatives or not. Yeah, it was bizarre, but we were grown-ups and we'd learn to deal with it. I was hopeful, anyway.

Mom went to bed, turning off the lights, and I put on my headset and plugged the flash drive into the correct port. The screen on my laptop went black and then lights began to form, arcs and lines and spirals of every color swirling and merging together to spell my name.

And before I knew it, I was being logged in to Dragon Epoch automatically. But it was unlike anything I'd ever played before.

I was standing on the shore of a beautiful lake, a sunlit mountainscape forming a jagged backdrop. The graphics were new and gorgeous. This was an unreleased part of the game, and I surmised that it would be part of the new expansion that hadn't yet been revealed to players. But as I used the controls to move my character around, words started to appear.

The interface of the game normally did not behave like this, so I deduced that somehow Adam had written a hack of his own game, taking the graphics that had already been produced and putting together a private experience for me alone, taken from bits and pieces of Dragon Epoch. My eyes flew to the words on the screen, snatching up every one as if it were food and I a starving woman dying for sustenance.

I know of no better way to communicate with you right now than through this medium of 0s and 1s that is my second nature. In this environment we met, interacted, and, without even knowing it, fell in love. And like this beautiful place where you are now standing, that love was new, fresh, pristine. An unfamiliar country for both of us. And we were reluctant explorers.

Until we lost our way...

And now the beautiful mountainscape around me began to fade, the screen darkening slowly but steadily until this idyllic landscape became consumed in a dark, murky fog and I couldn't see anything. Except for those words...they kept coming, even across the darkness.

Everything changed the moment we began to make mistakes, the moment we separated, and each mistake we made caused the previous one to look like nothing in comparison. I accept full responsibility for all the wrongs I did.

I am tormented by the way I screwed up then, but I did it because this is the place where you left me, Emilia. Completely, utterly in the dark.

I took a deep breath, continuing to read, bracing myself for more raw honesty. I had the heavy feeling that this wouldn't be easy to read.

"You are in a maze of twisty little passages, all alike."

I blinked, remembering the famous quote from one of the earliest computer role-playing games, written and played by thousands long before I was even born—Zork. The iconic quote accompanied a huge walled maze that stretched out in front of me as far as the eye could see in every direction. I recognized the place from a zone in Dragon Epoch—an impossibly infuriating zone, which featured a constantly shifting maze full of riddles and puzzles that needed to be solved. In that zone, there were no monsters to fight and defeat. The enemy was the mind itself.

The words formed again, scrolling across my screen, each sentence appearing when I took another turn down the impossible maze. My gut twisted with frustration when those turns led to the inevitable dead-ends.

Every turn I took, every choice I made was the wrong one. All I knew was that I wanted you back. I had to have you back, but everything I did pushed you further away. It was as disorienting as this trip through the impossible maze.

I finally judged that I needed to stop moving, because no matter where I turned, the maze became more and more bewildering, closing in on me and making me dizzy.

Can you find your way out? What if the person you loved most in the world was at the end of the maze and you had no idea which way to turn?

Yes, I was angry, resentful. Even after I found out everything. And because you were sick, that anger got buried deep inside and turned into guilt. You were sick and I had no right to be angry with you.

I sat back, sucking in a sob. I didn't like where this was leading. I put my face in my hands and read through cracked fingers, as if watching a horror movie alone in an empty house on a dark night.

The maze faded away and instead, a vapor-like vision formed in front of me. It was hard to see through the haze, but there were clouds. And the words formed again.

That guilt became excuses. I know you wanted us to go back to the way things had been. I know you were as clueless about how to do that as I was. So my anger and resentment and guilt came out as excuses—excuses to keep you at a distance.

The vision of puffy white clouds solidified and words formed across them. *"I'm tired."*

Then they darkened into storm clouds, accompanied by the words, *"I'm worried about her."*

Then rain started to pour down in torrents. *"We need to go slow, wait until she is healthy."*

Then lightning struck, over and over again, blinding me. *"I'm so angry at her, and I hate myself for it because she is sick."*

And then, the visions cleared and I stood in a graveyard. I recognized this place—a point of respawn—one of the first of many graveyards in DE, where your ghost goes after you are killed in the game. And the words, the most heart-wrenching of all: *"What if she dies?"*

But these were illusions I used to hide the real issue. The one I never even realized I had. The most difficult to discover and the most painful to endure...

Suddenly, I was back in the original, beautiful mountainscape, standing on the banks of a rushing river that flowed past my feet. I toggled my view screen to look up in the sky. New words formed.

I wanted to be the man to protect you and comfort you...instead I was the man who had harmed you...

I buried my face in my hands, my vision blurring with tears, my throat stinging with them.

But words were scrolling on the screen again and I quickly blinked, afraid that I would miss them, not sure how to see them again if I didn't capture them now.

I know you wanted a different answer from me that day, when you asked me about how I felt about the baby. I couldn't give it to you then. I still can't give it to you. The only thing I could think about was the risk to you.

I do feel guilty about the lack of feelings because I know it's something you really wanted. And I could only think of you.

But when I think about how close you came to choosing the baby's life over your own, the fear of that moment chokes me. Because it was completely out of my control and I was utterly at your mercy. I hate, more than anything, to feel helpless, but in that moment, I was.

What would have happened if you had chosen to have the baby—and then you'd died? Could I have been anything but a resentful and bitter parent to that child?

I know you suffered, physically, emotionally. I know that for you it was a terrible, traumatic decision. But I'll never be anything but glad you made the choice you did—and that makes me feel guilty, too.

And it makes me question and have doubts about our future. Because I wonder...will we ever be able to have joy that isn't weighted down with loss and guilt and tears?

I toggled my mouse button to pause the playback of the game. Sitting back, I stared at that last bit of text, unable to breathe. Was Adam breaking up with me for good? I put a hand over my mouth to muffle the sobs but found I couldn't. Mom rolled over in her bed and without looking up, she muttered, "Everything okay?"

I cleared my throat. "Yeah...sorry. I'm just fine. I'm, um, I'm going to do the rest of this in the bathroom. I don't want to keep you up."

But she was quickly falling back asleep and I was trying to curb the wild hiccupping of my stomach. I scooped up my laptop and slunk into the bathroom, where I sank down onto the floor and let the tears out—finally.

I bent, reached out and grabbed a massive wad of toilet paper from its holder on the wall, burying my face in it to muffle the sobs now unwilling to stay at the pit of my stomach. I felt like I was coming undone. My world was falling apart.

I didn't know how much more of this I could take. After Adam's bare and frank admission of his internal misery, his feelings of guilt. His helplessness. What could I say or do that could ever repair that? I stared at the laptop again, as if it were a wild animal about to jump up and bite me.

Knives stabbed at my throat, the backs of my eyes. I wiped my snotty face and took a deep breath. I'd come this far on his wild ride.

I might as well see where it led me—where it led *us*.

...And I know that it's important to you to have a child someday. If that's still true when the time comes, then we will find a way. But I was honest when I said that you are enough for me. When I found you, I found what I had been looking for without even knowing it.

Because my life without you...?

And the river, the mountains, the trees, the deep blue sky all faded and I was now in the middle of a barren, gray desert. The landscape was dotted with cactus plants, and sand stretched as far as the eye could see. A lone, arid wind howled through the bushes, blowing tumbleweeds under a blazing, relentless sun. I could almost feel the waves of heat rising off the sand.

It would be emptier, more desolate than this place.

I need you. I've always needed you. But that means nothing if you won't let me in.

The air rushed out of me with a rattle and a hiss, as if I'd been punched in the stomach. I was shaking, but I wasn't cold. My mouth was dry, but I wasn't scared.

And I couldn't look away. Because the desert was fading again and now I was inside a jail cell, a dark prison. Jagged, rough stone walls rose above me in every direction, with only one wall of bars on one side. I used the controls to turn myself around, this way and that. Only on the third try did I notice a small figure in the corner. I recognized her immediately from the latest portion of the secret quest that we had worked on for months.

This was the lost Elvish princess from Dragon Epoch, the one who was the object of the secret quest. She was thin, half-starved, dressed in rags, her face full of sorrow. Four magical bonds held her down, one on each of her arms and legs. She looked up at me with pleading eyes full of misery.

The cell dissolved and I was now in a room with two doors. Two choices.

Which one will you choose? If we are going to be together, we both have to pick the same one, make the same choice. We have to decide, in spite of all that has gone on between us in the past, in spite of how hard it gets, that our love is tougher than any of the obstacles that have almost impeded it.

Everything faded to black and there was nothing but an old-style green cursor, blinking against the black background with just one symbol at the prompt. A question mark.

I typed, wondering where it would lead. Would it send him a text or some other type of alert? Would it trigger some other crazy effect in this strange little game he had led me through?

With a deep breath, I tapped out the words.

I choose us. Forever.

My computer was at the desktop screen again. I waited, not really knowing where my message had gone or if I'd get a response. I thought through the strange, fantastic journey I'd just experienced, particularly moved by that image of the princess, pinned down by her bonds, looking up at me with misery in her brilliant green eyes. She was just like me—in a prison of her own making.

My eyes were half-closed in reverie when suddenly they flew open and I sat up straight with shock at that realization. The princess was just like me!

"Four bonds. Four allies," I muttered to myself, furiously typing commands into my computer. My heart was racing. Before I'd left for

Anza, we'd been stuck at what I was certain was the final step of the secret quest for weeks.

I punched in the commands to log in to the game and it came to the login screen, flashing the fancy intro graphics and video. In a frenzy, I hit the escape button to skip all that and selected my character from the screen.

The last time I'd logged in to the game with my friends, we'd made it to just outside the jail cell. We could see the princess inside, and I'd wondered at the time why she had four bonds holding her down while still locked inside a cell.

Eloisa has entered the world of Yondareth

My character was in the same location as when I'd last logged out, standing at the bars of the jail cell. In the past, our group had tried breaking into the cell with the help of the allies we'd gathered, but every time we'd done that, huge swarms of trolls had come into the room, overwhelming us in seconds. After countless tries at this, we'd deduced that the way to help the princess did not involve breaking down the doorway. But after that, we'd been completely stuck. In the meantime, I'd left for Anza and sworn off the game for a while.

I moved Eloisa forward to speak to the princess once again to see if I'd remembered her words correctly from the last time I'd spoken to her. She always said the same thing and only that one thing when she was hailed.

Eloisa says, "Hail, Princess Alloreah'ala."
Princess Alloreah'ala says, "I am bound by despair."

Four bonds. Four allies. Despair. The allies had to help the princess free herself. Somehow I had to convince them to do it.

After we had discovered that Sergeant GriffonShield had been waiting for us to ask him for help and he'd told us to gather his allies, we'd gathered the four closest allies to the princess and brought them with us.

I approached the princess's trusted maidservant, Maiden Liliannl'a.

Eloisa says, "Hail, Maiden Liliannl a."
Maiden Liliannl'a says, "What must I do?"
Eloisa says, "Use your love to free the princess from despair."
Maiden Liliannl'a says, "I will try."

Then, I watched as the maidservant approached her princess, curtsied and said, "My dearest princess. I love you and I wish to use my love to set you free."

I held my breath, waiting for something to happen.

Suddenly, the bond holding down her right foot glowed golden and vanished.

Holy. Shit.

The breath rushed out of me. I almost hollered in victory until I remembered that it was three in the morning and Mom was asleep on the other side of the wall.

I sucked in a quick breath, feeling giddy with excitement. I hoped that my group wouldn't hate me for doing this without them, but I couldn't wake them up at this hour. I hoped they'd understand why I had to have this finished before I saw Adam again.

I approached the three other allies, all in turn. First the bodyguard, who did the exact same thing the Maiden had done and freed her other leg. Then, the princess's best friend. She freed the princess's left arm.

The last one I approached was the princess's lost love—General SylvenWood, the broken-down man from the very first quest given in the game. He was the non-player character who I had figured out last year was the one who triggered the secret quest.

When I asked him to do the same thing, to use his love to free the princess from despair, he turned to me with sad eyes.

General SylvenWood says, "Alas, Eloisa, we once had a great love. But I made some terrible mistakes and so did she. Our love was not enough to save us from the heartache that life put in our path. We separated and the great evil used this separation to spirit my love away from me. Since she left, I am a broken man, a prisoner of my own despair."

Eloisa says, "Your love will set her free."

General SylvenWood hangs his head and sighs.

General SylvenWood says, "I will try."

The General approached the cell and, in similar words, professed his love. But instead of the bond glowing and breaking immediately, the princess looked up at him and said, "SylvenWood, my one true love. I thought you had abandoned me. All these years, I'd never forgotten you. But I thought you had forgotten me."

The general held his hands forward, as if pleading with her. "My one true love. I've suffered every day that you've been away from me. I never abandoned you. I just had no idea how to help you. I love you with all my heart."

Suddenly, the last bond dissipated and the princess weakly stood. With each movement, she appeared stronger, more powerful, until she made her way to the cell door and, with her own powerful magic, sent it flying open.

The allies gathered around her, cheering, hugging and kissing her. But as if remembering by happenstance, the princess turned and approached me.

Princess Alloreah'ala says, "Hail, Eloisa."
Eloisa curtsies.
Princess Alloreah'ala says, "Thank you for gathering my allies. Thank you for finding my true love. You will be rewarded for your kindness. And you will find that your one true love is waiting for you to find him, too, Emilia."

With a gasp, I fell back against the door of the bathroom, stunned. Had he written this all for me?

42
ADAM

I T WAS ALMOST MIDNIGHT WHEN I FELL BACK AGAINST THE
pillow of my bed and opened Emilia's journal to read what she
had written to me. I had to admit, I was both curious and a little
scared of what I'd see. And I also wondered if, at this very moment,
she was reading the messages I'd left for her...

Dear Adam,

*This evening, I am furious with you. I won't lie. I write this with a hand
that's shaking with rage and tears of anger in my eyes. Because today you
sent me away. You gave up. And let me tell you that makes me so pissed off
at you right now. Was this just your way of getting back at me for what I
did to you last year? Because I've been in a hell of my own making and you
didn't need to create a new one for me...*

I leaned forward, tensing. This didn't look good. I flipped through
a few pages idly, hoping the entire thing wasn't full of the same hurt
and anger. I didn't know how I could bring myself to read that. With

no small fear, I flipped back to that first page and forced myself to read every word she had written. Wasn't this what I'd wanted—what we'd both wanted? Open, honest communication?

I grabbed my reading glasses off the nightstand because I felt a headache coming on, and I'd taken to using the damn things in the hopes that they'd ward off the headaches. But I had a feeling that the real pain that would come from reading these pages wouldn't be in my head.

...How can I not feel guilty for what I did? Every breath I take, every day that I live comes from the lifetime that I stole from the person our child would have been. And I had no choice but to do it. My choice was robbed from me.

I closed my eyes and rubbed them through the lids with my thumb and forefinger. With a shaky breath, I willed myself to keep reading.

...Tonight, as I was undressing for bed, I took time to examine the scars and tattoo marks on my body. I studied them as if looking at them for the first time, through your eyes. They repulse me, but not for vain reasons. Not just for the permanent mark of imperfection, but because of what they represent. It's not just the scar on my flesh but a reminder of the way I wounded us. And like the one on my body, I'm reminded that that wound will never go away. I did this. I broke us...

...Part of me fears—no, scratch that—most of me fears that one day, when it becomes important to you, when you realize that I may not be able to give you a child, I'll lose you.

Dear Adam,

You once told me to put the burden on your shoulders. But it never occurred to me that you had taken all that on—and more. And in so doing, it had become an impossibly heavy load. How can one couple—even with all the love in the world—survive such a thing? We are broken, it's true, and not all that's broken can be fixed...

Dear Adam,

Today I had a long talk with Heath in the barn. He wanted to know what was going on with you and me. And, really, since I'd dragged him into this, kicking and screaming, I felt I owed him an explanation. So there I was, trying to explain, my mouth opening and closing like a fish. I had no explanation. We did things wrong. We made mistakes. Big mistakes. I did. And you did. We did this. And I lie here tonight wondering if we can ever get past this. Do you want to?

...And then I started to think about that goddamn bucket list and that night I forced you to sit down and write it when you were worried out of your mind about me. But you did—you wrote down everything I asked you to write down. I don't remember a thing about that, but I can't stop thinking about how unfair that was...

...And as I sit here making this new list, the thing that overwhelms me is the desire to do it all with you. Because if it's not with you, then it's not worth doing. What do you think? Anything to add?

My New Bucket List
- *Find something to laugh at, every day*
- *Remember all the things I'm thankful for every day*
- *Remember all the people I love*

- *Remember all the people who love me*
- *Know in my heart that I can't do this alone*

Dear Adam,

Tonight I'm missing you so badly that I almost called you on the phone, even if it meant just listening to your voicemail message. God, it hurts so bad that I ache with it. I just need to hear your voice. I just want to feel your arms around me. So tight. Tight, tight hugs.

...When I first met you, you intimidated the hell out of me. I didn't know what to make of you, but you fascinated me anyway. You saw things. You knew things. You noticed and you cared. And I couldn't stop thinking about you, wanting to know more. Everything was so thrilling and new then. The rush of fresh, new love. It was like a drug that I was addicted to.

...But that doesn't hold a candle to what I feel now. I still think about you. Every day. I wonder what you are doing. I wonder if you have kicked all your blankets off your side of the bed again and woken up cold. I wonder if you are so absorbed in work that you forgot to eat dinner again. I worry that your headaches might be coming back or that you fell asleep with your face on your laptop again. I look up at the moon every night—and the stars. And I wonder if you are looking up at them, too.

Dear Adam,

In less than two days, I'll be looking into your eyes again and I write this with a shaky hand, wondering what I'll see there—will those beautiful dark eyes be windows, or mirrors, or doors locked and shut tight to me?

I'm scared. I looked up at the sky tonight and I saw a shooting star cross over the constellation of Draco. That's a sign, right? A good sign? I made a wish, but of course I can't tell you what it is. But that wish is my hope. All my hope wrapped up in that one little instant of burning meteorite. It reminded me of this quote:

"The skies are painted with unnumbered sparks. They are all fire and every one doth shine."
–Julius Caesar, Act 3, Scene 1
(Don't be too impressed. I had to Google that...)

Those sparks are like my hope right now. Unnumbered. All fire. And I pray that you still have hope, too.

I read for hours, unable to put it down, and when I finished, I flipped back through the pages—back through her sketch recreating the shooting star through the constellation of Draco. Back through collages, articles printed out and glued into the pages, her list of quotes from our favorite movies and TV shows. Back to her new bucket list.

And then back to the last few lines of the last entry, written just hours before she'd wrapped up the journal and handed it to me.

...And so I have forgiven myself for what I once believed was unforgivable, but I give myself permission to be sad about that loss sometimes...

I closed my eyes and slept. And for the first time, I didn't dream of her. Or at least I didn't remember it if I did. She was no longer a ghost, a phantom of guilt that tormented my conscience. She was flesh and blood and real. And she was my future.

In the morning, when I woke up and checked my phone, I found a text message waiting for me...a special alert I'd set up from inside the game. Four simple words and I knew who they were from.

I choose us. Forever.

***

Just before sunset by the peaceful rocks overlooking the tide pools at historical Crystal Cove Beach, my Uncle Peter married Emilia's mom, Kim. They held hands and said informal vows to each other, but the ceremony only lasted minutes. We quickly congratulated them and sent them off to spend their first evening alone as a married couple.

But all through that ceremony, I could hardly concentrate on my uncle's happy turn of events because I couldn't take my eyes off the beautiful woman standing at the bride's shoulder. The wind ruffled her short, dark hair. Her skin glowed, radiant in the golden sunlight. She wouldn't stop smiling, and in that lace-edged white sundress, she looked like an angel.

But she wasn't a mere angel. Vibrant, full of life and strength from all that she'd overcome. She was a goddess.

And I do believe that she was just as unfocused on the wedding as I was, because she held the bride's tiny bouquet, smelled it often and stole glances at me like a shy schoolgirl in the back of class.

I'm sure she was just as overjoyed about her mom's happiness as I was for Peter's, but it was hard to concentrate on them when we'd had no chance whatsoever to talk. The two of us. Alone. And we had so many important things to say.

43
MIA

I LINGERED ON THE ROCKS AFTER THAT SHORT, HUMBLE ceremony. The family had spent time together on the beach and they were now following the happy couple back to the parking lot. But, having hugged, kissed and congratulated my mom already, I stayed behind and stooped, looking into the tidal pools at the anemones and hermit crabs, relishing a little quiet time to myself and hoping that Adam would wander back to talk to me.

I didn't have to hope it because I soon became aware that he'd never moved more than a few feet from me. He stood nearby, his hands in his pockets, looking out over the ocean and hovering near me like a sentry. I glanced up at him, squinting against the dying sun. "Hey."

He pulled his eyes away and looked at me, smiling. "Hey, cousin."

I made a face. "Do not *ever* call me that again. That is beyond gross."

He chuckled, taking a few steps toward me until he was standing beside me. I stood and climbed on top of the group of rocks next to us. "Someone said they saw a pod of whales swimming around out there earlier. I've been looking and looking and haven't seen anything."

He stepped up on the rock beside me, his eyes scanning out over the ocean. We were silent and though I was still looking for those whales, every inch of my body was aware of how close his body was to me. Just inches away, but it felt like miles. Like every cell in mine was calling out to every cell in his. My throat was tight and I forced myself to swallow.

"There!" I said, throwing out my hand wildly to indicate where I'd seen the spout from a blowhole. In my excitement, I'd thrown myself off-balance. He reached out to grab my shoulders, steadying me. His hands felt like heavy weights on me. Grounding me, electrifying me.

I hadn't felt his touch in so, so long and now his warm hands were on my bare shoulders. I shook slightly with excitement, with suppressed energy. I'd slept very little last night, winding through the puzzles of the game—solving the quest he'd rewritten for me. It had been like traveling through a twisting maze and finding his unguarded heart at the center.

In spite of all this running through my mind, I kept my eyes on the spot where I'd seen the spout and another one went up just after that. But he didn't look up at that one when I pointed it out. Instead, he kept his eyes on me. I could feel the weight of them, as heavy as his hands. And now his thumbs moved across my skin and my mouth went dry and I barely contained the whimper in my throat.

His head dipped and his mouth alighted on the juncture of my neck and shoulder. Heat shot through me and I did moan a little then, responding immediately. He didn't pull his mouth away, just joined that delicious touch with his tongue, trailing along the back of my neck and shoulder, his hands cupping my shoulders a little bit tighter. My eyes shut tightly and my left hand went to his hair, twining my fingers in it, pressing his head against me. I never wanted him to pull away.

My skin was tingling, sensitive, almost so much so that everything was near painful. Every time his lips moved across my skin, I had to fight to keep from jumping. I turned my head and he pulled his mouth away. We stared into each other's eyes for long moments. His hands slipped from my shoulders to my waist and then tightened his hold, encircling his arms around me. I fell against him with a sigh and his mouth landed on mine.

I opened my mouth to him but didn't wait for his tongue to enter. Instead, I pressed mine forward, exploring him. He sucked in a breath, probably surprised by my boldness. I turned in his arms and pressed my chest against his, fixing my hands around his neck. The kiss deepened and I was caught up, swirling as everything turned—like we were the axis of a world all our own and it revolved around us.

They say love makes the world go round, and that tiny world we had formed went around us and at our center, at that axis—*love*. My heart pressed against his. The world dimmed as the sun sank below the horizon, but neither of us seemed aware. The ocean continued to pound its endless rhythm, but it was nothing compared to our hearts thumping against each other.

When he pulled his mouth away, that dreamlike reality we'd formed around us continued. He pressed his forehead to mine and we stared into each other's eyes. My hands were on his cheeks, my thumbs caressing his exquisite jaw. He was even more beautiful in the violet light of dusk than he was in daylight, if that were possible.

"Emilia," he whispered, his eyes closing, and then he tucked me under his chin as he pulled me closer to him. "I missed you."

Missing him seemed such a weak way to say what I'd been doing for the past two months. Existing without him had made me feel lacking, incomplete, a whole huge part of me gone.

"I missed you, too—the way an ionized atom misses its last electron," I said with a laugh on my lips.

"You are such a nerd," he laughed, kissing my nose. "But that's the most romantic thing anyone's ever said to me."

Two atoms, sharing a covalent bond, melded together, forming a molecule—something better than each of the parts separately. And I couldn't help but think that that was like us. Separate, we were special, unique people; together, we formed something rare and precious and greater than our separate selves.

"So, I might have checked at the reservation desk early this morning and rented one of the cottages for the night...if you feel like spending the night here at the beach," he said.

I pulled my head away and glanced back at the line of cottages all along the shore. They were historic landmarks, these cottages, all here since the Depression era and inhabited by beach dwellers until the previous decade, when the state had retaken the homes, refitted them, and rented them out nightly to the public.

I nodded enthusiastically. Spend the night in one of these adorable cottages with Adam? Yes, please.

"Your bag is in your car?"

"Yeah. I was going to go back to the hotel tonight if—if you didn't want me to stay over with you."

He frowned for a minute, looking at me like I was crazy, then reached into his pocket and pulled out a key on a big keychain. "I rented the white one on the end." He pointed. "Give me the keys to the car and I'll go get your stuff."

We traded keys and he kissed me again before heading up the hill to the parking lot.

44
ADAM

I JOGGED UP THAT HILL AS QUICKLY AS I COULD ONCE I LEFT THE sand. The parking lot was a ways away, but I hoped that would give Emilia some time to settle in at the cottage while I grabbed her stuff. I was still pretty high from holding her on the beach, kissing her, feeling her body fall against me.

She felt more solid now...stronger. More like her old self but with essential changes that only made her more beautiful, mature, amazing. Or maybe she'd just always been that way and my time away from her had made me appreciate those things in her even more.

When I hit the parking lot, I saw that some of the wedding guests were still hanging out. The bride and groom had gone, but Heath stood at his car, leaning up against it and talking to Connor. When he saw me, he immediately straightened, glancing behind me. He'd been waiting to see if Emilia was okay.

"Hey, man," I said when he got closer.

"She's okay? Where's she at?"

I smiled. "She's okay. She's coming home with me."

Heath grinned. "Good. That's great to hear."

I slapped my hand on his shoulder. "I know we've both been a pain in your ass for the last few months. But thanks for being a great friend."

Heath looked a little taken aback. "No sweat, man."

"Here. I want you to have something." I reached into my pocket and held out my hand, pressing the keys into his.

He opened his hand, not understanding at first. These were the spare keys to the Porsche.

"Uh. Dude, you must be high," he said with a laugh and then looked up into my face and saw that I was dead serious. "For real?" His jaw dropped.

"Yeah. Drop it by my service guy whenever you need it taken care of. I'll cover it. But you better take good care of it or I'll kick your ass."

He held his hand out to me. "Adam, I can't take this. That car is your most prized possession."

I shook my head. "I love the car, not gonna lie. But you took good care of her when I couldn't...and I love her a whole hell of a lot more than that car. Thank you."

Heath paused for a moment, a confused frown transforming slowly into a goofy grin. "Well, then. *You* better take good care of *her*. Or I'll kick your ass."

I laughed. "I have no doubt about that."

Giving Connor a wave, I walked over to the Tesla that Emilia had been using for the last few months and opened it up to get her things before turning and walking back down the hill.

45
MIA

I TRUDGED ACROSS THE SAND AND LET MYSELF INTO THE cottage. It wasn't the luxury accommodations we'd had in Paris, but the quaintness of the place—and its stellar location—was not lost on me. I took a minute to explore my simple surroundings. There was a bedroom with a double bed and a loft up above. The kitchen had a microwave and a fridge and one big old wood-burning stove that no longer functioned and had been apparently included for ambiance. The floors were simple beam wood. And the décor was beach-themed, complete with a painting incorporating bits of shimmering beach glass.

When Adam returned from the hike to the parking lot and back, my bag slung over his muscular arm, I was lying on the bed, paging through the picture book that had been sitting on the coffee table. It recounted a complete history of the Crystal Cove area from prehistoric times until the present. "Did you know that they used one of these cottages for a Japanese language school during the 1920s?"

He dumped my bag on the small bench at the end of the bed and watched me, smiling. "Really? Fascinating." But I could tell what fascinated him was not the information I was giving him but what he saw on the bed before him. I smiled knowingly. His eyes had that unmistakable glow in them—that smolder. Swallowing, I batted my eyelashes at him.

I tapped on the cover of the book. "I can read you some more of this, if you like."

He smiled, that dimple forming at the side of his mouth again. He was so good-looking it stole my breath. He reached up and loosened his tie without taking his eyes off of me. I had already kicked off my shoes, but I closed the book and set it on the floor beside the bed. I leaned back and patted the bed beside me as he was unbuttoning the cuffs of his dress shirt.

"As you wish," he said with a laugh, coming around to lie beside me. We reached for each other at the same time, our noses colliding in our haste to kiss each other again. We both leaned back, laughing.

I rubbed my nose. "Och. It's just a flesh wound," I quoted from one of our favorites, *Monty Python and the Holy Grail.*

"She turned me into a newt," he said in his best imitation of John Cleese, the actor from that same movie.

"A newt?"

He smiled. "I got better."

I laughed. "Come here, you hot geek god, you."

He kissed me and pulled back. "Mmm. Yep, you really are a witch. And you've completely beguiled me. Toad curse and all."

"Did you turn into a toad while I was gone?"

"I was as miserable as a toad without you."

I stared for a moment and then started laughing so hard I snorted. "That is so completely non-sexy."

"Unlike that snort. That snort right there is utterly sexy."

I stuck my tongue out at him and he wrapped his arm around my waist, pulling me up against him. I put my hand on his chest, splayed out my fingers across the solid muscle. "Speaking of utterly sexy..." I said, and my hand flew up and quickly unbuttoned half the buttons. "Oops. Your shirt fell open."

He leaned down and captured my lips with his, his mouth sealing over mine with more insistence, more hunger than before. My heartbeat was a footrace inside my chest, galloping in turns and stumbling in others.

"Oops," he murmured in between urgent follow-ups. "My mouth fell on yours."

"Wow, we are so clumsy," I breathed against his lips.

He continued to kiss me, pressing my head back against the pillow. His hand cupped my jaw before his finger traced its way back to my ear and then down along the side of my throat. He drew the chain of my necklace aside, the compass flopping on the bed beside my neck. His touch was scalding hot and ice cold at the same time. I sucked in a breath.

His finger trailed across my collarbone and landed on the top button of my dress. Slowly, our mouths separated and he stared into my eyes. My breath faltered as he slipped the button through the buttonhole. I was at once mesmerized by his touch and utterly afraid for him to see what was underneath. And he clearly knew that. Pulling back and propping himself up on one elbow, he didn't stop. His finger slid down slowly across my skin to the second button. Before I could react or protest, that one slipped open as well.

But he wasn't looking at what he was doing. Instead, his eyes were fixed on mine. In minutes, the dress was unbuttoned past my waist. Adam pressed his finger against the notch at the base of my neck and slowly trailed it down across my chest, over my bra, between my breasts and down my stomach, until it landed at my navel. There, he traced a circle around it and a fire ignited in my belly, my body burning for his. A long breath of air hissed between my teeth as I concentrated on that one, simple touch.

His hand came up again to my shoulder. And in spite of the burning arousal, cold fear gripped my throat as he slowly slipped the strap of my sundress—*and* my bra—off of my shoulder. My breathing froze and I put my hand over his, stopping him before he brought the straps low enough to expose my scars.

He froze and our gazes held for endless minutes. I was sure he could see the fear, the uncertainty in mine. I saw the determined passion in his. Slowly, gently, he slipped his hand out from under mine, took my wrist and pulled my hand away from where I had stopped him. I didn't resist as he brought my hand down to my side, slipping it under my hips and pinning it there so I wouldn't be tempted to use it again to stop him.

My heartbeat was icy in my throat as his hand returned to what it had been doing. His other hand, as a precaution, gripped my free hand inside of it. All I could do was stare into those dark eyes, my breath coming faster as he succeeded in slipping the straps over my left arm. He pulled that side of my bra down and I was completely exposed to him. Hot shame bathed my face, but Adam hadn't looked there. He was still studying my face, holding my eyes with his dark ones. Then he shifted so that his leg pinned mine down, and with another tug on the other half of my bra, I was naked from the waist up.

He lowered his eyes and looked at me, and part of me wanted to curl up and die. Despite having gained back a bit of the weight I'd lost during chemo, I was still too thin. My breasts, as a result, were smaller than before, and the left one was still maimed and ugly, the angry red scars jagging over the skin, black dots tattooed across it. Slowly, as if afraid I might bolt even though I was held down, he raised his hand and with a butterfly-light touch, he traced his fingers over the raised scar. I shivered under him.

He shushed me, looking into my eyes again though I avoided his gaze. "Emilia. Look at me." And I did. I saw sincerity and admiration in his eyes. "You are beautiful. And these," he said, tracing the scars again with more pressure than before, "are your strength."

I blinked, my eyes stinging. I wanted him to touch me again. And he did. My breath shivered in my chest. He palmed my scarred breast, running a progressively firmer touch over it until my nipple puckered to a point, erect and begging for his attention. He lowered his mouth and kissed it ever so lightly.

I gasped and arched my back to meet him. He kissed it again, a light peck. And again, a little harder. Then his mouth opened and his tongue tasted, ever so slightly. And again, his tongue ran over and around my nipple until I was burning and writhing underneath him, unable to get enough of the feel of his mouth. He suckled and pulled, tasting and tugging until a small sob escaped the back of my throat. The first time his teeth touched my nipple, I jumped as if jolted with electricity. My hand, which had been wedged underneath me, pulled free and came up to weave my fingers in his thick hair, holding him to my attention-starved breast.

He turned and, while thumbing my once-injured breast, put his mouth to the task of similarly treating my healthy one. Time stretched—maybe a half hour or more, I wasn't keeping track—and he did nothing but lavish my chest with his careful, passionate attention. I was stunned to realize how close I was to climax just from what he was doing to my breasts.

He noticed, too. His hand slipped from my breast, across my stomach and into my underwear. His mouth was still doing indescribably wonderful things to my breast as his fingers found the swollen bundle of nerves and rubbed against it in gentle circles. I closed my eyes and arched to him, my entire being inflamed with his touch. I was so close...

He removed his head from my breast and pulled back. He pulled my hands out of his hair with his one free hand. "Touch them," he whispered, those glowing eyes holding mine captive. I hesitated and he stopped rubbing against my clitoris. I almost whimpered with the loss. "I want to watch you touch them. I want you to know what I already know—how hot, how beautiful your body is."

I trembled under him as I slowly put my own fingertips to my erect nipples, tugging at them lightly, crying out as his hand started moving across my sex again.

"You are so beautiful," he repeated over and over again as he watched me finger my own nipples. I closed my eyes tightly and gasped as he brought me to the edge, slowed and stopped again. I almost screamed in frustration.

"Open your eyes."

And I did.

Our eyes locked and his weren't mirrors, or doors, but corridors, leading deep inside. I gasped and he kissed my lips as he circled his hand over my sex. I pinched my own nipples and then arched my back as everything tightened inside of me.

He watched as he took me up and over the edge. I screamed his name and he gasped against my mouth, his lips pulling gently at mine. It had been a long time since I'd had an orgasm that pleasurable, that intense. My eyes rolled back as I continued to convulse with pleasure, continued to raggedly call his name. His hands tightened on me and I felt as if those ripples of ecstasy would go on forever.

I came down from that, my body burning and trembling with the intensity of my climax, but he didn't stop. "I'm going to make you come again," he uttered fiercely, his mouth now against my neck.

But I pulled myself away from him, trying to close my legs. "I want you inside me when I come again."

I thought he might object to that, but he didn't. He pulled his hand out of my underwear and quickly pulled my dress, bra and underwear off of me. I was no longer self-conscious about being naked in front of him and was anxious to see him naked, too. I unbuttoned the rest of his shirt and pulled off his undershirt while he unzipped his trousers. Soon, he was only in his tented boxer briefs. Before pulling them off, he reached into the pocket of his discarded pants and extracted a foil-wrapped condom.

He pulled off his underwear and rolled me onto my back. I could tell by the strained rigidity of his handsome features that he wasn't playing around anymore.

I swallowed as he slowly parted my legs, settling between them before rearing up to slide the condom on with one hand. I sat up on my elbows and watched him, though it only took seconds. He was well practiced at it, it seemed.

I hoped he wouldn't cut this short, like the other times. Would we stop now? Would that same fear come back?

I held my breath as if somehow breathing would break the spell of the moment. My eyes met his ferocious gaze and he lay back down against me, pushing me gently off my elbows so I was flat underneath him. His body hovered over mine, burning me with his heat. His erection pressed against me as he kissed me again—his tongue and lips and teeth claiming my mouth, forcing it open under him and owning every inch of it. There was hardly time for a breath before he was nudging his cock against me, pushing his way inside.

He gave a more insistent push of his hips until our pelvises rested flush against each other. I gasped at the familiar, wonderful feeling of him filling me up. I took a deep breath and he pulled his mouth away from mine to look into my eyes, his breath heavy, his eyes drunk with desire. "I almost forgot how fucking good you feel," he muttered hoarsely. Pressing his damp forehead against mine, he twitched his hips, sliding out of me before pushing home again. I moaned.

"I never forgot how fucking good *you* feel," I murmured. "I've wanted you inside of me every day for months."

He gasped but he never broke the rhythm. I wondered, briefly, if sex with the condom wouldn't feel as pleasurable for him as it had before, but my mind did not linger on that long because it was more than clear that he was enjoying himself. Soon he was reared up on his arms, my long legs draped over his shoulders, his eyes half-closed, on his own way to ecstasy as he pushed relentlessly inside of me and then pulled out again in a sharp, short rhythm.

He stopped again, pulling me up against him and leaning back so that we were both sitting up. He laid my thighs over his and we faced each other. He entered me again with a hoarse groan. As we moved against each other, his strong arms pinned my chest against his and he kissed my face—my forehead, my temples, my cheeks, everywhere.

Then his mouth was on my mouth, his tongue darting in and out with the same timed, relentless rhythm of our bodies moving against each other.

And my whole existence, for those moments, became Adam. Adam's smell, Adam's sweat mingling with mine, Adam's hot breath on my skin, Adam's body moving against me, Adam's hands gripping me, Adam's tongue in my mouth. Adam's cock sliding inside of me, claiming me. *Yes.* I was forever his.

His breathing grew more ragged as, his hands fixed to my hips, he dragged my pelvis over his, faster and faster until once again I was coming, my world shattering around me, my whole body convulsing. I threw my head back, shouting in ecstasy, but he didn't stop, sliding me over him again and again. With one last deep push, he stiffened against me, holding me still. And I felt his orgasm pulse through me as if I was coming again. He shuddered and he pressed his forehead to mine. Holding his breath we froze in time—one body, one soul.

With a gasp, he fell back against the mattress, staring up at me with sated eyes.

In that moment, our bodies still joined, my hands splayed across his cut, damp chest, I felt powerful, feminine, sexy. The most desired woman in the world. Adam had done that. And soon the tears were up and over their usual careful barriers, spilling out from my lower lids and down my cheeks.

He frowned, his dark brows furrowing. He reached up, tracing a thumb down the path of my tears. "What's wrong, sweet Mia?"

I shook my head, unable to speak. I leaned down and kissed his cheek, his neck, laid my cheek against his shoulder. "Nothing's wrong. I'm just happy. So, so happy."

His arms tightened around me and we lay like that, saying nothing, just enjoying each other, our naked bodies pressed to each other.

I wished we could just spend the rest of our lives like this. Never feeling anything but this protective bubble of love around us to keep life's sadness and hurt at bay.

"This feels so good. I could lay like this for a week," he murmured, his words paralleling my thoughts.

"I could be your blanket," I said.

"That sounds perfect. I could be yours sometimes, too."

"Mmm. Do you think that people will bring us food if we call them and tell them to?"

He brushed his fingers along my damp back, tracing my spine. He turned his head and put his nose in my hair, inhaling. "You are one amazing, intoxicating woman, Emilia Strong."

"You are one heart-stoppingly wonderful man, Adam Drake. And you keep me up all night, either with mind-blowing sex or your damn game."

"What?" he said, sounding surprised.

"After I went through your program on the flash drive, I figured out how to solve the quest."

His hand on my back stilled. "You solved it?"

I looked up at him and he was smiling. "Yes...the princess was bound by her own despair, and her allies had to use their love to help her set herself free. And then the princess gave me some advice. She told me to go out and find my true love because he was waiting for me."

Adam laced his fingers around mine. "Well, the princess was right, then, wasn't she? Your true love has been waiting for you all his life. And he sure is glad you've finally made it."

I sobered for a minute, then angled my head to look up into his face. "Adam...are we going to be okay? I mean, it's been months and we couldn't talk to each other and I know we've learned a lot about ourselves, but...what about us as a couple?"

His hand tightened around mine. "Well, we have learned a lot in the past couple months, but I think the biggest thing *I've* learned, anyway, is that this is a work in progress—that we keep working on it and we don't let things build up and fester. That we can't be afraid to talk about it."

"And we don't give up—even when things look impossible."

He let out a long breath. "Well, this certainly felt impossible not too long ago. And I'm sure it won't be easy. But it sure as hell is worth it."

We dressed and had a late dinner at the Beachcomber restaurant, set right in the inlet amongst the cottages and illuminated with tiny white lights. We were like new lovebirds, holding hands over the table while we talked about trivial stuff. Adam filled me in on the goings-on among our mutual friends while I'd been up in Anza. He did most of the talking. I listened, nodded and kept my new little exciting secret to myself for a few minutes longer.

After coffee, I mentioned that I'd like to go for a moonlit walk along the beach, and I thought I'd have to be more persuasive but he actually brightened. After paying the check, we walked out to where the waves were breaking against the shore, where the sand was packed tighter now that the tide was low and an almost full silvery moon hung overhead, casting an otherworldly glow over the sand and water.

When we got as far as the tide pools—not far from the spot where our relatives had married each other earlier that day—he turned to me. "We still have a lot to talk about, you know. I didn't want to be the downer to bring all that up, but..."

I stopped, nodding. "I know. I agree." He pulled me into a hug and I kissed his cheek. "But first I have something to ask you."

"Sure. Go ahead," he said.

"Well, it has to do with respawns."

"Huh?"

I cleared my throat. "A do-over. My do-over."

He still clearly did not understand. "Umm."

Gathering my courage, I swallowed my fear, took both of his hands inside mine and sank down on the sand in front of him.

He laughed for a moment, not understanding, and then his laughter died out when I looked up into his eyes and, squeezing his hands, I asked, "Adam Drake...I love you more than anything. Let me be by your side until the very end, whenever that may be. Will you make me your wife?"

He froze, his features sobering. I held my breath. I couldn't tell what was going on in his mind. And I guess that was what this question was all about. I trembled, cold fear seizing me, frightened beyond all thought that his answer would be "no".

46
ADAM

EMILIA HAD PRESSED SOMETHING INTO MY HAND. I TORE MY eyes away from hers to open it and look inside. In the dim moonlight, it shone like a tiny star itself and, without getting a really close look at it, I knew exactly what it was. I'd tried to slip a ring like this on her finger last fall.

My jaw tightened. "Stand up, Emilia."

She didn't say anything, but her eyes skittered away from mine, her features clouding. I tugged on her arms, and with a frown she slowly got to her feet, squaring her shoulders. We stood face to face, and I stared into her beautiful brown eyes. She was biting her lip, convinced that I'd rejected her.

"Why are you doing this? Why are you thinking of marriage now?"

Her brows drew together. "Because I know what I want and I don't want to wait, and if I've learned anything this year it's that I'm not going to defer my own happiness."

I nodded, relieved that she wasn't doing this out of a sense of obligation to make things up to me for last year. I took the ring out of the palm of my hand, took her left hand in mine and then dropped to my knee. She gasped and I had to hold on to her hand or she would have pulled it away in shock.

"No, keep it there," I said. Finding the correct finger, I slipped the ring on, pushing it past her knuckle. It was a perfect fit. It was, indeed, the exact same ring that I'd bought for her. She'd told me she'd sold it, but here it was, shining at me from the fourth finger on her left hand.

"Emilia Kimberly Strong, will you do me the honor of allowing me to become your husband?"

She stood absolutely still, and I realized I'd been too scared to look into her face as I asked it. And, God, wouldn't it be extra humiliating to have done this twice and get the same silence for an answer both times?

I raised my eyes to hers and saw that she was crying, shining tears trailing down her cheeks. She sank onto the sand before me and we were now at eye level. I wiped her tears away with my hand and she smiled, watching me. "I've never been more sure of anything before— ever. I love you. One thing I've learned in this last year is that this life can really be tough. It can throw such utter shit at a person. It can take you for an utter fool. And I've tried to be strong, but the thing I've learned above all else is that I can't do this alone. And I can't do it with anyone else but you...please."

But I only laughed at her. "I asked you, silly. But I'll take that as a 'yes'?"

She laughed and pressed her forehead to mine. "Yes. That's a big, big yes."

I pulled her into my arms and kissed her, holding her tight against me. Her heart thrummed against my chest and her arms locked around my neck. A surge of love washed over me and though she had instigated this, I was completely certain that she was my future. I wanted this amazing, strong, beautiful woman beside me for the rest of my life.

When our lips parted, I took her left hand in mine again, turning it over I looked at the ring. "I thought you said you sold it off to pay for your medical bills."

She nodded. "I pawned it. Fortunately, it was still at the shop last week when I bought it back."

I raised my brows and looked at her. "This is probably an indelicate question, but—"

She straightened. "I sold the blog, Adam. That's how I got the money."

I frowned, unable to find the words. I was more irked about her selling the blog than about her having sold the ring in the first place.

She laid a hand on my cheek. "Please don't be mad. It's something I had to do. I put a lot of myself into that blog and *Girl Geek* will always be a part of me...but there was a point where I wouldn't have been able to continue a lot of the features. You and I being together meant that there would have been some serious conflict of interest on what I wrote about. I would have had to change the angle of what I was doing anyway, so...I saw selling the blog as a way of making that final, ultimate commitment to growing up and leaving my old life behind."

"I would never have asked for you to do that."

She nodded. "I know. I asked it of myself. It's something I needed to do. Plus, with medical school, I wasn't going to have the time I used to before."

That was the other big question hanging between us, so I was glad she'd brought it up. "So you've come to a decision about medical school?" Relief washed over me. "I'm so glad you are going to go. My realtor found some wonderful properties in Maryland—"

I cut myself off at her shaking head. "I sent Hopkins my polite rejection."

I pulled away from her and sat back on my legs. "*What?*"

"I'm not going to Maryland."

"But—"

"I'm staying here. I'm going to go to UC Irvine."

My mouth hung open. She gave me a look of concern.

"Adam, are you okay? I'm kind of worried."

I shook my head. "I don't understand. UCI wasn't even on your top-five list."

She sat down in the sand next to me. "You're right. It wasn't. Until I started going there every week for my chemo. Until I met the staff and some of the teaching doctors and was so impressed by how they interacted with their patients. How they concentrated on our comfort, our emotional health and putting us at ease. To be honest, I'm not even sure about specializing in oncology anymore. I don't know if I still have the guts for it. But if I do, I want to be taught by those doctors."

I looked at her, still not quite able to wrap my mind around it. "Are you sure?"

She smiled and nodded. "I've given it a lot of thought. I had a lot of time up there in the desert to think."

I shook my head. "You are *absolutely* sure? Because I don't want you to regret it."

She looked up into the sky, fingering the compass around her neck. "So here's the deal... This last year has been, um, challenging, and I tried to do a stupid thing and power through it by myself because that's what I'd always done my entire life. For me, it was easier to do that than to get my heart broken by relying on other people who wouldn't come through. It was an idiotic way of thinking. You and I had started something special, but I was very much still in that old mindset."

She looked down from the sky and found my gaze. I leaned back on my arms, watching her. "So I've learned that very hard lesson. At any moment, your life can change for the worse or for the better. And when that happens, you need your allies. My people are here. Mom, my friends...and you. Even if I moved there with you, I wouldn't have everyone else. And I need everyone." She leaned forward and laid her cold hand on my cheek. "Some more than others, of course. But I need Alex and Jenna and Kat and William and Britt. Mom and Peter and Connor. And, of course, Heath."

"Hmmm." I shook my head. "I was afraid you were going to mention the big ugly guy."

She laughed and then leaned forward, looping her hands around my neck. "I need all of you. And I don't want to leave for that long. Being sick...having been through all that happened to us. It taught me a lot. It taught me what is really important. So it's better that that slot at JHU goes to someone who really, really wants it. As for me, I still want to be a doctor, and I think I'm going to be learning from some brilliant doctors at Irvine."

I reached out and pulled her onto my lap. She came willingly and clasped my neck, pressing her head onto my shoulder. "Adam..."

"Yes?"

"I just...I want to say that even though I have no idea what's in store for us in the future, or if we are even finished with going through these rough bits in life—I just want to say that whatever happens, the good or the bad, I'm so incredibly lucky to be sharing those days and nights with you."

I closed my eyes, turned and kissed her face. Her lips found mine and we shared a passionate kiss—one with enough fire in it to stoke the flames for more. I ordered my libido to calm the hell down because I wasn't going to wear her out tonight. She was still recovering, probably still weak, and we had to go easy for her sake.

Before I knew it, though, she had pulled me down in the sand on top of her, reaching under my shirt to touch my chest. "So about that old bucket list..." she said.

"Sex in public?" I said in a faux-shocked voice.

"The beach is public. And look—I brought some of my own." She pulled out a condom—the wrapping of a brand I didn't recognize. I squinted at it in the dim light.

"You can't read it but trust me, I conducted some research into the product testing these things have to go through, and this brand has by far the best record for breakage."

I laughed. Then I stood up, and when she tried to pull me down again, I swung her into my arms. "Come on—I'm going to make sweet, slow love to my fiancée in the privacy of my own cottage, thank you very much. Where there's no danger of sand getting involved."

She laughed all the way back to the front door. But when I put her down, sliding her slowly down over my hard body, she wasn't laughing anymore.

47
JORDAN

Six Weeks Later

I T WASN'T EASY GETTING MY ASS OUT OF BED THE FIRST DAY BACK to work after Comic-Con and goddamn, what a week it had been—parties, women and, oh yeah, the panels. I think I managed to squeeze in some serious business in the cracks between all the fun. It's good to be young, single and rich.

But even I had to go to work, and after a week of living as if I didn't have a care in the world, my first day back at Draco had me dragging ass. Good thing I spent most of it alone in my office, sipping my favorite hangover remedy and pushing paperwork around—even if done virtually on my laptop. I really didn't have much to complain about, in all honesty. I had a kickass job at a growing company that had made me a crapton of money at a young age. I may not actually have *been* a rock star, but I was glad to live like one. The parties, the women, the dream beach house. And the open, spacious corner office that had its own view of the indoor atrium. I had a nice office. I wasn't

427

going to complain about that, even on a day when I was feeling like death warmed over, laying my head on the desk for much of the morning and wondering if I could wander out a little early for the day to catch up on my sleep.

Just before lunch, I was finally feeling the first hunger pangs when our jackass publicity manager, Weston, poked his head into my office—without knocking, of course.

"Fawkes—need you in Adam's office, ASAP." He said it like a word instead of pronouncing all the letters, like that made him cool. He was a pencil neck and his habit of *only* calling me by my last name irritated the fuck out of me. He seemed to know it, too.

"Okay, Preston," I said, hiding the smirk as I deliberately messed up his name. He rolled his eyes and spun from the doorway, leaving it ajar as he headed to the CEO's office.

A few minutes later—long enough to make it known that I didn't jump and follow his orders whenever he snapped his damn fingers—I sauntered over to Adam's office, where our illustrious CEO was pacing in front of the wall of windows behind his desk, his hands shoved into his pants pockets.

He'd been on edge for the last few months. While he'd been tending to a sick girlfriend, he'd also been working on the secret project with me—a project that stood to make us all a lot more money and push him up into billionaire range if everything went down as we'd planned it.

And, of course, he'd just gotten engaged. If nothing else could stress a man out, I'm sure the thought of marriage would. Poor fool.

I stifled a yawn and sank into the chair facing Adam's desk. I was now hungry as hell. Checking my watch—12:30—I tried not to think about the lunch that was arriving any minute now via my luscious new intern assistant.

"So what's so important it couldn't wait until after lunch?" I asked as Adam settled in the chair next to me.

Weston flipped open his laptop that was sitting on the desk facing us. "A negative PR situation—and before you open it and start going on about how this doesn't concern you—it *does*." He held out a hand to stave off my protest. I closed my mouth and shrugged. "It concerns *all* of us because of the plan to take the company public."

I sat up at that. He had my full attention now. Anything that threatened my pet project needed to be stamped out immediately. I scratched my chin. "Okay, so what is it, then?"

Weston leaned forward to toggle the video player on. "It's from Comic-Con. The video has gone viral over the weekend."

A *video*? Dude had his panties in a twist about a damn video? What the hell? I had a corporation to run. What could possibly be in a video to threaten our bid to go public? Weston was clearly smoking something—probably the good stuff. I eyed him for a minute until the video started streaming. Then, I was distracted by the distinctive sounds of hot sex.

My eyes jerked to the laptop screen. A girl, her back to the camera and wearing no pants. A strange tramp-stamp tattoo with a skull and crossbones was clearly visible at the small of her back. She straddled a guy sitting on a chair. His hands gripped her hips so tightly that her skin under his fingers was white. She gyrated on top of him and both of them were moaning and breathing hard.

I shifted in my seat, loosening my tie. It was more than just an ordinary sex tape, though, because both participants were in full cosplay from head to toe—except, of course, for the girl's tight little bare ass. They were unrecognizable in masks, but their cosplay was clearly intended to depict characters from Dragon Epoch. The captured princess, Alloreah'ala, and Falco, a famous bounty hunter that the elf king had hired to go and find her, to no avail. The princess even had sparkly purple shackles hanging from her wrists and ankles. *Christ Almighty.*

I was distracted by a hiss of breath at my right shoulder. Adam leaned forward, his face flushed. That vein that stuck out on his forehead when he was pissed was currently dancing the Lambada between his dark eyebrows.

With a jerky motion, he pounded on the pause button. "That shit is *viral?*" he choked out.

Weston nodded, casting a cautious glance at the boss. "It's all over the place—Facebook, Reddit, Youtube, porn sites—you name it."

Adam jerked out of his seat, raking a hand through his hair. I crossed my legs and then uncrossed them, unable to get comfortable. I settled for lacing my hands together and staring at them fixedly. "C'mon, man," I finally said after clearing my throat. "It's not a big deal. It's a couple of idiots goofing around...probably drunk off their asses."

"Employees," Adam muttered, flushing even darker red. "*My* employees fucking on camera, dressed up as characters from what is supposed to be a fucking *family* game!"

Oh. Shit. I needed to calm him the fuck down.

I held out my hand. "You don't know for sure that—"

But Adam cut me off, jerking a long finger at the frozen screen, indicating something in the foreground—what looked like a Draco employee badge, the kind we all wore. I had one clipped to the pocket of my dress shirt.

Fucking hell.

"The name is obscured," Weston said, leaning in next to Adam to get a better look at what was unmistakably the logo of Draco Multimedia. "What's that thing blocking it out?"

"The chick's lace thong," I said drily.

Adam's hand closed into a fist that landed on the desk next to the laptop with a loud thump. "Goddamn it!" he hissed. "I leave fucking Comic-Con a day early to spend some time with my fiancée and all hell breaks loose." He turned his narrowed eyes on me and I swallowed nervously.

"You're not—"

"You need to find out who the fuck that was and make sure they are looking for another job before the week is out. This company cannot stand more negative publicity after last year's lawsuit and settlement. This needs to be nipped in the bud or we can kiss our plan to go public goodbye."

I held up a placating hand. "Adam, calm down. The ranting is not going to do your blood pressure any good. I've got this, all right? I'll handle everything. It's not going to affect our project. I promise."

He clenched his jaw. "I'm counting on you for that..."

I swallowed, sent him a confident smile I definitely didn't feel and nodded reassuringly. I was counting on me for that, too. Because three things had to happen. Number one, *nothing* could threaten our pet project. Number two, I needed to find out just how *and* why that video had been posted on social media. And number three, Adam could *never* find out that the dude in the video was me.

AUTHOR'S NOTE

Due to the subject matter of this novel, I felt it might be helpful to include a note about the research I conducted in order to portray Mia's illness and treatment with as much realism as possible. I did not want this to be a book about cancer, but rather, a book about how a young couple, already challenged with overcoming their own foibles, must find the strength to overcome those struggles, both external and internal, through their love for each other.

Nevertheless, I felt it was very important to not downplay the seriousness of Mia's cancer, the chemotherapy, and, above all, the difficult decision to terminate her pregnancy in order to seek life-saving treatment.

There were many resources that I consulted to learn more about breast cancer. Most heart-rending of these were the actual blogs and memoirs of cancer survivors and of those who, in the end, did not survive.

Some of my sources include:

Haily Peterson's youtube vlog chronicling her treatment and survival

Geralyn Lucas, author of the memoir *Why I Wore Lipstick to My Mastectomy*

Jessica of *Cancer, Baby* blog (archived after her passing)

Sylvia Soo of *Cancer Fabulous* (cancerfabulous.com)

Jennifer Smith of *Living Legendary* blog and author of *What You Might Not Know*

Jill Brzezinski-Conley of *Breast Friends* (Facebook) and subject of the documentary, *The Light that Shines*, A Story for All.

I urge you to seek out these sources if this subject interests you.

Thank you,
Brenna Aubrey

ABOUT THE AUTHOR

Brenna Aubrey is an author of New Adult contemporary romance stories that center on geek culture. She has always sought comfort in good books and the long, involved stories she weaves in her head.

Brenna is a city girl with a nature-lover's heart. She therefore finds herself out in green open spaces any chance she can get. A mommy to two little kids and teacher to many more older kids, she juggles schedules to find time to pursue her love of storycrafting.

She currently resides on the west coast with her husband, two children, two adorable golden retriever pups, two birds and some fish.

12104661R00260

Printed in Great Britain
by Amazon.co.uk, Ltd.,
Marston Gate.